Ciao, Bella

The Erotically Graphic Love Story

of

MR. N & Ms. O

MR. N & Ms. O

Cover by Jessica Bell Design

Images © Scott Maxwell, belyaaa, skiserge1

ISBN: 978-0-578-78618-6

AUTHOR'S NOTE

This is a work of fiction. Unless otherwise indicated, all the names, characters, businesses, places, events and incidents in this book are either the product of the author's imagination or used in a fictitious manner. Any resemblance to actual persons, living or dead, or actual events is purely coincidental.

Content contained or made available through this book is not intended to and does not constitute legal advice or investment advice and no attorney-client relationship is formed. The authors are providing this book and its contents on an "as is" basis. Your use of the information in this book is at your own risk.

The authors of this book are not financial advisers. The information in this book is not to be construed as financial advice. The authors do not make any guarantee or other promise as to any results that may be obtained from using the content of this book. You should never make any investment decision without first consulting with your own financial advisor and conducting your own research and due diligence. To the maximum extent permitted by law, the authors disclaim any and all liability in the event any information, commentary, analysis, opinions, advice and/or recommendations contained in this book prove to be inaccurate, incomplete or unreliable, or result in any investment or other losses.

This book is dedicated to my mother, who instilled in me the belief that I could be anything in this world that I strived to be. To my father, who taught me the best thing to be in this world is simply myself. And to my siblings, for being able and willing to call me on my bullshit with nothing more than a single glance.

To M, for helping me tame and domesticate that which I could not control in myself; N, for being the indefatigable impetus and positively charged source of energy I needed to encourage me to start this book; and T, for helping me realize just how much I valued communication.

But most of all to S, for showing me that which cannot be fully spoken can be far more beautifully felt. For showing me love was simply a word I believed I knew the definition of... until you came along and redefined it, giving my life new meaning in the process. No matter how big my dreams have ever been, without your love I wouldn't have known what I was capable of achieving. Thank you for believing in me. Thank you for loving me and allowing me to love you in return. Thank you... for being my best friend.

I look forward to living a life devoted to returning the favor.

This book is dedicated to my parents for providing me the best and most loving childhood a daughter could have, ensuring that I never wanted for anything as you simultaneously taught me the value of paying forward the excess you ensured I had left over to give.

And to my daughter, that she might live as freely as she has the courage to be, strive as far as she desires to go and to always love without regret...

And to my son, that he might understand the nature of his power and use it for good...

But most of all to N, for helping free me from myself.

I

Lust *n* **1 :** *an intense sexual desire* **2 :** *an intense longing*

Saturday

January 11, 2020

3:57pm, 73° & windy

Damn...

Tall. Handsome. Athletic. Serious... Fluid?

Probably in his mid-thirties, he stood at least six-seven or six-eight, putting him both a couple of years older and a good foot taller than myself. Having worked with more than a few professional athletes, I estimated he weighed between two-eighty to ninety, all of which appeared to be muscle. Yet as massive of a man as he was, his size wasn't what first caught my eye. No, it was the way he walked.

In a word lithe, he practically glided across the compact gravel parking lot toward Mickey's Pub & Pool where I sat watching from within. And much like anyone spotted walking on air, he was a sight to behold even before it happened.

Backdropped by the light cloud of dust, a deep purple aura suddenly began to outline his entire frame in a thin but majestic hue. Like an ember infused with electricity, the color brightened quickly, glowing into existence in a single pulse. Taking only a second or two longer, the subtle veil then dimmed almost as fast, thankfully leaving him in its wake.

I had never seen a man appear so simultaneously dark yet radiant.

But, my God, did it fit him to a T.

His head was shaved smooth to a shine. *So he takes pride in his looks.* Yet his tightly groomed goatee of peppered stubble contained a fair amount of salt. *Which means his vanity has its limits.* His shoulders were broad, topping a well-defined, but not overly large, chest. *So he obviously works out, takes care of himself.* While his black-on-black pinstripe button down narrowed in a V to his much smaller waist, contrasting nicely with his designer jeans over shiny black cowboy boots, a timeless style that seemed all his own. *And damn if he doesn't ow—*

My jaw dropped as I noticed the definitive bulge at his crotch.

Damn...

And just like that I knew. At least here at Mickey's, it was him or bust.

Simply put, I was a stranger from out of town and I desperately needed to get laid. It had been more than a year since I had last had sex. Making matters worse, the undeniable ticking of my baby clock was finally beginning to gnaw on my nerves. So six weeks ago I had made a vow to myself that one way or another my self-imposed celibacy would end tonight on this preplanned trip.

And come hell or high water it was going to... even if the odds were stacked against me.

Because scattered throughout Mickey's were no less than two dozen single females, many of them younger and more attractive than myself, a couple of whom were clearly on the prowl. Of course, the forty-five pounds I had packed on over the last year definitely weren't helping my cause either, even if I had been successful in shedding the first fifteen of them in the last month.

So while Deep Purple may have been a bit out of my current league, I was both looking and feeling better about myself than I had in quite some time. *And that has to count for something, right?* Mentally I shrugged off the question because, regardless of the answer, I had already quit on myself once in life and I was not about to do it again. And suddenly realizing that I was absentmindedly rubbing my sundress atop my stomach, I smiled.

Besides, I came here for more than one reason...

Cupping my glass of wine, I swiveled my bar stool to get a better view and plan my strategy. As Deep Purple stepped forward to hold one of the double glass doors open for yet another pair of pretty twenty-somethings who happened to be entering Mickey's at the same time, I noticed a couple of things.

First was how, had it not been for the quickened pace of his last few steps, all three would have arrived at the door at the exact same moment. Of course that was one of the great things about living in the South. It hadn't taken me long to realize that small acts of chivalry not only still existed, here they were also far more common than not.

But second to that, I also saw how he tried to appear oblivious to his effect on the clearly flattered coeds. And while they failed to notice, as a matter of occupational hazard I was trained to detect certain behaviors. Even though his overall expression remained neutral, I could tell by the almost imperceptible way he lowered his head that he sensed their shift in mood when they accepted his offer and giddily entered first.

A gentleman who likes to play coy. Good. Coy men could be easy targets if you knew how to play them right. *And I do...*

Watching as he ducked his head under the doorway, I studied Deep Purple's face to catch his initial reaction to the bar. While first impressions could tell a lot about a person, that which was significant enough to *make* a first impression *on* a person often told just as much.

If Deep Purple entered Mickey's and appeared disinterested might it indicate he was a regular already familiar with the place? And if so, would he immediately seek out his reason for being there, thereby belying a no nonsense nature as well? Or would he go directly to the daily specials on the menu board simply because he was hungry? Regardless, I knew whatever he did first held the possibility of mattering most and I wanted to catch it.

Curiously enough, just after entering his eyes focused high over the crowd in a back corner... then down for a second before darting high to the opposite corner of the room... then down again before taking in another high spot before looking down beneath that.

Seemingly satisfied, he stepped forward to the registration table, giving me a chance to follow where his gaze had been. And the only thing all three spots had in common were... illuminated red EXIT signs.

Interesting.

Was he a first responder? Or just overly safety conscious due to a previous trauma he didn't want to repeat? Whatever the cause, Deep Purple was obviously unnerved to the point that no sooner had he arrived his first thoughts were all about leaving.

As disconcerting as that might have been, I couldn't help but grin as he signed in just inside the front door. I was grateful to see that, like myself, he was here for the poker tournament. That would at least give us enough in common to break the ice. Now I just had to think of the best way to offer myself as an option because—taking another look around—here there were more than plenty.

Located off Highway 17, a few miles south of Jacksonville, North Carolina, Mickey's was your run of the mill local sports bar/pool hall/restaurant. The place was spacious yet segregated nicely, each with its own atmosphere, all of which were geared toward entertainment. Primarily a sports bar with big screen TVs, billiards, dart boards, Giant Jenga, foosball and shuffleboard tables in the back, there were also two large family dining areas in the front.

Of course each of these were separate from where I sat off to the side in the former cigar bar, now repurposed into a smaller but far more elegant, semi-private lounge. Not only did my vantage point serve my second favorite Cab, it also provided an unobstructed view of the entire place which was now occupied by nearly two hundred bar league poker players who had traveled from all over the state to compete for a trip to Las Vegas and a real money tournament.

When I first learned that the regional championship was to be played in Jacksonville, I thought it might be the perfect opportunity to kickstart reclaiming my sex life. As if being a second generation Irish-American in a bar called Mickey's wasn't a lucky enough omen, the US Marine Corps Base at Camp Lejeune was just a few miles away. Between the two, I had figured it would be easy to find some young, horny Leatherneck looking for some action and fool him into taking me back to his place to make my night by letting him believe I was there to make his.

Unfortunately, Mickey's was far enough on the outskirts of the city that the local clientele was far more family- than single soldier-oriented, so pickings were even slimmer than most of my female competition.

Only now as I watched Deep Purple sign in, I knew that none of that mattered. From what I could see, he'd more than do. While we might not get to play poker together, that didn't mean we couldn't play something else.

Provided I play my cards right...

Sadly, I had been the first player to bust out of the early play-in round on just my third hand. I had made the correct play, so despite losing I wouldn't change a single thing I did. But in poker it was often far more important to not become unlucky than it was to actually be lucky. And unluckily for me, my opponent beat the one in twenty-two odds I had stacked against him. Thus my tournament, which had started at noon, had been over since twelve oh seven.

Not that I truly cared. After all, I was there to get laid, not play poker.

Polishing off the last of my second glass, I punched the button on my smartphone. Just shy of four o'clock, I realized Deep Purple was here much too early as the final tournament didn't start until nine. This meant we were either both Type A personalities, he had a specific reason for showing now… or both. Regardless, I was just glad I had stuck around to find out.

After asking a bartender and two waitresses for recommendations then checking out their suggestions online, I had spent the last four hours narrowing down my choices to three bars, each much closer to the Marine base. I planned to call for a ride around five to check out the first bar because although there were plenty of available men at Mickey's, none were the type I wanted to touch, much less let tickle, my fancy.

At the invitation of my best friend, I had only joined the poker league just two months prior. At the time, the idea of playing cards for four to five hours one night a week in a semi-social setting seemed like a good way to meet more guys. But the bar poker league scene had turned out to be just as varied as any other, filled mostly with a wide cross section of males, from young to old, hapless to overdriven. Sometimes the asses outnumbered the gentlemen and unfortunately by the end of each night a few could be more than a bit drunk. In fact, in the last eight weeks not one guy had truly held my interest for more than five minutes. Though to be honest, most guys never did.

But as I once again gave him the once over, something told me Deep Purple was different.

For starters, there was the way he held himself. Shoulders back and chin up, if not for the goatee he could have passed for an active Marine. Even the way he casually studied the nearest tables of poker players bordered on respectful. I watched as he took notice of but never truly ogled any of the bar's most attractive females. That gave me enough pause to look for a wedding ring which thankfully he didn't have.

Then, of course, there had been his aura.

Describing it was difficult to explain. The best analogy I had ever come up with was the uniquely personal yet shared feeling of surrealism people experienced during déjà vu. Similarly, it was impossible to will an aura to happen so not everybody had one I could detect. But if and when I was able to catch a glimpse, it was like looking at a vibration of that person's inner energy level, as if their soul was so electrified the shell of their body could no longer contain it all.

As ethereal and otherworldly as it came across in trying to describe, I often found someone's aura to be an accurate indicator of the type of person they turned out to be. True to type, green meant jealous or insecure, red temperamental, yellow for timid and so on. Though I did my best not to prejudge, I had nevertheless observed this truth to play out in some of my patients during their therapy sessions.

With his registration finally complete, I watched as Deep Purple turned to survey the scene, taking in the place with a quick panoramic sweep of his eyes. Failing to find what he was looking for, he stepped further inside to check out the crowd in the back. Then, raising his hand in hello, he headed toward a couple seated at one of the poker tables, Abby and Greg Costello.

Yes! Yes! Yes! I could not believe my luck!

At forty-six, Abby was seventeen years my senior. While technically old enough to be my mother, she had instead become my closest confidant and occasional mentor after she and Greg had tracked me down five years ago. My best friends now, eight years prior both had been my patients.

While each to their own degree had once been a hopeless, miserable sex addict whose life was spiraling out of control, the two were now together in a Master/Sex Slave switch-style marriage that wasn't just consensual, it was also one of the happiest and healthiest relationships I had ever known. I had ultimately lost my job for introducing them, but it was a decision that I never once regretted.

The three of us had actually caravanned together from Charlotte earlier this morning. Hardcore poker fanatics, I knew they played Monday through Thursday nights, each at a different bar. I presumed they knew Deep Purple from one of their other locations... which meant he probably lived in Charlotte, too...

Hmmmmm.

The possibility didn't bode so well for me. My plan all along had been for a hit-it-and-quit-it type of night. Maybe even twice if the sex was worth it. *Though with my luck...*

Rolling my eyes, I shook off the feeling. Besides, I was getting ahead of myself. At its worst the probability of Deep Purple being a Charlottean was a minor, theoretical inconvenience. It was a big enough city that I'd probably never run into him again, especially if he was nothing more than a poker acquaintance of Greg and Abby's.

No, my main problem was my competition because as soon as Deep Purple had entered the bar, I noticed several women surreptitiously checking him out. Not that I blamed them. Even in a bar as large as Mickey's, filled with well over a hundred men, the man clearly stood out. And not just because of his well above average height.

Grabbing my glass, I downed the last gulp of my wine in one quick swig. Not very ladylike, but then again neither were my intentions. *And a little liquid courage can't hurt,* I mused as I picked up my clutch to make a bee line for Greg and Abby's table.

The tournament had just reached a break and all three were standing together chatting. I had no idea what I was going to say but I prided myself on being quick on my feet. I'd think of something. I always did.

Without bothering to wait for Abby or Greg to do it, I ended up surprising him right away by quickly saying hello and introducing myself. With one of the straightest, whitest smiles I had ever seen as well as two of the softest baby blues, Deep Purple politely shook my outstretched hand before introducing himself as Victor Maxwell.

Even his name was sexy.

Damn...

She looked at me as if she hadn't decided yet whether or not she was going to fuck me.

Which was a little preposterous because we both knew damn well that's what she wanted. That much was a given at this point. Which was fine because by now I wanted to, too.

So—seeing how we were at a poker tournament—I flashed her a grin with just enough gleam in my eye to let her know I knew she was bluffing. Nor did it matter.

Yeah, sweetheart, I'll fuck you later. So don't worry about it, we can both relax.

Unabashed at the obviousness of my thoughts, her eyes replied in kind as I chuckled silently to myself, amazed I was going to go through with it. I mean, she wasn't my type, at least not physically. Although I found every woman beautiful just by virtue of being female, on a scale of one to ten, nine people clearly would have deemed me out of her league.

And by my own admission, I wasn't all that much to look at in the first place.

I was in more than decent shape for thirty-five and—with the usual exception of Greg—was far better dressed than most of the guys in the joint. In a dive like Mickey's my boots alone were practically a fashion statement coup de gras. Hell, I'd seen more than a few slouches celebrating the unseasonably warm weather strolling around in shorts and sandals.

If I had been in the mood to try, truth was I stood a pretty good chance of scoring one of the hotter, younger twenty-somethings mingling about who were clearly in the mood for a good time. I was no manther, but a few of them had given me more than just a second look—including our waitress who was probably the hottest female in the entire bar—and the night was still every bit as young as they all were.

Yet Greg and Abby's friend—despite being completely nonverbal about it—was clearly offering herself to me now. I had received my fair share of I-want-to-fuck-you-and-I-want-to-fuck-you-now looks and vibes from women in my life, but none so undeniably direct as those she had been giving me from the moment we first met.

And I had to admit, there was *something* about her.

Her slightly plump face was girlishly cute so—though by no means a break-your-neck head turner—she actually was quite attractive. And even though her bright red with large white polka dotted sundress revealed her to be a good twenty to thirty pounds heavier than healthy, it also accentuated the fact that she was proportionally curvy in all the best places.

Her choice of a light lavender and chamomile perfume was a nice touch and the type of attention to detail I admired. Paired with her subtle selection of gold earrings, necklace and Saint Laurent clutch, it was obvious the woman knew how to accessorize with class minus any ostentations. Along with Greg and Abby, we had to be two of the most overdressed individuals in the entire place. To everyone else, we probably appeared to already be a couple.

But, given all that, it was neither her looks nor the looks she had been giving me that drew me to her the most. Instead it was her eyes.

More specifically, it was something *in* her eyes.

Under the soft, wavy tendrils of her long, dirty blonde hair sparkled two of the most unbelievably brilliant earthen pools of light I had ever seen. Umber orbs flecked by the kind of twinkles that seemed to constantly hint at a happy mischief deeper within. And accentuating her uniqueness, two faint moles graced her right cheek just below her eye. Somehow it seemed apropos that one beauty mark just wasn't enough.

But what surprised me more than anything else was the reassuring way her eyes looked at me—as if she somehow already knew each and every one of my secrets—making me feel like I had nothing I needed to hide. From the moment we met, her eyes alone had me believing she was the type of person I could say or reveal anything to while at the same time feel free of any judgment.

As if that weren't enough, she continuously exuded an inner calm that bordered on the surreal. Whether in the rise of her cheeks, the corners of her mouth or the shine in her irises, she was never more than a facial tic away from a chuckle or a grin. Even in her most neutral expressions her positivity was always there, brimming just below the surface.

Simply put she was the rare type of individual who had actually found their happy place in life and then never let it go.

Perhaps that was why—unlike most women I had ever met—she exhibited absolutely no self-consciousness, appearing neither insecure nor confident about her looks. On that front, she seemed at peace, possibly more so than anyone I had ever met. And over the last few hours, as our conversation flowed more and more effortlessly, I began to find myself wanting to know why she was the way she was. I wanted to know the secret of her serenity... because something about it was sexy as hell.

"So," I asked gently before sizing up my next billiard's shot on our table, "if you're not in the second round, you're done playing for the evening?"

I knew all too well that some players could be touchy about their knockout poker hand. She didn't seem like one of them, but I thought it best not to put too fine a point on it.

"I am," she smiled slyly. "Which means I am completely free to do *whatever* I *want* tonight."

I grinned at her implication even as I silently cursed myself once again for not knowing her actual name. Barbara, Betty. Maybe Bobby. I was positive it was something along those lines though embarrassingly I really wasn't sure. Not only had she introduced herself unexpectedly, the moment had been drowned out by a particularly loud segment of a song from Mickey's jukebox such that I couldn't hear her say her name very well. Though to be honest, on first impression I hadn't taken much interest so—like the ass I could sometimes be—I hadn't really cared to catch it.

But in my defense, I hadn't driven five hours to get laid. I was there to play poker.

Of course since then, we'd actually had a really great time as we rotated between playing foosball, throwing darts and shooting pool. Betty—as I decided to think of her—had more or less latched onto me at first, insisting I allow her to buy me a drink once Greg and Abby's break was over. Given the connection of our mutual friends, I didn't think much of it at first. But as we continued to chat and our small talk grew deeper, I quickly began to enjoy her company.

I found her to be highly intelligent, observant, easy going, and funny. She also had one of the quickest wits of anyone I'd ever met in my life. Most of her responses were so immediate, it felt like she knew what I was going to say even before I did. We got along so well, that within the first hour I couldn't remember the last person I had felt more comfortable and at ease around than her.

But taking a back seat to everything, there was no denying that from the moment we first met Betty was hotter than hell for me. I couldn't think of anything I had done to encourage her, but the eye she gave me every so often was enough to make me feel like I was being eaten alive. And the more she did it, the easier I became with it. I finally just accepted the fact that if she was down to fuck later tonight, so was I.

What the hell.

After mentioning she lived just west of Charlotte in the town of Belmont, I realized she, too, would have close to a five hour drive ahead of her. But that was assuming she was going home tonight which we both knew she wasn't. Which meant the only thing we had left to discuss was the logistics of where we were going to have sex. Of course by that point, it was as if she could read my mind.

"You know, as late as the championship round starts tonight and will probably end," she observed not so nonchalantly, "you might not get home until morning."

The wicked in Betty's grin matched that in her voice, both of which I did my best to imitate.

"I've got a hotel room around the corner."

"Good," she said without missing a beat, making damn sure I heard the undercurrent in her tone.

As her emphasis triggered a rush of blood to my crotch, I felt my cock press against the .22 Black Widow revolver tucked in the specially sewn pocket in front of my boxers. It was a sensation I might have enjoyed if not for the nagging suspicion that Betty could be a honey trap prelude to a future kidnapping. I highly doubted it, but no matter what I did, I couldn't discount the possibility.

I knew if Betty's ploy to bed me was a charade, the longer it went on the more likely my guard would drop. But I didn't feel that was her intent. Her interest seemed genuine even if her delivery was a bit unusual. Her openness to sex, while direct and obvious, was subtle and casual at the same time. She had a take-it-or-leave-it'll-be-your-loss-if-you-do kind of attitude that I thought was pretty cool.

Trying to cut myself some slack, I had to acknowledge she wasn't the true source of my paranoia. Regardless, I was thankful the revolver made me feel prepared.

So lighten up, asshole. Have some fun for once.

Smirking to myself, I gave Betty a playful wink to make sure she knew I had caught her drift. The wink and a smile she shot me in return made me wonder what I had done to get so lucky.

The hours quickly flew by as our conversation easily segued from one topic to the next. We talked about politics and religion, our favorite musicians and instruments as well as the authors and genres we enjoyed reading most, places we had traveled, bawdy jokes we knew, some of our worst fears and pet peeves, a few of which neither of us could explain nor help.

The variety of our discussion seemed boundless as almost nothing had been off limits.

Almost. But not all.

Interestingly enough, it wasn't long before I realized *both* of us were purposely avoiding talking about anything having to do with our occupations. I never spoke to anyone about mine, so at first I figured Betty was just politely reciprocating. But eventually it became clear that she didn't want to discuss her job either. I couldn't deny my own curiosity, but since I didn't want to be a hypocrite, I didn't press her on it.

With that one unspoken exception, our easy going banter about anything else easily gave way to several moments of good-natured teasing. And just like old friends, the couple of times we finished one another's sentences quickly began to end in shared laughter.

As the hours continued to pass, I realized there was something about Betty's energy that was almost magical. The intensity of her inner peacefulness seemed to transcend into an even more intense outer focus. Whenever it was her turn to listen, she gave me her complete and undivided attention, so much so that despite being surrounded by a crowd of a couple hundred, it often felt like we were the only two people there. In return, her focus somehow provided me with a clarity to precisely convey what I was both thinking and feeling. I didn't understand it, but—just like the proverbial moth fascinated by a flame—I couldn't get enough.

And I had to admit, it felt good to really relax and laugh again.

My relationship status was a bit complicated, made all the more frustrating because the woman I had planned to be with tonight had to cancel at the last minute. Alexis was a pharmaceutical sales rep in Columbia, South Carolina with whom I'd been in a semi-monogamous, no strings attached, sex-only relationship for almost half a year. Although she was married to a first lieutenant in the US Army based out of Fort Jackson, they practiced a TDY—temporary duty status—lifestyle so each were free to sleep with whomever they wanted whenever Alexis' husband was away on assignment as he had been for the last eight months.

The arrangement worked well, not just for her and him, but also for myself as I could no longer chance just sleeping around like I had in my past. Plus it didn't hurt that I was already familiar with the etiquette of TDY living during my brief stint in the Marines. It may not have been the most ideal lifestyle and I certainly couldn't have abided by it, but it worked for a lot of military couples and I wasn't one to judge.

Alexis and I, however, had never spent an entire night together even though it wasn't against her and her husband's rules. Since she had scheduled business in nearby Wilmington on Monday morning and because I would be leaving the state on Sunday for the next two months, the plan we had made over a month ago had been for her to meet me at my hotel later tonight.

Needless to say, I had been looking forward to this weekend—this evening, especially—for quite awhile. While there had been plenty of them, the last time I had actually woke with a woman in my bed was now longer than I could remember. Along with middle of the night sex, I missed first thing in the morning sex and this weekend was supposed to change all that. If nothing else, Alexis' unexpected cancellation after her husband returned home unannounced in order to surprise her definitely left me in the mood for a good grudge fu—

"Hey, you two."

Greg's unmistakable voice—a thundering bass damn near subwoofer level—suddenly boomed behind me. I turned to find Abby, as always, standing behind him with her head slightly bowed. And just as always, they startled me a bit and not because they both seemed to appear out of nowhere.

Two of the most physically polar opposite people I think I had ever met, Greg Costello was an absolute beast of a bodybuilder, especially for a black man in his late forties. Only five or six inches shorter than myself, he still outweighed me by at least fifty pounds, every one of which was all-natural, bro-certified muscle. And though he had tamed most of his heavy Brooklyn accent, his in-your-face brashness was still as thick as his traps.

What he hadn't toned down—at least not in the six months I'd known him—was his panache.

A crisp white button down complete with French cuffs, pressed and pleated black slacks, wing tipped shoes, along with a matching diamonds-on-platinum wedding band and pinky ring were Greg's standard dress base. What alternated each time I saw him were his matching sets of watches, tie bars and cufflinks, always using four, not just two, for his openly flared cuffs. Cooler still, he always color-coordinated his tie and suspender sets—like tonight's shiny blue paisley on a matte blue background—to match his wife's hair.

Greg's treatment of her—with some of the utmost love, respect, adoration and attentiveness I had ever seen—was, more than anything else, why I liked and respected him so much. Whether the remnants of his northern dialect sounded it or not, the man was at heart a true Southern gentleman.

Abby, by contrast, was a small wisp of a woman. Although she almost always wore heels, at most she was five one and a hundred pounds after a full day at a buffet. Just a tad younger than Greg, her hair was dyed a different stripe of the rainbow every other time I saw her. Tonight's electric blue was piled high, geisha style over an even classier blue silk kimono dress. I found the pink chrysanthemum pinned in her hair to be a nice touch. In fact, I thought her entire look was rather apropos and not just because it went so well with the near porcelain color of her skin.

Contrary to her always striking appearance, Abby was so timid and quiet in nature, I would have worried she was domestically abused if not for the level of love I saw in her eyes for Greg. I couldn't knock it. As different as they might have seemed, between their love, love for poker and a love for a heavy amount of graphic tattoos, they seemed to share more in common with one another than I did with most of the women I had ever dated... combined.

But if there were two things that stood out about Abby the most, it were her outfits and breasts. Everything she wore was so skintight, the woman couldn't help but ooze constant sex appeal, most of which was visually centered around her chest. Her breasts weren't overly, implant-obvious large, but set atop and relative to her diminutive frame, they were magnificently prominent.

Given my height, Abby's lack thereof along with her penchant for blouses with plunging necklines, it took a concerted effort to maintain eye contact whenever acknowledging her presence. That she always did the same while remaining quieter than a church mouse made interacting with her a little disconcerting. She was kind enough to always reply to me, but I never saw her initiate a conversation with anyone but her husband. And that was fine. Greg usually did all the talking anyway.

"We both got knocked out," he continued.

I shook my head even though it was obvious as the other players were still playing.

"Man, that sucks," I sympathized.

"Yeah, well, whatcha gonna do, you know?" Greg shrugged it off. "So we're going to head home." He turned to Betty. "Are you ready to go?"

I had been waiting for this moment. Dialing back my poker face to the most oblivious setting I could, I already knew that Betty had driven separately, so she didn't have to return to Charlotte with them if she didn't want to leave. I knew she didn't, but I had no idea how she would break the news to our mutual friends. Glancing briefly at me, her tone curiously gave away nothing of her true interest.

"No, I think I am going to stay a little longer. I have yet to win a single game against your buddy Victor here, but he is *not* as good as he thinks he is. Sooner or later, I will win one."

I did my best not to smile. Even though she had been knocked out of the first tournament early, Betty's poker face was perfect.

Abby's, on the other hand, tried to flash her a look of sisterly understanding that only two women can share. It was brief, but I caught enough of it to tell she knew what was up. Oddly though, Betty declined to acknowledge Abby at all.

In fact, there had been a strange dynamic going on between them all evening that I didn't understand. I could tell just by how highly Betty spoke of Abby that they were practically best friends. But whenever the four of us hung out during the tournament's scheduled breaks, Abby barely acknowledged Betty's presence. Even though she was polite about it, as quiet as the woman was I had never seen her be so standoffish to someone, even me.

Greg seemed to catch a whiff of something, too, but not enough to hold his interest. Accepting and dismissing Betty's answer with a quick head nod, he offered me his hand.

"Best of luck in there tonight, my man."

I paused before shaking. I wasn't looking forward to this. I really sucked at goodbyes.

"Thanks. And, uh, I wanted to say farewell to you and Abby. I won't be playing poker at the bar again, but I wanted you to know I really enjoyed meeting the two of you." I would have said 'getting to know the two of you,' but I honestly didn't feel like I knew Abby all that well.

Greg's look of genuine shock both warmed and disheartened me. We had become really good poker buddies and although I was sure he was unaware of it as we only saw each other for a few hours, one night a week for the last six months, he was actually only the second person I knew that I considered a friend... I didn't get out much.

"Awww, man, that sucks," Greg said, shaking his head, "because it's been really great hanging out with you. Can't say I'll miss your sunglasses though."

We both laughed. I only wore a pair of sunglasses whenever I played in a hand against Greg. Despite the light color of my eyes, he was the only person I'd seen recognize the uncontrollable dilation of my pupils and knew what it meant. He used that tactic against other players whenever possible and it frustrated him that I always countered one of his most effective skills. But rules were rules and I found those that could be taken advantage of needed to be in certain situations.

"I had to do something," I said. "You were crushing me when I first started playing. Which by the way, just so you know, your pinky ring? You slide it on and off when you're good but twist it around when you're not."

"Son of a..." Greg laughed. "Anything else you been holding out on me?"

I smiled. As genial as he was effusive, Greg often chatted—or at least tried to—with anyone who would engage him, keeping the players at the table nice and loose. And while that could irk the poker purists who preferred a game of quiet concentration, most loved the guy. But unlike those who stayed as motionless as possible, Greg's nervous energy kept him in the throes of some type of continuous physical movement.

"You're right handed and right footed," I continued. "You've got a good hand when you shake your left leg, but covering a weak one when purposefully shaking your right."

I could see the truth take hold in Greg's eyes. "Well, fuuuck me," he laughed. "I wish I had known all that five minutes ago."

"Well, now that I won't be playing against you any more..."

His grin growing slightly wider, Greg looked from me, to Betty, then back at me.

"Yeah, well, you never know. We might see you again sometime."

He gave me a quick smile before looking over to his wife. In the complete silence of just a few seconds, the two seemed to speak volumes. Abby nodded in agreement before turning to address Betty.

"You have our permission," she said solemnly to which, after a stunned beat, Betty replied with a small, curt nod of her own.

Greg chuckled. "Go easy on him, Doc. Just because he's a better poker player doesn't make him a player."

Doc? The word threw me for a second made all the more curious by the brief look of trepidation that flashed behind Betty's eyes. While it wouldn't surprise me if she was a doctor of some sort, I couldn't understand why she'd be reluctant for me to know. Before I could consider that or his odd admonition further, Greg turned to shake my hand again.

"And *you* take of yourself, my brother."

Accepting his hand again I was genuinely surprised when he used it to pull me close for a quick chest bump. Not only had I never seen him do that to anyone, no one had done that to me in at least fifteen years. And while Greg and I were tight, neither of us were huggers.

Or so I thought.

Wishing me luck, Greg and Abby began heading for the nearest exit. As my state of semi-shock slowly reeled off, Betty nonchalantly chalked up her pool cue until the Costellos were entirely out of earshot before turning to me with one of the most beautiful smiles I had seen in a long time.

"Soooo... you have a hotel room around the corner?"

Once again, the only thing I could do was smile in reply. The woman's bold directness was definitely refreshing. It felt like the perfect complement to what one of my former girlfriends had once described as my "quiet-man-of-mystery" nature. Giving her a quick once over, I wondered how Betty might respond if my persona changed behind closed doors.

Shit!

When Greg called me Doc, it was all I could do to maintain my composure.

Despite spending three ten-minute breaks with the Costellos over the last four and a half hours, I had managed to make it through the evening without either of them referring to me as such.

It had been my experience that men attracted to me solely because of my body or long blonde hair were often base enough that discovering I was a former sex addiction therapist only further enflamed their shallow interest. Which was precisely the reason I tried not to tell them.

But men like Victor, who were far more cerebral, were also far more likely to either not be swayed at best or intimidated at worst by my profession. And the way I saw it, taking a fifty-fifty chance when it came to a catch like Victor had no upside.

If that weren't bad enough, while I was extremely good at my job, I found it difficult to adequately explain to people exactly what it was I did for a living. Fighting through the individual preconceived notions and common misconceptions that came with the idea of someone being able to have a "sex addiction" in the first place often took up half the battle. Only if I was able to first win that one could I proceed to elaborate on the intricacies of my job... provided I still had enough patience left.

Shockingly though, my concerns were quickly sidelined as I saw Greg man-hug Victor with a chest bump. By then I had gathered that he had a great deal of respect for Victor. That, in and of itself, was unusual because despite both his appearance and brashness, Greg was neither arrogant nor disrespectful. He was simply a difficult man to impress. And for reasons which Abby and I were perhaps the only two people in the world to understand, he rarely made any form of physical contact with other men. And never had I seen him initiate it.

As his former therapist, to see Greg embrace Victor as he did was truly a *Wow!* moment for me. I tried to make eye contact with Abby, but as she had done all day, she avoided me even then... which not only further confounded but also irritated the hell out of me.

Everything had been perfectly fine between us before leaving Charlotte this morning and even after we had arrived at Mickey's. But she had slipped even deeper into her Sex Slave shutdown mode ever since I met Victor and I could think of no reason why. That she wouldn't communicate with me, either verbally or non-, was as bewildering as it was grating.

Abby knew my intention on this trip was to get myself laid. And she was damn well smart enough to realize by now that I had my sights set on Victor. But she had done her best all day long to give me zero feedback on how she felt about it.

Twice I tried to get her to go to the bathroom with me so I could not only privately pump her for any inside info on Victor, but also to tell her that I would prefer neither she nor Greg let him know that I had once been a sex addiction therapist. Every bit as intentional as uncharacteristic, she declined both my offers in such a way that I didn't bother thrice.

So just a few moments earlier, when Greg had asked whether I was ready to leave or not, it was all I could do not to throw the obvious in her face. While I could tell my answer provoked a reaction out of her, by then I failed to care how she thought or felt. I had given her more than enough opportunities to tell me where she stood on my desire to fuck one of her husband's friends. And not that I felt it had anything to do with it, but I knew we could always discuss why she rejected me tomorrow once she switched from Sex Slave back to Master mode.

After wishing Victor good luck and bidding us adieu, I wasted no time in getting back to matters at hand. And with Greg and Abby no longer in the building, it suddenly felt like Victor and I had more privacy. *Speaking of which—*

"Soooo... you have a hotel room around the corner?"

Batting my eyes, I did my best to strike a perfect balance between flirtatious and suggestive with just a touch of downright wanton. Given how much of a sucker I was for men with blue eyes, exercising my restraint on the last bit was the toughest.

Smiling at me but saying nothing, I reveled in how Victor seemed to enjoy catching my drifts.

As we shot a couple more games of pool, I couldn't help but wonder if he might now ditch the poker tournament altogether. I had to respect the fact he had driven almost five hours just to play in the championship round so I made sure he knew leaving early wasn't necessary. I'd certainly wait.

But what concerned me more the more I thought about it was what Victor might discover later by running a quick search for my name on the internet while playing poker. I hadn't seen him check his phone a single time all evening, but I knew he had one. I could see the outline of it in his front pocket right next to his even bigger bulge. Would he take the opportunity to look me up during the first private moment he was about to have since we met? And if he did, what would he think?

Just before nine, when he escorted me back to the lounge with a semi-awkward promise to return as soon as possible, I scrambled how to justify making a reasonable request for both of us to refrain from Googling the other. Even worse, I knew to ask at all might run the risk of stoking a suspicion he might not even have. So should I? And would he? *Because if... then...*

As my brain locked itself into analysis paralysis, it was all I could do to nod a weak goodbye as the rest of me began to panic.

Watching Victor walk away, it was all I could do not to scream.

After Greg and Abby left, Betty and I squeezed in a few more carefree games of pool before it was finally time for me to take my seat in the tournament. Not wanting to appear too eager by skipping it, I reluctantly left her in the lounge where she promised to wait for me.

Oddly enough, the last fifteen minutes before nine o'clock had filled me with an inexplicable sense of increasing dread. Even though we had only known each other for five short hours, I felt the uncomfortable awkwardness of our impending—albeit temporary—goodbye growing by the minute. There was a part of me that wanted desperately to kiss her but in our final moments together she seemed preoccupied by something. The last few seconds before I walked away just didn't feel right so I decided not to force it. Besides, I was sure we'd get to that later.

Much to my chagrin though, I caught a couple of Marines further down the bar checking Betty out just as I turned around. While I had full confidence that she wasn't going to meet and leave with anyone else while I played poker, it was all I could do to keep from snarling. My sudden flare of anger threw me off because I had never been the possessive type. To make matters worse, I could have sworn I saw the two jarheads give her the eye again just as I passed behind them as they laughed.

Before I knew it, my Krav Maga training kicked in and I watched helplessly as both my hands reached out, grabbed each guy by a side of their head before smashing their skulls together. Watching them crumple like dead weight, I blinked just in time to see them finish a swig from their bottles of beer. Gritting my teeth, I swallowed too, downing the uncomfortable lump in my throat along with the violent images my mind had so quickly conjured. *Get a grip, assho—*

"—Victor?!"

Despite doing my best to keep the desperation out of my voice, Victor turned to me with a semi-stunned look on his face. As he quickly made his way back to my side, I couldn't help but feel guilty for causing him to worry. I only hoped I didn't look as pitiful as I felt when he finally drew near.

"Is everything okay?" he asked.

He appeared more disoriented than worried which made me feel a little better.

"I'm... I'm sorry. I... I just wanted to ask you for a favor."

"Oh... Umm, sure. Anything. What is it?"

"I know this will probably sound strange... but I was wondering if... I'd like to make a deal with you. While you're back there playing poker and I'm out here... I promise not to Google you if you promise not to Google me."

Victor's look of confusion quickly gave way to what appeared to be slightly incredulous relief.

"You mean... you won't run a search for *my name* if I promise not to run one for *yours?"*

"Yes. Is that okay? Can we just not do that?"

Victor's smile overrode his chuckle just enough for him to speak. "You have my word, I will not do that... to you."

"Thank you," I sighed gratefully.

After studying me for a second, Victor leaned in closer. "You're welcome," he said.

And then he kissed me.

It started as a simple kiss.

Invading Betty's personal space for only a brief second or two, I leaned forward just slow enough to give her an opportunity to refuse my advance if she wanted. But sensing no hesitation from her in return, I touched my lips to hers.

Keeping my eyes open just long enough to see hers go glassy, I pressed against her mouth, splitting our crevices by taking her lower lip between mine as I felt her inhale deeply. Suspended together at the top of that moment, I savored her taste, the uniqueness of her wine tinged breath and did my best to capture the sensations in my mind even as I felt a small part of them work their way into my soul. Releasing her lips as she exhaled, I opened my eyes to find hers staring into mine.

"Don't go away," I smiled. "I'm coming back for you."

Almost as if she were too afraid to speak, Betty simply nodded.

Still reeling from Victor's kiss, I swiveled in my seat and tried to gather my composure as he walked away. I was swooning and embarrassed enough that I didn't want him to notice.

The man had no idea that he was only the seventh to ever kiss me. No idea that no man—boys, really—had ever kissed me with so much genuine affection. No idea that he was the first to ever kiss me with his eyes closed. No idea that for the first time all night... I was having some serious doubts.

I'd *never* had a love life and my sex life didn't extend much past the same. I'd long ago given up on the hope of ever finding someone of the opposite sex capable of relating to me. Or, if I was truly being honest, someone with whom I was capable of relating. But that was fine because I had also long ago made peace with my situation since I knew no one was to blame, not even myself really.

Yet I had to admit in just five hours of conversation, Victor had come closer than anyone I had ever met with regards to what I was looking for in a man. As this was unchartered territory for me, I didn't know what to do about it. And that was a feeling I definitely deplored.

Shaking off my anxiety about our Googling one another now that it was out of my hands, I found myself both saddened and relieved. Prior to saying goodbye we had been having such a good time that I didn't want it to end. I had made more than enough overtures for Victor to know I was ready to go back to his hotel room for sex so, while I did understand, I actually was a bit disappointed that he didn't ditch the poker tournament and take me up on my offer as soon as possible.

But at the same time, I also really enjoyed the feeling of how relaxed we both were about the whole thing. Each of us had understood for quite awhile that having sex tonight was a foregone conclusion. Victor had picked up on all my signals with relative ease and, after a brief consideration, returned them in agreement. After that, not having to worry about trying to seduce one another had simply allowed us to just be ourselves.

And that, at least for me, turned out to be the ultimate seduction.

As a doctor, I had spent so much time with patients that I had inadvertently begun to treat everyone I met in the exact same, listen-before-responding measured manner. In turn, I had forgotten what it felt like to interact with people from my own personally opinionated perspective and not just that of a doctor.

Engaging with Victor as myself, a woman who just needed to get laid and not as a psychotherapist, made me chuckle as the age old adage 'Physician, heal thyself' sprang to mind. Of course, if I felt bad about anything, it was how I had used my knowledge of behavioral psychology to get exactly what I wanted.

With regard to Victor, I knew that men with a tendency to play coy were often much simpler to manipulate compared to those too dense to even grasp the concept. You first just had to realize that most weren't *trying* to be coy, they actually enjoyed thinking of themselves as *being* coy.

To them, being coy was part of their hunt to capture a woman's interest and affection, much the same way women used it against men. But for a man, being coy wasn't so much a weapon they used as it was a shield they wore like a cloak of invisibility that allowed them to get closer to their prey without being directly detected.

But I knew if you let men like that know however directly or indirectly as needed that there was no reason to hunt and therefore no reason to chase because their goal was also your goal... then there was no longer a reason for them to be coy. This, in effect, often completely disarmed them to the point where they weren't sure what to think. And confused people were always the easiest to manipulate.

The tricky part was simultaneously getting such a man to realize you weren't willing to be preyed *upon.* It wasn't a one way street. They had to understand we were both hunters and we were both prey. Finding a man who could accept then handle that equality was, among a host of others, one of the main reasons I was still single.

Thankfully, Victor didn't seem to have that problem.

Sipping on the last of my Cabernet, I smiled as I thought back on our conversations... or, to be more precise, our one continuous conversation. With barely a lull, it seemed like the last five hours were over in a minute. I couldn't recall the last time, if ever, I had enjoyed talking with a man as much as I had Victor.

While at first I had been captivated by his aura and how handsome he was, those things were quickly overshadowed by all the small details I began to notice about him. Like the black flames of his peek-a-boo tattoos, mere clips showing just under the cuffs above each wrist and both sides of his collar along the front of his shoulders. From what little I could discern, the design was symmetrical and appeared to be calligraphy written within an overall tribal outline. The mystique alone was enough to make me think more than once about ripping off his shirt if nothing more than to discover what it said.

Then I remembered the first whiff I caught of his cologne. We had been shooting pool for about an hour and I hadn't realized he was wearing any until he excused himself as he slid past me to line up a shot. The expensive scent of airy yet well-oiled wood was absolutely intoxicating and smelled masculine as hell on him.

Lastly, though if I was being honest mostly, it was Victor's attention to me that had my head spinning. At first I wasn't sure if he was just being polite and returning the favor. But as the hours passed, I realized he truly took no notice of other women checking him out. He had become too interested in me to care. And while I'd never been a jealous woman, when I noticed not even our waitress—a much younger, really pretty, bubbly brunette—held his eye longer than it took him to place our order, I couldn't help but feel thrilled. As astounding as it was for me to believe... Victor was actually into me as much as I was him.

Shaking my head in amazement, I tried not to lament my unexpected predicament because by hoping for nothing more than to get laid, I had inadvertently screwed myself. It almost wasn't fair. I mean I hadn't planned on meeting anyone close to being Mr. Right tonight. All I wanted was a Mr. Right For Now. Instead I crossed paths with Victor, possibly the closest thing to Mr. Right I had ever seen, the type of man whom if I had met under any other circumstance I would have taken my time and tried to get to really know. True, I definitely would have wanted to throw myself at him as soon as possible, but I probably wouldn't have. Not that it mattered now because here I was and here I had with my only consolation that he had said yes.

Yet I really had no idea *why* he wanted *me.* While I knew what my motivat—

Oh, shit! My tattoo!

My fit of jealousy aside, my heart and head just weren't in to playing poker. Knowing full well that Betty was ready to go back to my hotel room to fuck took it out of me even more. A sad run of cards—which under normal circumstances I would have attempted to bluff my way through—and I had no problem tossing my last hand into the muck a mere seventeen minutes into the tournament, shoving all-in with the one fairly decent pair of cards—Ace-Ten—that had never won a single hand for me. Although this time was no exception, for the first time ever my loss made me smile.

Only after rising and wishing everyone at my table good luck before walking away did it strike me that I had just driven five hours to play amateur poker only to be the first player knocked out of the championship round... and I couldn't have cared less about it.

Oh, dear God, I can't believe I forgot!

Equally as bad as not wanting Victor to leave me at the bar, I now wanted him to stay gone. I needed time to think... think. *Think!* How in the hell was I going to explain my tattoo?

I had never allowed myself to entertain any possible scenario whereby I met a man like Victor therefore I had no decent explanation at my ready. Not a single one of the dozens I had rehearsed now seemed worthy... Or maybe I was having second thoughts about myself. Was I worthy?

Is that why I'm worried?

It was more than possible because truth be told, when it came to Victor there was only one scenario that came to mind. And just shy of my coming clean with the full-blown truth, it was the one I dared to allow myself to hope for the least.

But now that it's possibly here, what should I do?

I honestly had no idea. But what I did know was that more obvious than the contrast between my pale skin and my tattoo's fading colors would be that I had willingly allowed myself to be so glaringly branded. That my tattoo would silently scream my dedication for me. And *that,* I suddenly remembered, had been the point. I needed it to because not even I had the words to describe my own feelings and desires when it came to sex.

Of course like most people, my issues ran much deeper than that.

Simply put, like so many others in life I wanted to belong because I felt like I never had. My intelligence level as a child had meant I never fit in with kids my own age. I couldn't relate to them and the older ones I could relate to couldn't back to me.

For my part I could fake it, sure. Smile when I knew I should, laugh when I knew it was expected. But in so many moments and ways my life had felt like an act in which I just played my part as best I could in order not to draw attention to myself. Because deep down if there was one thing I feared above all else, it was that people would realize just how different I truly was.

Yet with Victor, for five straight hours I failed to feel a single iota of that fear. Or at least none that wasn't of my own making. The man had been neither overly opinionated nor judgmental. He seemed to evaluate then just accept things as they were. On a personal level, both his empathy and his rare conceit had struck me as being entirely void of ego.

Flashing back, I suddenly recalled a moment when our waitress had arrived a bit late with our drinks. After offering her apologies, Victor had graciously assured her we were fine before pointing out we were still nursing the ones we had. Asking for and then addressing her by name, he offered his sympathy for how busy the place had become as more and more poker players no longer playing were ordering food and drinks.

I had felt a twinge of jealousy in that moment especially as I recognized Victor acknowledge the sway his attention held over her. But when, as soon as she walked away, he sidled up to me and whispered, "I bet she won't be late with your drink again," I literally thought I might melt. His entire act of kindness toward her, though genuine, had really been for my benefit.

Glancing down at my torso, the last of my anxiety evaporated just as a tickle of butterflies began to take flight... along with my smile.

Screw it, I thought as I cupped my wine glass and looked around. *I'll think of something.*

Reentering the lounge area, I spotted Betty smiling and people watching from the same corner stool I left her. The voyeur in me instinctively slowed my pace to better observe the one in her. Sipping her Cabernet Sauvignon, I saw her pause to savor the flavor while studying a happy couple throwing a game of darts just as we had done earlier. Unfortunately, that also allowed me to see the secret double dose of appreciation written across her face fade a few seconds later when a passing waitress groaned loudly in frustration at something on her phone, breaking the spell.

Finally becoming aware of my approach, Betty's eyes lit up, making a part of me do the same.

"Are you ready to go?" I asked, pleased to see the look in her eyes.

"Hell yes."

Her eagerness was enough to make my cock start to swell, neither of which surprised me. Despite—or perhaps due to—our casual acceptance of the inevitability of sex, the sexual anticipation between us that had been slowly building all night was still at its peak. Thrilled to hear she was every bit as ready as I and before she could object, I passed the bartender enough cash to close her tab. Given what we both knew was about to happen, paying for drinks felt the least I could do.

"Thank you," Betty whispered. Her smile was demure and gracious, but something in her eyes clearly indicated she was touched even deeper than she let on. Seemingly embarrassed, she covered by turning to grab her clutch before following me toward the exit where it was my turn.

I had long hated establishments like Mickey's with standard entryways. The lower the header the more pronounced my ducking under them was obvious to anyone watching. And while I was over people's mixed looks of amusement and pity, I had no desire for Betty to be subjected to them.

Realizing our walk to leave was our longest stretch of shared silence, I shot Betty a quick, deadpanned glance once we were alone outside. Although I had had a lot of fun trying, nothing I had said the entire evening seemed to catch her unawares. So without preamble when I simply stated, "I need to stop at a gas station for condoms," her instantaneous retort should have been unsurprising.

"Do me a favor," she said. "Get two boxes."

Holy shit, she's fucking serious.

My jaw dropped a full inch. Without a doubt, Betty was more down to fuck than any woman I had ever met. And it was beyond obvious the woman knew what she wanted and even better how to get it. But her confidence was so nonchalant, it was unlike anything I had ever experienced in a woman. Simply outmatched, all I could do was laugh.

"Sounds more like 'Do *us* a favor' to me," I chuckled. Of course, by then I knew it would have been smart to leave well enough alone, but the idiot in me couldn't resist. "So tell me. Does the lady have a preference for ribbed, studded or spiraled?"

"I prefer it raw and hard, but I'll take whatever you've got."

Son of a bitch! I smarted. With nothing clever left in my think tank I squeezed my lower lip between my teeth. I couldn't believe it. Was this really happening? Sure, I'd had sure things drop into my lap before, but Betty was on a whole other level. Her approach toward sex was both more subtle and more blunt—and therefore, more complete—than anyone I had ever known, including myself.

There was an underlying beauty to her, yes, but on the surface she also seemed to be so girl-next-door wholesome. The pretty, cheerful but ultimately forgettable receptionist of some lobby type. And yet she wasn't. Not by a long shot.

Stunned, I followed her toward her car. Walking in silence I started to think her door might present another good opportunity to kiss her and nullify my sudden reticence. But as she pointed her remote and pressed Unlock on her fob, I saw the taillights flash on a white Mercedes AMG GT C Roadster. Even my best poker face would have failed to conceal my disbelief.

You've got to be shitting me... Is this some kind of joke?

Betty's car was a new but fairly rare and expensive masterpiece. A $150,000 showcase of some of the finest German engineering ever devised. I knew. On the other side of the parking lot was mine. Only mine was black.

I picked the same damn car to—

Shaking off the shock, I started to mention the coincidence, but quickly decided it would be far better to allow Betty to experience the same surreal realization once she saw mine. Grinding my teeth, I even managed to swallow my sudden overwhelming desire to quip, "Nice car."

Too stunned to remember my intention to kiss her, I opened Betty's door for her. After she slid in and I had given her the name of my hotel in case we became separated, I hesitated before shutting her door. Even if it was a bad idea, it was still the right thing to do. Plus, I just had to know.

"Before we go any further," I faltered, "I need to ask you something."

Betty looked up at me quizzically. As quick witted as she had been all evening, I knew she was oblivious to what I was about to ask her. And there simply was no other way for me to put it.

"What's your name?"

I was well aware most women would probably get pissed to be asked such a question by a man with whom they had just spent the last five plus hours. Especially one that they had unequivocally given every signal in the book to that they intended to fuck. But as her raised eyebrow and seductively spreading grin slowly confirmed, Betty wasn't just any woman.

"You don't remember? Hmmmm..." I watched her briefly contemplate the implication before the devilish look in her eyes caught up with her grin. "Good. The sex will be better that way." Pausing to let me take her words in, I nodded in agreement. "And besides," she continued, "I can always tell you after if you're still interested... provided of course I still am."

Shaking my head in laughter following her wink, I gently closed Betty's door.

Once in my own car, I decided to trust my instincts and removed the revolver from my boxers before locking it in the gun box bolted beneath the passenger seat.

Fifteen minutes later—after buying two boxes of condoms at a gas station along the way—I opened the door to my hotel suite, allowing Betty to enter first.

Sharing the same sly smile, neither of us said a word about our matching cars on the elevator ride up. That she, too, chose to allow our obvious yet coincidental connection to go unspoken for the time being... I honestly thought was pretty damn cool.

When Victor pulled out in front of me, driving the same Mercedes AMG GT C Roadster only in black, I thought I might die from the shock. That the man had money didn't surprise me. I'd spent much of my life working with the uber wealthy. Their personal tells, though variable, were obvious to a watchful eye.

No, my shock came from growing up a "car" kind of girl. From classic muscle, super cute Beetles and tricked out Hellcats to sensuously sleek Mercedeses, I loved almost anything automotive. My father's daughter through and through, I was a total gear head.

Still less than a year old, my Roadster was my one true extravagance in life. That it had ultimately been a failed attempt to lift me out of my funk notwithstanding, it was still my pride and joy. So, to know that Victor had chosen to purchase the same car, that our tastes could be *so* similar...

And to think, we've been talking for hours without knowing we had this in common, too.

My mind flashed back to when I first spotted Victor walking across Mickey's parking lot. Realizing I hadn't seen what he'd parked then, it suddenly dawned on me that he hadn't mentioned the coincidence when he'd opened my door for me just a few minutes ago. I remembered a briefly stunned yet appreciative look on his face, but I saw that look all the time on people trying not to gawk at my car.

No, he wasn't appreciating my car... *He was appreciating the* coincidence... *And he said nothing about it.*

The realization sent a thrill up my spine so intense I felt my nipples harden even further than they already were.

He's calculating me.

My mind slipped into overdrive. Victor knew I was about to discover what he drove as I followed him to the gas station and then the hotel as I was doing now. Under normal conditions, anyone would have mentioned the coincidence. It was *not* normal not to. But Victor *was* normal. So for him to act abnormally could only mean that he had an ulterior motive. But what—

He wanted me to feel it, too, I suddenly realized. *He wanted me to feel this... this... Damn.*

That meant Victor wasn't just thinking *about* me... he was also thinking *of* me... *Me.* A good thirty pounds overweight *me.* A not-at-my-best-right-now *me.* And—

Oh shit, my tattoo! How in the hell had my tattoo slipped my mind *again?!* And what was I going to tell Victor when he saw it?

Shit! Shit! Shit!

I couldn't believe I forgot again. From the moment I had first been inked, I had had no qualms with possibly telling one of my future lovers its origin. After all, that was the reason I got it in the first place. The idea, the *fantasy,* I was ready to tell about it actually excited me. But I had concocted my story for a stranger I never planned to see again.

Only Victor didn't feel like a stranger. He hadn't for hours now. And though when we first met I didn't see how his being from Charlotte or being such good friends with Greg and Abby was an issue, now I wasn't so sure... Or maybe it was just wishful thinking on my part. Maybe now that we had gotten to know one another I *wanted* those things to be an issue even though they still weren't? Because I had to admit if Victor was going to want to see me again after tonight, I would sure as hell like to see him, too.

I shook my head, realizing I was getting ahead of myself again. I needed to decide just how much I was going to tell Victor about my tattoo. It wasn't like I could hide it. The damn thing was plastered clear across my entire torso.

Tell him the truth... Tell him the story... Just... not all *of it. Not yet, anyway.*

The thought came out of nowhere. Like a bullet piercing my brain, it ricocheted inside my head, looking for a way back out. Finding none, I started to mull the idea over.

It was definitely an option. But if I went that route, it would be a deception by omission. Not a betrayal per se, but a definite leading the man astray.

Should I do it? *No. Probably not.* Could I do it? *Yes.* Would I do it? *I don't know... Maybe.*

A sudden desire not to answer my last question gave in to my confidence to make the right decision once in the moment. To trust myself to think on my feet. It had gotten me this far in life. And if it could get me Victor...

Get me Victor...

The thought was so natural I couldn't help but smile. The words had such a nice ring to th—

My reverie was broken by the realization that we were pulling into the hotel parking lot. I had been so deep in thought, I barely remembered stopping at the gas station. Now so close to finally getting what I wanted, my anxiety suddenly flared anew.

What am I going to do?

Trying not to fret, I pulled into the spot next to Victor, put my car in park and tried the only thing I could think of, something that I had advised many of my patients to do as often as possible. I took a deep breath... held it... then exhaled slowly. Then I reminded myself to keep it simple.

First things first. Relax. Then get yourself laid. Fuck his ever-loving brains out. And trust that the rest will take care of itself. With my confidence restored, I inhaled again. *You can do this.*

Exhaling the last of my fear, I tried to ignore the fact that it had been nearly a year since the last time I had sex. More importantly, I knew this was probably my last chance to satisfy my fantasy. In its own weird way, tonight had become now or never.

My heartbeat slowing, I grabbed my clutch from the passenger seat just as Victor opened my door. Surprised by it even though he had been a perfect Southern gentleman all night, I paused just long enough to look up into his crystal clear baby blues.

Oh, yeah, I smiled as I took his outstretched hand. *I'm going to fuck the hell out of you...*

Less than two seconds after she turned on the nearest switch for the light above the bed, my hands grabbed Betty's face, pulling her to me as quickly as possible. Restraining myself as best I could, I devoured her mouth with my lips and then my tongue, savoring her as she responded in kind.

Kiss for kiss, nibble for nibble and bite for bite we went at each other like teenagers experiencing passion for the very first time, the sexual tension and anticipation that had been building between us all night finally free. Fighting for control, my fingers threaded their way through her hair as her hands circled my waist, each of us drawing the other closer into a tighter embrace.

We fought furiously to cover as much surface area as possible, our lips and tongues greedily battling over increasingly wet turf. It didn't take long for me to realize that I couldn't remember the last time I had kissed anyone this way. I had forgotten what a true coupling felt like, for heat to explode into more heat, a chain reaction where one fire multiplied and ignited others, each hungrier than the last as they spread throughout our bodies in search of more fuel to burn.

With Betty's head still firmly ensconced in my hands, hers began to rub me all over, exploring my arms, pressing across my back and stomach before pawing along my chest. The hardness of my nipples seemed to really turn her on, sending shockwaves through me.

Highly sensitive, my nipples stayed perpetually stiff. I loved to have them played with and sucked on. But since few women ever took their own initiative to do so, I always figured I was just odd that way and so more often than not just silently went without.

But not with Betty.

Over my shirt she pinched both of my nipples, rolling them between forefinger and thumb as her crotch parted to straddle my leg. With her pelvis grinding slowly against me, her hands seemingly reached their breaking point as she tore them away, gliding them down across my stomach then back to my ass.

Most men, I knew, would have had her naked by this point. But both because the kissing was so damn good and that I took a certain sense of pride in not being like most men, I resisted even though I knew without a doubt she was ready to fuck. The sheer heat coming off her body told me I probably couldn't make her any wetter than she already was.

But as the passion of our kissing increased, I felt myself absorbing her excitement and loss of control. Taking it in, I actually gained more as I lost less of my own. And the dynamic of *that* was incredible.

As Betty's lips, hands and body began to plead with me, each in their own way to please, please tear off her clothes and fuck her, my kisses wordlessly replied *No.* Countering each of her silent protests with renewed concentration and vigor, I continued to explore her mouth with my tongue, moving her face and head in flowing rhythm with my own.

But when the frenzy of her roaming hands told me she couldn't take it anymore, I suddenly wrapped my tongue around hers like a snake, gripping it in an almost suffocating coil, pulling it out of her mouth and forcing it as deeply as possible into my own.

Betty's eyes went so wide I knew she had never felt anything like this before. She froze momentarily as I pointedly met her gaze with my own. Locking eyes, I watched her expression as I slowly began to give her tongue a blow job.

Round and round I went, up and down, in and out. Quick became slow only to become quick again. Whenever her tongue began to soften in the least, I sucked it harder, gripping it like the muscle it was and stroking it back to rigidity. Without saying a word, I made her realize I wanted her tongue to stay as stiff as she could manage and keep it that way. In a daze, she finally began to comply.

And that's when I truly began to tear her up.

I closed my eyes and focused all my energy on orally pleasuring just that one, single part of her body. Varying my intensity to her overall response, I made love to, had sex with and fucked her tongue with my mouth over and over again. And as I did, ever so slowly, little by little her knees lost enough strength to where I was practically holding her up.

I don't know if she watched me or lost herself in the fellatio I performed on her but, after only a few minutes, I could swear she came. Nothing earth shattering or body wracking. Just a slight but sudden tensing before her entire body relaxed as if she could take it no more, the fight in her momentarily drained.

So as Betty's spindle began to soften, I matched it. Ramping down from the hard sucking motion of a torrid vortex to the gentle swirl of a caress, I slowly released her tongue, satisfied that both it and she were completely spent. When

I finally opened my eyes, I found that hers had turned to glass as she did her best to focus on me. Planting one final kiss, lingering only to pull on her bottom lip with both my own, I released her from my grip, allowing us to gently separate as she regained her footing.

As the immediacy of our passion subsided, the residual intensity of the moment filled the void. In a long, single look, each of us silently acknowledged the extent of our chemistry. It was clear whatever impersonal ideas we had about tonight being just a one night stand were gone, leaving us standing there, gazing at one another in newly appreciative shock.

Damn... who is this woman?

When, after several seconds the smile in Betty's eyes spread down to her mouth, she slowly took a step back followed by a deep breath... then began to undress for me.

Walking into the hotel suite first, it suddenly felt like I was in a movie when Victor grabbed me from behind by my arm and spun me around. And just like in the movies, I was every bit as ready for it.

The surprising thirst and hunger with which he quickly kissed me was so strong, it almost bordered on desperation. I felt the sexual tension between us that had been pent up for hours pour forth from him like a swollen lake breaching its levee.

But there was more than that.

As Victor's desire saturated me, I also sensed his incredible *need* for me. I couldn't explain it any more than I could deny it, but it was there, fused within the heat of his passion. And as much as his need flooded me with such a profound sense of unexpected relief, my body was forced to relax even further in order to expand and make room inside myself. The sensation was almost overwhelming.

I had offered myself to Victor so freely, so easily, that I couldn't blame him if all he intended was to use me. In fact, there was a very large part of me, of my desire, that wanted nothing more.

Yet as our evening had progressed, wanting more from Victor was exactly what I found myself wanting. I wanted to know more about him, see more of him, be more with him. And the way he kissed me... he had already given me *more* than I ever expected.

Victor had me in the throes of a heat I had never before experienced and I wanted him to know just how responsible he was for it. Yet as the minutes continued to pass and all he did was kiss me, my desperation grew uncontrollable.

But given not just his size but how my head was cradled in his hands, he controlled almost everything about us. The direction of our mouths, the proximity of our bodies... the pace of our flow, back and forth and back and...

Each feverish burst of his frenzy sparked one of my own, increasing the heat gathering between us. And as the energy centered around our mouths built, I finally began to short circuit. No longer able to contain itself, the electricity spread down my arms to my hands.

Searching for an outlet, my fingers rubbed their way down the muscles of his arms and up the creviced spine of his back. With nowhere else to go, my hands pressed themselves smoothly down the tautness of his obliques, across the unbelievably flat ridges of his stomach then up to his chest.

Wasting no time, my fingers went straight for his nipples and the moment I realized they were already hard a huge surge of heat and wetness diffused itself between my legs. Unable to stop myself, I spread them, wrapping my groin around one of his legs to grind against him.

But the more I rolled, squeezed and practically pinched his nipples, Victor seemed to still. I didn't understand his reaction. I knew he was turned on. I could sense it in the way he was breathing, feel it in between my fingers and there was absolutely no denying the unbelievably hard bulge in his pants. Yet it suddenly felt like a competi—

Victor's tongue suddenly wrapped itself so forcefully around my own that, for the briefest of seconds, I thought I might have done something wrong. As he pulled my tongue deep into his mouth, I froze. Desperately wondering what was going on, my eyes refocused just enough to find Victor purposefully staring into them.

As his tongue began to slide up and down my own, I became lost in the sensation. Coiling around it, again and again and again, with each of his pulls I felt the energy drain back up my body, traveling from my knees through my loins, past my chest until finally exiting my mouth through my tongue.

Sucking even harder, Victor fixed his eyes directly on my own.

Though my head was gripped securely in his hands... my legs straddled his... my tongue held captive by his... and though my hands were latched firmly onto his body... at no point were Victor and I more connected at that moment than we were in our eyes.

Never had I had any man communicate so wordlessly yet so completely as Victor did with me in that moment. Stunned by my own comprehension, I made my tongue as stiff as I could as he so obviously desired. When he closed his eyes, I had to follow suit in order to keep from fainting.

The feeling of his tongue scrolling up and down my own, wrapping, coiling, licking, sucking me from base to tip... over and over again... It was impossible not to recognize the similarity between what he was doing to me and fellatio.

My God, no wonder...

It took all the strength I had to keep my tongue as firm as it was. But try as I might, eventually I couldn't continue. With each bob of his muscle, more and more of my heat and energy and every ounce of my resistance were slowly sucked into Victor's mouth. My entire body held out as long as it could until *I* could no longer.

As Victor acquiesced, relinquishing his control over me, my focus slowly returned. I gazed up at him in appreciation for several seconds, bathing in our connection... before suddenly remembering I had a surprise of my own.

Stepping back, I slipped out of my high heels, thankful to see Victor follow my lead. Although I was quaking on the inside, his eagerness gave me enough confidence that when it came time to take off my sundress, I barely even paused.

Here goes nothing... Moment of truth...

Eyes locked on one another, I was glad I was already excited because to be perfectly honest, from what I expected Betty with less clothes was going to fail to excite me further. I felt a little bad about that yet also forgave myself. As good as our kissing had been, I couldn't fault human nature. What turns us on, turns us on and what doesn't, doesn't. And I was as guilty as any man at becoming visually excited by what I saw... And I was sure Betty's body wasn't exactly going to do that for me.

For as long as I could remember because of my own height I found myself inexplicably attracted to tall, slender females. And on the rare occasions when shorter women captured my interest, I preferred them petite.

But despite how often my predilection could make me feel like the most callous asshole on earth, the truth was chemistry trumped everything for me. So while my libido might have had a narrow range, my mind and soul, and therefore my body, had one which was far more expansive.

And if our kiss was any indication, chemistry was something Betty and I most definitely had more than enough of.

Reveling in anticipation of what was about to come, I unbuttoned and removed my shirt as she pulled her sundress over her head. From experience, I was fully expecting to watch Betty's eyes widen as she got her first real look at my tattoo.

Instead, my eyes were the ones to go agog.

As her sundress lifted past her midriff, the tattoo scrawled across her torso leapt out at me like it was on fire and screaming in agony. Three spheres, each a different size and color, were arranged in a triangle then connected by straight, dark lines of various thickness and number. Only the three dimensionally shaded circles appeared to be melting from some invisible heat as their lines dripped what looked like radioactive blood.

Taken altogether, Betty's tattoo was a visualization a mad chemist might conjure during the worst acid trip imaginable which, after being interpreted by someone who spoke only in tongues, was then drawn through the eyes of a serial killer. The entire image was strategically placed so that anything less than a full one-piece bathing suit would fail to hide what was easily the most unique, oddest yet undeniably most hideous tattoo I had ever seen in my life.

Why the hell would anyo—

"Cool tat," I muttered, trying to hide my confusion. "Uhh, I've never seen one like it before." *So much for hiding.* "Does it mean anything?" *Stop talking, you idiot!*

I knew how stupid the question sounded before it escaped my lips. Virtually no one had a tattoo that didn't mean something, if to no one else then at least to their self. But I was so taken aback, I couldn't think of anything else to say. Thankfully, it didn't matter as the sultry smile in Betty's voice alone practically oozed that of a Cheshire Cat.

"That's my Sex Slave tattoo," she purred.

Sex. Slave. Tattoo.

The words echoed through the sudden blankness of my mind as my pulse began to race. Which I guess is oddly what happens when your heart skips that many beats. Of course, if Betty hadn't been surprising me at every turn all damn night, it probably would have stopped altogether. Instead, I somehow managed to take it in relative stride.

"You're... into being a Sex Slave?"

"I am," she preened as she unclasped her bra.

Her words barely registered over my surprise. I wasn't a breast man. I had been with so many women that only the best impressed me. Because of this I often found myself more enthralled with a woman's nipples. And all four of Betty's were exquisite.

Her breasts were just a little too large for her frame, which fit my idea of perfection. I figured her push up bra had given them their high firmness but there was almost no droop to them. Yet they weren't fake. And her nipples—raised erasers precisely centered inside her soft pink, perfectly proportional areolae—were the most beautiful I had ever seen in my entire life.

But as I drank in the vision of sexuality peeling away her clothes before me, two lines of thought began to whirl in my head.

Selfishly, the first concerned my penchant for raunchy sex. I doubted I was into anything so extreme to which a woman who obviously enjoyed being a Sex Slave might have an objection. Admittedly, it had been way too long since I had truly let my freak flag fly, but even my hedonism had a limit. And because of that, I figured no matter what I did I was probably going to leave Betty wanting for more.

Yet my second thought troubled me even further.

She's pretty... beautiful even... But is she so insecure about her appearance—or maybe just her weight—that she feels the need to be a Sex Slave?

I knew it was a horrible thought, but no matter how little we knew much less cared about one another, I wasn't into one-sidedly using women for sex or anything else for that matter.

I was too empathic. Great sex for me meant that I felt everything I was making my partner feel. I would consciously take their excitement in, then give it back and take it in again, amplifying it each time I did so until it became an unconscious, natural act. Much like our kiss moments ago.

But if Betty was into subjugating herself as a way to compensate for her looks, for her being somewhat overweight... that wasn't something I had in me to tolerate much less be cool with.

Yet there was nothing insecure about her. No lack of self-respect. No self-loathing. From what I had observed all evening, Betty's sense of dignity and self-esteem weren't just perfectly healthy, they were admirably so. That the two characteristics could so peacefully coexist in one person whose overriding sexual desire appeared to be to be used solely for another person's benefit felt like an incongruous assumption. And it unnerved the hell out of me.

Then again, being unarmed didn't help either.

"So, where's your Master tonight?" I tried to ask without sounding as worried as I suddenly was.

"I don't have one at the moment."

"Oh."

I breathed a small sigh of relief as my mind pivoted from one uncomfortable idea to the next. This was uncharted territory for me. The thought of some jealous sadist suddenly banging on our door trying to reclaim his property... I stopped my brain from going there.

"And your tattoo?" I asked as nonchalantly as I could. Despite my distraction, I carefully watched Betty's face as I slowly began to pull down my boxers. "They signify what you're in to?" I stepped out of my boxers, continuing as if nothing was unusual. But it was. It always was.

"They... they do," Betty stammered.

Attempting to recover from her momentary shock, I watched as she finished slipping out of her panties. With the exception of a thin, faint strip above her clit, she was completely shaven.

"And... what... um, what are you in to?" I asked as my mouth watered in anticipation. *Dear God*— "What turns you on?"

The girlish giggle that escaped Betty's lips before she spoke continued to echo within her words.

"Being made to feel like a dirty little slut."

As Betty smiled at my shock, I realized that her words, the sound of her voice and the gleam in her eye were all things I would never forget.

Whatever misgivings I had had at that point vanished as I suddenly understood. The confident woman standing naked in front of me was simply more sexually liberated than any I had ever met. She knew what she wanted and she obviously knew how to get it. I had seen it in her eyes all night and now I heard the undeniable confirmation of it in her voice. And for the briefest of moments I felt like I had died and gone to heaven. As a sudden rush of lust swelled within me, I fought my own instincts to keep it from raging beyond my control.

I had never wanted a woman so badly in my life.

And she was mine for the taking.

So I took her.

Staring straight into her eyes, I reached around Betty's back and quickly ran my left hand up behind her head. Playfully but firmly gripping a fistful of hair, I fed two fingers from my right hand into her open mouth. She was so willingly compliant, my cock stiffened even harder than it already was.

As my fingers slid in and out of her mouth, Betty purred and cooed for me, eagerly licking and sucking as one of her hands slipped between her legs while the other took hold and began stroking my cock. Within seconds, her hands synchronized with mine, both daring and pleading with me for more.

Rising to the challenge, I fucked her mouth with my fingers, increasing the pace of our rhythm like a maestro conducting an orchestra. Up and down her one hand pumped as in and out her other fingers went. Building us both to a crescendo only to slow to keep from cresting felt so natural it was almost organic.

The power alone was intoxicating. To be given control of a woman's masturbation intensity—and to both of us, no less—was not only unlike anything I had ever felt before, it was something I had never even been able to imagine.

Realizing what I had, what she had given me, I did my best to ignore the pleasure and expertise of her one hand while trying to exploit her other. Slow...

fast... deep... shallow. One finger... two fingers...

In less than two minutes, just as I sensed Betty on the edge of orgasm, I slowly began to decrease our mutual tempo back down to a natural standstill. As mind blowing as the experience was, I needed to see how far I could take things with her before proceeding further. Sex Slave or no, I was unsure of just how far she'd be willing to go for me. Although one thing was for sure.

She doesn't have a problem talking dirty. So—

"Wetter. Make my fingers wetter," I commanded, pausing just long enough to allow her to gather her spit with which she obediently slathered my fingers. "So," I teased, purposefully dropping my voice a few octaves to a shade I knew probably matched the look in my eyes, "whose description of 'dirty little slut' should we use? Yours? Or mine?"

Never flinching, Betty looked me straight in the eye, slowly withdrew my dripping fingers from her mouth and in a tone more hungry than my own said, "Yours," before she resumed sucking.

There are moments in life where you just want to hit the pause button and soak it all in.

I'd been with nearly a hundred different women in my life. But none of them had ever offered themselves to me so carte blanche or with such abandoned fervor.

Images of unfulfilled, bucket list fantasies began to flash before my eyes. The things I could do to this woman. The things she would not only be okay with but actually might *want* done to her.

Yet the only sounds I could hear over those images were Betty's girlish giggle and the words 'Being made to feel like a dirty little slut' echoing again and again.

Dirty, huh? Let's see about that...

Gently but forcibly, I used my fingers in Betty's mouth to push and guide her down on to her knees. Her eyes went to my cock but when I wouldn't remove my fingers from her mouth, she finally looked up at me, her disappointment and confusion clear.

I did my best not to hesitate. I enjoyed the control she was offering me, but I was still unsure just how far she'd allow me to take it. Yet in that moment, I was torn. Push her too far and I could potentially bring the chemistry we had developed to a screeching halt. Or fail to take a chance and probably regret it for the rest of my life.

Luckily, I'd never been the kind of man to waste an opportunity.

"Nothing says 'dirty little slut' to me," I said, "more than a woman with cum all over her face."

If Betty's words had been heroin to me, mine were like crack to her. Her eyes went wide as she spit my fingers out as fast as she could. I wanted to be the one to shove my cock in her mouth but she was quicker. And the hunger with which she devoured me was beyond indescribable.

My cock was extraordinarily thick or "girthy as fuck" as one of my former lovers so eloquently liked to put it. It wasn't overly long, but it was still long enough that I had never been fully deep-throated—especially given my width. Most women were too scared to try and the few who dared had all choked.

Yet Betty managed to inhale me completely in a single gulp, her lips both stretching and gliding in one fell swoop all the way down to surround the lowest base of my shaft just as her eyes rolled briefly to the back of her head. She even paused just long enough for me to feel her throat muscles give the head of my cock one brief but amazing tug that rendered me helpless.

"Ohhhh my God, yessss!"

Temporarily powerless against the pleasure that had swallowed me whole, my head rolled backward as I finally experienced what had to be one of the best sexual sensations in the world.

And Betty was just getting started.

Using the pointed tip of her tongue, she flicked under and along the head of my cock, rimming and exploring me at all the right angles and intervals until her teasing eventually gave way to nothing but pure sucking. With her head bobbing up and down while twisting side to side, she corkscrewed both her mouth and tongue around my cock as best she could. Pulling me deeply in and out, over and over and over again, her mouth coiled ever tighter as she wrapped herself around me.

Allowing my eyes to roll back into my head, I closed them hard. Denying myself the sense of sight increased my sense of touch as the feel of her mouth became even more concentrated. Seconds became so many minutes that I lost track of time before realizing Betty hadn't forgotten my command for "Wetter" as the sound of her slurping suddenly caught my attention.

I opened my eyes and looked down to see a trail of saliva running from Betty's cheeks, mouth and chin over to the entire length of my cock. Her eyes partially rolled back, I could swear the woman was enjoying herself more than I was. It was almost as if I wasn't even there. My cock in her mouth seemed to be the only thing giving her pleasure as the rest of me had become irrelevant. The sight of being used like that, solely for her gratification, was such a complete turn on, I actually wondered if she could do it.

Can she make me cum?

I wanted to so badly, not just for me but for her, too. Unfortunately, I knew something Betty didn't, that it was extremely rare for any woman to ever suck me off. Though she had me close, for that to happen, I had to be in control. She was getting me there and for a brief second or two I thought about allowing her the chance to see how long and far she could go, if she could succeed.

But I also prided myself on reading a woman's moods, being aware of her signs, especially when it came to sex. So just as I saw the first sign of insecurity begin to cross her face for not being successful despite what was obviously her best efforts, I began to take charge.

"Look at me," I softly commanded, waiting for her eyes to find mine. What I could not say with words, I attempted with my eyes, hoping my look would convey everything I wanted her to know.

It's ok. I want you. Yes, I want you. But I want to give you something. The something you say you want.

Once the look in Betty's eyes changed from slight confusion to one of trust and understanding, I knew she was ready.

Cupping my left hand behind her head, the fingers of my right began to trace a line. Starting behind her left ear, I gently caressed her cheek, slowly trailing my hand below her chin, then up and over to her lips. Turning slightly to the side, I dragged the head of my cock against the inside of her right cheek. Pulling it out of her protesting mouth with my hand, I slapped her face with it, playfully but solidly. The easygoing giggle and smile that suddenly engulfed her face told me she absolutely loved it.

"Open your mouth again for me."

Looking up at me in a slow burn, when Betty's eyes finally met mine it was like I was looking at another woman. Her cocoa orbs that had just been filled with unexpected mirth were now clearly filled with lust. More lust than I had ever seen in a woman.

"Yes... *Master.*"

Or heard. *Fuck meee!*

Yet there was more than just lust in Betty's tone. As she called me Master, it also sounded as if she was challenging me. And damn if I wasn't up for the challenge.

Gripping the back of her head with both my hands, I proceeded to skullfuck her for the next several minutes as hard as I possibly could. I jackhammered her mouth over and over, yet never penetrating deep or long enough to even try to make her gag even though that seemed impossible. Instead I focused on my speed, attempting to slide my cock in and out of her mouth as often as I could in the shortest amount of time.

Harder and faster I kept at it, my cock using her mouth the way her mouth had used my cock only moments ago.

Her eyes glassy again, Betty glanced up at me as often as she dared. And as I watched each of her glimpses of my heat become too much to take for too long, I slowly realized I had never been with a woman who was so turned on by *my* passion. The harder and faster I thrusted, the more she seemed to love it. But it was more than mere physical enjoyment as she seemed to mentally lose herself, temporarily abandoning and devoting her entire being just to service me.

As my urge to cum began to boil, I knew I couldn't hold off much longer. I had to make a decision and I had to make it fast because with each passing second, I had less blood to think clearly.

No, not yet. Don't do it. Not until you know for sure.

Aggravated by my own moral code, I suddenly ripped my cock from Betty's mouth as quickly as it had just been thrust. As confusion slowly crept across her face, it was all I could do to prevent myself envisioning what she would look like if I had allowed myself to mark her. God knew she was beautiful enough already.

And gazing down at the incredible woman on her knees before me, so did I. Which settled it.

Reaching down, I placed my hands under Betty's elbows and gently helped lift her to her feet. Our eyes locked, I watched the surprise on her face as I moved in to kiss her. Tenderly. The way one lover shows the other their appreciation.

Once I was done and began to pull away, Betty expressed her own with a well-sated *Hmmmmmm.*

I smiled and brushed the hair back from her left ear into which I leaned down and softly whispered, "Now I want to watch you walk over and lay on the bed for me, face up. Then I want you to spread your legs and show yourself to me. I already know how beautiful you are. But I want you to show me. I want to see even more of you... I want to see you... *All* of you."

For the first time, a pause preceded Betty's obedience. As I pulled back from her ear, I found her eyes staring directly into mine. The connection we made in that moment was almost indescribable. Her heat for me was still there, but something had joined it.

Appreciation. Adoration. Contentment. Happiness... Peace.

I watched as she both saw and felt herself through my eyes as she looked right into me, through me, and back at herself. She inhaled and exhaled slowly, three or four times, each slower than the last. It was as if she was willing time to slow down so she could drink in and savor the moment for as long as possible. God knew I was.

Because watching her do that... was a far too brief... yet far more beautiful eternity...

But since all good things must...

As much as I enjoyed seeing myself through Victor's eyes, my body ached to obey him. So, slowly I turned and walked toward the bed, doing my best to saunter and sashay as subtly yet sexily as possible with each step.

Over the years, many men had commented on how beautiful they thought I was. Especially my ass. But not a damn one of them had ever said it in a way that truly made me feel special. Desirous? Yes. An object of their lust? Yes. But special? No.

But Victor's words in my ear. *I want to see you.* My God, the way he had said that literally made my knees too weak to obey him right away. Instead I tried to stall by looking up and staring into his eyes. Yet within seconds the connection we made had me feeling as if I was looking back at myself. Seeing myself through his eyes. And what I saw shook me to my core.

Awe. Wonder. Adoration. Appreciation. Beauty. Passion. Desire. Lust. Want. Need. Ache...

The feelings Victor so obviously had for me, and I for him, continued without end and though indescribably wonderful, the intensity of it was more than I could handle. When I was finally able to turn away, I had to steady myself.

Being the object of male desire was something I had been accustomed to since puberty. But having a man desire me such that I knew just by the way he was looking at me that he truly appreciated all the things he thought he saw in me... I had never felt anything like it before in my life.

And so soon...

I gave my head a little shake. While my heart and soul rang euphoric and my entire body thumped increasingly hornier, my mind was infuriatingly confused.

How could this be?

I made this trip hoping for nothing more than a mindless fuck. After nearly a year of celibacy, I just wanted to feel a purely physical pleasure that wasn't provided by myself or any of my toys. I didn't plan to actually *feel* anything for someone. To make a connection like this.

And yet here I was, sopping wet between my legs, trying to put on a show for a man I had just met... Trying to make him fall for me like I was falling for him.

I'm falling for him...

The truth hit me just as I reached the bed. I was. I was falling for Victor. There was no denying it. But instead of slowing me down, my body acknowledged my admission by instinctively transforming it into a fuel that began to naturally ratchet up my seductive kitten act several notches.

Because if I was falling for Victor, I damn sure wanted him falling for me.

Climbing up diagonally on the foot side of the bed with my back to him, I crawled on all fours as slowly as I could. With my knees spread, I arched my ass into the air as I lowered my face into the pillows, pausing to display myself for effect.

"Show yourself to me," he had said. "I want to see you."

Here I am, Victor... See me...

Ever so slowly, I dropped my pelvis until I lay completely flat, pausing again just long enough to let him view me this new angle before rolling onto my back, finally doing as I was told.

Looking over, I found him standing there like some sculpted god, watching me. With the eight pack of his stomach muscles rippling down across his hips in a V pattern all the way to his groin, his right bicep flexed up and down as he slowly and methodically pump-stroked his dick.

The sight was erotic as hell.

Fully clothed, it had been clear that Victor was in great shape. From the raised veins above his hands to the taut muscles of his neck that stretched across his cheekbones and the length of his jaw, every exposed inch of his skin screamed serious fitness buff. But fully naked, I could tell he had the type of body that could only have been sculpted by years of serious dedication.

And then there was his dick.

Of the six lovers I had had in my life only one had been longer than Victor. But I had never seen one as thick as his. Not even in porn. He was easily twice as wide as any man I had been with and when he first dropped his boxers my first thought was *Oh, shit!*

In that moment, I knew what I was about to say to Victor. I also knew the type of questions my tattoo would more than likely evoke. I had even practiced the delivery of my various answers over and over in my head for the last couple of weeks. I had no idea which I was going to use until I did, but I knew that if I was lucky enough to meet a man anywhere near the caliber that Victor seemed to be, then I was going to go all out. Finally take the chance I had been fantasizing about taking.

If you're gonna get a little you might as well live a little, girl!

I tried not to roll my eyes at the memory as all I could do now was hope that if Victor was into anal sex that he also knew how to handle his monster.

Speaking of which...

Lowering my eyes just a touch, I continued to watch as Victor slowly and firmly pumped his shaft. Like a mechanic he kept his tool hard, but as the seconds passed I could tell that it wasn't his own hand that was giving him pleasure. It was me. And the lust in his eyes was so palpable that his gaze alone felt like fingers stroking my body.

With my eyes locked on his, I dug my heels into the bed and pushed my head up onto a pillow. Ever so slowly, I spread my legs and bent my knees. Just as I felt my labia open up, I paused for the ultimate dramatic effect. Then I allowed my eyes to smile.

Now see me more...

The sight was greater than any mortal man should have to bear.

As perfect as Betty's breasts were nothing had prepared me for my first true glimpse of her ass. As she finally walked away, I could see her rear was part swayback, part heart-shaped shelf and all bubble. It stunned me to realize that the polka splotch of her sundress had somehow camouflaged the outline of her curves, curbing and blurring their edge while never exposing the slightest clue of the two mesmerizing cheeks concealed beneath.

Unable to tear my eyes away, I continued to ogle Betty as she strutted over to the bed. Unable to touch her, by the time she reached it I was touching myself, torn between my actual vision of her and those which I wanted to do to her. By the time she rolled over and slowly spread her legs for me I was almost at my breaking point.

The beautiful tulips of her pussy parted ever so slightly, I could actually see her wetness glistening from twelve feet away. With her entire body bathed by the light above the bed, her come hither look practically challenged me to continue holding my ground.

But no man is that strong.

Taking one last mental photograph, I dropped my hands to my side. With my cock standing at attention, I allowed Betty's eyes to drink in my body as I slowly strode to the foot of the bed. Positioning myself between her legs, I fought the intensity of my growing hunger as I leaned down and kissed the inside of her right knee, allowing my hands to slide along the smooth outside of her legs and down to the sides and then underneath her buttocks.

Momentarily shocked, I became distracted by just how perfectly each of her ass cheeks fit in the palms of my hands. Purely by reflex, my fingers massaged her flesh, reveling in the feel of her for a few seconds as I kissed the inside of her other knee. Holding her firmly, my mouth began its search down her inner thighs, kneading and suckling as it drew closer and closer to what I wanted most.

Enjoying the taut yet supple softness of her skin, I kissed my way down her legs, reveling in the look on Betty's face as she watched me. Her legs were shaved so smooth, I couldn't resist petting them, stroking them back and forth with the back of my hand or side of my cheek. And as my mouth delved closer, inch by inch toward her center, a part of me wanted nothing more than to linger.

But a larger part of me wanted so much more than that.

Despite how wet she was, I was four inches away before Betty's aroma finally pleasured my nose. The female of her scent was, as always, personally unique. Heady yet light, she was so inviting I couldn't help but inhale deeply, sampling her before tasting her.

Betty inhaled, too, her breath quivering as her body tensed in anticipation of my mouth which could no longer deny either of us.

My upper lip dabbed her clit just before my tongue lapped her from the bottom up, parting her completely and sipping as I went. Her nectar tasted even sweeter than she smelled.

My God, this is the one.

My head spun because I knew where my mind was going. I also knew if I went with it, I would lose focus and become hopelessly lost. So I perished the thought by pausing to take a moment to get my first close look at Betty's holiest of holies.

The softest color of pink set against naturally pale skin, her pussy was an absolute work of art, every bit as beautiful as it was perfectly formed. Peaking from under its hood, her clitoris, though small and dainty, was clearly swollen in arousal while her soft, perfectly proportioned lips dangled just slightly, as if their entire reason for existing were to be spread and suckled upon.

Shelving my admiration along with my other thoughts, I licked her, savoring the folds of her lips as I lightly brushed her clit with the bridge and tip of my nose. Forcing her to moan ever louder with each pass of my tongue, I gripped her ass tighter, pulling her to me so I could plunge deeper and deeper within her womanhood. I couldn't give her enough because I couldn't get enough.

She truly tasted better than any woman I had ever been with.

Given how well Victor had used his tongue on mine earlier, I figured his cunnilingual skills would be phenomenal. I just had no idea he would be capable of the same level of desire to match. But as I glanced down between my legs and felt him tease the edge of my G-spot with the tip of his tongue, I honestly didn't know which was greater, his expertise or love of oral.

He was lost in me, his eyes closed as the low moans that emanated from his throat escaped softly through his nose. The deeper he searched, the greater my urge became to spread myself. What he was doing to me was too much yet not enough, both at the same time, causing my mind to scream, alternating between *Yes! No! More!* and *Stop!* over and over again as my hands clenched the bedsheets, balling them in my fists. I had never been so wet from receiving oral sex in my life and it wasn't long before I could tell that Victor's face was absolutely covered in my juice.

He didn't seem to notice yet he had to be paying attention to my body because he hit every erogenous spot I had, focusing on each just long enough to bring me to the brink of orgasm before gently moving on to assure the next that it too would get a turn. By the third time his mouth covered my clitoris, I grabbed his head with both my hands to keep it from going anywhere else.

As if sensing my desire for release, Victor acquiesced by concentrating all his efforts right where I held him. But he quickly retaliated by both clamping down and stimulating me with the fastest tongue flicks and full-on, smash mouth rubs I had ever experienced, eating me alive both literally and figuratively.

Bucking harder and harder against him, my knees and hips began to rise on their own. As my heels dug into the mattress, I struggled to keep my fingernails from digging into Victor's scalp. But the more he left his mark on me, the less I cared about leaving my marks on him.

Higher and higher I rose, only slightly aware that the few times I had experienced this much oral pleasure in the past I had also weighed far less. Despite Victor's intertwined fingers applying such a firm, downward pressure as they laced themselves across my lower stomach, I vaguely knew that it may have once been easier for me to arch my pelvis so high... but damn if I could remember it that way.

Ten seconds before my first orgasm, I found Victor's eyes watching me intently. Moving his mouth slightly to his left, the rougher, side edge of his tongue began to scrape across my clitoris. I was so sensitive I could swear I felt every taste bud he had. The angle was different from anything I had ever felt before, making me feel as if my body had just discovered an unknown erogenous zone.

And that's when the shudders started.

The first time my body jerked, my mind was still being blown by the new sensation. But the second shock wave drowned out my brain entirely. The trinity of my mind, body and soul coalesced into one as my body triumphed, reigning supreme, wracking itself again and again against Victor's mouth as my tremors radiated outward.

I had always been one of the lucky ones, a multi-orgasmic woman who was easy to please which was one of the primary reasons I had always enjoyed sex so much. But this was something totally different.

The orgasm Victor induced in me at that moment was more complete than any I had ever had.

As I allowed Betty's hips to lower slowly to the bed, I did my best to be gentle with her. Keeping my mouth a mere inch away from the sweetest smell in the world, I inhaled deeply while alternating my exhales, hot through my mouth and cool through my nose.

Around my seventh or eighth alternation, when I saw goosebumps begin to rise on the finest hairs of her legs and torso, I knew she was still excited yet relaxed enough to continue. Kissing my way past her clit before slowly nuzzling a trail through the soft curls of her landing strip, I allowed the tip of my nose to trace a meandering path to her tattoo.

Up close, each sphere appeared incredibly faded and I couldn't help but wonder how long she had had them. Yet the first thoughts accompanying said wonder weren't ones I wanted to have so I quickly moved on, up to her right breast where I rubbed my nose against the unbelievable firmness of her nipple. Aware that her eyes were keenly following my every move, I stilled, drawing out my tease but also allowing her slightly winded breathing to slow enough to catch itself.

Fixing Betty's unsure gaze with the controlled look of my own, I allowed the tension to build. Once her eyes widened such that she was practically begging for my mouth, I snatched her nipple quickly, so fast and unexpectedly it accounted for at least the first half of her gasp. The second half came from the slight gnaw of my teeth followed by the suckling of my lips and teasing of my tongue.

Knowing the distraction this would be, I used the opportunity to slide my right hand up to her left breast. Using her groans as my guide, I covered and kneaded it with both rough and gentle squeezes. It felt so perfect in my hand that several seconds went by before I realized I could also feel the staccato beating of her heart, pulsing rapidly just below.

Remembering her fascination with my nipples, I consciously made the effort to return the favor, spending several minutes with each of hers. Not that it was difficult. I had never been more turned on by the sight of a woman's breasts or nipples in my entire life. Which surprised me.

Yet another reason I had never been a "breast man" was because a part of me looked down upon men who unapologetically were. I found those who openly leered at the most protruding part of a woman's body to more often than not be shortsighted misanthropes who failed to peer any deeper for a woman's true self or worth.

Not the type of man I had ever aspired to be.

Yet I couldn't help but gaze in appreciation at Betty's breasts. She had been so physically blessed I felt obligated to do my damnedest to worship them as I felt they deserved. So as I pleasured my mouth with one, I pleasured my eyes and hand with her other. And as her chest slowly flushed red, I watched in delight as her other nipple appeared to grow even stiffer.

Every bit as beautiful as her breasts, her nubs were truly stunning. Shaped like slightly oversized pencil erasers and just as pink, each were so hard and sensitive that every flick of my tongue elicited an audible moan. Realizing just how much she enjoyed my mouth, I took my time, varying my pace and intensity in tune with how her body and mouth reacted.

Round and round I went, using my tongue and lips, gnawing her breasts and nipples gently with my teeth and firmly with my fingers and hands. Sucking turned to tugging. Pinching to pulling. Gripping the back of my head to press me tighter, the pitch of her ecstasy slowly began to rise higher and higher until this time she left no doubt; Betty came.

The tremors that shook her body were slight, not much more than quivers really. But they were real.

I had been with enough women to be well aware that once most had achieved orgasm, numbers two through however many they could handle often followed their first quite easily. I had even read that some women could achieve orgasm via breast and nipple stimulation alone and it excited me to no end to know that Betty was one of them.

Relenting my intensity by withdrawing my mouth, I allowed her time to catch her breath while my fingers and hands delicately stroked the curves in the cups of her tender skin. Marveling at their shape, I felt Betty's hand slip further down the back of my head so that she could pull my face to hers.

With our eyes the closest they had been to one another since our kiss, a look of mutual understanding crossed between us. We both knew this was something special. We could see it in one another's reflections. We were on a path toward a level of chemistry that most lovers would never achieve in a lifetime.

And yet we still hadn't fully consummated our evening.

Parting her legs, Betty reached down to take my cock in her hand. I could see the pleasant surprise in her eyes as she discovered I was still fully hard. As she pumped me in delight, her legs spread a little wider. In a moment of slight panic, I began to suspect she might be thinking of forgoing a condom.

It'd be dishonest of me to say I didn't want to as well. But I was torn. There simply was no way I could have sex without a condom with a woman I had just met who enjoyed being a Sex Slave. Even though I had inspected her as thoroughly and orally as I could, I just couldn't take the chance. At least not until I could reconcile all the inconsistencies going through my brain.

Not wishing to tear myself away and ruin the moment, instead I whispered softly.

"Are you ready for me?"

"Yes. Please."

With a nod, I rose from the bed to retrieve a condom. Betty's eyes stayed glued to my cock as I rolled the prophylactic on as quickly as I could. Due to my size, the largest store-bought condoms were such a hassle that I had custom ordered my own for years. Struggling with the tight fit, I mentally kicked myself for unpacking them after Alexis' cancellation.

Few things irked me more than the feeling of being unprepared.

Once the condom was on, I made my way back over to the bed where Betty willingly spread her legs further. I positioned myself slowly above her, just close enough to run the head of my cock up and down between her slit in order to reignite her excitement before going further. As her breathing grew more and more ragged with each passing tease, I fixed her with my gaze. I wanted her so badly, but there was just one more thing I wanted first...

No, it was one more thing I *had* to have.

"I can't have sex with a woman whose name I don't know."

Her body clearly aching, Betty's voice finally cracked, "Can't? Or won't?"

"Both," I assured her.

"Bella," she panted. "Bella Rose Qui—innnnn..."

As I exhaled my last name, Victor split me in two as he pushed himself completely inside me. The power and perfectly timed swiftness of his thrust caught me by surprise as pleasure and pain fought one another between my legs. I was wet enough, true. But he had used no fingers to taper me first and because none of my vibrators were as thick as he was, I was as tight as I could possibly be.

The walls of my vagina quivered around him, clenching and releasing again and again in tiny, uncontrollable spasms as they attempted to accommodate his girth. Everything happened so fast, my body didn't have a chance to defend itself. Not that I would have wanted it to.

I had never felt so filled by a man in my life and the feeling was incredible.

"Are you okay?"

I opened my eyes, not realizing they had closed to find Victor's face peering down at mine. His look of concern touched me so deeply that my mind delivered my body from its ache.

"Fuck me, Victor," I moaned, grabbing his head and pulling his ear to my mouth. "Please, just fuck me..."

Thankfully, Victor Maxwell wasn't the type of man that needed to be told twice.

I'd never know how he was able to slam into me a second time without my feeling his first withdrawal, but he did. Over and over, harder and harder his thrusts came as I tried to spread my legs for him as wide as possible if for no other reason than to keep my pelvis from shattering.

Letting go of his head, I gripped the underside of the headboard and held on for dear life as Victor began to use me for all I was worth. As I felt myself become looser and wetter, the frequency of his thrusts intensified as did the sound of our bodies crashing together. I tried to meet his eyes, but all it took was a simple glance to see the man was gone.

With the dilated pupils of a wild animal, Victor's entire demeanor was one of pure, unadulterated lust the likes of which I had never seen. Momentarily shocked, my body reacted first, turning on even more and instinctively flooding my vagina with more heat and wetness than I had ever felt. Within seconds, the unbelievable sloshing and slurping noise emanating from between my legs became so loud I actually felt a tinge of embarrassment.

Not that Victor noticed.

Pounding me relentlessly, all the tenderness and desire he had shown to please me had been replaced by a man possessed. From his dick to his body to his facial expression, everything about the man was now harder than stone. In that moment, he appeared to care nothing for me. I had given him permission to use my body as he pleased and every ounce of care and concentration he had for me was now wholly centered where we were joined.

That realization, the look upon his face, the rhythmic sound of his body so forcefully slapping against mine and the thickest thing I'd ever had inside me were more than enough to trigger my next orgasm. Reaching up, I grabbed Victor's head with my hands, pulling my mouth up to his ear and latching on as my pelvis began to shake and shiver uncontrollably beneath and against him. Despite my best effort to stifle the high pitch of my moan, I came so hard my body's vibrations reverberated through our din.

Unable to take anymore, Victor thankfully slowed his thrusts as I sensed him tense his pubococcygeus, intentionally contracting the muscle to stave off his own orgasm. Then, just as my shudders slowly began to subside, his mouth collapsed on mine, an erotic kiss of lips and tongue, hot and wet, passionate yet gentle, his need still evident.

Looking into his eyes, I returned his kiss, adding my own fervor. Slowly taking control, an unexpected burst of confidence the likes of which I had never felt suddenly spurred me to clench Victor as firmly as I could between my legs and push upward, rolling him to his side and on to his back until I had him straddled. He offered so little resistance, it was as if our bodies and minds were dancing in unison, each willing to lead or follow as the other required.

I watched as both of us drank in the visions from our new vantage points.

With his tattoos spread across the top and sides of his long, muscular arms like the wings of some fallen angel, I imagined myself mounted on a demigod whose hard-bodied chariot had been sent to transport me to another world. This beautiful man was clearly, at the moment anyway, so far out of my league I didn't know what to think. But that he was mine, at least for this moment, meant I didn't have to... so I didn't.

Instead I enjoyed watching as Victor's eyes trailed slowly away from my own, pausing at my hair, my mouth and then my neck. I watched with delight as his pupils expanded at the sight of my breasts, his lips parting to smile, eager to savor. But restraining himself by folding his fingers behind his head, his eyes continued to trek further south, across my stomach until he found the pleasure of where we were joined.

Suddenly slowing the upward pace of my rising hips, I slid myself up off Victor's dick, releasing him inch by excruciating inch until only his head remained inside me. Pausing until he could stand it no longer, I allowed him to arc up once, slamming into and filling me entirely once again.

The pleasure was so intense I couldn't help but to lean forward and shove Victor's face between my breasts as I gripped his head in ecstasy. But pushing down with the full weight of my hips, I lowered us both as I released his head and waited until his eyes found mine. With one look, I left him no doubt that he was mine to ride. And with one look in return, he acquiesced to my demand.

The effortlessness of our nonverbal communication and our sexual synchronicity was such a complete turn on that my wetness began to flood our bodies once more.

Up and down, in and out I began to slide, grinding my pelvis and clit firmly against him with each undulating roll of my hips. As his hands began to explore my stomach, breasts and nipples, I slowly increased my tempo. I wanted Victor to cum, but I wanted to know it was my actions that triggered it. I wanted to take him to that place were he had no more control, much as he already had taken me.

Faster and faster I went, acutely aware of the ever increasing sound of wetness slapping between us. Despite how badly I wanted to cause his climax, with each passing minute I lost more and more control as my own orgasm began to once again overtake my body. Well aware of the rising tide inside me, I fought it as best I could. Yet when I came, it was out of nowhere.

But this was no ordinary orgasm.

First came a rush of blood down my inner thighs that traveled all the way to my knees, turning my legs into torches. Though brief, the heat was so intense I actually feared our skin singed one another wherever we touched. Then came the spasms as muscles deep inside me began to pulse and throb more vigorously than I had ever felt. In rapid succession, I gripped Victor's dick in my vise before letting loose only to clench him again and again and again.

I had never felt an orgasm so strongly before in my life.

Wailing in euphoria, my nipples became so erect they actually hurt. And as I watched in amazement, Victor suddenly exploded without warning inside me. The surprise in his eyes as the intensity of my contractions practically milked him dry was made all the more pleasurable by the perfect rhythmic unity where our bodies remained connected.

Riding the wave of the longest orgasm I'd ever had, I lost track of time as every squeeze I gave produced a pump as his every pump induced another squeeze, over and over again. But as the strength of both eventually subsided, I watched the shock momentarily render Victor to the point of being dazed. Unsure of what to do with his hands or mouth or any other part of his body, he stilled and did nothing...

I'd never experienced an orgasm more strongly or unexpectedly in my entire life.

I had become used to women being overly impressed by the girth of my cock. But as that was no personal accomplishment, I took no true pride in it.

I did pride myself, however, on my level of self control when it came to my own orgasms. I had been exercising my PC muscle for almost fifteen years. Three times a day every other day, I did fifty repetitions for five to seven seconds each. On that level, I was an absolute machine.

In fact I had become so good at controlling my orgasmic impulses that I often made a game of trying to discern just how many orgasms my lovers could handle before they neither wanted nor could take another. Only then would I allow myself release.

But Bella's contractions were like nothing I'd ever felt before. Not only their strength, but their rhythm. It was as if we were perfectly in sync in a way that not even my mind was capable of comprehending.

After my body exploded of its own accord along with hers, I lay there in awe, gazing at the visage of beauty and lust astride me as we continued to pulse in unison. Her burning eyes locked on mine, Bella slowed the rhythm of her hips as the span of time between her shudders decreased to a point that finally allowed her to gently lay down atop me. Curled on my chest, I wrapped my arms around her.

Beautifully aware that I was still fully inside her, neither of us moved nor spoke a word.

As a full minute lapsed, I began to wish she would fall asleep, her nestled in my arms, me nestled in her. Stroking her hair with one hand, I pulled the bed's comforter over us with the other. When Bella didn't stir, I began to think that this is what Heaven must feel like as the afterglow of our energy enveloped us, cocooning us both safely from yet deeply within the universe.

Every need of my body completely sated, as the moments continued to pass and blood returned to my brain, it oddly dawned on me that I'd never known a woman who hadn't jumped up to race to the bathroom less than a minute or two after sex.

Inhaling the scent of her hair, I smiled as I reminded myself, yet again, that she wasn't just any woman.

And to think all this time her name was Bella. How appropriate...

I laid above Victor without a thought or care in the world. I was in the present moment so completely it was as if neither past nor future had or would ever exist. And all I wanted to do was to stay right there, for the rest of my life. In that moment. That one, perfect moment.

I didn't want it to end and inexplicably felt if I didn't move, didn't speak, didn't interrupt or disturb the magic... the now might go on and on, carrying and keeping me in it.

Not even Victor's hand stroking my hair or covering us with a blanket could pull me out of that moment. Though I did offer him a *hmmmmmmm* of a purr and gentle twist of my hips to let him know I was aware he was still ensconced inside me.

As he slowly grew softer, I took a few minutes to simply enjoy being before I raised my head to find him looking at me. Speaking across our shared silence, we gazed deeply into one another's eyes.

"Yeah," he finally said softly.

"Yeah," I had to agree.

Using his fingers, Victor brushed back the largest curl crossing my face and laced it behind my ear. Then he kissed me. A simple, sweet thank you, his kiss felt so natural it was as if we had already pressed our lips to the other's more than a thousand times.

When I finally opened my eyes, I became aware they had been closed for quite a few seconds. I had become lost in the moment, in the afterglow so completely that once again I had lost track of time. Waking from my semi-consciousness to still find him looking at me, I felt momentarily embarrassed.

How could a kiss from a man I just met make me feel so deeply?

Realizing that the soft intensity with which Victor was studying my face mirrored that which I performed on my patients, I tried to look away but couldn't. The feeling was just too wonderful.

He's calculating me again...

"What is it?" Victor asked.

"What is what?"

"Whatever it is you're thinking that's making you smile."

"Oh..." I paused to inhale, unsure of how truthful I should be. *Completely!* "I was just thinking you were looking at me the same way I imagine I look at my patients from time to time."

Victor smiled. "And you liked that."

In that moment, I liked that Victor felt confident enough to make a statement instead of asking a question which made it feel like he knew me... and it felt really nice to feel known.

Although I'd felt that way all night, starting soon after we met, it had surprised me at first just how quickly we had become comfortable around one another. Like picking back up with a long lost friend. And that feeling permeated everything, from the way we talked to even the way we looked at one another. I don't know why I was so surprised that our mutual ease had carried over into bed but it definitely had.

Allowing my smile and exhale to serve as my response, I took a few more seconds to drink in Victor's baby blue eyes before turning my attention to the rest of his body. As amazing as his physique was, the first thing my eyes went to were his tattoos.

While the overall outline of the design was tribal, the tattoo itself was split into what appeared to be two identical pieces. Symmetrical images of black flames extended from the top of his shoulders, licking the lowest curve of his neck, down along the outsides of his arms until they ended just beyond his wrists. Bizarrely, both the letters and words on his left arm were transposed backward so that they mirrored those on his right. Peering closer I realized that not only were the two outlines written in Latin... so was the overall calligraphic inscription contained within.

What the hell?

Staring into Bella's face, I seriously began to question if I was falling in love.

I'd never been in love before. I'd had a childhood love—a puppy love, yes—

but I'd never been in love as an adult.

I'd tried. I did want it, but time and time again, love had simply never materialized for me. So to think I might be feeling such a thing for a woman I had known for less than a third of a day—*a Sex Slave no less*—I shook the thought from my head.

Though Bella eventually looked away, I couldn't tear my eyes from her face. I began to notice so many little things like the slight ski-slope angle of her perfect nose... the gentle play of incredibly faint freckles across her face and neck... the flowing silkiness of her beautiful blonde hair... and of course the two uniquely alluring beauty marks just below her right eye.

And then I noticed that she was taking note of me.

As she studied the design of my tattoo, Bella's face began to show signs of both recognition and confusion. Still clenching my cock inside her cradle, she rose above me a bit higher to get a better view.

"Temet?" she asked, indicating the first half of the tattoo running from my left wrist to shoulder. "Knosce?" she finished, going from my right shoulder to wrist. "Both in mirrored writing?"

I was too shocked to do anything but nod. No woman had ever noticed the overall design of my tattoos were words that could be read. I had painstakingly disguised the adage as best I could, first by drawing both the words and their letters backwards, as if viewed in a mirror, then by camouflaging the tribal font within a maze of curling tendrils. The damn thing took me almost a full year to create.

Peering even closer, Bella began to read the calligraphy I had further embedded within the letters of Temet Knosce. From my right wrist to my shoulder, she began to read.

"Quod plures intelligentes facti sunt mihi, et minus intelligentes Intellego me."

Moving across my chest, she continued from my left shoulder to my wrist.

"Scio me esse minus intelligentes, certo fore intelligentiores..."

Overcoming my astonishment, I began to translate for her.

"The more intelligent—"

"—I become," she softly interjected, "the less intelligent I realize I am. The less intelligent I realize myself to be, the more intelligent I strive to become."

I exhaled the sharp intake of breath I failed to realize I was holding. I couldn't believe what I just heard as I suddenly realized that over the years I'd grown to become self-righteously smug because no one had been able to detect much less read my tattoo. Humbled didn't begin to describe the depths of what I was feeling.

"I'm a doctor," Bella explained with a sheepish smile.

Dumbfounded by both her admission and sudden change in demeanor, I recalled what Greg had called her. *Still*— "Not all doctors know how to read and speak Latin."

"No, but—"

Jerking upright I kissed Bella fully on her lips before she could say anything else. As the protest of her words gave way to the relaxation of her body, I wound my fingers through her hair. I had never allowed myself to dream of meeting a woman who could interpret my tattoos, so I didn't know what to do except kiss her. When I finally pulled back and opened my eyes, I found her staring into mine.

"You closed your eyes... again," she whispered so quietly I almost didn't hear her.

I smiled and reached to brush back the curl of her hair that kept falling from her ear. As beautiful of a look it gave her, I preferred to see her full face, her every expression.

"I didn't want to be distracted by your beauty."

My words were as simple as they were true. Their effect, however, was a surprise.

"Okay, I think I'm going to have to call BS on that," Bella said, rolling her eyes and using the opportunity to roll off of me.

As my cock ached from the cold shock of her sudden absence, I started to protest but then realized what she was doing. Not only had I genuinely embarrassed her, she was giving me a chance to remove and dispose of our condom without any awkwardness.

As she padded toward the bathroom, I pulled the prophylactic off, careful not to create more of a mess than we already had. It had been quite awhile since I had slept in the wet spot. Thankfully, Bella had made sure it was going to be worth it for me. Chuckling to myself, I tossed the condom into the trash can by the room's desk just as I heard her pause at the bathroom door.

"Would my Master care to join me?"

Though both sweetly and softly spoken, Bella's words instantly stirred my blood. I knew well my own refractory period so I also knew the first possibility of my next erection was still another few minutes away. But when I turned to find her standing in the doorway—with only half of her seductively hidden beyond the frame—my entire body flooded with desire. That I could sense the blood reach all the way to my groin was a huge surprise.

As my nipples hardened and my cock began to swell again ever so slightly, it was all I could do to keep from running across the room. Not bothering to wait for my answer, Bella had the shower running by the time I ducked under the door and pressed myself up behind her behind.

While the water warmed, I encircled her waist with my right hand. Smoothing it along her stomach, I quickly slid my way up to her magnificent breasts. Caressing, cupping and molding each in turn, I used my left hand to sweep her hair off her right shoulder to reveal her neck line, which I gently kissed my way along and around, up to her jaw line, back to her ear, down to her clavicle, all the while pleasuring her chest while purposefully avoiding her nipples.

Delighting in her moans but realizing the water was steaming, I relented long enough to reach for the faucet to dial it back. To my surprise, Bella stopped me, quickly stepping into the shower and its stream.

"I prefer it hot. Is that ok?"

I smiled as I realized that even if it wasn't, I would probably have lied and agreed it was. I preferred the water hot, too, so while it wasn't a sacrifice, it did make me wonder what else I was already willing to give up for her.

As the water drenched her hair into an even darker honey, I struggled for a second to think of an answer. But then I realized there was a beautiful, wet, naked blonde standing in front of me.

And there wasn't enough blood for thinking when a man has that.

Standing in the shower, I began to experience the first true pangs of self-consciousness I had managed to keep at bay all evening.

Although visual stimulation had played a larger part in my life and my sex drive than in the vast majority of most women, that was before I had put on so much weight. If Victor hadn't looked so damn fine, I might have made the rare insistence on sex in the dark. My lust for wanting to absorb everything about him was the only thing that had allowed me to overcome my self-consciousness.

But now, with the passion of our initial encounter subsiding, here in the bright light of the bathroom there was no hiding how I looked. No hiding my tattoo, no hiding the extra pounds I had packed on over the last year by letting myself go. No hiding every dimple of cellulite on the back of my legs. It was all there for Victor to see and my only saving grace, that I had gained weight uniformly and not just in any one specific area, did little to ease my anxiety.

Thankfully, Victor really didn't seem to care. But that I didn't know *why* he didn't gnawed at me. The man was the epitome of male fitness and at the moment I clearly wasn't his female counterpart. I had been once, but that was a bad year ago. If I had met him before then—

—But you didn't...

And of course, even if I had it wouldn't have changed anyth—

I shook the useless thoughts from my head as I inhaled and tried to return to the present moment. But when I closed my eyes, all I could think about was the silence Victor and I had shared in our afterglow.

The entire sexual experience from start to finish had been the best of my life. Whether he realized it or not the man had just set the bar for me by which I knew I would measure all sex in my future. The feeling was every bit as wonderful as the knowledge had the potential to be depressing because deep down I knew if I couldn't make Victor mine...

For some reason the memory of Victor's face as I read his tattoos suddenly flooded my brain. His look of surprise had grown increasingly touched with each word I spoke. The thought lifted my spirits enough to make me smile.

Perhaps he already is mine...

Yet as I opened my eyes and looked down to see my own tattoo, my anxiety flared anew. Fighting to prevent it from overriding the moment, I resolved to come entirely clean to Victor the next time we met.

If there is a next ti—

Just then Victor pressed his hard-on between my ass cheeks, fitting himself perfectly up and down between them. I held my breath for several seconds, waiting for his next move as he teased me relentlessly. Slowly and rhythmically, he slid through me and the soap to the cadence of his own steady breathings as his soapy hands roamed my body while he kissed my neck in ways that were both tender and seductive.

He'd been leisurely playing with most of my body for the last couple of minutes as I just stood there and let him. I thought at first, given how erect he was, that he might take me from behind. But he seemed more than content to simply keep us casually aroused, even going so far as to avoid my nipples and groin every time his hands strayed close. The slight ache lingering between my legs was grateful that he wasn't attempting to get me as worked up as he clearly was again so soon. Even the corners of my mouth were still a little sore.

Under other circumstances, I might have been disappointed. But I had made it clear, for the moment he was my Master and I was his to do with as he pleased. After all that's what I wanted...

Isn't it?

I closed my eyes to help quell my thoughts. Feeling only where I was being touched, my muscles slowly began to loosen and relax under Victor's obviously well-practiced hands. At the pace he was going, he might take all night. Hmmmm.

Fine by me...

Try as I might, Bella wasn't the only one distracted in the shower. I could tell she was thinking about something but of what I had no idea. What the hell did Sex Slaves think about? What exactly did women like her want?

With her 'dirty little slut' comment still echoing in the back of my head, I started to worry I was being too gentle with her, that I was thinking more about her pleasure than my own. Because though it was her body that was being touched, I was far more aroused.

If she wanted harder and raunchier sex, I could give it to her. That was my preference anyway. In fact, the last time I had felt really close to any woman was longer than I could remember. My current situation notwithstanding, I had pretty much neither needed nor wanted to forge any personal attachments from which one day I would in all likelihood wish to walk away. The more emotionless the sex was the better it was for me. And more than any woman I had ever met, Bella was offering me the epitome of emotionless sex.

But such an extreme lack of intimacy for years on end had slowly sunk its fangs until it had bitten me fully in the ass and refused to let go. Because try as I desperately wanted to deny it, I had certain sexual fantasies that I refused to allow myself to fulfill. The type that I felt I could only experience with the most intimate of partners.

And although she had no way of realizing it, Bella had already connected more intimately with me in the last six or so hours than any woman had possibly ever. The thought that she could be the one woman I had been waiting to find made me a little fearful. Intimacy, after all, was not really one of my fortes. Yet the idea that I might have finally found someone with which to experience my most extreme fantasies began to counterbalance my worry.

Looking Bella up and down, one thought began to consume me more than all others.

The things I want to do to you.

But did I really want to?

Fuck yea— No... No, not yet.

Part of me wanted to, yes. But there was a part of me that wanted to wai— No, there was a part of me that *needed* to wait. Because *that* part of me didn't want to do all the things I wanted to do to her yet. It was too soon. I didn't know Bella well enough. And I knew if I gave in to myself too soon, there might be a part of me that would never care to get to know the rest of her.

And that was definitely *not* what the fuck I wanted.

Bella was clearly special and not just because she had the unique desire along with the lady balls to allow herself to be used as a Sex Slave. If she wanted me to play and be her Master, fine. I could do that. But we were going to do it on my terms, too, not just hers. After all, she wasn't the only one who had specific needs.

And even more to the point, just like me... she still didn't really know with whom she was getting involved.

As Victor kneeled before me, I gazed down and tried to focus on just how beautiful he looked from this angle. With the width of his chest and back further accentuated by the narrowness of his hips, the balls of his shoulders curved deliciously down into the cut of his biceps. I watched in delight as the cords of his elaborately tattooed muscles stretched and relaxed in tandem with those along his forearms.

Dear God, is he sexy...

With most of the shower head's water splashing across my chest, droplets of spray beaded Victor's head as he gently scrubbed my feet. Looking down on him from above, I was just beginning to think of how flawlessly perfect he was built when I noticed something.

Right behind each of his ears was a small scar. Both lines were less than an inch long, the remnants of former incisions long ago stitched and healed. Before I could stop myself, their location made me think of the winged god Mercury. Was that who Victor was? A fallen angel, clipped of his wings, here to relay some sort of message to me? I shook my head.

Even more surreal than the absurdity of my thoughts and how Victor had thus far washed and rinsed nearly my entire body was how he had changed washcloths just before washing my pubic area then used another one to specifically wash my feet. If this was the way he treated his one-night stands then I couldn't begin to imagine how he treated the women who were a more permanent fixture in his life.

When he stood to grab the last clean washcloth from the rack at the back of the shower and began to soap it, we both knew there was only one area left on my body for him to wash... And the thought of what that meant both excited and scared the hell out of me.

I waited until he looked me in the eyes before daring to speak.

"Victor... I'm sorry. I can't. You're... too big."

His smile was so immediate, the look of concern in his eyes so deep, my entire body relaxed despite my apprehension.

"I'm not going to take you there," he said gently. "Not tonight, anyway."

Relief flooded me from opposite directions. I had only let two of my lovers know that I enjoyed anal sex. I was more than happy to let Victor be the third. And while I was glad that he was so understanding, what thrilled me most was that he had said 'Not tonight, anyway' in such a way as to imply that there was going to be *another* night.

I allowed myself a smile even as confusion began to set in. After all, if Victor didn't plan on taking me there, why was he still—

—Oh... Ohhhhhh...

An hour and a half later, Bella and I lay sprawled across the bed utterly spent, trying to catch our breath. I had selfishly lasted a bit longer than I sensed she wanted me to so I could only hope the multiple orgasms I was pretty sure she had made up for it.

But the real truth was that I just didn't want the sex to end.

Every moment I was inside her, she was mine. And whether or not she realized it yet, I was already hers. In fact, I'd only ever hungered for one woman in my entire life as much as I already did for Bella. Not only had that relationship taken time to develop even then it had felt nothing like this.

Especially when it came to the reciprocation of our connection.

Hugging Bella gently against my chest as our breathing slowed together, I pushed my distant memory away by replacing it with one more recent, a snippet of our conversation from earlier at Mickey's...

... I remembered watching Betty/Bella line up a difficult shot on the nine ball. Losing and bored with eight, I had thought she might like to try her hand at something new.

"So my father and I kind of used to play this word game," she said just before missing her bank shot completely and leaving me perfect from where I stood. After rolling her eyes, she looked over at me. "Would you like to try?"

"Sure," I said before bending down to sink the nine, ending our game. "Doesn't seem fair though. Seeing how *I've* never played this game of *yours* before."

Bella lowered her head and eyes in a slow burn. "I have not won a single game in anything yet. I think your ego can handle one little lady bruise in your L column."

I couldn't help but laugh at the implication. "Cocky much?"

"Well..." she demurred with a grin, "it is *my* game."

Relinquishing the pool table, we moved over to sit at the one with our drinks. After ordering another round, Bella made a face.

"Is pineapple juice the only thing you're going to drink tonight? Come on! At least get a shot. Have a real drink with me."

As it was her third time prodding me, I gave in and told our waitress to add some SoCo. Bella waited until she was gone before needling me further.

"What is it with you and pineapple juice, anyway? This makes what? Your fourth?"

I shrugged as nonchalantly as I could. I didn't want to weird her out by delving into the matter any deeper than necessary. But I knew saying nothing might appear even stranger so, "With the exception of whisky, water, coffee and an occasional glass of wine, pineapple juice is the only thing I drink." Try as I might to nurse my juice as slowly as Bella did her wine, I couldn't. "But I'd hate to make you feel you were drinking alone."

"You Southerners and your chivalry," she quipped before rolling her eyes much more playfully than the last. After a quick pause, she added, "Thank you."

"You're most welcome... my lady."

Bella chuckled seemingly despite herself. "Look, it's not that I'm not grateful..."

"Buuuuuuut..."

"It's just... pineapple juice hardly counts as drinking now, does it?"

"It has its benefits," I said as casually as I could while finding it hard not to grin. Watching Bella's eyes cast her suspicion, I tried to change the subject. "So, this game of yours. How's it played?"

Bella's eyes widened in excitement. "It's a word game called... *Eruditious...*"

I cocked my head as she paused to let the word hang in the air.

"But 'eruditious' isn't a word," I pointed out.

Bella grimaced. "I know. But when I told my father I'd never heard of it he said, 'So what? Just because you've never heard of something doesn't mean it fails to exist.' So I tried looking it up. Then, when I couldn't find it in the dictionary, he told me, 'Let that be your second lesson. Just because something sounds like a word doesn't mean it is one.' It felt like a trick at the time but he was right. They were good lessons. Of course, in my defense I was only seven."

I raised my glass in salute and waited until Bella did the same. "To precociousness."

Bella smiled graciously before her expression toughened.

"So," she started, "Eruditious can be difficult to play yet it's easy to understand. Basically, it's a cross between a game of Bullshit and a vocabulary test. We challenge each other with, let's say twenty words, ten apiece, that are either real or not. Correctly guessing whether the word is real or imaginary is worth one point. But being able to define a real word is worth a second point. High score wins."

"You're right, it sounds simple. But what happens if we tie?"

Bella tried not to smile. "At the risk of sounding conceited, I do not lose when it comes to word games. Nor have I ever met anyone who could tie me."

"So you're not used to being dominated or tied but willing to risk it. Good to know."

I watched the surprise in Bella's brain stutter step across her face. It was amazing how fast she recovered with a simple shrug. "Just because I am not used to it..."

I allowed her implication to marinate for a second before acknowledging her point with a nod.

"But when it *comes* to Eruditious," she grinned in continuation, "should we tie we will then go word for word until one of us wins."

"Okay," I chuckled. "And these words we choose for one another, when real they—"

"—have to be found in a dictionary, any dictionary. English only. Those are the only rules."

"So any dictionary?"

"Any dictionary."

"No matter how obscure?"

I tried to make my question sound casual, but Bella's squint showed just how much I failed. I wasn't used to being read by anyone else so quickly... though to be honest, it felt kind of cool.

"For purposes of intellectual decorum," she relented after a few beats, "not to mention how I have already had my fill of it enough to last me two lifetimes, let's deem the urban dictionary disqualified. But for any other English dictionary," she nodded, "yes, no matter how obscure."

I pretended to think it over. "So basically, what you're saying is you'll stick your tongue out and I'll stick my tongue out just so we can see who has the bigger... lexicon?"

Bella wrinkled her nose a smidge. "In so many words... yes."

"Hmmmm. Sounds like it could be a fun game." Smiling pointedly, I lowered my voice just a bit. "Let's *do* it."

Bella let out a small squeal of delight. It almost made me feel sorry for her.

"I should warn you though," I continued, "I'm fairly well versed when it comes to etymologies."

Pausing for several head shaking seconds, Bella finally smiled. *"That,* Mister Maxwell, might just be the best pick-up line I have ever heard."

Gazing at her knowingly, I leaned closer. "Makes it even better that we both know neither of us needs one at this point, doesn't it?"

Bella's eyes widened. "Brutal honesty. Well *played...* I can see I am going to have to keep more than just my eye on you."

"You do that," I said with a quick wink.

Bella smirked at my challenge. "Cocky much?"

I paused a longer, much more pointed beat. "Much doesn't begin to describe it."

Bella's pupils dilated as she did her best to hide her excitement. "Hmmmm. I guess time will tell... Okay, my first word for you is... petrichor."

I did my best not to smile in condescension. However...

"Did you forget what I said about etymologies? Why? Did something I say after distract you?"

"What? No, I..." Bella's expression contorted as I watched her switch from one thought to another. "Oh, petri- as in petrified. Damnit," she rolled her eyes.

"Actually, the petr- part refers to neither wood nor trees but to rocks like those in petroleum. The -ichor half comes from Greek mythology."

Half shocked, half impressed, Bella smiled. "Hmmm. Is that so?"

I nodded gently. "It was believed that because they were immortal, the gods had no need for blood. Instead, they had this ethereal fluid called ichor running through their veins. Put them together and petrichor is the wonderful way the earth smells after a much-needed rain. The smell of earth's lifeblood as it were."

Bella pursed her lips and narrowed her eyes as good-naturedly as she could. "Good job. I guess I need to up my game. Your turn."

I paused and pretended to think even though I already knew what I was going to say. Giving her the once over before smiling as seductively as I could, I leaned forward, lowered my voice... and whispered, "Apodyopsis..."

"... What are you smiling about?"

My question broke Victor's reverie. I had been running my fingers lightly through the soft curls of what little chest hair he had as we relaxed on the bed after sex.

It amazed me just how different Victor was from all my former lovers, one-and-dones, most of whom had been gym rats, all shorter and most younger than myself. And whether due to age or steroids, I couldn't recall any having chest hair. The only thing I was sure of was that I had never cuddled after with any of them.

Lost in thought, Victor hadn't even been aware I was watching him think.

"I was just thinking about *Eruditious,"* he said. "Did you really play that with your father?"

I wrinkled my nose. "More or less. I modified the game for the bar."

"What was it like originally?"

I preened, secretly tickled Victor wanted to know more about my life.

"Well, when I was in... maybe second grade, my dad started giving me twenty words on a sheet of paper every Monday morning before school. They were my 'words for the week.' I had to look them up in a dictionary he gave me and memorize them. When he got home from work on Fridays, the first thing he would do was quiz me by randomly selecting five. If I knew the definitions for all five *and* how to spell each correctly, my allowance for the week would be doubled." I shook my head fondly at the memories. "He was always devising different ways to further my intelligence, especially with regard to my vocabulary."

"I'd say he was successful. I've noticed you don't use a lot of contractions."

Surprised that he noticed, I prolonged my pause into feigning ignorance. "I don't?"

"No, you—," Victor's face fell flat. "Good one," he deadpanned.

I couldn't help but laugh. "Sorry. But I *couldn't* resist."

"No, I bet you *could* not," Victor said before sticking his tongue out, making me snicker. "Seriously, though, you're lucky. He sounds like a loving father."

"He is... What's your dad like?"

"I don't know. I never really had one. Not for long, anyway."

Oh. Damn. "Oh, I'm... I didn't realize... I'm so sorry."

Victor's smile and shaking head quickly helped dispel some of my embarrassment.

"Don't be," he said. "Really, it's okay. My parents adopted me when I was a newborn. But they died later in a car wreck when I was still a child. I barely remember them and only bits and pieces of the actual accident."

Oh, God. "You were in it, too?"

Victor nodded. "We were sitting at a stop light when a car tried to turn left in the intersection in front of us. A truck going in the opposite direction swerved to miss it, but not enough. He clipped the car and the speed and angle sent the truck straight into us. My parents died instantly. Being in the back seat was the only reason I survived."

"How old were you?"

"I was in first grade, so five or six."

A melancholy smile spread across Victor's face as he obviously relived something from his past.

"I found out later in life that my adoptive parents were actually from France. They spoke English but with a heavy accent that I had as well. I got teased for it a lot as a kid."

I nodded. Despite the difference in our reasons, I knew the feeling well.

"Anyway," Victor continued, "after my parents died, I became a ward of the state and placed into foster care."

"That had to be a tough way to grow up."

Victor shrugged. "I'm sure I had it worse than some, but from what I saw I had it better than most. I got through it without any real horror stories to tell. A lot of my guardians were people who simply needed the extra money. They were more or less indifferent to my presence as long as I didn't cause trouble which I didn't. But bouncing around the system like that was no way to live so one day I decided I'd had enough. I arranged to get my GED early then petitioned the court to grant my emancipation. That allowed me to enlist with the Marines on my seventeenth birthday."

I couldn't stop a grin from spreading across my face.

"Now what are *you* smiling about?" Victor teased.

"Two things actually. From the moment I first saw you I figured you might be a Marine."

"And why's that?" Victor asked as he tucked a lock of hair behind my ear. Despite it being the fourth or fifth time he had done so tonight, I still swooned from the ease of his familiarity with me. Just a few hours old, our relationship already felt like it had spanned years. The feeling had me in such a tizzy, I had to swallow and clear my throat before I could continue.

"I recognize the type. My father is a Marine."

"Hmmmm... So a loving father *and* a good man."

I smiled. "He is. He's a recruiter, back home in—"

"—Dublin, Ohio."

I was as immediately impressed as I was flattered. I barely remembered mentioning offhand where I was from earlier in the night in reply to Victor telling me he was a rare, native Charlottean.

"Good memory," I said, trying not to swoon some more.

Victor shrugged sheepishly. "Just because I didn't catch your name doesn't mean I wasn't paying attention to everything else you said."

A wave of heat flushed throughout my body. *How does he always manage to say just—*

"What about the other thing?"

What other— Oh... I paused a little too long. The second thing was a commonality I wished I hadn't mentioned. But I had, so... "I graduated high school early, too," I finally admitted.

Victor studied me for a few seconds. "How young were you?"

I gritted my teeth. *How did you—* "Thirteen."

"Thirteen? Wow. That's... quite an accomplishment."

"Thank you," I said, painfully aware of how terse I sounded.

"Bella, it's nothing to be embarrassed about."

"I know, but..."

"But what?"

"But... nothing. I'm sorry, I just didn't have a great childhood. I couldn't wait for it to be over." *And the last thing I want to do is complain about it to someone who grew up in foster care.*

Victor nodded sympathetically. "It seems we have a lot in common."

"We seem to..."

Running my hand down across his six-pack, Victor inhaled as I palmed his dick, standing it up. I loved how heavy it felt in my hand.

"Do you jelq?" I asked.

"Do I *what?"*

"Never mind. If you don't know then you don't... Nor do you need to."

"Ohhhh-kaaaay."

Gently laying him back down, a better tease suddenly came to mind. "Can I ask you a personal question?"

"Sure."

"Why didn't you cum on my face?"

Victor's eyes widened. I couldn't tell whether he was shocked more by my boldness or the sudden change of subject. But after a few seconds, a funny smirk of admiration spread across his face.

"I like how you keep surprising me," he finally said.

"I know," I said behind a small smile of my own. "Truth be told, I like that you like it. And I like that that's why I find myself doing it... Now stop stalling and answer my question."

Victor made a face. "You know, you're awfully bossy for a Sex Slave."

"Known a lot of us, have you?"

"Touché... Okay then." Victor paused for a few seconds to consider his answer, something I found myself appreciating more the more he did. "You know, this might sound weird but—to me, anyway—doing that to a woman, marking her that way, is either entirely impersonal or it's an act of intimacy. We only met, what? Six or seven hours ago? I don't know how you feel, but I think we're well past any impersonal stage. But we haven't had enough time yet for... this... us... to be considered completely intimate either."

Slightly stunned to hear Victor use the word 'us,' I struggled to catch my breath before he noticed. "Fair enough," I said to fill the silence. "And, for what it's worth, I agree."

Us? Did he really say—

"Good," he said. "Now it's my turn. Your question. You sound a little disappointed that I didn't. Does it really turn you on that much?"

I hesitated. I could see where my answer to this line of questioning might lead. I didn't want to lie, yet I didn't want it to go much further either. *But fair's fair...*

"I don't know whether I would enjoy it or not. The thought turns me on, but I've never allowed it before so..."

The confusion on Victor's face was immediate. I started to continue, but unsure of whether to nip our conversation in the bud or try to explain myself at the risk of making it worse, I stayed mute. Watching the wheels turn in his head, I breathed a little easier as I saw Victor try to figure the best way to pose his next question. That he was once again taking the time—

"If you don't mind my asking... how many Masters have you had?"

He asked so gently, all I wanted was to come completely clean. I hadn't lied to him, not once. But his confusion was justifiable. Only our night wasn't over yet, so neither was my fantasy. And the way things were going, Victor had me wanting more than I had ever dared allowed myself to fantasize.

I had to try to keep things going. I'd never forgive myself if I didn't.

"I'm sorry, but I don't feel like answering that at this time," I said as gently as I could. "As you said, we haven't reached a stage of complete intimacy... yet."

Victor smiled. "'Yet'... I like that... But..."

"Yes?"

"If you've never allowed it before, with anyone including your former Masters..."

Oh. "Why did I decide to let you? Someone I just met?"

"Well... yeah?"

Continuing to run my fingers through the softness of Victor's chest hair, I took a few seconds to consider my answer. I had parsed my words far enough already. He deserved a better explanation.

"It's like playing poker, I guess. You evaluate the situation and then play your hand accordingly... Try not to let this go to your head... but you are the first man I have been with that I deemed worthy of something like that. That you chose not to, at this time and for the reason you stated, only validates my decision... But who knows? Perhaps when next we meet..."

The speed with which my words made Victor smile gave me goosebumps.

"So... there's going to be a next time?" he asked coyly.

"Unless all you want from tonight is a one-night stand. Or maybe you have an objection to being my Master?"

Victor's reply was immediate.

"God, no..." he said, his voice trailing off as he inhaled both slowly and apprehensively.

Uh-oh... "I sense a 'but' coming on."

I got it. Or at least I thought I did.

Bella's desire for a life of sexual servitude was entirely voluntary. That much was clear. No one was putting a gun to her head or forcing her to feel the way she did. And I certainly wasn't judging her for it. If anything, I envied just how deep her devotion and decisiveness to what she wanted ran. And that was *despite* how distracting her God-awful tattoo was every time I happened to catch a glimpse of it.

But the idea of taking on the role, actually becoming her Master on a more permanent basis was a little too far outside my comfort zone. Could I do it? Hell yes. Despite how there seemed to be a few limits to the things Bella would or would not do, the idea of on-demand-sex was still a huge turn-on. But could I commit to keep doing it? To actually *be* the type of Master she wanted? If I was being honest... no, I didn't think I could.

Or that I even wanted to.

After all, provided it was with the right woman, vanilla sex was good enough for me. The only times I'd ever felt it necessary to let my freak flag fly was to compensate for a lack in certain aspects of the basic necessities. Mutual growth, emotional companionship, intellectual connection, sexual chemistry. Time after time, whenever I perceived a deficit in my overall satisfaction with a relationship, I tried to fill the void with something sexually new and exciting. Sometimes that might mean focusing on a specific kink or fetish for a while. Other times it meant exploring particular fantasies.

But they never worked and given enough time almost always made things worse.

Now I was at a point in my life where, because I so often found it difficult to find the right woman, I was also unable to find one who was either as sexually enlightened as I had become or—far more importantly—one who was still open to exploring her sexuality in an effort to become so.

Because nothing excited me or made me feel alive as much as sex did.

Not the endorphin rush of a great, adrenaline-fueled workout. Not the "Aha!" moment that came from learning something new. Not even the warm, fuzzy feeling I got every time my non-profit donated a house to a disabled vet. Hell, I had actually been robbed at gunpoint once and I could swear I felt my heart slow from the momentary boredom as I realized it wasn't as big a deal as I had ever envisioned the experience would be.

So with one of the most beautiful souls I had ever met basically offering herself to me to make all my sexual dreams come true, I should have been jumping for joy.

But I wasn't.

It wasn't so much that I was worried about the unknowns that a Master/Sex Slave relationship would entail. In fact, I was fairly certain I'd be fine with whatever ideas or rules Bella had concerning what she wanted in bed. That part I could handle.

It was *why* Bella felt the way she did that I didn't get. But sooner or later I would need to because deep down I knew *that* unknown had the potential to drive me crazy. Bella's motivations, her life story, whatever got her to the point she was at now, I was eventually going to have to know for there to be any chance of us working out.

Only I knew I wasn't going to find out tonight.

No matter how well Bella might be able to articulate her thoughts and feelings on the subject, I knew my ability to understand something that personal could only come with time. But did I want to devote what little time I had left to finding out? That was the real question I had to ask myself.

And looking down into Bella's expectant eyes as she waited for my reply... I knew my answer was yes. Well, mostly, anyway.

As Victor finally exhaled, I could feel most of the tension leave his body. Most... but not all.

"Listen Bella, what you're offering, the sex, especially if you're offering me the opportunity to be your Master... the idea alone feels like a drug. Which to be honest, I'm not sure I can handle."

Wow... Victor's explanation hit me by surprise. Especially given all the ways he had manhandled me over the last couple of hours.

"You've done an excellent job, so far," I assured him.

His smile was gracious but tight. "That's because right now, I care about your pleasure. I've enjoyed satisfying you. I've enjoyed making you cum, feeling your orgasms. And after tonight I'd love nothing more than to experience it again..."

I held my breath as Victor paused. It took every ounce of energy to not put my finger to his lips and stop him right there. Because in that moment, I realized I'd never been with a man so in touch with his own thoughts, his own feelings, his own words. And as much as I wanted to hear whatever else he had to say... what he had just said was all I wanted to hear.

"But at the same time," he continued, unknowingly ruining my moment, "I know myself. I know my good side and my bad. What you're offering me... I know it's what turns you on, I get that... But you have to understand I'm afraid eventually I might start using you. And I mean really using you. Viewing you as nothing more," he struggled for a second before admitting, "... than a collection of holes I have the option to fill."

I was stunned. While the first half of what Victor said jibed with the man I had gotten to know, none of the second half did. It took me a second to figure out what he was trying to say.

"So you're saying what? You're afraid you'd switch to some... dark side you think you have?"

Victor nodded. "I am. A selfish side, anyway. That kind of constant control. I don't think I could handle it without turning into the kind of person I don't want to be. I won't lie and say I don't enjoy the power..."

"But with great power..."

"Exactly. Role-playing I can handle," Victor said as I watched his eyes briefly take in my tattoo before quickly looking away, "but as a way of life... I'm sorry. I just don't want that responsibility. If I'm looking for anything, it's more of an equal... not more of a servant."

Damn. The man was worthier than I thought.

"Despite not wanting the responsibility... you'd make a great Dom, you know that?"

I did my best not to grit my teeth.

Dominance and submission. A Dom and his Sub. Ever since the quintessential books and subsequent films had been released almost a decade ago, nearly every other woman I had been involved with had wanted a taste of the experience. To role play a way of life as if life itself wasn't good or special enough.

I had acquiesced to their desires, of course. But by and large, I found that most women wanted a dominant man more than they wanted to actually be dominated *by* a man. And that was fine, too. After all, I was a firm believer in a woman's prerogative to split a few hairs before they changed their mind.

But to me that type of indecision was indicative of instability. And I had grown up with enough instability to last a lifetime. I didn't feel a need to court more.

Of course, when it came to Bella—a woman so obviously dedicated to a life of sexual servitude that she had allowed herself to be permanently tattooed—I didn't see that becoming an issue. Of her choice, she was certain.

She was also right about that other part.

"I can't say it's the first time I've been told that," Victor admitted seemingly despite himself.

"Hmmm. I bet not..." I paused, allowing the awkward stalemate of our conversation to sink in for a second before attempting to resume control. "So, if you don't think you could handle me on a more permanent basis, yet this isn't just some one-night stand... where exactly does that leave us?"

Victor's smile loosened.

"I'm glad you asked because before we go any further, there's something I need to tell you," he said before taking a breath. "Not only was I not going to play poker with Greg and Abby anymore... I'm scheduled to fly out of Charlotte tomorrow. I'll be gone for the next two months on business."

I must have made a face because Victor continued on, as quick as he was apologetic.

"Believe me, Bella, I'd postpone if I could, but I can't. Not with everything I have lined up."

I... I... I knew this was too good to be true. *Damn.*

"Would it be too much to ask you to wait for me?" Victor asked.

Wait for you?... Wait? Wait what?! My head started to reel. *Did he really just—* Wait for him? *For two months? Damn... What kind of busi— Wait, that would give me time to— Wait—*

"What do you mean by 'wait' for you?"

Victor smiled playfully just before grabbing me around my waist and flipping us both over until he was on top of me. His face suddenly inches from my own, his cheek brushed softly across mine as he whispered.

"I mean I want you... And I don't want anyone... to come along... and take you from me..."

Like music to my ears, his gentle kisses began to float, dancing across my neck as his mouth began to roam. Nuzzling me with the warmth of his breath, his lips pled his case between each step of their waltz.

"Not while I'm gone..." Victor purred. "Not until I've had time... to think things through... Not until I've had time... to get to know you better... We can write... We can call and text... We can even video chat... every... single... day... if you'd like." He pulled his head back to look me in my eyes. "If I promise to wait for you, will you wait for me?"

I've already waited this long—

"I can wait two months," I said, hoping I didn't sound too eager.

The smile in Victor's eyes before he leaned down and kissed me was enough to leave me breathless. As one of his hands cupped my face, his other ran through my hair as I relaxed against his lips, content with the tender level of passion with which he thanked me. It wasn't until his kiss ended and he pulled away that I realized we were both opening our eyes at the same time.

How in the hell did I get this lucky?

"When I get back," he said, "how does a weekend together in bed sound?"

A whole weekend in bed? With you?! "Please!"

Victor smiled as he brushed another strand of hair from my face.

"Good," he said. "And at the risk of offending you... how about next time we go someplace that has room service?"

"Room service?" I smiled, secretly pleased that Victor was worried what I might think about meeting in a hotel again instead of at his or my place. "Hmmm... You really are a hedonist."

"You have a problem with that?"

I paused just long enough to give Victor my best smile.

"None whatsoever... Master."

Master.

I did my best to remain emotionless to the word. I had to admit that despite my misgivings the thought had a certain appeal. But on-demand, limitless sex? Hell, that might be the *only* thing that could ruin sex for me. And sex was the last thing in life I wanted to take a chance and become jaded on. Not to mention I had built my entire house around my swimming pool and part of me was still unsure I could get used to seeing Bella in a bikini, her tattoo glaring at me for the rest of my life.

'Rest of my life?' Where the fuck did that—

I shook my head. I was thinking crazy again. And being honest with myself was only making it worse. I needed to change the subject.

"So... what do you want to do next?" I asked before turning on my side. Trailing my fingers lightly from Bella's neck to her chest, I could only hope I wasn't too transparent.

"Believe it or not, I'd like to keep talking," she said, smiling wryly.

Shi— "Hmmmmm. Okay. But why wouldn't I believe it?"

"I was referring to myself."

"Oh," I laughed. "Yeah, guess I should have caught that." I gave her right nipple a brief tug with my left hand. "But I was distracted."

I noticed Bella inhale, but the look in her eye told me I wasn't getting off that easy. *Damn.* I gave up and stopped playing with her body.

"What do you do for a living?" she exhaled.

Shit.

Out of all the most obvious, unanswered questions of our night and the last in the world I wanted to hear, Bella just had to pick now to pose the one. Of course, it was my fault for bringing up my business trip and not hers that I was so out of practice being asked my occupation. After all, until now I'd done a damn fine job of preventing most people from getting close to or familiar enough with me to feel comfortable asking.

Until now...

Victor was uncomfortable with the idea of being my Master. I got that. He didn't want to discuss it further. Fine. But if I was going to understand his reasoning better, I needed to know him better. I didn't really want to open this particular can of worms yet, but if it worked...

"What do you do for a living?" I asked as plainly as possible.

As intended, my question clearly caught him off-guard. The rattled look on his face almost made me feel sorry for him. Almost.

"Yes," he said suddenly after a lengthy pause.

Umm— "Excuse me?"

"You asked me what I do for a living. My answer is 'Yes.' Because you name it, chances are I do it or, at at least one point in my life, I *have* done it."

Victor's answer was so pat, it almost sounded rehearsed. Regardless, he was definitely deflecting... I needed to take a different approach.

"Judging by your car, you must do it very well."

"Ditto," he said without hesitation.

Damn. "Though accurate, that might be the least informative touché I've ever heard."

Victor took a deep, measured breath before continuing.

"Listen, I'm sorry... but I have certain reasons why I rarely talk to anyone about my work, especially with someone I've just met." His expression softened as he seemed to consider his own words. Finally, he managed a small smile. "But in your case, I'd be willing to make an exception... but only if you go first."

Damn. I chewed my bottom lip, trying to appear as if I was pondering his proposal even though my mind had long been made.

"Then if it is okay with you," I finally said, "I would like to wait a little while longer... My job, my *former* job to be a bit more precise... it tends to distort the minds of men. Their expectations anyway."

"Well... that definitely sounds intriguing enough to be worth the wait."

"As does yours."

Victor smiled at me for several seconds with an expression bordering on appreciation. Even though I could almost see the wheels spinning in his head, I had no idea what he was thinking. But I was grateful when whatever it was concluded with a softening behind his eyes before he continued.

"So we agree then. We'll wait until you're ready."

His statement was as decisive as it was gentle. That he could manage to be both at the same time gave me goosebumps.

Who is this man?

Who is this woman?

'It tends to distort the minds of men.' What the hell could that mean?

Was Bella a private escort in between Masters? She could be. Without a doubt I imagined the woman's deep-throating skill alone could command some serious bank. Not that I had any idea what the going rate would be. I'd never paid for sex and never would, but that also meant I had no idea what a high price escort was really like in the first place. All I knew was—minus her physical beauty—Bella didn't fit any expectation I had ever had of one. Which meant—

—*No. She's a doctor,* I suddenly remembered, recalling not only what Greg had called her but that she had said as much when she revealed she could read Latin. How I had forgotten already... *Wait a minute.*

That didn't make sense. What the hell kind of doctor is hesitant to admit being a doctor?

Solely on stereotype, chiropractor was the first thing that sprang to mind but I knew that was ridiculous. Given my height, I'd met more than a few over the years and juvenile jokes aside they were all proud of their chosen profession. Besides, nothing about chiropractics distorted the minds of men. When the word 'proctologist' struck me next, I stifled my chuckle and tried to stop thinking altogether. I was starting to feel foolish, even if only I knew why.

All I knew for sure was that I felt a bit like a hypocrite for even being curious. I guarded what could be considered my occupation as much as possible, so I couldn't blame Bella for doing the same. And while I sincerely doubted she had as many reasons to be equally secretive that didn't mean her reasons weren't as valid as my own.

"So we agree then," I finally decided. "We'll wait until you're ready."

Kissing Bella on her forehead, I resigned myself to our crossing that bridge when we got there.

Immediately after kissing me on the forehead, I watched Victor clench his jaw to stifle a yawn. Earlier at Mickey's we'd discovered we were both the early-to-bed-early-to-rise type and at the moment I was more than a little grateful. We'd had sex five times, using an entire box of condoms plus two from the second. While I wouldn't say no to more, I was really hoping to save the last one for the morning which, hopefully like myself, was going to come soon enough.

Turning around to spoon, I shimmied my ass against Victor's crotch as I pulled his right arm over me, tucking his hand beneath my chin and whispering good night.

"Yes, it was, thanks to you," he whispered with a chuckle. "Good night."

As Victor shifted into a more comfortable fit behind me, warming my back, my habitual side fought against the unfamiliar timing of my excitement. Despite how my mind was constantly in motion, I normally drifted off to sleep almost immediately once my head hit the pillow.

But tonight had been anything but normal... and I had too much to think about.

In a number of various situations during my therapy sessions, I found it often helped to speak with an air of clairvoyant certainty, if for no other reason than to give the impression of establishing my bona fides. Researching my patients online beforehand greatly aided my ability to do that effectively. Whether I needed to forge a seemingly simple yet coincidental personal connection or maneuver our conversation in a more productive direction, what I secretly knew about a person could be a tremendous help to the both of us.

But with Victor I was flying blind, knowing only what he told me and what I could observe.

Drifting a little deeper toward sleep, I played back the entire evening in my head. Along with his purple aura, I recalled just how well the kissing had boded. Amazingly, every time we had sex was preceded by a make out session that was hard to stop.

Then there was the sex which was fantastic, but incredibly wasn't the best thing about the night. While a couple of my orgasms had bordered on the unimaginable, the first for its strength and several for their duration, they were just highlights.

No, the moments that followed like this moment here and now were what I had been dreaming of and desiring more than anything else. The peace and quiet. The stillness... Moments where my mind was finally at complete rest. Here was my happiness.

I smiled into Victor's hand. Despite my plan, I really hadn't wanted to just get lucky. I'd have settled for it, it would have been good enough for the night, but deep down I knew I had been truly hoping for something more. And while never in a million years could I have expected a unicorn man to come along, here he was... lying next to me in bed...

Closing my eyes I wondered, would he still be in the morning? Or was this all just a dream?

Falling asleep... part of me didn't want to... while another part... couldn't wait... to wake up... just to... find... out...

Using my hand tucked under Bella's chin, I drew her a bit closer to me, snuggling us tighter. When my cock began to stiffen reflexively, I altered my position to minimize our physical contact, allowing it to subside. Even though my body didn't want to, I knew we needed to stop at some point.

The room's illuminated alarm clock showed quarter to two which was well past my typical bedtime of eight. Normally, I'd be waking in two hours—and still probably would—to hit my gym. Yet as tired as I should have been, I couldn't help but recap my day.

From the moment we met, the bar games we had played, Eruditious, our laughter, flirting and all our talking to say nothing of the unbelievable sex... I'd never had a day and an evening like this one in my entire life. The idea that I could have more, nay, all I wanted and desired... I shook my head in disbelief.

While the first half of my life had been everything just short of tragic, the second half had been absolutely golden. Yeah, I'd known some good times early on just as I'd had to overcome a few obstacles later. But by and large the two halves of my life had been night and day. I'd gone from darkness to sunshine and I didn't want to go back. Theoretically though, allowing Bella into my life could do just—

Pushing the negative possibility from my mind, I thought back instead to the moment Bella told me her name for the second time just as I entered her for the first. The coincidentally perfect timing of my thrust inside her as she moaned Quinn.

As my cock started to swell with the memory, I tried to distract myself by shifting the focus of my thoughts to the origin of her names. While I figured Quinn to be more likely Irish than Scottish and Rose to be from the Latin *rosa,* I knew for a fact that Bella's etymological root was Latin for both beautiful and fair.

A beautiful fair-haired rose.

As her breathing relaxed into a soft snore, I thought how aptly the woman tucked under my arm had been named by her parents. But neither her beauty nor her fairness were what had me chuckling as I kissed the back of her head.

"Ciao, Bella," I whispered softly before closing my eyes and falling asleep alongside her.

Sunday
January 12, 2020
10:19am, 62° & sunny

The strip club was too dark and smoky to see well or far. Few understood as did I that that was by design. Forced to move closer for a better look, our patrons often felt more of an obligation to pay for their perceived reward of faux intimacy.

Dancing around my pole in sync with the thump of the bass, I took care not to bump into the chair positioned just a few feet away on the stage. Every girl had one which, just like mine, was also empty. Not that I cared because, just like them, I was bored. So bored I didn't bother making eye contact with any of the men in the crowd below us.

But I wasn't too bored to notice the girl furthest from me suddenly strut her stuff with a little more enthusiasm. A fish was nibbling on her line and she was trying her best to reel him in by enticing him with some of her better moves. Given how little she had on, she might land him, too.

Not that I was worried. I was in better shape and a better dancer than most everyone else. Only my outfit wasn't as risqué as any of the other girls. I was more American pie than International skank. And if that was what he wanted, she could have... hmmmmmm.

I could see him... but not his face. He was tall, broad shoulders... and obviously unimpressed as he slipped silently through the clouded, strobe-lit air to the next girl. She, too, began to gyrate with more energy, more purpose. Yet once again, Faceless moved on.

Girl after girl after girl he glided by, each trying to outdo the last until finally he stood before me, his shaved head bowed, his face and eyes avoiding mine...

Yet he seemed familiar... I felt like I knew him... I just didn't know how... from where... or most importantly why.

What I did know was an attempt to impress him didn't. So neither did I.

Of course, I was no longer bored. I couldn't fake that. But just because my curiosity was piqued didn't mean I was going to perform for him like some trained monkey on an invisible leash. No, the way I danced was for me. Aligning my body with the rhythms and vibrations of the music as they pulsed through me was how I enjoyed myself. How I made it through my workday.

If Faceless wanted to watch me, fine. If he wanted to pay to watch me, even better. But my dignity wasn't for sale.

The scarlet filter rotating to cover my spotlight, temporarily changing the color of my hair, gave me an idea. Wrapping my leg languidly around the pole, I slowly twisted my hips, allowing my head, shoulders and hair to follow their path. Given my pale skin and blue bikini, I closed my eyes and corkscrewed around, spiraling my body like I was the most seductive barbershop helix ever made. Again and again, around and around and—

It startled me when my leg brushed against his. Enough so that I opened my eyes to find him sitting in my chair, gazing up at me as I continued to dance.

Victor...

The cerulean glints in his eyes were magnificent. Transfixed to mine, they never roamed. Not to my glutes as I performed a perfect squat. Not to my breasts as I bowed them forth. Not even to my crotch which began to flood as I backed up to my pole, pressed myself against it and started sliding up... and down... up... and—

"—Oh, God..."

I wasn't pressed up against a pole. I was on my back. But with my legs spread, there was something definitely still pressed between them.

"Oh, my God," I moaned again as both Victor's face and fingers pressed further into my flesh.

Waking on the verge of orgasm, I was overcome with emotion. As my body screamed for more, my brain did its best to protest.

Wait! I didn't give you permission...

I had never awakened in bed with a man before. This was all new for me. Didn't he have to ask me first? Could he just do this? Whatever he wanted? To my body? *My* body?

Oh, God, please don't stop...

Pressing forward, my pelvis tensed just before my dam broke. Small tremors quickly grew into giant quakes as my lower torso convulsed again and again. Operating with a mind of their own, my hands gripped the back of Victor's head and pressed him solidly against what felt like the center of my entire being in a desperate attempt to either quell or prolong my orgasm. I couldn't tell which I wanted more and the dichotomy of my competing desires was an utter mind scrambler.

Make it stop! No, don't, please do it again! Right there! Oh, make it ohhhhhhhhh...

Shuddering in ecstasy, the frequency of my spasms decreased as an extra second or so began to separate each from the last until my legs finally gave out and laid flat. After relaxing for several seconds, I summoned the last vestige of my energy, stretching my neck and body, fully splaying myself before collapsing yet again and giving in to the totality of how sated I felt. My muscles turned to jelly as every ounce of remaining tension I had drained away, carrying my consciousness in tow.

Closing my eyes, I felt Victor's breath between my legs but lost track of time between then and when I last felt him kiss my cheek.

"Go back to sleep," he whispered. "I'm going to shave and shower."

Incapable of anything more than a perfunctory *hmmmmm,* I murmured my acknowledgment to the sounds of Victor's words. But as the fog of my mind obscured their relevance, my eyes grew even heavier, preventing the sense of sight from intruding on my body's happiness... and its warmth... its warm... warmth... wait...

Sleep?... Shave?... Shower?... Shower?!

Exiting the brief slumber I was unaware I had entered, the sound of a running faucet stirred my curiosity just enough to rouse my consciousness. But then it stopped... And then it started again... until it stopped... And then started...

Getting the better of me, I forced my eyes open. From my position on the bed, I could see a dressing mirror on a wall, the angle to which allowed me to see the bathroom. The door was cracked just enough for me to see Victor, his head and face covered with white shaving cream. To my surprise, he was using a long, wood handled straight razor. With each long scrape, a strip of white foam would disappear from his head before being rinsed off into the sink.

Unaware I was watching him via the mirror, my eyes traveled down Victor's body, delighted that I could see the muscles in his ass as he twisted, leaned forward and flexed. But disappointment came when I realized I couldn't see his dick because at that moment...

Sliding quietly out of bed, I tip-toed over to the door, startling him when I pushed it open.

"Hey," he said apologetically before turning to face me. "I'm sorry if I—"

Without saying a word, I dropped to my knees and scooped Victor's dick into my mouth. The tile was cold and hard, but I didn't intend to be on it for very long.

Gripping Victor's ass with both my hands, I pulled his entire body forward as I looked up, directly into the shocked wide white of his eyes. Extending my tongue at the same time I opened my throat, I made sure Victor was watching as my lips travelled all the way to his groin until my nose pressed into his abdomen.

"Fuck," he moaned as his head rolled backward.

Pausing a quick beat, I slowly drew back my own, working against the suction created by the tightness of my lips.

I could literally feel the blood drain from my brain as Bella's mouth coaxed me hard.

One minute I'm shaving my head, wondering if I really had it in me to satisfy the depths of desires a Sex Slave probably possessed and the next my cock was well past her tonsils. All I knew was I had to think and I had to think fast while I still had the available blood supply.

Reaching down, I grabbed a couple of towels from the shelf under the sink and dropped them at Bella's knees.

"Here," I mumbled. "For your knees."

Ignoring the towels, Bella quickly swallowed me whole again, almost in defiance.

"Fuck!"

Fully erect now in one direction, it took everything I had to keep my knees from buckling to remain so in the other as Bella wasted no time making her intentions clear. Given the pressure and speed of her mouth, she wasn't just trying to suck me hard. This time she was going to suck me off.

Closing my eyes, I did my best to relax as I enjoyed the firm pump of her hand paired with the soft, wet heat of her mouth. Obviously remembering how I liked it, she began to alternate her loud, throaty sounds between wet, hissing slurps. Closer and closer her frenzy drove me on until I finally felt the familiar rise of my balls as my cock swelled even more in anticipation.

Purely from force of habit and without even looking, I reached down and grabbed the back of Bella's head. Almost instantaneously both her hands gripped my wrists, flinging my arms aside as her fingernails dug into my skin. Shocked by her strength, I looked down to find her leveraging her new position to the fullest. Our arms spread like two, wind taut sails pulling in opposing directions against me and my mast, her head snapped and whipped fore and aft, bobbing upon me as furiously as she could. Over and over and over again.

Until suddenly I came. Spectacularly.

Shot after shot after shot I pumped into her mouth. Yet for the more than twenty to thirty seconds that followed, Bella never slowed her pace. My body shuddered in waves, jerking spasmodically as I could swear I felt the pressure in her mouth increase until my cock felt like it was a straw. I wasn't just shooting my load, it was literally being sucked out of me faster than my testicles had the strength to pump it.

Sapped of energy, I braced against the counter just as my knees began to shake like they were going to buckle. As unbelievably wonderful as Bella's blowjob actually felt, I suddenly found myself reveling in the fact that just because I was done coming didn't mean she was done sucking. It took her at least another half a minute to gently ramp her pace down to a complete stop, a full thirty seconds of bonus ecstasy that seemingly stretched itself into eternity.

Doing my best to catch the first glimpse of her eyes, I realized Bella had swallowed almost none of my cum, allowing it instead to escape her mouth and spill over her lips to slide down her chin before oozing all over that beautiful chest of hers. With a slightly glazed look in her eyes—almost as if the experience was her first—one thing was certain. The woman knew how to make a man feel special.

And even more so when the realization fully hit her as she swallowed what little was left.

Locking eyes, Bella withdrew the head of my cock completely from her mouth. Following the flourish of a final suckle, she purposely gave it one last kiss before releasing me from her hold.

"Sweet, isn't it?" I asked, causing Bella's eyes to widen despite herself.

"Very," she admitted with a smile.

"See? I told you pineapple juice has its benefits."

"You are kidding me," she said with a bit of a weird look on her face as I helped her stand.

"Does it taste like I'm kidding?"

"No. No, it certainly does not. It just surprises me you know about that. Most men don't."

Her comment caught me off guard... but not because it was true.

"I guess how pineapple can make a man's cum taste sweet is fairly common knowledge in the BDSM community. I take it that's how you know about it?"

His question caught me off guard. I wasn't ready for a conversation like this. Not yet.

"Not exactly. I mean it is common knowledge, yes. But no, that's not why I know." *Think!* "I'll tell you what," I finally said, doing my best to sound agreeable, "how about we save this conversation for the drive back to Charlotte? You are bound to find out whenever you Google me anyway."

Victor's expression quickly contorted into a funny look. "Why's that? Are you famous or something?"

With a half-smile-half-shrug, I paused as if it was a possibility.

"Well, like they say, if you have to ask, then no. But if you can wait until we're on our way, I promise to explain everything. Well, almost everything. After all, a girl's gotta have her secrets."

Glancing at my reflection in the bathroom mirror, it was obvious Victor was admiring my ass.

"Why do I get the feeling," he started, before turning to look me directly in the eyes, "that just as there's a few other things you've definitely got more than most... secrets are also one of them?"

Acknowledging his compliment with a quick nod, I shot Victor a wink, forcing his face to soften to a smile.

"Deal," he said.

And then he leaned down and kissed me.

Gazing down at Bella, a flood of emotions began to reverberate through me, each radiating further outward as they rippled away from my core.

Being allowed the privilege of continuing to spend time with her, if only by phone, was good enough. That she was alluding to revealing more personal details about her life was far better. But that she was standing here, naked, before me now, I suddenly realized was the absolute best. And all I wanted to do was kiss her.

So I did.

Just before Victor had begun to come earlier, I realized I had a decision to make. Despite how badly I wanted to swallow everything he had whole, I was almost too lost in the moment.

When his hands grabbed the back of my head, something instinctual in me had screamed out *Hell no!* Although I thoroughly enjoyed how he had fucked my mouth last night, this time I was adamant. I wanted to be the sole cause of his orgasm.

So when I suddenly found myself holding him back while doing everything I could to usher him forth... all I could think was *Don't stop, keep going* because I honestly had never been so lost in the act of fellatio before.

Of course, I had sucked a couple of guys off in the past. Always slowing as they came. Waiting to see how they tasted first. Whether I needed to swallow immediately or, provided they tasted okay, perhaps tease them a little by letting them watch me savor their pride. I knew how to put on a show and I pretty much knew how cum tasted after all.

Or so I thought.

Given everything I knew about sex, that a man's ejaculate was directly affected by the foods he ate was one of the most surprising. While it made sense, it still shocked me a bit. I mean I knew a diet high in red meat could make cum taste fairly horrible. But that a man could alter his own flavor by consuming enough of the right foods to make himself taste sweet? Wow.

But that Victor did so on purpose was even more mind blowing. After all, what kind of man does that? None I had ever known.

So when Victor leaned forward to kiss me it wasn't just my fascination that made my eyes pop.

His cum was still clearly on my lips. I could taste it so I know he had to, too... Yet as he kissed and continued to kiss me, I could tell it made no difference whatsoever. He was neither turned on nor off. He simply wanted to kiss me and wasn't going to let something as trivial as a tiny bit of his own spunk on my lips stop him.

Realizing just how secure Victor was in his own sexuality, especially compared to the relative boys I had been with, was an unexpected and enormous turn-on. A fact I couldn't help contain.

Kissing him with increasing passion, I reached out to find his cock not entirely flaccid. And when, after just a couple urgent yet well-timed strokes he regained rigidity, I knew it was on again.

Damn.

An hour later, after one last round of unbelievable sex followed by some soul-filling, life-invigorating afterglow, we were both finally dressed and prepared to leave. Well, almost anyway...

"Sit down on the bed for me," I asked every bit as gently as I commanded.

Sex that had started in the shower but ended in the bed had left us with barely enough time to dress before checkout. In our haste, I had managed to secretly scoop Bella's panties into my jacket pocket without her noticing. Thankfully, she had quit trying to find them, finally chuckling with a, "Screw it, I'll go commando," crack that I approved of with a grunt.

But now, trying to discern my intent, she searched my face for a few seconds before acquiescing and doing as she was told. Bending down on one knee, I gently lifted her left foot as I pulled her panties from my pocket. The grin alone that spread across her face as she shook her head was totally worth it.

"I should have known."

Slipping her panties over her feet without a word, I watched her watch me as I slid them slowly, higher and higher, up under the skirt of her dress until they reached the point where her legs met the bed. With my fingers still firmly hooked in the sides, I took a moment to gaze upon her figure.

As sexy as Bella was, the sight of her covered breasts and curve of her hips had me wanting to rip her clothes back off. What my hands weren't touching, I caressed with my eyes. Down her body, then back up to her face.

"Stand for me," I again asked and commanded.

By that point it was apparent Bella's obedience stemmed more from her own desire than mine. That I had the power to turn her on so easily was absolutely intoxicating. The more I used it, the more I wanted to use it more.

Pushing up off the bed, she rose above me. As she towered to her full height, I slowly began to stand. With my fingers still hooked in the sides of her panties, I let my face trace its way up her stomach and through the valley of her breasts until we were eye to eye. Pausing just long enough for her anticipation to build, I continued to stand until I was completely upright.

Without saying a word, I raised her panties up until the sides were just above her hips as I felt her spread her legs just a bit for a better fit. Then, with my hands still up her skirt, I gave Bella my best smile.

"Now I want something from you."

"Hmmmmm. And what would that be, Master?"

Instead of speaking, I took my right hand and began to slowly rub between her legs. Little by little, I pressed her panties deeper within her folds, massaging and stroking as I went. My eyes firmly on hers, I watched as Bella's deep inhales exhaled in staggered breaths, becoming small pants that ultimately gave way to the softest of moans. Within thirty seconds both her panties and my fingers were sopping wet. Realizing I had her close to her tipping point, another thought occurred to me.

Slowing my pace so as not to deflate her too fast, I eventually withdrew my hand. Still looking deeply into her eyes, I allowed her to watch as I licked my fingers clean. But when she began to speak, I cut her off.

"I'm not finished."

Reaching back under her skirt with both my hands, I slowly peeled her panties back down, lower and lower until they fell to the floor around her feet.

"Step out of them, please."

Bella did and I bent down to pick them up. Gathering them to my nose, I inhaled her scent one last time. Then I took great care to reverently fold her panties before slipping them back in my pocket. While the last thing I knew I was was a perverted, panty sniffing weakling... deep down part of me knew I was probably going to smell them at least once before we saw one another again. The thought of two months without her made me want to sigh.

"Now we can leave."

"Are you sure you're in no rush?" Victor asked as he stood outside my car door. "Because we can take the highway—"

"—No, taking the back roads sounds nice," I said just as my retractable top finished stowing itself in the trunk. "It's not like I have to be back at a certain time."

At that moment I honestly couldn't have cared less about which route we took home to Charlotte. I was, however, keenly aware of how deliciously sore my entire body was, a loose, relaxed ache the likes of which I had never felt before. I couldn't remember the last time my mood had been so mellow yet alive.

"Okay then, what about lunch? I know this great restaurant just off I-40 in Wallace."

I wrinkled my nose. "I think I'll be okay until I get home... if it's all the same to you."

The truth was I'd probably be starving by the time I returned home. But with only two months before seeing Victor again, I was already planning my diet. And restaurants were no longer included.

"Okay, then just follow me. I'll call you as soon as I finish a few phone calls I need to make. Shouldn't take me much more than an hour."

As Victor turned from my car door to head toward his own, mellowed or not I couldn't believe the man's audacity. Wasn't he going to at least kiss me goodbye? *How dare he?!*

"Victor Maxwell!" I huffed loud enough to stop him in his tracks. "Do you mean to tell me that after last night *and* this morning that you are just going to walk away without so much as a polite goodbye?"

A bemused look crept across Victor's face. "Who said this is goodbye?" he asked before smirking even further. "Although you are correct. I am forgetting something." Stepping back to my door, he reached in and took my left hand. Bending over as he pulled it up to his lips, his eyes held mine the entire time. "Ciao, Bella," he said with a smile before releasing my hand.

I lowered my eyes to hide my blush as my mind spun. I mean, *Who does that?*

While Victor walked to his car, I donned my sunglasses, fired up my seat's scarf heater and looked up at the sky. Though still a touch on the brisk side, the morning was bright and cloudless. Taking a deep breath, I began to revel in my newfound situation.

Following Victor out of the parking lot, I almost wanted to pinch myself. Twenty-four hours had yet to pass in what looked like the beginning of a new phase of life for me. I had, at least to some extent, a new man behind me, a new path in front of me... but no panties on me. And while I had no idea what I had gotten myself into, I couldn't have been more excited. My future had never seemed more unknown or limitless while at the same time being filled with nothing but the most positive of possibilities.

Yet a large part of me still had a hard time believing it.

Turning my body over to Victor to do with as he pleased with no reservations whatsoever had shockingly come easy enough. After all, I knew going in that it was probably only going to be for one night. But given the way Victor had been with me, not just using me for his pleasure but also taking such great care to focus on my own… I knew I was facing a lifetime of regret if I didn't both ask for as well as offer him more.

But now I was neither regretting nor facing any at all.

And all because I just took a leap of faith and offered myself to be a Sex Slave to a man I just met. Was I freaking crazy? Who does that?

Abby did was, of course, my first thought. Because like it or not her relationship with Greg, out of all that I had ever known, was the one I envied most. And my parents had set a pretty high bar.

I had grown up watching my father do things like spontaneously grab my mother and begin whisking her across any floor, enticing her to dance at a moment's notice. I often reminisced about listening through my bedroom wall as they ended each night, talking and laughing as they recounted their day to one another. I'd even seen the look in my mother's eyes each time my father surprised her with a gift, usually something she had only mentioned in passing. But they were my parents.

And thinking of them in any other way was just… *Ewwww.*

So things were understandably different when it came to Abby and Greg. Their joy and contentment, excitement and love—to say nothing of their insatiable lust for one another—were just a few elements of their relationship that made my heart race whenever they didn't have it melting. They were so perfectly matched the psychologist in me knew it would have been unhealthy to deny my own simple truth: *I. Want. That!*

And staring at the back of Victor's car I knew at a bare minimum I now had my best shot at obtaining it. I'd never met a man who could excite much less satisfy both my intellectual and sexual senses as well as he had.

A shift in my seat sparked a tinge of excitement to run through me as I rubbed against the physical freedom beneath my dress. The sheer pointlessness of underwear flickered briefly through my mind before I found myself wondering if I'd ever get them back. Segueing to remembering they were my favorite pair to realizing I couldn't think of anyone I'd rather have have them than Victor, part of me wondered what if anything he'd do with them. Smiling, I glanced ahead at his car.

Anything he wants, I purred to no one but myself as I settled in for the ride.

Leading us deeper through the rural back roads of the eastern half of the state,

I quickly noticed Victor was keeping a leisurely pace. Normally I drove like a bit of a speed demon, pushing the limit wherever I safely could. I loved revving the AMG's throaty vibration beneath my seat whenever possible. The feeling of being in control of something so powerful was always exhilarating.

But with no place to be and no time to be there, I was more than content to take in the sights while waiting for Victor's call.

Having grown up in Ohio before attending college at Notre Dame followed by Boston College, I had never lived in a place as lush as North Carolina. No matter the time of year, the trees always seemed to be so green and full of life. At least compared to what I was used to.

From the hotel parking lot, it didn't take long before the swamps and bogs of the tidewater gave way to fields of mobile homes and solar farms dotting the coastal plain. Along the horizon, the remnants of dormant Bradford pear, dogwood and cherry trees framed the edges of the occasional cotton or lavender field. Though not in season, the mild winter coupled with the week's false start to spring had more than a few plants speckled in premature bloom. Set against the warm backdrop of the Carolina blue sky, the soft palette of pastels in various shades of white, pink and purple somehow seemed even more magical.

In the blink of an eye, the perfect night had become the perfect day.

Basking in the sun, I realized it had been quite a while since I had last soaked in some natural vitamin D. It felt so good, I began to wonder why Victor hadn't dropped his top and done the same. Of course, without sunscreen on a day like today his head would probably burn. And I bet he thought the same.

Hmmmmm... I wonder what else he's thinking right now?

Oh my God, what the fuck *am I doing?*

It wasn't that I didn't know. After all, I had been here countless times before.

I had long lost track of the number of women I'd met, struck up a conversation, realized we had some chemistry, pursued our conversation further, then mutually realized our chemistry went even deeper than it had upon first impression. We'd then acted on it, ended up sleeping together far too soon, only to realize far too late that we had missed or flat out ignored all the warning signs that we weren't right for one another.

A mistake I had let happen time and time again.

I had given in to the aggressive size queens who were all too aware that height correlated well to length. Given in to the admiration of a suggestive smile and the definitive possibility of so much more. Given in until there wasn't much of me left to give. And for what? To turn into a man who damn near took sex for granted.

Because like it or not my problem was sex had always come easy for me. Before I was in my 20s, I realized that being halfway decent looking and better than decent acting—not to mention being a great deal taller than average in height—had that effect on women. So much so that while most guys looked forward to two days off a week from work, I had to *schedule* two days off a week from sex.

I remembered how the constant, revolving door of women once had me jokingly thinking of myself as a carousel in a park. And it started getting to my head, had me believing I was somehow special. I mean, they could have been collectively lying, but the reviews most were giving me sure had me feeling like I was on top of the world long after we got off the top of one another.

Until one day, I caught a cold. A bad one which was odd for me because I was rarely sick. But suddenly I was when it dawned on me I had no one to turn to. No one I wanted to, anyway. And so I suffered my cold alone which, thankfully, was better than anything a doctor could have ordered. Nursing myself back to health gave me enough time to swallow a heavy dose of self-evaluation. My life, my way of living... sucked.

Of course, it wasn't any woman's fault that I had allowed myself to become something next to nothing. Wasn't their fault that I allowed myself to belong to almost any woman willing to open her legs for me. Wasn't their fault that I had lowered my value until I was cheap enough to belong on the clearance rack. And not only wasn't I special, sadly I had allowed sex to become even less so.

Glancing in my rearview mirror, a small part of me worried whether or not I was on the precipice of a repeat. I honestly couldn't remember feeling a stronger connection with anyone in such a short amount of time or ever having a better sexual encounter than I had with Bella. And while the degree might have been foreign, the circumstances were all too familiar. Meet, connect, mix well, fuck.

All parts I had no problem with.

It was the possibility for a repeat of what came after that I wanted no part of.

I didn't want to wake up one day and regret the warning signs I failed to see. Things, I was a bit ashamed to admit, like Bella's unsightly tattoo. Not only could I not ignore seeing it, I wasn't sure even if I came to understand it how I might feel about it.

Of course, thinking or worrying about that could come later. Right now, I didn't want the high I was riding, this feeling I hadn't felt in far too long, to end. Yet at the same time I knew all good things—

Shaking my head, I rattled off the hold my manic-depressive thoughts were trying to grab upon my heart. Enough at least for me to concentrate on what I needed to do next.

Having exchanged cell numbers earlier, when I told Bella I needed to make a few calls before phoning her, I wasn't completely lying. While I couldn't fill out the necessary paperwork or file my flight plan until getting to the airport, I still needed to schedule my jet's fueling and servicing in advance to minimize my delay. And I needed to call and let Alexis know I was ending our relationship.

Yet mostly I just wanted some time to think. But first things first.

"Call Rick," I said after punching the Phone button on the steering wheel. Surprisingly, the call rang twice before connecting.

"Boss."

A man of few words unless you got him going, Richard Crockett was the closest I came to having a best friend. And though I did my best to try and remember he was more a personal assistant, it irked whenever he reminded me of my role in the equation.

"What have I—" *Never mind.* It was pointless anyway. And my fault for not learning. "Hey. Are you busy at the moment? I need a favor."

"Nope. Name it."

"I need the address for a Dr. Bella Quinn in Belmont."

"Business or—"

"—residential," I said, cutting him off before he got to personal. "I'd do it my self but I'm driving."

Rick paused for just the slightest beat. "Got it."

I shook my head. Despite my effort, I had no doubt he did. It wasn't just that my request was more than a bit unusual. Rick was just that smart, his thick, lapsing North Carolina country boy drawl be damned.

"And I need a quick dive on a Greg and Abby Costello of Charlotte."

"Depth?"

I thought about it for a second. I hated taking up the man's time on such a beautiful day. "No more than half an hour each."

"Degree?"

"All legal. Public records only."

"Budget?"

I paused. Rick was asking questions faster than I had given consideration. Regardless, I saw no need for hard inquiries. "Zero," I said after deciding I could dig deeper later if the situation warranted.

"Deadline?"

"Whenever you find the time. But if you'd text me the doctor's address asap, I'd appreciate it."

Another beat. "Done."

"Thanks."

"No problemo, jefe. Anything else, mon frère?"

I shook my head. That's what I liked about Rick. When the man wasn't all over the place, he was all business. And when he wasn't all business he was usually bouncing back and forth between any of the three different languages he spoke.

"Not today. Speaking of which, you enjoy the rest of yours, okay?"

"Roger, dodger."

I started to sign off when I suddenly remembered— "Hey, how's Nixie doing by the way?"

Nixie was a retired bomb sniffing Belgian Malinois that Rick was fostering for one of the guys in his former unit. She'd lost both her hind paws to an IED in Afghanistan a few months back. Naturally her handler thought of Rick first to take care of her.

"She's good. Still a little wobbly on her new feet but I bet she'll be about runnin' on 'em by the time you get back. Definitely by the time my buddy gets back to retrieve her."

"Good."

"Yeah, it is. Which reminds me. You gotta sec?"

"Sure."

"Another friend of mine contacted me yesterday. Have you heard anything 'bout a flu going around in China?"

It took me a second. Not only did I know Rick still had contacts throughout the military, I remembered hearing some— *Oh, yeah.* "You mean the one in Wuhan? Yeah, I heard it mentioned last night on the news, but I didn't pay it any attention."

"You might wanna. My buddy says it's a lot more severe than's bein' reported. Like to the point of bein' purposefully downplayed."

Okay. "So nobody wants to cause a panic. What's new?"

"Nothin'. Except maybe the BioSafety Level 4 facility in the middle of downtown Wuhan."

I gritted my teeth a bit. One of Rick's only character flaws—at least in my opinion—was how taken he could be when it came to conspiracy theories. A little too easily excited, if he got going on a rant, it could be hard to get him to calm back down. Fortunately, he typically had enough self-awareness to keep from broaching such subjects on his own. So for him to bring this up...

"Email me what you know. I'll take a look."

"All I'm saying is if we need to start thinkin' about locking down To Fish—"

"—I said I'd take a look."

Thankfully, Rick picked up on my tone. "You're the boss, Boss."

Shaking my head, I said, "Call me if it's necessary. Otherwise, I'll see you in two months."

"Good. In time for openin' day, right?"

Oh, damn. I forgot— Shaking my head harder, I resolved to work out the scheduling conflict later. *One thing at a time.* "As long as everything goes according to plan, I will be."

"Well, then I hope it does."

I gritted my teeth again. The only people who knew what I was doing for the next two months were those on a strict need-to-know basis. Despite how close Rick and I were, he wasn't. Not yet anyway.

"I'll talk to you later," I said. "And hey, I'm serious. Don't spend too much time diving. It's too nice a day outside. Get out and enjoy it."

"Roger, dodger."

Disconnecting, I rolled my eyes. Reality sucked. Life had been so much more fun in bed with Bella. Not that I had time to reminisce about my latest lover. After all...

I still had to call Alexis.

Even if she wasn't my woman, I was still a one-woman man. It was only right for Alexis to know as soon as possible that she'd need to find a replacement for me. She already knew I was going out of town, so our two month hiatus would be no surprise. How she was going to take my call to extend it permanently, on the other hand, I had no idea. Yet after politely explaining I had met someone, she was more than gracious even going so far as to wish me the best. Along with a caveat.

"Just... do me a favor," she appealed, her voice sounding tinny over the phone, "and give me a call back if it doesn't work out, okay? I mean, I was prepared to wait two months anyway but—hey, wait a minute... Is she going on your trip with you?"

"Uhhh. No."

"And you just met her?"

"Yeah. Yesterday actually."

"And... she's willing to wait two months for you, too? And you for her?"

"Ummm. Yeah."

"Wow. Wow, that's great. She must be really something. Understanding to say the least... I'm really happy for you... I hope it works out."

"Thanks."

"Just, uh... Like I said, let me know if it doesn't, okay? I mean, who knows what could happen in two months? And besides, I'd rather wait awhile before... taking a chance on somebody new. You know what I mean?"

I tried not to sigh. While Alexis had every right to her disbelief—and probably more than enough justification—I just wasn't in the mood for the negativity of her doubt, especially when I was more than capable of conjuring enough of my own.

Of course, at the same time I couldn't help feeling a bit sorry for the woman either.

Although I had only served a year in the military, I knew how the constant goodbye of the TDY lifestyle made some couples more lonely than others, which in turn made some more inclined to agree to extramarital sex. That part didn't bother me. To each their own had always been my philosophy. After all, until we found our answer, we were all just trying to figure out what made a relationship work. Which unfortunately seemed to be especially true for couples in one which only partially did.

Along those lines, as unorthodox as it might have been, my no strings attached relationship with Alexis had seemed to be more than enough for her to stay true to her husband.. I'd done my part to see to that. But I'd been upfront from the beginning. She knew I could end our arrangement at any time for any reason. Though even I had to admit, I hadn't seen anything like Bella coming.

"Okay. I will," I agreed. "You take care of yourself."

"You, too. And, hey, Chuck?"

"Umm... yeah?" I tried my best not to stutter. Despite how impersonal our entire relationship had been, Alexis and I had grown familiar enough to stop saying one another's name so long ago that I forgot I hadn't even given her one of my real ones.

"Thanks... for everything."

"You're welcome. And thanks to you, too."

I hit the disconnect button on the steering wheel, thankful to be done with one of the most awkward phone calls of my life. It wasn't Alexis' fault, of course. Though our agreement was mutual, I had been the one to create then stayed adamant about sticking to certain rules like no kissing. No sex acts or positions that she hadn't already experienced first with her husband. No contact other than on our assigned days for sex with the exception to cancel or reschedule. In short, no going down any path which might lead to any emotional attachment whatsoever.

And for me it had worked. At first, anyway. The problem was I hadn't just denied Alexis. I had ended up denying myself.

Maybe that was why I was so easily hung up on Bella after just one night. Because like it or not, I knew deep down she might represent my last chance of finding those things I did my best to deny I really wanted most. Love, affection... companionship.

It was Bella's desire to be a Sex Slave that was throwing me for a fucking loop.

And now she wants to get to know me better.

Delaying the inevitable, I inhaled deeply as I pondered how to handle her wanting to know more about me... which inevitably meant my past. I would tell her, of course. Eventually, anyway.

But which one? And how much?

No one knew Joey Dahl was still alive and the last time I had been in touch with anyone who knew me as Joseph Beveaux was almost two decades ago. While that left my last eighteen years as Victor Maxwell, I typically did everything I could to maintain both the lowest personal and public profiles possible. I purposefully didn't have friends by avoiding the cultivation of any relationships beyond professional. And with the exception of my weekly poker night, I kept my casual acquaintances to a minimum.

I was a hermit by design if not desire. And for the most part, I was okay with it.

Yet here I am...

Glancing in my rearview mirror before I resumed making phone calls, I noticed Bella's beautiful blonde mane blowing in the wind around her, whipping about wild and free.

And there she is...

Watching a smile spread across her face, I found myself wondering what she was thinking.

Hmmmm. I wonder what she's doing?

I pushed the button on my steering wheel. "Call Abby."

Within the first two rings, the video call chime suddenly interrupted which triggered my automatic eye roll. Abby knew I kept my phone clipped to my car's air vent. She also knew I hated taking a video call while driving. Annoyed, I stabbed the green Accept button. Abby's answer was almost as immediate as her question.

"So... how was it... slut?"

As usual, the woman wasted no time getting straight to the point. Despite the unusual staccato of her words, I consciously avoided looking at her on my screen while keeping my eyes on the road. It sounded like she was winded while exercising.

"Wouldn't you like to know?"

"Daaa... ha... ha... hamn!... That good... was it?"

"Better," I preened.

Stealing a peek at my phone, I saw Abby staring at me from her treadmill. Knowing how the woman interrupted her workout routine for no one, I felt a bit honored that she had even taken my call. Pressing a button on her machine, she began to decelerate her run.

"I can tell... You look like ass."

I tried to suppress the laughter in my scoff. "Biiitch."

"I'm serious... How much sleep... *didn't...* you get?"

"Not much. But I slept like a baby..."

"And woke up like a woman... with a lap dog between her legs?"

I froze. *How the—*

"Ha! Thought so..."

"How did—"

"—I got Greg to talk Victor into doing a couple... shots of tequila with us one night," Abby continued, answering the question she knew she'd prompt. Out of the corner of my eye, I saw her pause to get off the treadmill before grabbing her phone.

"Why?" I asked.

"Because Victor was always too much of a gentleman to ever say anything sexual around me—I've never once caught the guy checking out my tits, by the way. Can you believe that? *My* tits!"

I did my best not to snicker. Abby could be full of herself sometimes, but if what she said was true then Victor's restraint was more than admirable. Hell, even I couldn't help but to look on occasion.

"Anyway, I left them alone at the bar for a while, but the only thing Greg could get Victor to admit to was a penchant for oral."

"'A penchant?'"

"Greg's words, not mine... Actually, he thought Victor sounded a little obsessive about it."

For some reason, my brain immediately flashed back to when Victor told me his parents were French and how Freud's theory of a child's psychosexual development was delineated by different stages. During each phase, libidinal energy—the fuel of our sexual desires—would concentrate for varying amounts of time on a specific erogenous zone. If a trauma occurred during any one of these periods, the child could develop a sexual fixation with that particular part of their body.

And although I hated to resort to stereotypes, I knew the French were more than fond of kissing. It was easy to believe Victor's mother was the type to kiss him mouth to mouth. There was also a very high probability she was the last female to do so for a very long time. From a purely psychological standpoint, his oral fixation would make perfect sense if his libidinal energy was interrupted during its development by his mother's death.

"I am sure he has his reasons," was all I offered before realizing on second thought that not even Freud's theory could account for the level of Victor's affinity for cunnilingus. The man had given me at least five orgasms using his tongue alone. And that was before we fell asleep.

"I was a little worried he might be trying to compensate for something," Abby continued, "but I can tell by that shit eating grin of yours he obviously wasn't... Soooo?"

Grinning because she didn't know the half of it, I was also confused and a bit bummed. As my best friend and former patient, I knew almost everything about Abby's sex life before Greg. A big part of me was finally looking forward to a conversation where we could switch roles and I could do some of the revealing. But her know-it-all-already attitude was taking some of the fun out of my surprise.

"Soooo what?" I asked, trying not to pout. *Which reminds me...* "And hey, by the way, I'm still mad at you. Why wouldn't you go to the bathroom with me all day yesterday?"

"Why? So you could try to pry me for information on Victor?"

"Yes! Exactly! What else did you think I was trying to do?"

"That."

"So why didn't you want to tell me anything?"

"Trust me, you were doing more than fine on your own. I saw the two of you together. You didn't need me to jinx it by telling you everything I know."

"What do you mean jinx? And hell, you obviously know even more than I thought you did."

"Oh, I know that..." she said with a small smile. "But I'm still waiting."

I didn't like the way Abby was acting. I knew she wanted to know more... but something wasn't right. Her voice had become steadily calmer even though it was Sunday. Sunday, Monday, Wednesday and Friday weren't her quiet, submissive Sex Slave role playing days. Those were Greg's. So for her to act like this... she wasn't just fishing for details. She wanted something else.

"What exactly are you waiting for?"

"For starters, a thank you would be nice."

"A thank you for wha—" *Oh my God!* I couldn't believe it hadn't dawned on me sooner. *"Victor's* why you wanted me to come to Jacksonville?"

"You know, for such an uber successful yet sexually repressed psychotherapist, you aren't very smart sometimes." Abby's tone softened just a bit as she leaned closer to her camera. "Bella, Victor's the *only* reason I suggested you play poker with us in the first place. God knows bar poker's not your kind of scene."

I was momentarily stunned as my mind tried to put the pieces in chronological order.

Greg and Abby had known Victor for about six months. Soon after they met, Abby had begun inviting me to play poker. After a month of badgering, she finally stopped. But a few months later I remembered thinking that joining them might be a decent way to ease myself back into society at large.

But Abby had probably realized I wouldn't want to drive so far just to play at the same bar Victor did, so she invited me instead to play at one in downtown Belmont, closer to my house. And as my best friend she had known full well my competitive nature meant that ultimately I'd want to also compete in the regional championship... where I might meet Victor. Meaning she had surreptitiously set me up just as I had once done for her.

My heart melted as I looked over at my phone. "Oh my God, *thank you,* Abby."

Abby's facial expression turned uncharacteristically poignant. "You introduced me to Greg and lost your job because of it. Although it worked out better for you in the end, for a while there you gave up your livelihood to give me the love of my life... No, Bella. Thank *you.*"

I don't know if it was the lack of sleep or because it was one of the kindest things anyone had ever done for me... all I knew was that I suddenly wanted to cry.

"Don't cry on me, you fucking wimp."

I couldn't contain my giggle. *Aaaaaand she's back.* Despite her heart of gold, Abby never had been one for sappy moments. Bitch was usually tough as nails.

"I won't," I sniffled.

She rolled her eyes before grinning. "How'd your tattoo work? What'd Victor think?"

"Hmmmmmmm." Thankful for the change in subject, I couldn't stop myself from smiling. "You were right."

"Did he realize the truth about it?"

"Oh—"

Caught by surprise, I thought back to the moment Victor's face was a mere inch from my stomach, just after he had first gone down on me. Thankfully, he hadn't lingered long. In fact, he hadn't looked at my tattoo much the entire evening. Which, despite how horrendous it looked, now that I gave it more thought, seemed odd...

"I don't know," I said, shaking off the feeling. "It's so faint it only stands out because I'm so pale... We never specifically talked about it at all actually."

"Interesting. You'd think that'd be the first thing most men— Wait a minute. You never *talked* about it? Meaning you didn't *explain* it? Which means Victor still thinks... "

I forgot how adept Abby could be at matching actions to motives. Of course, she'd been through enough therapy sessions to learn how all the dots typically connected.

"At the moment..." I said.

Refusing to look, I could feel Abby peering at me nonetheless.

"Bella, you know as well as I do, the longer you let him think..." Her words trailed off as she read right through me. "*Daaaaaaamn!* 'That good' indeed!"

All I could do was grin. *Hell yes!* Even though it was only one blissfully perfect night, I had no doubt Victor was the type of man I'd love to be my Master... if I could get him to accept it. While it was the kind of opportunity I figured most men would jump at, that Victor *wasn't* jumping at it, that he wasn't like *most* men, was what gave me the best kind of butterflies.

"Holy crap, I know he's hot and your type and all, but—"

"—But yeah," I agreed. "I know. Believe me, I wasn't expecting it either. Remember, all I wanted was to get laid. I certainly wasn't expecting to make a connection with anybody. You of all people know that."

I remembered how great it felt to finally contrive Abby and Greg's accidental meeting. After months of in-depth therapy, I knew they were so perfect for each other that it had come as no surprise when they realized it, too. They were so well-paired that nowadays they were hardly ever apart, that rare couple that had no problem being around one another twenty-four, seven. Of course, I wasn't hoping much less expecting the same for Victor and myself... not yet anyway.

"Okay, so back up a minute," Abby said. "You two obviously hung out together the entire time before Greg and I left last night. How'd that go?"

"Oh, that was ah-*mazing,* too. You know the seven-minute lull? Never had it. And every time we switched subjects all we did was find out we had even more in common. It got to be a little ridiculous actually... Speaking of which, I can't believe we drive the same car!"

Abby scrunched her nose in confusion.

"What are you talking about? Victor drives one of those sport utility pickup trucks. Granted, it's a really nice one. Greg told me he thought the thing cost about eighty grand, but it's nothing like your Mercedes."

"Well, trust me, I'm following him right now. His car is exactly like mine except it's black."

"Wow, I knew the guy was money," Abby teased, "but who knew he was Bella-money?"

I rolled my eyes.

Together, Abby and Greg owned eight small but upscale fitness centers catering exclusively to Charlotte's young and affluent banking community. Greg had owned a gym on the rougher, west side of the city when they met, but with Abby's guidance they had rebranded and expanded. With locations in uptown, the neighborhoods of Ballantyne and Myers Park, the towns of Waxhaw, Huntersville, Cornelius, Mooresville and their latest near me in Belmont, they had all of the wealthiest sections and suburbs of Charlotte covered. The Costellos were rolling in it. Abby just enjoyed ribbing me that at twenty-nine I could afford to work almost entirely from home as infrequently as I did.

"Listen, Bella, I'm really happy for you. I'm pleasantly surprised, but... I just hope everything works out. That's all I'm saying."

There it was again. Abby's surprise... along with something else. Apprehension maybe. Whatever it was, something about her hesitancy didn't make sense.

"Why exactly are you surprised?"

"Well... I guess... mainly because I've only ever been around Victor on Thursday nights. I only really know him through Greg."

Ahhhh... Part of what she said made sense.

Since Abby and Greg were switches, they alternated their Master/Sex Slave roles pretty much every other day. But like many switches, their roles weren't strictly limited to the bedroom. Depending on how devoted to the lifestyle participants were, each person's role could permeate anywhere from a few to all aspects of their life. When an unaware, casual observer, found a switch to be unusually quiet one day as opposed to another, they often just chalked it up to them being at best "in a mood" or at worst "a total schizo."

With such limited interaction, Victor wouldn't have felt comfortable opening up to Abby as much as he obviously did with Greg. In turn she had probably observed Victor well enough to set us up, but not enough to expect how well-matched we might be.

Only I knew Abby better than that. She didn't hesitate about anything unless she was truly confused about something. Which she rarely was. I shot her an eye.

"Whaaaat?"

"Ab-beeeee," my psychologist voice admonished.

Abby threw up her hands. "Fine. You're going to find out anyway."

"Find out what?"

"Victor... He's a ghost."

"A what?"

Over the years I had grown accustomed to how Abby could unexpectedly say something completely off the wall. She had done it more times than I could count, more often than not just to try and get a rise out of me. But I could tell from her tone, this wasn't one of them.

"A ghost. Online. There ain't shit out there on him. No social media, no history, damn near nothing since he quit playing poker almost ten years ago."

"Wait. He played poker? You mean professionally?"

"Yeah, he didn't tell you about it?"

"No. He never mentioned it."

"Well, according to the internet not only did he, he won a good six figures per year doing it. But there's very little record of his life either before or since then."

Having used the internet so often to gather background on my patients, I knew it was rare for anyone to leave little to no trace on the web. While introverts like Victor and myself tended to have less truly personal information floating around online, everyone typically had something. But so what if Victor didn't? It still wasn't all that much to get worked up about.

"So he likes to keep his private life private. *You* do the same thing."

"Trust me, if I thought that's all there was to it I wouldn't mention it, but that's not all," Abby continued. "Victor's employers are even more of a ghost than he is."

Now that's interesting. "What do you mean his employers? What does he do for a living?"

"You mean he didn't tell you that either?" Abby huffed loudly. "Excluding Greg, I saw him talk to you more in half a day than he has with anyone in the last six months and his job never came up?"

"No, I asked but all he said was 'Yes.'"

"Oh, my God!" Abby squealed. "That's all I've ever heard him say to anyone! He really said that to you, too?"

Suddenly I remembered how Victor's 'Yes' had sounded somewhat rehearsed. *No, not rehearsed. Repetitive.* The realization made me feel a little better, but not much. Unhappy that my 24-hour high was suddenly swinging low, I tried to counter by rationalizing. "So? So he doesn't like to talk about his job. Neither do I. It's not a crime."

"No, it's just weird. And since you mentioned it, yeah, kind of the same way you don't either."

"Oh, really? And when's the last time you or Greg elaborated on what you two do for a living?"

Fully self-aware as to what she looked like and given his record, Abby and Greg had hired a mid-level bank executive to moonlight as the 'face' of their fitness centers. Cutting the guy in on half a percent of the profits allowed him to legitimately masquerade as the owner while they ran the business in the background. The guy was an absolute dick, but their strategy was so successful I really couldn't knock it. I also hated being defensive while trying to make a point, especially knowing I wouldn't score one. Still...

"That's different and you know it," Abby shot back. "We have our reasons for—"

"—As does Victor in all likelihood."

"Maybe, but that doesn't explain why Victor's employers—"

Exasperated at getting nowhere but in a worse mood, I snapped.

"—You haven't even told me who his employers are, but you know what?! I don't want to know! Victor can tell me when the time is right just as I'll do the same."

Abby paused, backing off and making me feel even worse. I wasn't one for snapping. Lucky for me that wasn't what concerned her most.

"So you really don't want me to tell you?"

Yes. "No. I'd rather wait for Victor to tell me."

Abby gave me a lip shrug. "Fair enough. But can I show you something in the meantime?"

It took every ounce of strength I had not to roll my eyes which made me feel kind of crummy. No matter what her reason, I knew Abby was only trying to help.

"Sure."

"Okay, give me a second. I'll text it to you," she said just before my screen turned dark. Still connected, I could hear her fidgeting with her phone as she quietly mumbled something about a map.

Grateful for the momentary silence, I exhaled a long breath I hadn't realized I was holding. It was my own fault really. I knew full well that Abby could be a handful sometimes. I also knew like most people prone to addiction, once she got her hooks into something she had a tendency to take it to the extreme. I had no idea what she wanted to show me, but my shaker of salt was ready.

"Okay, I'm sending the photo... now," Abby said just before reappearing on my phone.

I tried not to roll my eyes. I hated distractions like this while driving and she knew it. Luckily Victor and I were approaching a four-way stop just as her text came through. Two quick taps later and I was staring at a...

That's weird.

On my screen was a satellite image that looked to be roughly a full square mile wide. Based on the number of trees, the land was rural, somewhere in the countryside. While a large, outdoor pool completely surrounded by a house the size of a mansion took up the left side of the picture, the right was occupied by five evenly spaced houses scattered among the trees. In the center was a barn and several large buildings situated between a large pond and several acres of farmland.

But what stood out most was the ring around it all.

A light green thicket surrounded the entire area, creating a barrier around the majority of the property. The line of unbroken foliage stood in stark contrast to the dark green trees as it cut a path through the woods that must have been over half a mile long on each of its four meandering sides. The view from up above gave the entire place the appearance of a compound. Whether designed to keep people in or out, either answer begged a follow-up question. Or two.

"So what am I looking at?" I asked as I turned my focus back to the road. "And why?"

"You said you didn't want me to say," Abby's disembodied voice replied.

It took me a second. *"That's* Victor's employer?"

"His employer, his home, homes... I don't know, but the whole place is listed under one address. Maybe he'll tell you more than I've been able to discover." Reaching over I quickly tapped my phone to bring Abby's face back up so she could see me. "It's weird looking, huh? That ring of trees?"

I cocked my head and brow slightly. "I'm sure there's a perfectly good explanation for it."

"Not a natural one. Trees don't grow in a pattern like that. Someone bulldozed a path through those woods and planted them that way. Probably for a reason."

"Abby," I said, shaking my head.

"Okay, okay. I get it. I'll stop. I just..."

I waited until I no longer could. "You just what?"

Abby sighed. "Now that you've had a chance to form your own opinion, as your best friend, I just feel it's my job to warn you."

Warn me? "Warn me, what?"

"Victor. There's something... *different* about him."

"Yeah. I know," I said curtly. *It's one of the reasons I like him.*

"Yeah, well, it's obvious you don't know everything, no matter how big that brain of yours is. And before you get offended, that wasn't a dig. I meant Victor is different in the same way you are."

I rolled my eyes. "And what way is that?"

"I don't know. For lack of a better word, he's... esoteric. Like you."

"Esoteric?" I did my best to sound nice. What I often lacked in street smarts I made up for in academia. On the other hand, what Abby made up for in street smarts she pretty much completely—

"Yes, *esoteric.* Like the funny way you both tend to talk sometimes. Or hell, the different way you both seem to look at things for that matter."

"Things like what?"

"Well, take your tattoo for starters. Or that puzzle room of yours and why you did what you did. I mean, I understand but still—"

Rolling my eyes again, I finally rued the day I let Abby in on my secret. While I couldn't deny her assertion, part of me was peeved she had enough gall to bring it up... *I mean of* all *people—*

"—I'll tell you what," I interrupted, "how about I call you once I get home? Whatever Victor hasn't told me by then I promise to let you fill me in on. Okay?"

Abby pursed her lips reluctantly. "Okay. Just... I don't know, be careful, okay? I mean, I don't think Victor's a serial killer or anything but... just be careful."

"I will... I'll call you when I get home."

Hanging up, I shook my head. I might not have liked Abby's negativity, but I would never doubt her sincerity, loyalty or intent. Her friendship was one of the things in this world I was most thankful for.

Glancing ahead at the back of Victor's car, my mood immediately brightened. *And now I have another one,* I couldn't help but smile... even if it wasn't quite as big as before.

Ending my call with the airport, I glanced in my rearview mirror to check out the front view of Bella's Mercedes. Although the color was different, to see the same car on the road was still a treat, especially models like ours with the Panamericana grille option. I'd forgotten just how aggressive-looking the car appeared to others. And while it definitely wasn't the fastest car I owned, the AMG's 550 horsepower engine was still a beast.

To know that Bella was driving the one behind me—panty-less no less—gave me an even bigger thrill. And as I realized our taste in vehicles was only one in a series of similarities we seemed to share, I couldn't help but grin from the personal satisfaction that came with the comfort of familiarity.

What are the odds?

Half of my garage was full of investment vehicles which excluded their use for trips as long as the one to Jacksonville. Out of the other half which I used for personal and recreational purposes, only three were convertibles capable of taking advantage of the unseasonably warm weather that had been forecasted. Since both my Prowler and CJ7 were the same color but far less comfortable over long distances, the AMG had seemed like the lone man out as well as the perfect choice.

So a one in twenty.

Looking back again to catch a glimpse of Bella, I smiled.

Led me to a one in a million...

Shaking my head, my thoughts segued into acknowledging a lot of luck had gone my way over the second half of my life. I was lucky not to have been aborted, lucky to have been adopted and given a wonderful foundation of both love as well as a love for education. I was also lucky not to have been killed in either the car wreck that claimed my adoptive parents or the one thirteen years later that left me no good to the Marines, myself or anyone else. Hell, I was even lucky to be in the right place at the right time during the early days of the poker boom almost twenty years ago.

But none of that seemed to hold a candle to the stroke of luck I had come across in Bella.

My Sex Slave...

I couldn't deny the idea sounded a bit more palatable than the actual description.

The more I thought about it, the more I believed I could handle the duties of a Master. Putting aside my own narcissistic modesty, there was a part of me that actually felt born for the role. To provide for a woman's needs—especially the sexual ones she couldn't satisfy alone—I had to admit gave me great joy. But to have one so fully devoted to me in return?

Despite my heart and body's desire, the jury in my head was still out on that one.

But looking in my rearview mirror, I smiled at which way the foreman was leaning.

Damn...

Waiting for Victor's phone call after ending mine, I couldn't stop thinking about what Abby had said. And what more she might have if I hadn't stopped her. Not that I completely regretted my decision.

Whatever Victor did for a living was mystery enough. The last thing I needed to add were the perspectives of Abby's suspicions. Coupled to my firm belief that at best most people were only very narrowly defined by their jobs, there was a large part of me which actually enjoyed how even now neither of us really knew the other's exact vocation. True, Victor knew I was a doctor. But the medical field was so vast for all he knew I could be a chiropractor.

Unencumbered by any misconceptions, I felt as if Victor had thus far grown to know me in the proper light. Who I was, what I thought, things that held my interest. Not what I did for a living.

And while I knew the bliss of our ignorance wouldn't last forever, I was grateful Victor had obliged my unorthodox request to extend it until I was ready. Still mentally unprepared for its end, I looked around and tried to find something distract my mind.

Unfortunately, my immediate surroundings were of little help.

Our drive had long become boring. It seemed we were forever on nerve-wracking two-lane roads with few to no passing opportunities. And though the North Carolina countryside was still beautiful, there were only so many dilapidated double-wides one could pass without succumbing to the osmosis of depression. While a truly extravagant but completely out of place all-brick home or two popped up here and there, by and large my predominant view had become a montage of rural poverty.

Sadly, the dreary scenery was better than my mood.

Part of me couldn't shake Abby's warning. While one of the main reasons I was so attracted to Victor was that he was so different, I knew different could also be a forewarning of something not-so-good. And hearing the admonition in Abby's worried-Mom voice didn't make things any better.

Of course, there was a simpler explanation for what I was really feeling.

As much as I wanted to curse Abby for bringing me down, I couldn't. After all, nobody stays elated forever. While I didn't know why I thought I was any different, I surmised it was because for awhile... I was.

I've never had a night like the one just past, I hummed to myself as the impromptu lyrics sprung to mind. *One so high I forgot it wouldn't last...*

Smirking at the thought, I exhaled in a long huff. Two lines and I was already tired of my own pity party. So when Victor's call suddenly came through, I wasted no time in answering.

"I was beginning to wonder if you forgot about me."

"My apologies," Victor replied, the sound of his voice both reminding and making me instantly aware of just how much I missed it. "My phone calls ran a little longer than expected. Plus, I thought you might enjoy a little alone time in order to think."

"Why?" I teased. "Is that what *you* did once you were done with your calls?"

Victor's silent pause went on for so long I almost felt sorry for making light of my observation. I had to remind myself he still had no idea of my exact profession. Not that I had one of his yet either.

"Was I that obvious?" he finally asked.

"Yes, but it's okay," I assured him. "You were right. I did need some time to think. I mean, after all, it is not every day that I offer myself to a new Master."

"Yeah, well, I don't know if I'd go so far as to calling myself a Master, Bella."

"Pfff. Master, Mister. Tomato, potato." I rolled my eyes. *Damn lyrical mood.*

"How do you do that?" Victor asked after a beat.

Hmmmm. "Do what?"

"Take… something so serious so lightheartedly?"

Good question. "Well… I guess it's because I figure if I am wrong then I am wrong. But if I am right then I am right. Worrying over either changes neither."

The Mercedes' speaker system was so good I could actually hear Victor's chortled snort over the wind. "Have you always been so blasé when picking a new Master? That is how it works, right? It's a mutual choice. I mean you're not so hardcore into it you can be traded without your consent?"

Does he really think—

"Yes, that's how it works," I said quickly. "No, I have never been traded without my consent."

"Good."

Suddenly realizing just how far into left field Victor must be perceiving my situation to even suggest such a thing, it took me a second to think of a reply that was both good and appropriate.

"Listen, Victor… when it comes to the Master/Sex Slave lifestyle, just understand that no two relationships are the same. If you decide to accept my offer, then *we* will create whatever rules we decide to abide by… together. But in the one I want, we won't be writing down any rules. There'll be no contracts to sign. Our commitments will be as verbal as they are binding and they'll be filed away in our heads and hearts. But if you'd like me to be more specific," I took a deep breath, "here goes.

"My rules are simple. No pain. No humiliation, either public or private. You won't be deciding *what* or *when* I eat. In fact, our rules will only pertain to the bedroom or anywhere *we* decide to have sex. And while anything goes once we start, if you go too far, I'm gone. The tricky part is it's on you to figure out just how far I can be pushed. If you get it wrong, then you aren't the man for me and I'm not the woman for you. And so what I'm offering, what it *basically* boils down to, is this. If you take care *with* me, I'll take care *of* you."

Victor was quiet for a second. "Anything else?"

"Well… in case it's not the given I think it is, as long as we're together, we're monogamous."

Victor went quiet for a little longer. And while there was more I could say, I waited and let the onus lie with him.

"I'm not opposed to anything you just said."

I could hear it in his voice. Although Victor meant what he said about my answer, he still had questions.

"Good. In the meantime, just know this. The only Master you need to worry about is yourself. And to your earlier point about being blasé, no, I have not been... But before we go any further I think you need to know something else... While nothing I have told you has been a lie, it sounds like you've misinterpreted some things I've said. But it's not your fault. Trust me, though. I have my reasons for revealing things about myself as slowly as I do... As, I am sure, so do you."

My final words surprised me. I didn't mean to put the shoe on the other foot. It wasn't exactly fair... but I did feel it might help his perspective. After all, I wasn't the only one who was holding back.

Victor was silent for a few seconds before I thought I heard him smile.

"Do you know what you look like right now with your hair blowing in the wind?"

The sudden realization that he was watching me in his rear view mirror made me grin before I had the chance to catch myself.

"No," I said as I regained my composure. "What?"

"Like a beautiful banshee chasing me down, trying to claim my soul."

Butterflies fluttered in my stomach as this time there was no stopping my smile. *Did he just call me—*

"How poetic," I deflected, trying not to blush. "Thank you."

"You're welcome."

Wanting to not ruin the moment by pointing out that a banshee was a harbinger of impending death, I cleared my throat. "So, we still have more than three hours to go. What shall we talk about?"

"Honestly... I want to know more about you."

"Well, that's good because I definitely want to know more about you, too. Why don't you start and I'll finish."

"Hmmmmm. Normally I'd insist ladies first. But I guess satisfying your wants first qualifies, too." Victor let his innuendo hang for a second. "What would you like to know?"

Hmmmmm, what wouldn't I? I thought as Abby's picture flashed inside my head. *No, not yet.*

"How about anything and everything," I said instead. "Along with anything and everything in between everything and anything."

"Oh. Is that all?"

I could hear Victor chuckling almost as loudly as I could his playful eye roll.

"You know what I mean."

"I do. But honestly, Bella, I'm afraid I wouldn't know where to start."

Having made the same request and received virtually the same reply from so many of my patients, the muscle memory of my response kicked in before I could stop my mouth.

"Well then, don't start with where, start with when," I said, cringing inwardly that I was using the same words and cadence that I did with my patients. Of course, Victor wouldn't know that, but I still found myself crossing my mental fingers for him not to notice.

"What do you mean when?"

His tone was far more nonchalant than inquisitive. *Thank, God.*

"I mean, start by telling me your very first memory and then the one after that and the one after that. Then, when you get to too many memories to talk about them all, start skipping around to whatever you feel is important. I mean, other than how you lost your parents in a car wreck, grew up in foster care, graduated early and enlisted in the Marines at seventeen, I honestly don't feel I know much else about your life. And just to be clear, I'm not trying to pry. So tell me only what you want to tell me, leave out what you don't want me to know."

Victor's pause held for a little longer than I expected.

"Yeah, I guess I could do that," he finally said.

"Good. So your earliest memory. Go."

"Well, I can think of two that occurred right around the same time, close to my fourth birthday... Are you sure you want to hear this?"

"I am. And I'll make you a deal. You tell me those first two memories and I'll tell you why both are probably negative, okay?"

Wow. How in the—

"Wow. Yeah. They both were," I heard myself stammer. "I'm not sure how you knew that, but your offer definitely sounds worth it to find out." Stunned, it took me a second to gather my thoughts.

"The earliest was the worse of the two. I remember it was fall. My parents and I were living in an apartment complex and I had gone outside one morning. Our apartment was on the ground floor so I was allowed to go play for short periods of time without supervision.

"But when I got to my usual spot there were two other boys who lived in the building across from mine already playing. They were brothers, the oldest just a bit younger than me. And they were black... I think they were playing with Matchbox cars while I was digging in the dirt. Or vice versa. I don't really remember. All I know is we were all just kind of doing our own thing...

"After a minute or two this other kid—blonde haired and white like me—who lived in another building, he walked up to us. He had one of those geodesic climbing domes behind his apartment that we played on whenever I was allowed over to visit him.

"He might have invited me at that point, I'm not really sure. All I remember was standing up next to him and announcing to the two brothers that we were going to play at the blonde kid's house and they, the brothers, couldn't come with us."

Thirty years later and I still remembered it like it was yesterday. Bella was right. It was definitely a negative memory.

"To this day," I finally continued, "I don't know why I did that. I mean I was never a mean child and I can't remember the brothers ever doing anything wrong to me. And it wasn't something I learned from my adoptive parents. I might not have known them long but I certainly don't remember them being racist. All I knew at that moment was that myself and the blonde kid were alike and the brothers were different from us.

"But I also knew instantly that what I had done was wrong. In fact, I remember the very next thing I did was look over toward my apartment to make sure no one had heard me. And I can still remember how my dad was standing in front of the living room window in his blue, terry cloth robe with a mug of coffee in his hand... and the pissed off look on his face.

"Probably took him all of ten seconds to run outside, yank me up by one of my arms and haul me back inside. As mad as he was he probably spanked the hell out of me, but I can't remember... But I do remember just how wrong I wronged those boys."

Suddenly I released an exhale I didn't realize I had been holding. My shame didn't go with it.

"And you were four at the time?"

Bella's question startled me. "Ummm... yeah."

"It's amazing when you think of it, isn't it? Thousands of years and the human race hasn't evolved that much. But in thirty years... one human definitely can."

Bella couldn't see my smile. But I had the feeling she could feel it.

"So you're right. My very first memory was a negative one," Victor finally continued. "My second was too, although thankfully *my* ego was the only one hurt that time... It happened later that winter. My parents had a set of Encyclopedia Brittanicas stacked together on the bottom shelf of a bookcase in the living room behind our couch.

"One day I must have felt like I had some privacy because I remember I had the V volume open on the floor in front of me. Somehow I had managed to both know and memorize that under the pages of the Victorian Age there was a drawing of a rather... Rubenesque young woman."

"Rubenesque?"

"So they used to say," Victor teased. "And as you might suspect, she came complete with the most exposed not to mention ample cleavage I had ever seen."

"Did she now?" I teased back, wondering why Victor classified his recollection as negative.

"She did. And I remember I used to love looking at her. Well, two parts of her, anyway."

I laughed. The thought of a four year old Victor ogling a semi-nude woman was adorable.

"Of course," he continued, "I also remember my mother peering over the top of the couch that day to see what I was doing."

Oh, my God! "No, she didn't!"

"I tell you I'm probably the first four year old in the history of the world to ever be sexually mortified by his mother."

"Oh my God, that is too cute!" I laughed.

"No, it's not," Victor groaned as he tried to keep his chuckle from joining me further. "Trust me, it's really not."

"Yes, it is!"

Losing it, he bellowed with me, "You're not making it better!"

Laughing together for a few seconds more, I finally relented. "Well, if it helps, I'd say you've recovered nicely."

"Gee, thanks."

"And for the record, that was your id that was hurt, not your ego."

"Ah, well, what's a little Freudian slip of the tongue between friends?"

Laughing to myself, I admired how quick-witted Victor could be as I preened at being thought of already as his friend.

"So tell me," he continued, "how did you know both my first memories would be negative?"

Hmmmmm... "Well, I could answer that, but then we'd be talking about me. And as far as I'm concerned, we're not through talking about you yet."

Somehow, I actually heard the face Victor made. "Sounds to me like you're breaking our deal."

"And it sounds to me," I countered, "like you should read the fine print a little more carefully next time. Our deal never specified *when* I'd tell you how I know what I knew. Or how I knew what I know. Or... Oh, you get my drift."

"Mmmmmm," Victor hummed, "I do. But I'd definitely prefer getting something else of yours right now."

The unexpected interjection of sexual innuendo suddenly heightened my awareness of my skin as my entire body flushed. Shifting in my seat to scratch my itch against the constricted fabric of my panties, I was shocked to realize I had become comfortable enough to forget I had none on. Realizing just how easily I could touch myself, my pussy responded by growing damp.

"Is that so?" I asked as I lifted my skirt. Steering the car with my left hand, I started to steer my body using my right.

"Very much so," Victor said.

It might have been my imagination, but I thought his voice sounded a bit deeper. Huskier. Lustier... Regardless, by the time my fingers finished their third trip around my clit, I felt my eyes wanting to close as I gave in to the pleasure. Pulling my hand away in frustration, I placed it back on the wheel. The last thing I wanted to do was run off the road and die like an idiot. Especially now.

"Well then," I sighed, "I guess two months can't come soon enough." *Though neither can I.*

"No, it can't," Victor agreed.

His words as quiet as they were emphatic, I reveled for a few seconds in the sincerity of their unspoken desire.

"So," I said, resolving to resume our previous conversation, "you are a naturally bigoted, promiscuously curious four year old with a predilection for thick girls—"

"—Heyyyyy!—"

"—who, thankfully enough for me, has resolved only one of those issues—"

"—You are not that thick, Bella... but you are most welcome."

"Yes, well, I'd rather cum well than be welcomed, but I'm sure we'll get to that eventually. For now, why don't you tell me how you got from there to here. Tell me, who is Victor Maxwell?"

Bella couldn't see my smile, but it thrilled me to know that she was already anticipating our being together again two months from now.

Pressing my seat's massage button, I relaxed and began to consider how best to fill her in on as much of my life as I could without provoking too many questions. In the back of my mind I already knew what parts were and weren't safe to talk about. For the moment, those aspects were the givens I couldn't yet give.

The funny thing was, despite how unique my life had been, I really didn't see it all that differently from anyone else's. Everyone had stories to tell, experiences and lessons that stuck with us, moments we wished we could remember and regrets we wished even harder to forget.

Most of us had been places where we stuck out and others where we had fit perfectly in. And while my height had garnered me far more of the former, it had been a long time since I felt a need to seek more of the latter. At this point

I was content walking through life a loner and—because I had less time left than most—the last thing I needed was anyone slowing me down.

But those were issues I could address with Bella later. For now...

"As I told you," I finally started, "after my parents died, I was placed in foster care. I remember I was allowed to take just one toy with me from my house. I chose a model car my father and I had built shortly before the accident. It was a '63 Corvette, his favorite."

"That's nice that you remember that."

I tried not to sound too dejected. "Hard to forget. The model was rated for kids 12 and up and I remember feeling so proud my dad thought I was mature enough to build something made for kids twice my age.

"But what I really remember was the lesson he taught me that day which was to always follow the instructions. He said instructions were the best shortcut ever made for how to do something. And he said there were instructions to everything in life, no matter how big or small... His point was if we took time to find the instructions first, then things would be much easier when we attempted to do them."

"Simple. But wise words," Bella said. "Of course, the two usually do go together."

I nodded even though she couldn't see me. "You know, if life had gone on normally for me, I probably wouldn't have remembered that lesson. It would have been like a lot of the others my parents had been teaching me. But maybe a week later, at their funeral, the only person I knew was my teacher. He was a big, black man, reminds me of Greg actually. But he was much more soft spoken. As gentle as he was giant.

"I remember he pulled me aside to talk in private. He said he knew my parents well and how much they loved me and cared about my education. He told me if I did my best to remember as much as I could that they had taught me, I'd be okay. Then he handed me a book called *All I Really Need to Know I Learned in Kindergarten* and said something I've never forgotten. He said, 'This book is the shortcut to almost everything in life.'"

"What a beautiful coincidence. So, what did you do?"

"I read it. As best I could anyway. I mean it was written for adults but as a first grader I remember thinking anyone who had graduated kindergarten should have been able to read it. So I did, over and over and over again. And I did my best to learn it and my father's lessons well.

"To this day, before I attempt anything new in life, I make sure to find a set of instructions whether written down or on YouTube or something else. Because my father was right, there's always a set someone has created somewhere and spending a little time to find them first can save a ton of time later... And if there's one thing that's precious to me in this world, it's time."

Bella stayed quiet for several seconds before softly asking, "And why is that?"

I paused, unsure if I wanted to give her my full reason, but then thought *Why not?* After all, what did I have to lose?

"How tall do you think I am?" I asked her.

"Ummmm, gosh. I don't know. Six-six, six-seven?"

"I'm six foot eight. Now tell me, how many six-eight sixty year olds do you know?"

"Not many," Bella replied, even more gently than before.

I knew exactly what Victor was trying to say.

It was suspected but not yet proven that the same factors which led to higher than average growth were also behind those leading to premature death. If tumors developed on the brain's pituitary gland before it began to produce hormones initiating puberty, that process could run amok. The excess growth hormone not only led to gigantism, the extra doses also gave the heart a real beating which was why heart failure was the leading cause of death among the world's tallest individuals.

"Not many is right," Victor said. "But luckily for me, I learned this at an early age."

Interesting... "Why did learning that early in life seem lucky to you?"

"Well, for starters, it's a great motivator to always make the most of my time. It's led me to do everything I can to maximize the parts of my health I can control... But it also led me to a pretty fascinating discovery which has led me to have an even better life."

"And what's that?"

Victor was quiet for several seconds. While I was pretty sure he was thinking before speaking again, I was certain he had no idea what a turn-on it was.

"Do you know how people say the older you get the faster time seems to pass by, too?"

I nodded, forgetting he probably didn't see me. "I do."

"Well, I saw an experiment one time that not only showed why, it showed me how to... negate that process."

"Really?"

"Yes and it was actually pretty simple. I watched a computer screen as six black dots swept completely across, from right to left, one at a time. Each paused in the exact center, all for the exact same interval, before moving off to the left. But between dots 5 and 6 a white triangle was inserted. It, too, stayed on the screen for the exact same length of time, but it *seemed* like it remained just a bit longer, like a fraction of a second. The reason was my brain was suddenly processing new information which, in turn, gave the appearance of time slowing down.

"What I realized was that if I wanted to give myself even more time to live—even if it only *seemed* like I had—one of the best ways to do it was to always fill my brain with new information."

"Negating the process of feeling like time was passing faster and faster. Smart."

"Thank you."

"And has it?"

I heard Victor's smile in his words. "Why don't you tell me."

Ummmm... "What do you mean?"

"Well, at the risk of sounding sappy... we've known each other less than a day now. Does it seem like less or more time has passed?"

Oh. My—

Victor was right. Not only was the last twenty-plus hours one of the fullest days of my life, without a doubt one of the hallmarks of our time together had been the sharing of all new experiences and the exchange of personal information with one another. I couldn't believe we'd still only known one another less than a day when it felt more like we'd known one another seemingly forever.

To think that Victor had spent much of his life purposefully trying to replicate this feeling...

Wow.

And what was even more special was that he had implied it about... us.

Just. Wow.

Skipping over most of the horrors of my life in foster care—especially that of my second name change—I told Bella about the head trauma I suffered only a year into my stint with the Marines.

"I was in a rollover accident while heading to a training exercise with a couple of the guys in my unit. We were running late and our driver took a curve too fast."

I explained how I was ejected when our Jeep rolled over. Although temporary, the injury to my brain was so severe that less than two months later—despite my best efforts to the contrary—I was awarded an honorable discharge with partial disability.

"The way I was lashing out back then, I was lucky I got either, much less both. Of course, that was over fifteen years ago. I'm better now," I assured her. *For the most part, anyway.*

"I saw two old scars by your ears when we were in the shower. Are those from the accident?"

"Yeah."

"If you don't mind my asking," Bella inquired a little more cautiously, "what part of your brain did your doctors determine was damaged?"

"My amygdalae. They're responsible for our—"

"—Emotional responses and decision-making abilities. They also help form, store and process the memories correlated with the most emotional moments of our lives." *You. Idiot!*

"Ummmm, yeah..." Victor stammered. "That."

I wanted to kick myself. I wasn't prepared to get into this yet, but I knew I needed to explain. *And apologize.* "I'm sorry for interrupting... I... started college intending to become a neurosurgeon."

"Just *intending?* It sounds like you would have made a great one."

"Thanks."

Victor was quiet for several seconds, but when he spoke again, he sounded cautious. "I take it you didn't pursue it to completion?"

"No."

"Hmmm."

Victor's sigh of relief unnerved me enough to continue explaining.

"I tried, but the deeper I got into the curriculum the more I realized that I was a brain studying a brain. Pun fully intended, it was a little too mind-boggling for me to wrap my head around. The more I did, the more I disassociated which felt unnatural in a weird sort of way… It wasn't long before I felt like I was the living embodiment of Nietzsche's quote about staring into the abyss only to find it staring back." I paused to exhale. "Anyway, that's why I know so much about the amygdalae."

Of course, I knew a great deal more such as the amygdala was an incredibly essential part of our brains, affecting everything from our compassion and arousal to our fight-or-flight responses, even our susceptibility to paranoia. Suddenly remembering what Abby had said, I recalled damage to the amygdala had been known to produce not only hypersexuality but hyperorality as well.

So was that the reason why…

Thinking back, I remembered how lucky I felt to encounter a man so passionate about cunnilingus. There was a moment during the first time Victor had gone down on me when I saw an unfamiliar look in his eyes, one as equally enraptured as it was lost. A total abandonment I had never seen before on any of my lovers who had performed the same. Victor was definitely the first with whom I had ever experienced such a thing.

But was I the first for him?… Or has he always been like that during cunnilingus?

Unsure and not wanting to think about it, there was something I nevertheless was and did. I was positive I had glimpsed at least a hint of the same glazed look in Victor's eyes even before that moment in the hotel room. Oddly, it was when we were interrup—

No, not we. *I* had been the one to interrupt the moment by pointing out the shuffleboard table was open. The moment the President had been speaking. *Something about a level playing field. But there was something else... Wasn't there?*

What was it Victor had started to say?

I wasn't sure what to say in response. But I knew I needed to say something.

"Well, while I'm sorry you had to go through all that, I'm actually kind of glad you understand the amygdala better than most people. But just for the record, I really am better now."

"I... believe you," Bella replied.

As she fell silent, I continued to explain how my injury led to bouts of uncontrollable anger made worse by there being no real treatment option better for my brain to heal than time. And how, in hindsight, I realized the Corps did me a favor by forcing me out.

"But when you've just lost the best thing that's ever happened to you it sure as hell doesn't feel that way. So, eighteen and pissed at the world I packed my bags and headed to California."

"California? Really? Don't tell me you wanted to be an actor. You don't seem the type."

"Maybe not but then again there's not a whole lot of acting in porn. Although on second thought, sometimes there's probably too much."

"Porn? Oh wow *this* I have to hear. You went there to become a pornstar?"

"Yeah. Well, I tried anyway."

"You 'tried?' Victor. I just spent an entire night with you. How the hell could *you* fail at *that?"*

"Like anyone else," I laughed at the compliment. "I didn't try hard enough."

"Yeah, well, I'm pretty sure the operative word wasn't *hard."*

"No, my problem was nothing like that. My first day on a set I was taken just to get an idea of what it was like. Not to perform. The shoot took place at one of those mansions up in the hills with a ton of different rooms. The crew spent all day filming several scenes. Trust me, being behind them takes a lot of glamour out of it."

"I bet. But did something go wrong in particular? Or was that enough for you to call it quits?"

"It was a bit of both. It was a shock to see people having sex around others like it was no big deal. Not to mention the way some used drugs so openly. The way no one seemed to care about either rubbed me the wrong way. Then came the last scene of the day."

Bella must have heard it in my voice.

"Ooooh. That bad?"

"The worst. Though it shouldn't have been. It was the simplest. Boy on girl. Only the actress was a complete diva. She was late to set and everyone was already in a bad mood. They'd been dreading and grumbling about working with her all day long. Making snide comments. That sort of thing."

"Did you have any idea who she was before then?"

"Yeah," I admitted. "I'd seen a few of her scenes before if that's what you're asking."

Bella chuckled but said nothing.

"She was never the biggest starlet in the industry," I continued, "but she was decently famous at the time. Probably because she was one of the most beautiful. Your typical six foot tall, California bleached blonde. Unfortunately, she was also a total robot. I mean the woman had no passion, no desire and no acting skills whatsoever to even fake an attempt at any excitement... Still, I was looking forward to seeing her in the flesh, so to speak."

"So to speak."

I laughed. "Anyway, she and her guy get to the end of their scene and move into position for her facial... which she *hates.* I mean you can see it written all over her face—"

"—Literally and figuratively from the sound of it."

"Oh, yeah. And then some because it was a pretty good one even by porn standards. But after several seconds, she just couldn't take it any longer. She jumped up and absolutely screamed for a towel. Of course, the pissed off director screaming 'Cut!' even louder didn't make things better."

"I bet not... So what happened after that? With you?"

"Well, as bad as I felt for her in that moment, I felt even worse as I watched how everyone else seemed to react with glee. It made me sick to see someone do something for money which she obviously hated doing and it made me sick to be around the kind of people who took delight in someone else's misfortune... So I decided porn wasn't for me."

Bella was quiet for a couple seconds. "Did that scene have anything to do with why you didn't cum on my face?"

I considered it for a second. "Probably... You're different, of course. Your desire, your permission, they're all there."

"But like you said, you only want to ever mark one woman like that. Your woman."

I paused a beat before responding, "Correct."

Bella was quiet for several seconds. "Okay, so porn was a no go. Then what did you do?"

I smiled. I could only imagine what she was thinking, but I loved that she had the wherewithal not to press the issue during a phone conversation.

"At first," I continued, "I took a job as a private investigator's assistant. It only lasted a few months but I learned a lot. After that I took on work how and wherever I could find it. Carpenter, courier, bartender, personal trainer, masseuse. You know, jobs that paid the bills."

"'Yes. You name it, chances are I've done it.' Or something to that effect I believe you said."

I smiled. "That I did. But in my downtime from... *doing it—"*

"—Mmmmm, nice one."

"Thank you—I discovered something else. It was legal to play poker at eighteen in California casinos. And I was good at it. Real good, actually."

I continued to explain how as I made more and more money I eventually started playing poker full-time. And my timing was almost perfect. The entire industry had just started to boom after an amateur poker player parlayed an $86 online poker tournament into a $2.5 million win. Suddenly every home game cowboy in the country was itching to try their hand in a casino against the professionals, convinced they could do just as well.

Of course, most of those weekend warriors were no match for even the average full-time professional poker player. But with such a large influx of wannabes, the different games and their varied formats also grew in size. Suddenly there were more than enough tournaments for the professionals to play primarily within their particular area of expertise.

"And what was yours?" Bella asked.

"Mmmmmmmmm... Can't you guess? I played my best poker in the *deep* stack events."

"Wow. I can't believe I didn't see that one *coming.*"

The sound of Bella's chuckle told me I needn't explain that deep stack poker tournaments gave players more chips and time to play than an average game. I excelled in them because they allowed me to leverage my patience. Most amateurs just didn't have the stamina to play in a 12- to 14-hour day, multi-day tournament. And those that chose to try were often easy pickings for guys like me who played in them all the time.

"I assume you aren't still playing," Bella said.

"Professionally? No. I only joined the bar league just to relive some of the fun for a while." *That and to get out of the house,* I didn't say.

"So how long did you play until your next job?"

"About a decade, I guess. It was a great way to spend my 20s, living in my RV, traveling the country, playing different circuit events. I settled in Las Vegas for a year or so near the end. By then like most professionals I was also playing online."

I paused. Maybe I had a change of heart. Maybe it was because I had reached the point in my own story where it just made sense. Or maybe because it was Bella. Either way, I just kept talking.

"But when the law stepped in and shut down the three biggest online poker sites, I packed up, moved back to Charlotte and started a private, non-profit charity organization called the To Fish Foundation. I'm the executive director. It's what I do now."

And just like that, he told me.

No fuss, no muss and about as anticlimactic as anything I had ever experienced.

What the hell?

Victor's revelation had me at a complete loss. The executive director of a charity organization? What was surreptitious enough about that to compel him to avoid talking about it for so long? The only justification for his silence I could imagine might be a reciprocation of my own reluctance.

But absent that... what was the big deal?

"So... what exactly does the To Fish Foundation do?" I asked as nonchalantly as I could.

"More like what don't we do," Victor said, the evident pride in his voice mixed with what sounded like a bit of relief. "The name comes from 'Give a man a fish and you feed him for a day—"

"—Teach a man *to fish* and you feed him for a lifetime.' That's clever."

"Thank you. I thought so."

"Really? *You* wrote that?"

Before ceding me a "Touché," Victor laughed so loud I thought he might break my speakers.

"I'm teasing, of course," I relented, "but it is a catchy name. What made you choose it?"

"It's kind of what we do. The foundation more or less has three parts. The largest part is a charity geared toward wounded veterans. We provide free housing and job training for those who can no longer do for themselves so that they can get back to it. The second part is an animal rescue and veterinarian center. And the third is an orphanage specifically for children who have lost their parents."

"It sounds perfect for you."

"I've certainly been blessed to have found my calling. And to make matters even better, I more or less get to work from home."

Sensing an opening, I moved in. "So do I for the most part... but my house isn't big enough to hold all that."

Victor laughed. "Neither is mine... What I mean is the majority of the foundation is on my property. The orphanage and rescue center and a few families, anyway."

"Sounds like quite a property to contain all that."

"It is. Maybe when I return, you'll let me show you around."

Abso— "Sure... It's a date."

"Mmmmmmm, good."

Smiling through our shared silence, I lifted my chin to enjoy a little more of the sun which suddenly felt even warmer for some reason.

"So," Victor continued, "enough about me. Let's talk about you. Or is that fine print still in effect?"

Sensing Victor's sass, I decided to hand it right back. "Hey, nobody forced you to agree to that deal. You entered into it willingly... Just like I let you last night."

"Oh, my, no you didn't."

"Oh yes we did. Or have you forgotten already?"

Victor paused before his voice deepened. "Your taste is still on my lips, Bella. So no, I haven't forgotten. Have you?"

Flustered by his abrupt directness, it took me a second to respond. "Liked it so much you saved some for later, did you?"

"But of course. You wouldn't expect anything less from a libertarian who likes to have his cake and eat it, too, now would you?"

Oh my, God! That's it! "That's what I meant to ask you about!"

At the sound of the word *libertarian,* yesterday's fuzzy memory that had been nagging at me suddenly rushed back into focus. One by one, as the crystal-clear images began to materialize, I remembered...

... After seeing Victor stare at one of the TVs above the main bar for more than a few seconds, I turned to see what was so distracting. While most of the screens were dedicated to one of the day's playoff football games, he was watching the only one that wasn't, a cable news channel replaying a snippet from the White House press conference earlier in the day.

Doing his best to look presidential as he fielded questions from behind a podium, the President was flanked by two men. The younger on his right sported an equally dapper, custom-tailored outfit along with a bit of a smirk while the older gentleman to his left donned both the dour suit and expression of a lifelong bureaucrat.

Whatever the event concerned it had been the first and only real thing to divert Victor's attention from me all night. Which might have been why, when he caught me watching him, he turned a bit red in the face.

"Sorry," he said. "I don't watch much—hell, any—TV really."

I shook my head. "No need to apologize. I just wasn't aware you were interested in politics."

"I'm not," Victor said quickly before looking back up at the screen just as the President finished speaking.

"... going to make sure we have a level playing field," the President said. "For everyone."

Watching Victor smile slyly at the President's last words, I suddenly realized that was the very first time I had seen his secretive, insider-like grin spread across his face.

"Mr. President," I heard a reporter say in the background, "what can your administration tell us concerning reports of a new strain of the influenza virus originating out of Wuhan, China..."

As Victor turned to give me his full attention once again, I was a bit perplexed.

"So, if you're not into politics," I asked, "why were you watching so intently?"

With the look of a man trying to determine whether or not to say anything, Victor paused for a few seconds before speaking.

"Because that 'level playing field' the President was talking about... I'm pretty sure he was referring to cryptocurrency."

Just then the shuffleboard table behind Victor finally became free of players. I had been watching it for more than an hour because if there was any game in Mickey's I had a chance in hell of beating Victor in, it was shuffleboard.

And I was beyond ready to have a taste of at least one victory tonight.

"Come on," I said as I grabbed my clutch and wine glass. "Shuffleboard's open."

Victor shrugged with a shade of pity in his eyes. "If you insist."

Determined to make him pay for his condescension, it was a few minutes into our game before I remembered how I had caught him listening to the President. While in my excitement, I couldn't remember where that conversation was going, something he had said made me curious.

Pausing with a puck in my hand, I turned to stare at Victor for a few seconds, prompting him to finally ask, "What?"

"I was just thinking about how you sounded with regard to the President a few minutes ago... and despite not being interested in politics, I was trying to determine who you would have voted for in the last election... even if you didn't."

"Oh, I'm no anarchist. I always vote," Victor snorted humorously. "But don't bother. You'll never figure it out."

"Is that so?" I said, my tone rising to the challenge with me.

"Trust me, it is. I can even give you a hint and I'd bet you still won't figure it out."

Something in Victor's voice told me he wasn't kidding, but my competitive side was unable to resist. Especially considering his offered advantage. "Ohhhh-kay... you're on."

"Are you sure?"

"Bring it, Too Tall."

Victor laughed then shrugged again. "Well... as long as you're asking for it."

I flexed my eyes at the insinuation.

"Okay," he continued. "I am every bit as fiscally conservative as I am socially liberal."

I cocked my head at his riddle. "Which means on a scale from one to ten both could be zero and your statement would still be true."

Victor grinned but said nothing, each of which were mildly infuriating.

"So, you're a man," I said slowly trying to draw out any tell, "who likes to have his cake and eat it, too." Gleaning nothing, I took a stab anyway. "You voted for the libertarian candidate, didn't you?"

Victor's second humorous snort was a bit more derisive. "No."

Damn. "And why not? You don't have anything against libertarians, do you?"

"Not at all. They seem like fine people. But I mean, you know what they say. Once you've met one libertarian—"

"—you've met *one* libertarian," we finished in unison before laughing together.

"Okay," I said. "I give, you win. And you don't have to tell me who you voted for... unless you want to."

Victor looked sheepish for a split second before replying, "I voted for myself."

What? "No, you didn't."

"I did. Wrote my name in the write-in slot. There was no way I could vote for the other two."

All I could do was stare incredulously which after a couple of seconds made Victor turn even more sheepish.

"It's just..." he hesitated before continuing, "well, I think I'm smarter than the one and more compassionate than the other. Not that it took much of either, you know?"

In my shock, I was a bit taken aback. "Well, that's a little misogynistic, don't you—"

A little too late, I caught myself but not before Victor began cocking his head at me.

"I guess it depends," he said. "Which description do you think describes which candidate?"

Damn...

... Shaking off the memory, I was thrilled to finally remember what had been nagging me so much.

"That's what I meant to ask you about!" I exclaimed.

"What's that? My faux libertarianism or quasi narcissism that spurred me to vote for myself?"

"Neither one," I laughed. "Do you remember when you said the President was referring to cryptocurrency after he said something about 'a level playing field?' What made you say that?"

I could hear the smile in Victor's voice almost before he spoke.

"Do you recall the two men standing behind the President?"

Dapper and dour immediately sprang to mind. "Yes."

"Well, one was the Secretary of the Treasury and the other the Chairman of the Federal Reserve. And although he didn't say so directly, in that particular moment the President was actually sending a message to China."

I could hear it in Victor's voice. The more he spoke, the higher his tone rose. Something about the subject really interested him. I couldn't claim the same, but I recognized the symptom often enough in my addiction patients, people who even at their calmest could still be fervent. And I had learned whenever the pitch of their voice climbed higher, the best thing to do was simply prompt them with an open-ended question or two. After that, there was no telling how long they would talk.

Or better yet what they might reveal.

"And you think his message had to do with cryptocurrency? Why is that?"

Bella's question gave me pause for more than one reason.

First off, I knew just because I found cryptocurrency interesting didn't mean she would as well. In fact at one point last night, when she casually mentioned that her mother was an economics professor, I got the distinct impression Bella failed to share in her interest with regard to anything having to do with finances. Though even if she did, it wouldn't have mattered. With virtually no practice, I had little confidence in my storytelling ability to boot.

Yet my hesitation wasn't because I didn't know the answer.

Though no expert, I had researched, listened to others explain and subsequently forgotten more about cryptocurrencies than most people would ever begin to comprehend. Almost the entire wealth of my blockfolio had been built by completely immersing myself into the space for the last decade, living and breathing all things crypto until they damn near consumed me. Not only was I reluctant to open up the same rabbit hole for anyone else, I knew the financial risks associated with trading or investing in cryptocurrencies paled in comparison to the potential physical risk of accruing that particular type of wealth.

Consequently, I was so paranoid about anyone finding out how I had made my money that I had never made a single attempt to tell anyone the story myself. I was nothing if not diligent when it came to covering my tracks, first and foremost of which meant keeping my mouth shut. And while I didn't want anyone to know about my involvement including anything I knew about cryptocurrencies, that didn't mean I couldn't tell Bella what anyone could discover on the internet on their own.

The problem was I had no idea where to start. Even the most obvious beginning wasn't truly the beginning.

Despite my sudden apprehension though, I actually started to feel excited.

Regardless of the extent to which I was about to say anything, at the very least I was on the verge of voluntarily revealing something only a select few in the world knew about me. But if one thing was certain, if I was going to even begin to entertain the possibility of becoming Bella's Master, there were things she needed to understand about me first.

Realizing my quiet had stretched on a bit too long, I suddenly felt it appropriate to begin my answer with a question. *Might as well get one of the most confusing parts over with first.*

"Have you ever heard of Satoshi Nakamoto?"

It was odd.

Although we had known one another for less than a day, I felt like I could discern just as much from the cadence of moments when Victor fell uncharacteristically quiet as from when he spoke. Even under the din of my overactive imagination, I could clearly hear the stutter step of the man's brain as he tripped over his own thoughts, unexpectedly falling out of sync with the wavelength we shared.

In short, it felt like I knew him.

So much so that when Victor finally ended his silence by clearing his throat, I knew my hunch had been right. Whatever he was about to say was extremely important...

"Have you ever heard of Satoshi Nakamoto?"

... just not enough to stop either his question or tone, both barely shy of reverence, from catching me off guard.

What the— "Ummm... no. No, I don't think I have. Who is he?"

Victor's nonchalance was audible almost before his answer wasn't.

"Hmph. He, she, they. No one knows for sure. The general consensus is he's a he, but it's also possible he's a front for the CIA or NSA. Not that it really matters. All of Satoshi's communications were online only but they stopped altogether about ten years ago and no one's heard from him since."

"Ohhhhhh-kaaaaay," was all I could offer in reply, prompting Victor to laugh apologetically.

"I'm sorry. I know a lot of that must sound... confusing."

I tried my best to agree politely. "You could say that."

Sensing Victor's exasperation, I was thankful when he tried starting over.

"Let me ask you something else. Have you ever heard of bitcoin?"

Ahh! "Yes. Now actually, *that* I have."

"Good. What do you know about it?"

Ah. "Not much I'm afraid, just what I've read or seen in the news from time to time. But it's a cryptocurrency, right?"

"Hmph. Some people say it's *the only* cryptocurrency."

I don't know why, but the idea made me chuckle. "Hmph. It sounds like *some* people are pretentious."

I don't know what I was expecting in reply, but Victor's howl of laughter caught me by surprise. "Yeah, some of us have been," he admitted.

Oh, God— "I'm so sorry, Victor," I said. "I honestly don't know enough about it to have made that comment. I was just joking. I meant no offense."

Victor's laugh turned gracious. "Trust me, Bella, it's okay. Besides, the last thing someone should be offended by is the truth."

My smile and I couldn't have agreed more. *Hmmmm.* "So, I take it that means you know a thing or two about bitcoin?"

Victor hesitated. "I do."

"Well, enlighten me then."

"Are you really interested?"

"Not exactly," I admitted. Like a lot of kids, whenever my parents had talked about their work I tended to tune them out. Two decades later, financial talk still bored me. "But I've always loved listening to people talk about things that truly interest them. So tell me, what does Satoshi Nakamoto have to do with bitcoin?"

"He created it," Victor said reverently before clearing his throat. "You see, back in late 2008—during the height of what was still just the start of the world financial crisis—someone posted a link to a whitepaper on an online mailing list for cryptographers. The whitepaper described how an electronic, cash-style system using a new digital form of currency could be securely created using cryptography."

"And this 'new digital form of currency' was bitcoin?"

"It was."

"And the whitepaper's author was Satoshi Nakamoto?"

"Or his alias or pseudonym. Hell, some people think Satoshi might even be a drop—uh, though I personally doubt that."

The sudden falter in Victor's voice might have caught more of my attention if not for my own confusion. *What's a—* "At the risk of sounding stupid, what's a 'drop?'"

"Ummm..."

"Ummm... Uhh..." *Damnit! Think, you dumb—* "A drop is a real person behind whose identity someone hides whenever they do something online... Usually something for which they don't want to take the blame."

Holding my breath, all I could do was hope Bella would lose interest in the subject as quickly as possible. I felt like an idiot for mentioning it in the first place. *Because if anyone should know bet—*

"—So, a drop is like... an internet patsy?"

"Exactly."

"That's just... wrong."

"Yeah, I know," I agreed, hoping the less I said the more likely Bella would let it go. But after a long, contemplative pause...

"How do you know so much about drops?"

Though we had experienced a few brief lulls in our conversations, most had occurred only to give our impending answers room for thought. This one was different.

Starting with his stutter, Victor continued with the tone of a man who seemed as reluctant to speak as he did regretful to have spoken. With echoes of Abby's admonition still ringing in my head, I started to wonder how much more there was to what she had intended to say... and if it had anything to do with what Victor was now intending to not.

As the balance of silence between us began to tip, I couldn't contain my curiosity.

"How do you know so much about drops?"

Damnit, I moaned despite having a decent backup excuse. All the better because Bella already knew this part was true, I still wished I hadn't let the word slip.

"From my time working as that PI's assistant."

"Hmmmm..."

Comforted by how Bella seemed content to actually let the matter go and because one of us had to break the silence, I felt emboldened to try and explain myself a bit further. Plus, it felt like my turn. "Of course, that was back in the early days of the internet when careers like that were among the first to become obsolete. I mean, why pay someone to find someone else when you can do it yourself for free, you know?"

"True... But you only worked there a couple of months, right?"

"Right. But it was more than enough to learn more than I wanted."

"Oh yeah? About what?"

I tried not to roll my eyes at the memories. "Nuances of different laws. Surveillance techniques. The importance of burn phones. How you could find almost anything you wanted in underground and online black markets." *Especially false identities.*

Grateful Bella couldn't see the smirk on my face, I remembered first realizing the only thing better than having a second identity was having a third. And thankfully enough back then I had had not one but two extras at my disposal, both of which were at least partially legitimate—at least as far as the system was concerned.

Not that Bella needed to know about any of that... not yet, anyway.

"Believe it or not," I continued, "for the right money or reason there are people in this world who are *willing* to be a drop and take the fall for a lot of different things that they didn't do. I don't think either of those conditions apply, but there's an even bigger reason why I don't think Satoshi Nakamoto is a drop."

"Which is?"

Just out of curiosity, I'd given the same question plenty of thought over the last decade. And if there was one thing my time as a PI's assistant had taught me it was that often more important than following the money was following the motivation. So the best answer I ever arrived at was...

"Because I honestly don't think it's the type of Machiavellian ruse the creator of a benevolent form of money would be likely to employ just to cover his tracks."

Equally polite as incredulous, Bella did her best not to laugh at my reply. "'A benevolent form of money?' You make it sound like bitcoin's capable of intent."

Well— "Yeah. I definitely feel its purpose is."

"And what purpose is that?"

"Well, unlike the system we use today, bitcoin was designed to be a way for money to be equitably created and distributed before being used. But more importantly, it allows anyone, anywhere in the world to make private, online monetary transactions... but without involving a bank or any other type of financial institution whatsoever."

"What?"

"It's true. Bitcoin cuts banks completely out of the process."

What?

While I understood most of what Victor said, I had a hard time putting it all together.

"Are you telling me someone using a pseudonym created a form of money that doesn't require using a bank or even something like... a credit card?"

"I am. In fact, bypassing banks is really bitcoin's whole reason for existence."

"But that can't be legal. I mean, something like that could be used to avoid taxes. Or for money laundering or God knows what else."

"People do those things now using cash. You don't think cash should be outlawed, do you?"

"No, but..." *Damn.* Unable to argue with the logic, I didn't know what else to say.

"Trust me, cryptocurrency is no different," Victor continued. "And bitcoin, in particular, is just as legal because, due to the way it's primarily being used, it's not considered money. At the moment, it's been deemed property which is how it's taxed."

While I could hear the truth in Victor's voice, I still had a hard time believing him.

"So, what you're telling me is a private citizen at best or a... a... an anonymous group of what—government hackers—"

"—Actually, if anything they're more than likely just some highly skilled programming coders."

Oh, is— "That doesn't sound like it makes a difference. Not if what you're trying to tell me is they have *legally* been allowed to create their own form of money which anyone can use?"

I tried not to feel annoyed, but the more nonchalant Victor's responses came, the more bewildered I felt.

"Well, like I said, even though it *could,* it's not exactly *being* used as a form of money. Not at the moment, anyway, or if ever for that matter. But yes, as for the rest of it, that's exactly what I'm saying."

"That doesn't make any sense. I mean, what's to stop *anyone* from doing the same thing?"

"Nothing," Victor said, continuing to sound completely unfazed. "In fact the last time I checked there were over five thousand different people or groups on the internet that have."

"What?"

"They're called altcoins. Coins alternative to bitcoin."

"You're serious? There are over five thousand different forms of *legal* money floating around the internet that anyone can use? Anyone, any *coder,* can create?"

"For the most part, yes. But it's not just private individuals and companies that are doing it. China has something called a CBDC—a central bank digital currency—that is already live and in use. It's still in the pilot phase but globally that gives them first mover advantage."

Ahhh... Finally, Victor said something familiar. "Is that what the President's message was referring to when he talked about a level playing field?"

"In a way it was, but the playing field part is more about the kind of system to be used."

"And what kind of system is that?"

I laughed.

The way my mind worked—and didn't—boggled me sometimes. Perhaps it was my reference to a system. More likely it was how the events of last night were still so fresh in my mind. Either way, my brain married the two into an appropriately inappropriate analogy.

"I apologize," I started slowly, "if what I'm about to say comes off as sexist, but I'm reminded of something that feels like it was a rite of passage among boys. I guess it could have been for girls, too, I don't know. But when I was about ten or eleven, one of my classmates brought some coins to school that he found in his father's dresser. They were about the size of a quarter but the color of a dull brass. He probably had three or four of them. All of which were engraved with a naked couple engaged in different sex acts."

"Ha! Are you talking about nudie booth tokens? The kind they used to use in the old porno arcades for peep shows?"

"I am. Of course, none of us knew that at the time."

Bella chuckled. "What made you think of those?"

"Well, those tokens are only good within the one system for which they're designed. But the world is full of different systems and in order for them to interoperate, a protocol has to be agreed upon by its participants. Like the internet. It uses https—HyperText Transfer Protocol Secure—which is strictly for sharing packets of information. It works because all who use it have agreed to the same standards for sending and receiving those packets.

"But when it comes to money—whether its traditional fiat, CBDCs or cryptocurrencies—a new protocol needs to be created and agreed to for the same interoperability to be achieved. It needs to be neutral or *level* and anyone using it needs to have equal access. While other countries have been working on their own protocols for years, sadly enough the US government has failed to develop any competing technology. We literally have nothing on the books so to speak."

I tried to follow Victor's logic.

"So you're saying what? In order to compete we'll have to turn to the private sector?"

"Why not?" he asked. "What do you think the Federal Reserve is?"

At that moment I was more than happy Victor and I weren't face-to-face as mine flushed beet red. Kicking myself for not paying closer attention to my mother's financial ramblings, I knew the Federal Reserve wasn't a branch of government unto itself. But...

"Isn't it a government agency?" I asked.

"No. The Federal Reserve is a private entity, owned to varying degrees by the very same banks which are its members. In essence, it's a hundred plus year old company in which the United States has placed all its trust to maintain the stability of our financial system."

Yikes. "Given how much the US is in debt, I'd say they aren't doing so well."

"Exactly. And when one system doesn't work... it's only logical to eventually try another."

While I could hear in Victor's voice the unmistakable implication he already knew of another, I felt like shaking my head in mental exhaustion. I couldn't remember how we had transitioned from talking about his failed day in porn to a discussion about cryptocurrency and the world's financial system. But even though he felt as passionate about the latter as I did about him, there was still only so much monetary talk I could take.

"Okay, *not* that I am bored with the subject, but I'd like to get back to talking about you."

"Actually," Victor countered, "I'd like to talk about you for awhile, if that's okay. I mean, other than that you're friends with Greg and Abby and that you're from Ohio, I don't really know much about your life before yesterday. So tell me. Who is Bella Rose Quinn?"

I felt my blood drain, even from my brain. Hearing my full name come from Victor's mouth coupled with the familiarity in his tone gave me such an abrupt thrill that despite the warmth of the sun I still got goosebumps. "I'm... I'm not sure what to say... or where to start..."

"Well then… don't start with where, start with when."

"Mmmmmmm, nice one."

Victor laughed. "Thought you might like that."

"I did… Okay, let's see." I thought back to— *Oh, yeah. Hmmmm.* "This might sound strange at first, but bear with me," I started.

"You're not going to top my nudie booth story, are you?" Victor interrupted with a laugh. "Because I'm not sure I can come up with something stranger than that."

I laughed. "No. I think you're safe with that one for awhile."

"Good."

I shook my head before continuing. "Like I said, I grew up in Dublin, just outside of Columbus, Ohio. My father, as I told you, is a Marine recruiter and my mother is an economics professor there at…" I stuttered, still unable to bring myself to say it even after all these years, "… the nearby university."

I could hear the wince in Victor's laugh. "Don't you mean *The*… Nearby University?"

"Exactly," I laughed, glad that he understood the ridiculousness of which I refused to speak. "So one day my dad came home early from work." Having heard my father proudly retell the story so many times over the course of my life, I smiled as I realized this was my first.

"I was sitting on the floor of my bedroom putting a puzzle together and apparently he watched me awhile before saying anything. He said I had the outline already framed, but I also had all of the remaining pieces laid out individually so that not a single piece laid on top of any other. Half of the pieces were face up while the other were still face down."

Inhaling, I couldn't help but reminisce.

"I remember I loved literally letting the pieces fall where they may. Although I moved them just enough to uncover those underneath, I made sure they stayed face up or down, however they landed when I dumped them out of the box. The puzzles were a bit more challenging but far more interesting that way."

"If you say so," Victor playfully interjected.

"Well, they were. And, as it just so happened, my father had recently read that a hallmark of a high level of intelligence in children is the ability to recognize patterns far earlier than most. So he stayed quiet and watched me for a few minutes.

"He said I never got frustrated at finding an incorrect piece nor would I touch one until I was almost certain it was right just by identifying it with my eyes." I paused to take a deep breath. "Because of what he saw, my parents arranged for me to take a Mensa test a few weeks later... It turned out I had an IQ of 162."

I let my words hang there, afraid to say more.

"Wow, Bella, 162 that's... literally off most IQ charts I would imagine... but I'm guessing you already know that."

"I do."

"That's... more than impressive."

"Thanks," I said before holding my breath and waiting for the inevitable.

Over the years, the relatively few men I had trusted to know such an intimate detail about me had all become immediately intimidated thereafter. Even the ones I thought sure could handle it. Unfortunately each ended up changing significantly enough that our relationships were never the same. And although all of those relationships had been strictly platonic, I hadn't thought I still held out any remaining hope of ever finding a man who could come to grips with knowing I was almost always going to be the smartest person in the room... but I guess I still did.

"So what happened next?"

Wait? "What?"

"I said what happened next," Victor repeated. "Your parents discovered you were a child prodigy which, quite frankly, I'm sure they probably suspected for other reasons even before they discovered you could do puzzles upside down. Then what?"

My God...

I could hear it in Victor's voice. *Nothing* had changed. I had just told the man I was a certifiable genius... and he didn't balk. He wasn't intimidated or scared. Nothing changed.

Whether he knew it or not, that it wasn't a big deal to him was a huge deal to me. But...

"Ummm... then nothing," was all I could think to say.

"Nothing? You mean you were a child genius with an IQ of 162 and that's the end of your life story?"

I couldn't help but laugh. "Well, when you put it that way."

"If I'm your Master, don't I get to put it anyway I want it?"

"Mmmmmmm..." I loved how easily Victor intermittently referred to himself as my Master. That he was warming to the idea was a good sign. I just hoped his openness could survive two months. After all, a lot could change. But... "That does *come* with the deal, yes."

"Nice one... Okay so you're a precocious child savant who later be*came* an adult with a predilection for deviant sex—see, two can play at these games—"

"—So I see. *And* get two in one, at that—"

"—but what happened in between?"

Glossing over a childhood spent feeling unrelated to thus isolated from my peers, I explained how after entering the University of Notre Dame as a sophomore, I crammed three years into two by taking full course loads in the intervening summers. Then...

"After earning my Ph.D. from Boston College a couple of years later, I accepted a job offer in Charlotte."

"So..." Victor said with a pause. "What exactly do you do for a living... Doctor?"

I took a deep breath. *No fuss, no muss.*

"I am a cognitive behavioral psychotherapist. And I once specialized... in sex addiction."

"... Cognitive behavioral psychotherapist..." Psychotherapist... A psychotherapist... She's a psychotherapist? She's a fucking *psychotherapist! You gotta be fucking kidding me.*

As the world began to recede in all directions, I felt myself grow inexplicably smaller. Alone in the hollow of its center, Bella's words sounded every bit as distant as they continued to drone on.

"... in sex addiction."

How in the hell had I not picked up on her occupation? *Probably because I didn't want to.*

"... but I've spent the last year transitioning..."

Psychology was the one doctoral field I failed to even consider.

"... to working exclusively with children..."

There's a word for it, right?

"... suffering some type of severe trauma..."

Does it really matter?

"... although to be entirely honest, most of my clients are rich, spoiled brats simply acting out..."

If it didn't matter, no one would have bothered creating a word for it. So, yeah, it matters.

"Victor..."

What the— Oh, yeah. Avoidance. It's called avoidance.

Well, there was no avoiding it any longer. Bella being a psychotherapist explained everything. How she knew what it took to induce a feeling of connection. How to make me feel like she could read my mind because for the most part she probably could. And hell, with an IQ of 162 she probably even knew the easiest ways of all to seduce me. But why? Why would she do it? And why me?

"Victor..."

I ran my splayed fingers across my scalp, mildly shocked by the sensation of tight, bare skin. Half rolling my eyes, I was vaguely aware the involuntary reflex was a nervous habit I hadn't had in years, a throwback to a time when I still had hair.

A psychologist. No, a psychotherapist. Who cares? There's a reason both words start with psycho. Remember? I shook my head. *No, that's not how it went down. That was my fault.* Not that it mattered now. *How the fu—*

"—VICTOR!!!"

I don't know what finally cut through my fog first, Bella's buzzing in my ear or the sight of the eighteen wheeled logging truck barreling down at me in its own lane. Curling my right wrist clockwise just a bit, I calmly veered my Mercedes back across the center lines allowing us to slice past one another. Thankfully, the Doppler effect mitigated the continuing blare of the trucker's horn. I thought the level of his pissed off reaction seemed a tad bit excessive given our near full foot of final separation. Not to mention *I* was the one who would have died.

Shrugging off my brush with mortality, I consciously focused on the beat of my heart for a couple of seconds. *One one thousand. Two one thousand. Three one... Yep.* No chang—

"Oh, my God! Are you okay?!"

The sheer terror in Bella's voice jolted me back to reality. Eerily trembling a bit on the inside despite not shaking on the out, it took me a second to realize I was experiencing Bella's reaction and not my own. Only then did I feel my heart rate sink for what I had just inadvertently put her through.

"Umm... yeah. Sorry. I... I..."

I chickened out. How could I explain why I spaced out? As a psychologist she'd be more than capable of understanding the effects of my injury, but her expertise would only arouse even more of her suspicions, possibly enough to scare her off, the thought of which worried me even more. Besides, I had a handle on it. Didn't I? *It doesn't matter.* Because even if I didn't, there was still only one cure for the problem I had.

And since it never hurts to ask for help...

"Do me a favor..."

Victor's voice was so surprisingly small, I wasn't sure I heard him.

"Okay?"

"I'm going to hang up now," he said, the sound growing stronger, "so I can concentrate on driving. I want you to follow me somewhere. It's only about fifteen minutes away. Keep up, okay?"

"Umm... Okay..."

Killing our connection, Victor's speed suddenly increased. Too confused to think straight, he had a full three second jump on me before my foot obeyed my body's command to not let him get away.

As the engine roared to life, I sank down into my seat and allowed the sudden additional burst of adrenaline to course through me. The part of me that was still in shock from watching Victor almost die quickly gave in to newer bewilderments.

Where did he want to take me? What kind of place was he familiar with way out here in the boonies? And why had he veered over into the other lane for so long? What was he doing or thinking when that happened? Could it have something to do with the damage to his amygdala? Was his trauma more severe than he had let on? He'd exhibited no other problems from the moment we'd met, so I doubted it was that. The problem was I didn't know for sure. Which meant as always it came down to an issue of trust.

Did I trust Victor? And more importantly, did I trust my own judgment?

Yes and... yes. Afterall... *Wasn't that partly what last night was about?*

With my mind clearing and resolve returning, I sat up straighter. The feeling of relief coupled with the AMG's revving vibrations and the freedom of being sans underwear soon had my entire body tingling. And the unfamiliar anticipation that came with being even further outside my comfort zone began to feel invigorating.

As Victor wove us faster and faster through the countryside, I glanced ahead for any law enforcement before remembering it was Sunday. Most sheriffs would be stationed nearer the churches in their towns at this time of morning. Not that it mattered. I had no idea where we even were until my navigation system displayed the town of Lumberton and I-95 just up ahead.

A few twists, turns and minutes later in the town of Pembroke, Victor suddenly pulled into a small business park... that appeared to be deserted.

Hmmmmm...

I'd passed by the business park more times than I could remember, usually whenever I decided to take one of the scenic routes on a Sunday returning from my house in Corolla on the Outer Banks.

And, just like every other Sunday, the place was completely deserted.

Arranged in a U pattern, the three single story buildings were subdivided into offices for solo practicing dentists, accountants and divorce lawyers, none of whom worked Sundays. Though all three buildings shared the deserted common parking lot in their center, I knew the paved alley running along the backside of the middle one offered the most privacy. Scanning the entire area for any signs of activity, I deemed the coast clear as I parked behind the center building and waited for Bella to pull up next to me and do the same.

It was clear enough, anyway.

As Victor swung my car door open, the look in his eyes intensified. The man was in heat.

Taking his hand, he helped me out before reaching down to promptly scoop me up, his right forearm solidly beneath my buttocks. Instinctively I pulled myself up around his neck, suddenly aware that I couldn't remember the last time a man had lifted me so bodily into his arms.

I felt so tiny. So vulnerable... And yet so safe.

Even more contradictory, in the back of my mind I couldn't help to notice how despite being alone we were obviously still in a very public place. Although they seemed vacant, anyone could open any of the building's back doors any moment or come driving around the corner any minute. Under normal circumstances, either of those possibilities would have been a dealbreaker.

But Victor was anything but a normal circumstance.

Gathered so firmly in his massive arms, the shallowest depth of my desire was more than enough to drown out one of my deepest fears. Overriding any urge I had to take flight from the negligible discomfort, all I wanted in that moment was for Victor to take me any way he wanted me.

As our mouths began to furiously devour one another, he shut my door with his knee, turned and carried me swiftly away. I had no idea where he was taking me, couldn't care less and could have done even less than that about it had I known. Feeling the man's sheer physical strength, how effortlessly he held me aloft, was such an immediate and immense turn-on that I felt myself flush wet.

Five, maybe six steps were all it took before he held me above the front of his car. By then my legs were wrapped firmly around his torso, his bulge so undeniably evident all I could think about was how badly I wanted him to fuck me while holding me in his arms.

Instead, he uncoupled, laid me gently on the hood and slid me back toward the windshield. Reaching down beneath my skirt, he pushed me even further using the back of my thighs as his face dove quickly under the loose fabric as he spread my legs.

Thankful he didn't have to waste time pulling off my panties, for the briefest of moments I found myself cursing how in half a day Victor had picked up on how I preferred to be eaten so slo—

—Ohhhhh...

I had to be quick. *Correction.* We had to be quick.

I figured Bella's window of comfort could be held open only so long before her instinctual fear of public humiliation might chill the fire burning between us. Hoisting her into my arms, I was grateful when the shock in her eyes quickly gave way to an undeniable look of passion reinforced by the deliberate press of her pelvis against my own. By the time I laid her across the hood of my car the frantic pace of her kisses alone had left zero doubt to her desire.

The problem was I knew from the night before that Bella preferred to be warmed up slowly.

Making sure the back of her skirt offered her bare skin protection from the heat of my hood, it took every ounce of strength I had not to clamp my mouth immediately upon her clitoris. With the front of her skirt bunched above her waist, I almost couldn't believe what I was seeing.

Like late morning dew still adorning the petal of a flower, sunshine actually glistened in the moisture between her folds. Never in my life had I seen a pussy look so picture perfect. So artistic. Or so unbelievably edible.

Fighting my urge to drink from her, I feathered the tip of my tongue up and down her outer edges, whispering my way through the faux protest of her body's squirms. While she writhed in torture from the anticipation, my left hand sought out her right. Just before clasping it, I distracted her by pressing the flat of my tongue against her clit and flooding her with my saliva.

Hearing Bella moan as she arched her neck and bucked against me, I pulled her hand down then pressed her fingers atop her button. Releasing her to work her own magic, I cupped her buttocks, raising her hips while driving my tongue into the sensitive spot just under her clit. Between her manual manipulation and my oral, fifteen, maybe twenty more seconds was all it took before she came.

Arching her back, her entire body bucked as she wailed, abandoning herself to the bliss. While the stifled moans emanating from her mouth were different from any she had made the night before, I could only hope being so exposed in the open temporarily allowed her to feel free in the same.

Prolonging her orgasm with several last licks, I drew her down slowly until she finally laid flat once again against my hood. With the somber acknowledgement that this would be my last opportunity for two months, I inhaled her scent deeply despite knowing full well I had already committed this among so many other aspects of her to memory. And as her panting slowed and breathing returned to normal, I exhaled gently in an attempt to cool her just a bit faster.

The difference in temperatures alone was more than enough to make my entire body ache. With my nipples frozen solid, the rest of my skin was on fire... but not from the hood of the car.

I could feel my blood both pulse and pulsate with every beat of my heart, flowing, racing, expanding my veins and capillaries, increasing the outward pressure under my skin until every square inch of my flesh had swelled to the point of becoming ultra-sensitive.

And that was just the start.

My mind rushed alongside my body, made hyper aware by a level of exhibitionism I had never known I was capable of achieving. Inundated by my surroundings, my senses hovered just short of a full overload.

The sounds of birds chirping pierced the slightest rustles of the wind as the intermittent hum of traffic, safely in the distance, faded in and out. The powder blue sky above me was even more vivid than before, streaked now by a few random clouds, each stretched by an invisible jet stream out toward the green pines on the horizon that somewhere in my head I swear I could smell. I felt enveloped by it all, as welcomed and open amongst it as my legs were to Victor.

In that moment my entire being was alive.

And it wanted more.

With Victor's face still so close to my hand, it took very little effort to slip behind his head and pull him up to me. Covering his mouth with my own, I reached with my other hand for his belt buckle... and became thoroughly confused when he stopped me.

Opening my eyes, I found him looking at me, his expression soft though he clearly was anything but.

God knows I wanted her.

But it wasn't how I wanted her to remember me or us for the next two months, humping on the hood of a car behind some building we'd probably never see again. And although I knew the mental advantage of always leaving a woman wanting for more, emotionally I knew the best way to accomplish that was to leave her unable to handle anything else, especially when she would always be able to do so again later.

Of course, our later was about to take longer than most. *Still...*

Reluctantly raising back off the hood of the car, I pulled Bella by her hands to stand beside me.

"That," I said, looking her deep in the eyes and allowing my meaning to take hold, "I did for *both* of us. But what you want right at this moment and what I want are two different things. You may not understand this, Bella, but I no longer want to leave for the next two months to go do what I have to... yet my life can't go forward until I do. I know that might not make a lot of sense, but if you'll wait for me... starting now with a denial we freely agree to together and not one which we are forced... I promise I'll make it up to you when I return."

In my wildest dreams I never thought I would hear a man say such things to me. Especially one I had known for less than a day. Whether it was the restraint in his actions or the compassionate sincerity in his voice, my head was swimming. All I could do was nod as I gathered my thoughts.

"Listen, Victor... you've given me more than you realize. And if you really want me to wait for you, I will... on one condition."

"Name it."

I pursed my lips. "This might sound weird but... no video chatting."

Slightly confused as I knew he might be, Victor started.

"You may have noticed," I said before he could say anything, "I am a bit more susceptible to visual stimulation than most women."

Cocking his head, Victor smiled and said, "Actually I'd say more than most *people.*"

"That's probably true, too. Which is why if I can't have you for the next two months, if we can't have each other... then I'd prefer not to drive myself crazy."

Victor peered at me slightly. "As long as that's all it is," he said.

Saying nothing, I tried not to smile any further or blink... but failed at both.

Victor chuckled. "Okay, I'll guess we'll have to address that later then," he agreed, graciously choosing to not press me further.

Grateful not just for his understanding but how he had decided to momentarily handle the situation, I reached up and pulled his head down for a kiss.

"Thank you."

"You're well *cum*," I said playfully, causing Bella's smile to break out even further.

"Well, I certainly came well," she admitted with a laugh.

It was good to see her breathe easier. I didn't understand why she wanted to forgo video chatting over the next two months probably any better than she had an idea why I had just declined to fuck her over the hood of my car. But that was fine by me. There was still so much we didn't know about one another. Two more wouldn't hurt.

"Well, I promise you there's more where that *came* from," I said with a wink.

Bella's eyes grew wide. "I hope so."

Flashing my best smile, I took her by the hand, walked her back to her car and opened the door for her knowing full well the next part was going to suck. Two goodbyes in two days to people I cared about. As bad as I had dreaded it, I was better prepared for the first. This one was going to hit harder. Even if there was really only one thing left I could say.

Kissing her as passionately as I could without allowing it to go any further, I finally tore my lips away from hers and waited until she opened her eyes.

"Ciao, Bella."

Back on the road with another two hours ahead of us, Bella continued to fill me in on the details of her career. How a year ago she had transitioned from focusing on sex addiction therapy to working primarily as a child psychologist while occasionally serving as a marriage counselor. She didn't find her subjects as personally interesting, but as she explained it, that was also a good thing.

"After all, as doctors we are not *supposed* to be personally invested in our patients, anyway."

"'Not supposed to be,' huh? Why does it sound like you disagree with that?"

"Probably because I do," Bella said. "Don't get me wrong. I understand the advantages of remaining personally detached, not just for doctors but also for our patients. But when the primary motivating factor for becoming a therapist in the first place is caring *about* people, it is incredibly hard not to also care *for* them. Especially when some of them can be so incredibly interesting."

Hmmmmm. For some reason Bella's choice of words sparked a memory.

"That reminds me," I started. "Last night, just before they left, when Abby said, 'You have our permission.' What was that all about?"

I knew I had said too much as soon as I said it. Even worse, deep down I knew Victor was intelligent enough to pick up on what I purposefully left unsaid. *Leave it to me to make an unspoken slip of the tongue.* Momentarily frustrated, I rolled my eyes as I tried to rationalize my own forgiveness. Though in all honesty, perhaps I was being too hard on myself.

After all, I had never really met a man like Victor before. One I was just as attracted to out of bed as I was in. One who not only checked all the boxes but created then filled others on his own. One who after only one night and morning of the most intensely personal passion I had ever known had me seriously contemplating a lifetime of voluntary sexual servitude.

Ironically, perhaps that was why I felt free enough to drop my guard whenever we talked. Of course, it also might have been because my body was still free-floating in panty-free, post-orgasmic bliss while a large piece of my soul was still clinging to the hood of his car. Either way, Victor had the same effect on me. He was freeing.

And wasn't that the point?

Smiling privately, I acknowledged just how much it was. That as hard as it was to explain, virtually my entire motivation for wanting to offer myself as a Sex Slave had been to free my mind. To rid it, no matter how temporarily, of all requirement for thought or responsibility. To give it a rest.

Yet now that I had it, now that I was freed to speak not just by Victor but by Abby and Greg as well, ironically it was *I* who felt the need to apply the brakes. After all, only I knew where the most truthful answer to Victor's question could lead. And I still wasn't ready to go there, not just yet. But I could be in two months. That was long enough. So, until then... I took a deep breath.

"Abby and Greg were giving me permission to tell you that several years ago they were both my patients. In fact, I introduced them. Well... kind of."

Before Victor could inquire further, I explained how it was standard protocol to keep private sessions between sex addiction patients separate. If not by day then at least by appointment times. True, patients could always meet during then choose to interact with one another after a group session.

"Call me crazy," Victor gently interrupted, "but putting a bunch of sex addicts in the same room together, even if it is for therapy, doesn't sound like a bright idea."

"You are correct. For certain people," *Abby,* I couldn't help thinking, "it's not. But for some patients, especially those who've exhibited a great deal of progress, a group session can offer a layer of additional, collective support to their recovery making relapse even less likely."

I explained that only after getting to know the particulars of Greg and Abby's cases extremely well did I realize each could be a partial solution to what the other needed. While I felt ethically bound not to leave the two alone in a room together, those binds weren't strong enough to prevent me from scheduling back-to-back appointments where they could pass one another in the reception area where I worked at the time. I figured if nature didn't take it from there, then it wasn't meant to be.

"But I take it nature took?" Victor laughed rhetorically.

"You've known them for six months," Bella replied. "I'm sure by now you know."

"They are quite the couple," I agreed, warming to how we shared the same opinion so strongly.

Sensing Bella had more to say even though she wasn't, I let her continue to do most of the talking. But as she filled me in on the particulars of her career, every so often I had to shake my head.

I can't believe she's a psychotherapist.

The idea was taking a little longer than normal for me to absorb though of course that wasn't Bella's fault. Although she now knew about my accident, I hadn't told her that in addition to my head trauma, it was a psychologist that had effectively screwed me out of the Marines.

If not for the damage to my brain I probably would have gotten over my dismissal long ago. But I had truly loved the Corps. At the time my unit was the first real family I felt I had since losing my own. So back when I felt it slipping away—to yet another vehicular accident, no less—I tried everything I could to convince the doctors on base that I was fit for duty.

Even though it had taken me a few days to fully recuperate, physically I had been fine. It was mentally and emotionally where I just couldn't keep it together. Petty crap began to set me off far too easily, sending me into a blind rage at the smallest illogical events. Never a good trait for any Marine much less a squad's best marksman which at the time I was.

So after my second run-in with the MPs inside a week, my CO ordered me to see the base psychologist. And though I was under the impression my initial consult went well, at the end the doctor informed me that he was going to keep me "under observation." While all he really meant was he'd be checking in with my superiors every once in a while to see how I was doing, the phrase triggered an overwhelming sense of paranoia I'd never before had.

Despite spending more than a decade in foster care including a horrible bout fighting chronic insomnia, for the first time in my life I was a nervous wreck as each day somehow seemed worse than the last. Convinced someone was following me at all times, I couldn't go anywhere without literally looking over my shoulder. Unable to sleep, I ended up making small mistakes which in my mind were bigger problems than they actually caused. Then, constantly beating myself up over my own stupidity, I lashed out at anyone and everyone until I voluntarily scheduled my own follow-up appointment with the psychologist.

Feeling like my career was on the line and desperate to hold on to my "family," I opened the floodgates to my soul, telling the good doctor anything and everything about my entire life. Minute by minute as I realized the deeper my catharsis went the freer I felt, I purposefully began to let myself go until I was wallowing uncontrollably in the throes of a full-blown emotional breakdown.

Bad decision.

By the time I made it back to my bunk my CO was waiting for me with an ultimatum. I could accept an honorable discharge with a partial disability... or an honorable discharge with nothing due to my newfound unsuitability. The choice was easy. Hell, I couldn't even argue with the designation once I was informed unsuitability meant "Unsatisfactory behavior due to personality problems beyond a soldier's control." Which at the time was definitely me in a nut shell.

Yet despite the undeniable truth, I blamed the psychologist.

"... for three years."

What? I shook my head to snap out of it, instantly annoyed with myself for having tuned Bella out again, even if only for a couple of seconds. "I'm sorry, what did you just say? I didn't hear you."

"I said I also hosted a podcast for three years," Bella repeated, "the last of which I also had a YouTube channel. It's... it's kind of what I didn't want you to find out about me last night when you went to play poker."

Why not? "What was your podcast about?"

"Well, in terms of subject matter, sex addiction. But... the show kind of took on a life of its own. It ended up a bit bawdier than I intended. Though if I am being completely honest, that was also the reason for its success. A lot of times I just talked about whatever my listeners wanted to discuss."

I nodded to myself. While I had very little experience with podcasts, Bella's description matched my own. Akin to pirate radio shows they were loosely formatted and had a tendency to run off on unscripted tangents. "It sounds interesting."

"I like to think it was. You should give it a listen if you find the time."

"I'll do that. It's been years since I've heard a good, entertaining podcast."

"Oh? You used to listen to some?"

"I've heard a few, but mostly I just listened to one really. As a matter of fact, it was where I first heard about bitcoin."

"Really?"

"Yeah, it was a poker podcast that was popular with all the circuit grinders. One of the hosts was extremely pro-bitcoin because of its potential. There was a lot of speculation at the time about how instead of using dollars, poker could be played online with and for bitcoin, in effect circumventing the law which said it couldn't be played for real money."

"But I take it said nothing specifically about whether or not it could be played for bitcoin?"

"Exactly. I remember thinking how right the host was and not just because it was the perfect legal loophole. Remember, I already knew just how large the underground black market was from my days working with that private investigator in LA."

"Wait a minute," Bella interrupted. "Wasn't there an online black market that used bitcoin? One that the government shut down because people were buying drugs and guns and all kind of other illegal stuff on there?"

"Yeah, it was called Silk Road. I remember when it launched was the first time I really thought about buying bitcoin. I figured it was going to take off."

"But you didn't?"

"No. It didn't sit right with me at first. It was obvious demand for it would increase and drive up its price, but I just couldn't bring myself to buy a form of money I knew criminals were using because at the time it was pretty untraceable. It wasn't until I gave it some more thought that I realized criminals use cash to commit crimes all the time but I certainly wasn't going to stop using cash just because of that."

"So then you bought some?"

"Not right away. Its legality was still in a little too much of a gray area for me.

But then, as I told you before, a couple of months later I was playing a poker tournament in Vegas when Black Friday went down."

The confusion in Bella's voice was hard to miss. "Black Friday? The day after Thanksgiving?"

"No. In the professional poker world, Black Friday refers to the day the FBI seized control of the three largest online poker sites running in America. Along with all their players' money."

I filled Bella in on how I spent the day watching so many distracted online players fret over the sudden loss of a large chunk of their livelihoods. Whether lighting up Twitter to share information, checking various poker podcasts for the latest developments or just playing live like me simply because they suddenly had nothing better to do for the day, one thing was clear. In order to continue, online poker was going to have to do something different.

And that meant using bitcoin.

"The players eventually got their money back from the federal government," I explained, "but by the time they were reimbursed the money was almost beside the point."

"Why was that?"

"Because a lot players were out of business by then. To them, money is a tool. It's no different than how a carpenter views a hammer or a doctor a scalpel. It's the instrument they *use* to *make* the money they live off of. It's just that for professional poker players—and bankers, too, for that matter—the tool they use happens to be money itself. So when their tools were seized, it really was no different than having their entire business confiscated. And I knew when they eventually rebuilt—"

"—they would rebuild with bitcoin... which would help its value to increase."

"Exactly."

"So that's when you bought your first bitcoins?"

"I guess you could say it's when I started to dabble," I said as casually as I could through my smile. I was pleased that I had been able to explain things well enough for Bella not only to understand but also for her to see where they were going.

Speaking of which...

Realizing we were only minutes from Charlotte and that time was passing far too quickly, I began to ponder what I could do to slow it down. Figuring the rest of my story could wait until later, I glanced ahead where I spotted a sign on the side of the road. Even if it was a sudden change of subject, the timing was perfect. "Do you see the next exit coming up?"

"The one for Highway 601?"

"Yeah. That'll take you to Midland about ten minutes north of here. Charlotte's identity owes most of its existence to a seventeen pound gold nugget discovered there in 1799."

"Hmph," Bella uttered, clearly a bit disinterested. But I wasn't done explaining.

"A kid named Conrad Reed found it in a creek that flowed through his family's farm. He didn't know what it was, but he thought it looked interesting enough to lug home. Unfortunately, his father, John, didn't share his son's interest... so he put it down on the floor and used it as a doorstop."

"You're kidding."

"Believe or not, I'm not. But, after a few years went by John decided to see if he could get something for it from a jeweler in Fayetteville. The jeweler, of course, recognized it so—I imagine as magnanimously as one could in such a situation—he told John to name his price. John, not knowing its true value, asked for about a week's worth of wages, around $3.50 at the time." I let my words hang for a few seconds. "Want to guess how much that gold doorstop of his was really worth?"

Bella hemmed and hawed for a second. "I don't know. $350?"

"Add a zero."

"$3500? Wow, that must have been a fortune back then."

"Oh, it was. At $3.50 a week John's mistake cost him the equivalent of *twenty years* worth of work. But, after coming home and discovering what gold was really worth, he set up a placer mining operation—which is really just another way of saying scouring the ground—that eventually paid off. Just a couple of months later one of his slaves found a twenty-eight pound nugget, making it the first documented commercial gold find in the United States.

"When word got out, America's first real gold rush was on. By 1830 there were so many mines in the area that transporting all that gold to the nearest mint in Philadelphia became too much of a burden. So they set up a mint in

Charlotte which in turn led to the need for places to store it."

"Hmmmm," Bella mused. "So that's how Charlotte became such a banking capital."

"It's how it got started, anyway... I haven't bored you, have I?"

"What? No. Why?"

Victor's question caught me off-guard. While I couldn't say I was riveted by his story, I thought I had been somewhat successful in trying to pay attention and follow along.

"It's just... well, along with not being interested in financial things, I remember last night you also mentioned something about not really being a history buff. And I just realized that's all I've been talking about for the last couple of hours."

I didn't know whether to chuckle or preen. Either way, Victor's concern was touching.

"No, you haven't bored me. But I can't help to wonder why you're explaining all this to me."

"Well, I guess it's because of how you found your patients' stories easier to understand when they started at their beginning. And I couldn't agree more. I think historical context is important. An overabundance of gold led to a need for the creation of banks. And the creation of cryptocurrency's story started as a response to the problems brought on by the banks... Speaking of which, take a look."

Clearing a small rise in the road, the city of Charlotte suddenly came into view ahead to our left. Having worked in uptown a few years back, I knew the stately line of white granite and black glass buildings well. But jutting through the winter canopy from this distance and direction, the perspective was new to me. And while it might just have been the angle of the midday sun, from this side the cityscape appeared a bit more picturesque.

Continuing down off the foothill a few seconds later brought a twinge of sadness. Not only did my postcard view disappear, I realized we were only about twenty minutes from the airport. While I was glad Victor had bypassed the quicker outer belt, the thought of no longer talking with him until who-knew-when again was one I didn't want to have. The feeling left me with a need to hear his voice.

"So, what do banks have to do with cryptocurrency?" I asked.

"At the moment, not much," Victor continued. "When it comes to change, banks are as slow as they are conservative, especially when it comes to new technology where they're about as risk averse as it gets. Making matters worse, there's also far too much regulatory uncertainty right now. Until that changes, it's only natural for them to steer clear of cryptocurrencies. Of course, that's also understandable given how *most* coins are designed to put them out of business."

I could hear it in Victor's voice, the slight emphasis he placed on the word 'most' whether he meant to or not.

"'Most?' Meaning not all?"

I shook my head, bewildered yet delighted once again that Bella could read me so well. *If only she knew,* I thought unfairly before remembering so few actually did.

"No. Not all. In fact, there are some coins in particular which have been developed specifically for banks to use. Especially when it comes to cross-border payments made between two countries. Banks aren't using them yet. They can't even legally accept custody of them like a deposit, but eventually I think regulations and laws will be created which allow them to."

"And if they don't?"

Approaching the inner beltway at just that moment, I gazed in appreciation at the edifices soaring above the tree-lined horizon.

Centered geographically at the intersection of two Native American trading paths, I knew all of uptown was neatly bound within an area less than two miles square. Monuments to the city's immense wealth, the majority of Charlotte's skyline was dominated by some of the largest financial institutions in the country. Architecturally beautiful, the banks had long been the brightest jewels in the centerpiece of the Queen City's crown. And despite how much I once believed in bitcoin's mission to replace them, I had to admit...

"It would be a shame to see them go."

I heard Bella let out a small, incredulous snort before catching herself.

"You don't really think cryptocurrencies are that powerful, do you? That they could one day negate the need for banks? To actually put them out of business?"

I tried to tamper the smugness of my smile as I realized just how little Bella still knew. How so many different areas within the crypto space were on the cusp of mainstream adoption. Automated smart contracts, CBDCs, stable coins, decentralized finance and trade. The list went on and on with more being built every day.

"For a couple generations," I said, "there was a land-based telephone line in every house and every other street corner in America because the technology was just that crucial. Then a new technology was developed and the companies behind the old way of doing things became obsolete. But life went on and in many ways got better by becoming more efficient."

I shook my head at the analogy, knowing how not even it began to describe the magnitude of what was likely to happen.

The coming paradigm shift was going to be so tectonic in scale that hundreds of thousands of people like myself had already made an obscene amount of money off the first few ripples of the coming tsunami of change. I knew that what the internet did to post offices and libraries, blockchain, distributed ledger technology and especially CBDCs, were about to do to commercial and retail banks. And the probability of their demise brought on just by the potential of cryptocurrencies alone...

With the right regulations and technological upgrades...

"So, yes, cryptocurrencies could render banks obsolete in much the same way," I assured her.

A couple seconds of contemplative thought passed before I heard Bella mutter softly to herself.

"Damn."

Driving for several more in silence, uptown disappeared from our view off to our left just as my exit entered on our right. Even if we continued talking, I reluctantly acknowledged our physical proximity to one another was about to go bye.

"Well, this is my exit."

"Wait? What? I thought you were going to the airport?"

"I am. I fly out of Concord," I said simply, hoping Bella wouldn't ask me to elaborate. Her mention of a fear of flying last night at Mickey's had been brief but strong enough that I had no intention of informing her I was a pilot with my own jet. Not until I had to, anyway.

"Hmmmm. You know, somehow I did not peg you for a budget traveler."

I chuckled. While the smaller regional airport hosted the discount airlines, it was just as equidistant to my house as the larger international—and far busier—Charlotte-Douglas. But since it was also a cheaper place to park my jet, Bella was at least half right. I'd let her live with that for now.

"Yeah, well, never judge a book by its cover. Plus," I added, "I'm not one for crowds or delays."

Not to mention goodbyes.

"What I hope you're not one for is one-night stands. You're going to call me, right?"

The words came out of my mouth unbidden. If our impending separation hadn't been so sudden, if I had had more time to think it through I might have parsed my words a bit more carefully.

Given Victor's response, gladly neither was the case.

"Oh, trust me," he said. "I plan to do a lot more than just call you. In fact... I already have."

Ignoring the mystery, the level of assurance in Victor's voice alone was enough to quell almost the entire flare of my anxiety. Glancing to my right as I passed him on the left, I caught his wink just before his last two words extinguished the rest.

"Ciao, Bella," he said as he blew me a kiss farewell.

After reaching cruising altitude and completing my checklist, I settled back as best I could and pulled out my phone. With my Honda Elite on autopilot, I had about two hours before beginning my descent into Kansas City. On any other occasion I'd spend the entire flight sightseeing and soaking in what every pilot knew, that no matter how bad things were below every day was a sunny one above the clouds. Only now neither interested me as much as Bella did.

Jonesing to discover what the internet had to say about my wannabe Sex Slave, I typed "Dr. B" in the search bar and was shocked when Bella's full name became the first to fill the dropdown menu.

'*If you have to ask,' indeed,* I chuckled.

Tapping her name, I was amazed at the total number of results that popped up, the majority of which involved her podcast. Scrolling down, I noticed the *Images* thumbnails section was filled entirely by her pictures, the first of which was more than enough to catch my eye.

Sporting a dark, classy business suit and black rimmed glasses, Bella's hair was piled high behind her head in an elegant chignon. Two long, curling tendrils hanging down—one on either side of her face—rounded out the sexy scientific researcher vibe she most definitely exuded. And while at first I thought having her hair pulled back had given her face a slimmer look, on closer inspection I could tell that she had indeed been thinner all around.

Damn!

As beautiful as I already found Bella to be, nothing could have prepared me for how smoking hot she once looked. Gone were the plump roundness of her cheeks and the bulkiness of her shoulders, the absence of which made her neck appear even longer and more graceful. And even though she was seated behind a fairly nondescript desk with framed pictures of the *Mona Lisa* and Taj Mahal behind her and a decently large broadcast microphone in front of her, I could still see her waist was once smaller which made her breasts seem even larger.

Slowly scrolling through the various pics, it didn't take long to realize Bella looked much the same in all of them. From her fashionably conservative attire to professionally chic coif, she appeared the epitome of success. What she did not appear to be was a Sex Slave. And given what I knew I found it even more difficult to reconcile that under her collection of Albert Nipons and D&Gs was one of the most stupefying tattoos I had ever seen.

My mental disconnect was so strong I was a dozen pictures deep before I realized almost every image was a still shot taken by someone during her podcast. Curiously, just as I began to wonder who might have been behind the camera, I swiped left to find a large silhouette staring back at me.

Positioned behind heavily frosted glass, the backlit figure was a large, muscular male with a shaved head. And though the lighting obscured the color of his skin and the thumbnail description labeled the man "The Invisible Andy," my immediate impression was that Greg was behind the partition.

Puzzled by the designation as well as the unexpected association, I tapped back to the search results and selected the first url directing me to Bella's official website. Standard enough, I found links to her bio, podcast and YouTube channel along with her Instagram, Twitter and Facebook pages. Additional tabs highlighted her photo gallery, contact page and the array of psychotherapy services she offered as well as one with an index of chapters for a charity organization called "Doc's'Dicts" along with one for what looked like a message board labeled Dear 'Dicts.

Unsure where best to begin, I remembered Bella's advice about the beginning so, figuring her bio probably contained the oldest information, I tapped the link.

Presented bullet-style, the page was a chronological list of her educational background as well as her work history and certification credentials. Filling more than two scrolled screens, it was hard not to be impressed by all her achievements. The woman had accomplished more by twenty-five than most people did in a lifetime. But disappointingly bare of any uniquely personal details, none of it was what I was hoping to discover.

Backing out, I decided to alter my search method. Scanning each link on the main page I soon realized Bella's initial podcasts were dated the oldest out of everything on her site.

And a quick perusal showed them to be extraordinarily well organized.

A live, weekly podcast, *Dr. Bella Quinn's Sex aDDDictionary* ran from the end of 2015 to that of 2018 with a concurrent YouTube channel opening at the start of her third and final season. Running down the list of shows, I was both heartened and dismayed by the sheer volume. While her earliest episodes clocked in around an hour, by the end each ran closer to three. Averaging two hours apiece with fifty episodes per season spread out over three... doing the math in my head I was looking at roughly three hundred hours worth of material.

No matter how much I wanted, there was just no way I could devote five hours each day for the next sixty to listen to Bella's entire show.

Luckily, every episode had been broken down and was available in standalone snippets. With the list arranged like chapters, it was interesting to see how the overall show had evolved. It was clear only a few of her earliest segments survived all three seasons as others developed and took hold. Based on their descriptions, each appeared to follow a similar format with Bella and Andy alternating control.

Doubling as the episode's title, Bella opened with a word and its definition before delving into each show's primary subject aka "The Man Meat Of The Matter." This was followed by Andy with his "Fun Facts & Odd Things You Never Knew About Sex (But Will Now Never Forget)," before Bella took back over with a discussion on "Doc's Term Of The Day" which was then countered by "Andy's Neologism Of The Day." A lengthy "In With Quinn" call-in segment took up more and more time, extending the show as it grew more and more popular. Then, wrapping up each episode, Andy offered his final thoughts under "Leave It To A Man" before the episode concluded with Bella's "Take It From A Woman."

At some point in the second season a collection of "Andy's Diddle Riddles" was randomly tossed into the mix while in the third the occasional "The Balls Of Ballin' Ballers" turned into a far more regular installment as Bella began guest hosting names I recognized as professional athletes. And at the very bottom of the podcast list I was surprised to find a curiously titled, bonus compilation chapter, *The Very Best of Andy du Payne.*

Scrolling back up to her opening episode, I tapped Play and leaned back to relax as a twenty second mix of intro music began to fill the cockpit. Snippets of five or six songs, all sexual in nature, filtered down one into the next before fading out to the last few bars of Marvin Gaye's *Sexual Healing.*

Nice one...

A brief silence then filled the air before being broken by Bella's unmistakable lilt.

"Sex addiction. An affliction whereby an individual lacks the ability to manage or control their sexual behavior. A condition characterized by an often overwhelming persistence of sexual thoughts, sex addiction often negatively affects an individual's ability to maintain relationships, to work in a productive manner or even to complete simple, everyday tasks. Sex addiction is also known as compulsive sexual behavior, sexual dependency or hypersexuality.

"Hello, everyone. My name is Doctor Bella Quinn and I'd like to welcome you to my podcast."

Following her greeting with a brief rundown of her qualifications, Bella quickly turned her focus back toward her audience.

"So, you might be asking yourself with a title like *Sex aDDDictionary,* what this podcast is all about. Well, that's simple. It's going to be about sex. Sex. And more sex. It will also be about sex addiction as well as defining and exploring various terms and facets associated with sex and sex addiction, especially those that are lesser well known.

"As for the title itself, I want you to know I put a great deal of thought into it. I culled through several edits to select just the right one and I would like to explain why. It's not just because I know sex sells. I do and I unashamedly and intentionally named it so in order to drive traffic to my site and attain listeners.

"But I ultimately chose the title because words are also what I intend for my podcast to be about. After all, you can't talk about sex if you don't know what you're talking about and you can't know what you're talking about if you don't know the proper definitions of the words you use. So I invite you to sit back, relax and prepare to be educated on a subject I'm sure you probably think you already know all about... but which I will prove you don't. But don't worry. I promise, it *will* be fun.

"Which, of course, if you knew me you'd know that's a pretty big deal because I was taught as a therapist to never make promises. And if you think about it, that's pretty good advice. After all, a person can't fail to keep a promise they never make. But you know what I bet you will find even more surprising? I was also taught as a therapist to never *give advice* either.

"Now you are probably saying to yourself, 'But I thought that was what therapy was for, to get advice on how to get better.' Well, guess what? *It's not.* No, a therapist's job is to offer their patients a better, more complete understanding of what caused them to think what they did before they acted in such a manner that ultimately motivated them to seek help. Because even though it's an easy thing to say *after* a mistake that someone didn't think *before* they acted, that's not true. In fact, it's never true because the truth is we think all the time. We think while we're awake in the forms of thoughts and daydreams and we think while we're asleep in the forms of dreams and nightmares. True, sometimes we think less than others, but we are *always* thinking. Including just *before* we make mistakes.

"*Why* we think what we do or thought what we did is what psychotherapy is all about. It's simply a tool which professionals such as myself use in order to help guide our patients so that they can make their own decisions which are better than the ones they would have made without prior guidance.

"If you really think about it, a therapist's job is a lot like that of a parent of a teenager. While there are specific instances when parents need to intercede and instruct their teens on *exactly* what they should do, more often than not a parent's job is better spent *guiding* their child in such a way that the child makes the correct choice all by their self. That way, once their child begins to enter adulthood, they won't continue to expect another person—be it their parent or a significant other—to constantly rescue them from their poor choices.

"Along those same lines, therapists try to give patients enough leeway to make their own decisions, empowering them—just as a parent does their child—to feel even more confident when they are faced with making decisions in their future. In other words, our job is not to enable our patients. It's to *make them able.* And that, in a nutshell, is what I do."

Bella paused for a few seconds as it sounded like she was taking a sip of something.

"But why do I do it, you might ask. Why did I choose a career not just in psychotherapy in general but with a focus on sex addiction? Well, I did it because someone once told me it's always a good idea to pursue a profession that is recession proof. They warned me people whose livelihoods depend on the economy often go through periods of misery due to a factor beyond their control, leaving them feeling trapped and helpless.

"Of course, when you think about it, there are very few occupations which don't fall in this category. So instead of focusing on an occupation, I focused on the subject. I asked myself which occupations concerning *what* subjects were the *least* recession proof.

"The first answer I deduced was a no-brainer. Sex. I mean, necessity for the continuous reproduction of life aside, in an everchanging world our species' actual *desire* for sex is the most naturally reliable constant we have. Sex is one of the very few things that transcends all human culture. No matter how fragmented we are or might one day become, sex is the one language, the one form of communication everyone on this planet understands.

"However, my second answer—addiction—I could see where that might surprise people a bit more. After all, when the economy is good, less of us feel the need to turn to things like drugs or other crutches to get by which, in turn, leads to less work for people like myself. And let me state wholeheartedly right now for the record, I would *love* to live in a world where I was put out of work for that reason. I would love to be forced to find something else to do with my life because my help is no longer needed.

"Only I realized something. You see, *all* human beings at all times are addicts. And what we're addicted to... is *happiness.*

"Now, like all addictions, our desire to be happy is acquired. But what sets it apart is its natural development when, just after birth, our bodies begin to learn that certain external stimuli trigger the creation of dopamine, serotonin and endorphins. These chemical reactions are the pleasures our brains reward us with to make us happy, rewards which promote and reinforce the choices that, in return, maximize their own production... Not that that is an addiction I think needs a cure, of course."

Pausing again, this time the sound of Bella drinking something definitely filled the air.

"Please excuse me, everyone. I am not used to talking this much. Typically, I am the one that does all the listening. So if you hear me take a sip of water every now and then, well, now you know why... Okay, so switching gears, before I go any further I want to address a bit more specifically the 'Sex aDDDictionary' title of my podcast and I would like to start by asking you something. When you were scrolling through the list of podcasts just now to choose from and first saw how I spelled the word 'a-D-D-D-i-c-t-i-o-n-a-r-y,' did you immediately think of a woman with large breasts because the triple Ds jumped out at you?"

"If they didn't before, they certainly will now."

The voice came out of nowhere. Masculine, deep and hypnotic, the electronically filtered sound reverberated down as if emanating from a deity above. Which was almost as surprising as the manner with which Bella half-ignored it.

"Regardless," she continued, "I spelled the word that way not just for provocative marketing purposes but also for it to be thought provoking. I knew if anyone were only to hear the word 'addictionary' spoken, they probably wouldn't have thought of it being spelled that way. But guess what? Spelling it that way is how many sex addicts would have envisioned it immediately because that is the way they think. To a sex addict, almost everything in life does or can carry a sexual overtone.

"If you find that difficult to relate to, think of it this way. Have you ever owned a pair of sunglasses which had tinted lenses of a particular color, perhaps pink or blue? When you put them on, what happened? Everything you saw took on a pink or blue hue, right? Well, the lenses that sex addicts view the world through are always *sex* tinted. And because it's a huge part of who they identify as an individual, unlike an actual pair of sunglasses, theirs are very difficult to remove.

"If you need another example, think for a second what it feels like when your mind and body are both turned On with a capital 'O.' Over the course of our lives, most of us have experienced a full range of sexual intensities, from a little to a lot. We can compare different moments within our range to times when we are decidedly turned Off for various reasons and not interested in sex whatsoever."

All of a sudden, the deity coughed, pointedly and derisively.

"Hey, it happens..." Bella retorted. "But, as I was about to say, sex addicts on the other hand often have no such switch and the ones that are lucky enough *to* have one often find theirs stuck in the On position. For these people, everyone they meet that falls within the range of whom they are willing to take on as a sexual partner is not only fair game, for them it is always Game On!

"Sadly, society tends to denounce these people. Yet the surprising thing is all human beings are addicts in one way or another. Look around you anywhere you go and what is everyone doing? Staring at their smartphones. At work, at the dinner table, in the car, in the bathroom, first thing in the morning and last thing at night. Drawing a conclusion that almost every human being who has one is addicted to their smartphone might sound reasonable... But are we really addicted to them?

"Dig a little deeper and the truth is we are actually drawn not to the phone itself but to the *information* they allow us to access. And why not? At one time or another we have all experienced our own Archimedes-running-through-the-streets shouting *'Eureka! Eureka!'* or Thomas Edison's light-bulb-popping-on-in-our-head kind of moments. And we love that feeling, don't we? The feeling of suddenly becoming smarter? We do which is why we love our phones because in their own way, they are the easiest shortcut for us to mainline dozens of small hits of that euphoria to our brains each day.

"Because when you dig down to the heart of it *that* is what we are all addicted to. The euphoria, the happiness. Not the phone, not the information, but those *feelings* of happiness that, let's face it, we can never get enough of. And it's not just some of us that feel that way, it's everyone. In fact, addiction to happiness just might be the most universally intangible thing all human beings have in common. Which makes perfect sense because when it comes down to it, most of us just want to be happy in life. And in the process, we have become addicted to the feelings associated with the chemical reactions in our brains to, as I said earlier, dopamine, serotonin, adrenaline, et cetera. And just as pharmaceuticals fall into various categories like narcotics, opioids, analgesics—"

"—Laxatives—" the deity boomed.

"—Leave it to you to always be right on top of any anal angle," Bella shot back.

"Hey, you're the one who said 'anal-gesics' for crying out loud."

"Wow. That easily triggered today, are we?"

"Trigger was a horse. Horses have *huge* dicks."

A lengthy silence of wtf filled the air. That's what it sounded like until Bella sighed, anyway.

"Well, ladies and gentlemen of our listening audience," she started, "first let me say I *had* planned on introducing you to Andy when the time was right. But since *someone* obviously can't keep it in their pants and since you've already met—"

"—Helloooo, everybody," the deity butted in. "My name is Andy du Payne. Ooooooh, did someone say the word... *'body?'*"

"Aanndyy..."

"Yes, yes, I know it was me," Andy said. His electronic voice suddenly soft and sincere, the rapid switch in tone from playful to apologetic was more than slightly jarring. "Sorry, Doc."

What is wrong with this gu—

"It's okay," Bella replied. "Actually, you've done me a favor by inadvertently proving my point. Every*one*... Andy is a former sex addict... even if on days like today he appears to still be in recovery."

"Oooooh, was that a compliment?"

Although I couldn't see her face, I just knew Bella was rolling her eyes. While she seemed to take pity on the schmuck, the manner in which they riffed off one another, rapid-fire, like lifelong friends struck me as bizarre, not to mention the way Bella either addressed or ignored the guy was comical to say the least. Despite the picture I had seen earlier, the more Andy spoke the less I felt he was actually Greg, if for no other reason than I had never heard Greg sound so flippant or contrite. Or downright spastic.

It made me wonder who Andy really was.

"Of course, Andy du Payne is not Andy's real name," Bella continued as if uninterrupted. "So who is he then, you ask? Well, for lack of a better term, Andy is my side piece. *No,* not that kind of side piece. As it stands, I don't have a main piece, but even if I did, Andy still wouldn't be my side piece. But—"

"—Did you just say—"

"*—Stawwwwp!*—for purposes of this show, I will be treating Andy accordingly. Isn't that right, Andy?"

"I don't care how you treat me, Doc, as long as you keep treating me."

"Don't you worry. I will. After all... you need help."

"Hey!"

"Stop. You know you love it."

"Yeah, I do."

"Anyway, ladies and gentlemen, Andy is also my sound technician, phone screener and chat room moderator. He will be running all the boards, playing all the music and funny little noises you hear, sending us to commercials. In fact, he will be directing every element of the show except for me. So be nice. Around here he's the gate keeper."

"Oooh! Can I be the key master instead?"

Bella paused. "Okay."

"You have no idea what I'm— You know what? Forget it."

"Ohh-kaaay... And now that we've dispensed with the formalities, let's dive right in, shall we?"

Chuckling to myself, I began to realize one of the many reasons why Bella's podcast might have been so successful. While I had the feeling that utilizing words like 'we' and 'our' whenever possible as well as treating Andy like a semi-annoying interloper might have been by design, the rest of her delivery was completely natural. Like all great orators, she seemed to have a knack for making her listeners feel as if she was speaking exclusively to them.

I just wasn't sure what else to expect out of her podcast. Not to mention her sidekick.

"Now, for our very first episode," Bella continued, "I've decided to discuss a topic aimed directly at what is likely to be our biggest demographic. Males between the ages of 18 and 35. Which is why our very first segment is all about... jelqing."

Suddenly recalling what Bella had asked me in bed, I perked up what little I could in my seat.

"So, for those of you who have never heard of it, jelqing is a Middle Eastern penis enlargement technique. It's an exercise which stretches the penis, elongating it almost one and a half inches in length as it expands one inch in girth. But how likely are *you* to get those results? Well, studies have proven jelqing to be 87% effective. That's right, guys. There is a bona fide technique that exists to actually make your penis longer and larger that has an 87% success rate. Now, I know what most of you are probably thinking. Bullshit. If there was something *that* effective every guy on the planet would be doing it. To which I say bullshit. Allow me to explain.

"Are you a guy that wishes you had rock hard abs and big muscles? If you don't already have them, then probably so. I mean we all want to look our best, right? Strong. Virile. Masculine. Well, guess what? I'm sure you know that if you eat right and exercise properly and regularly, there's almost a 100% chance you could have that body. So why don't you? Because it takes dedication and since most guys aren't capable of it, most don't have it. Pure and simple.

"Well, the same is true of jelqing. But if you'd really like to add up to about an inch and a half to your length as well as one to your girth, listen up because you need to understand that in order to see *anywhere near* those types of results, this technique requires approximately ten to thirty minutes of *daily* dedication for at *least* two months. While the average workout is just one set, it's also anywhere from one to two hundred reps.

"And here, in a nutshell, is how it works.

"Just as the same with all exercising, you need to begin by warming up. The good news is a jelq warm up is super easy. Take either a warm bath or soak a towel in warm water before applying it to your penis. You can even use a heating pad if you want. All that matters is you increase the blood flow down there until you start to get a chubby. But *do not* get hard. You want your penis to be semi-tumescent or semi-erect. If you are too soft and limp or too hard and erect, jelqing... will... not... work. So do what it takes to get yourself right in that Goldilocks zone between the two.

"Then, once you are ready, lube yourself up with something like baby oil, but keep the bottle open and close. You'll most likely need more before you are done. Next, take the hand you rarely masturbate with and grip yourself as close to the base as possible. Using your fingers, form a circle. You want your grip tight, but not too tight. The point here is to prevent blood from escaping the lower confines of your penis *without* cutting off your own circulation.

"Then with your other hand form the same ring with your fingers around your penis, placing them above the fingers of your first hand. Once your grips are complete, keep your first hand stationary at your base and milk your penis with your second hand from the base to the head. Go slowly enough so that one full stroke to the tip takes about seven seconds. You want to feel yourself pushing your own blood forward. Now, as you decrease the space between your upper hand and your head, you will feel the pressure build. That pressure is *blood* and *it needs to go somewhere.*

"So as you pull forward getting closer to the head, relax the grip of your fingers just enough for the blood to slip past and return below it. But try not to let it escape beyond your first hand. Again, you want that hand tight but not so tight it cuts off circulation. New blood still needs to be let in and old out...

"But basically, that's it. That's how to jelq. Of course, jelqing is not the only method..."

With time running out before I needed to begin making preparations for my descent, I turned down the podcast while shaking my head in disbelief that more than one technique was necessary. Ready to learn something else, I opened my email from Rick... and got one of the biggest shocks of my life.

Greg Costello had once been incarcerated for rape only to be exonerated fifteen years later.

The last fifteen minutes of my drive home were a blur.

As soon as Victor and I hung up, the words *What have I done?* began to blanket my mind in a neverending echo. Sadly, every feeble attempt I made at an answer was quickly smothered by yet another question which only made things worse.

I wondered if Victor would view the distance of our separation, in both space and time, as an opportunity to reconsider my proposal? If so, what could I do about it? Or maybe I should have just done something differently altogether? Oh, God...

Did I blow my only shot?

Had I moved too fast? *Probably.* But if I had moved slower would we have gotten as far as we had? *Probably not.* So what's the answer? *I don't know... What's the question?*

Turning onto my street I let out a small, exasperated sigh as I banged both fists on the steering wheel. Considering how much oxygen my brain had been consuming as I beat myself up, it was a wonder any was left for my breath to be taken away.

And yet there was.

Waiting for me at my front doorstep as I pulled into my driveway was a deliveryman holding a large bouquet of flowers. Under any other circumstance, I would have immediately assumed he had the wrong address. But the moment I saw the irises I started shaking as an offhand mention I made to Victor last night during a conversation about gardening that they were my favorite came back to me. Too much to be coincidental, I couldn't believe he had remembered.

After apologizing for not carrying cash for a tip and being told not to worry about it, I carried the vase into the house and straight to my dining room table. Slipping the envelope out of its holder, my heart beat so fast I could actually feel it. What was th— *Oh, yeah. Rubatosis,* I thought with a smile as I plucked the card free.

Thank you for an evening that was every bit as memorable as it was enjoyable. Until tomorrow.
Victor

I stood still for several seconds in the childish hope that just this once time would finally choose to stand with me. I'd received flowers before but never in a romantic capacity. I had no idea if this would be the last, but as it was my first...

I wanted to savor the moment for as long as time allowed.

In 1989, at the age of eighteen, Gregory Thaddeus Costello was arrested for first degree rape in his hometown of Brooklyn, New York.

Compared to the post-internet world, the number of news articles devoted to the crime and trial were scant at best. In fact, had Greg's accuser—a twenty year old white woman by the name of Marci Warner—not been so publicly vocal in her condemnation, the case likely wouldn't have garnered as much attention as it did. Not that there was much to tell.

Marci claimed to have woken to find a stranger in her bedroom who forcibly raped then beat her with a bedside lamp, leaving her for dead. Details beyond how she positively identified Greg from a lineup were murky. Worse still, he apparently had no verifiable alibi for his whereabouts that night.

What was abundantly clear was Greg's conviction and sentence of twenty years to life.

Thankfully, updates to forensic technology led to his release in 2004 when a man previously arrested in Texas was found to be a genetic match to DNA evidence collected in Marci's case. Awarded a decent settlement for each year he served in prison, Greg didn't resurface—at least not on the internet—until he opened his own gym on Charlotte's westside in 2006.

Quickly scrolling through the rest of the information I learned he and Abby married in 2013, created a joint venture in 2014 to rebrand and open more gyms... then took on a third partner in 2015.

A man by the name of Andy Chastain.

A quick Google search revealed Andy was a twenty-nine year old marketing underling for one of Charlotte's biggest banks. He was also a hardcore weightlifting buff with a shaved head and bulked up bodybuilding physique like Greg's.

Unlike Greg, however, Andy was short, white and—judging by the extreme number of daily selfies posted to his Instagram and Facebook pages—also a bit of an insecure, full-of-himself douche. Even sadder, whether he was trying to look important by leaning against his Maserati, posing with random women or sporting his newest piece of designer threads, the guy never smiled. Unlike Bella, whatever Andy was looking for in life he obviously had yet to find.

Annoyingly, it wasn't a stretch to reconcile the images in his pics with the voice on the podcast. Electronic or not, I could see Andy Chastain having a deep voice.

But staring at one of his gaudier photos—of him in a gossamer, gold and black zebra print club shirt under matching Fedora—I failed to see Bella being involved with anyone who could have ever oozed so much idiot in just one picture, much less Greg and Abby going into business with the guy. Granted it was four years ago and a great deal of maturity could be gained between the ages of twenty-five and -nine, but still. It made me wonder.

Andy Chastain... Andy du Payne.

"Yeah, maybe," I muttered to no one but myself.

Determined to ignore Andy for the moment, I flipped back to Rick's email and began reading over what little info he had found on Abby.

After pausing long enough to take in and smell my irises, I fired up my laptop and Maps.

A simple search for the To Fish Foundation gave me the same satellite image Abby had texted. Only now I could zoom in.

Focusing first on the strange ring of trees surrounding the property, I realized whatever the fauna was it was both dense and leafy. The meandering line of light greenish-yellow was uniformly tight. No stray trees had sprouted anywhere outside its neatly formed perimeter. But unable to discern anything further about what it was, I moved on.

Concentrating next on the biggest structure, I was surprised to see that the main residence was fairly octagonal in its overall shape. A veranda stretched around several of its outer sides, most of which led to a large garden of landscaped flowers. And while a cobblestone driveway looped around a large, circular fountain offset in front of the house, a second snaked its way to the rear where, based on the dimensions, a ten-car garage appeared to be inset, perhaps even under a portion of the house.

Yet nothing was as impressive as the enormous swimming pool in the center of it all.

Completely surrounded by the house, the private wading area was an absolute oasis. With a waterfall grotto and an actual sand-strip beach serving as bookends to the Olympic size pool between them, I counted no less than four palm trees with two hammocks stretched between them and a pair of cabanas among the lounge chairs arranged along its sides. And that was in addition to the large outdoor cooking and living areas occupying the remaining space.

Allowing my eyes to briefly calculate the mental geometry, I realized a house at least four times the size of my own could fit in Victor's pool area with plenty room to spare. *Damn.*

Zooming out, I slid the image over before focusing back in to examine the rest of the property.

The five other homes on the far side were large but nowhere near as spectacular. Each had a pool and plenty of privacy and while two had yards, the other three were secluded by woods. All were fairly close to a few other nondescript buildings in the very center of the entire property near what appeared to be a barn and a horse field, both adjacent to a large pond. Everything looked normal.

But zooming back out and sliding around it wasn't long before I noticed something odd.

Grabbing my phone, I called Abby… who of course called me back via video.

"Can't you just answer the phone like a norma—never mind," I caught myself, a bit too late.

"You'd think for someone so smart sooner or later you'd get it," Abby replied.

"You're home?"

"I am and I want to ask you something. I'm looking at the satellite image for the To Fish Foundation—"

"—Holy crap, Victor told you who he works for?"

"Yes."

"Damn. You're good."

"Yeah, well I'm not good enough to figure something out. Where's the entrance?"

Abby grinned. "You see it, too, huh? Or don't see it I guess would be more accurate."

"No, I don't. I don't see any way to drive through that ring of... whatever that is. What are they? Trees?"

"It's Golden bamboo. You know, the fishing pole type? Those there are about twenty feet tall."

"What?" I peered at the image closer. "How can you tell?"

"Are you looking at the same picture I showed you earlier?"

"I am."

"Look in the top left corner. See where the ring cuts outside the tree line just a bit, closest to the power lines running at the far edge of the property?"

"I do."

"That's where you can see the bamboo from the highway, further to the left."

'*See the bamboo from the highway?'* "You drove out there?"

"Yeah."

"Why?"

"Because like you I couldn't find the entrance either. That, plus not knowing what that weird tree ring was were both bugging me. So I went there and tried to kill two birds with one stone. But I only got one. I still have no idea where the entrance is. As you can see the taller trees eventually obscure all the other driveways. I guess there could be a break in the ring in one of the spots where the line disappears beneath the trees, but you'll never be able to tell from this picture."

I was silent for a few seconds. Humbled. *Wow.*

"You really went out of your way to try and vet Victor for me, huh?"

"Well, it's not like I could get him to sit down and tell me his life story the way Greg and I did with you... Speaking of which, did you eventually tell him about us?"

I inhaled. In all the years I had known Greg and Abby, I had never met anyone that knew about their BDSM lifestyle. They were extremely low-key about it so to have been given permission to reveal that fact to someone wasn't just an honor. It was a privilege.

"I did," I said reverently. "But only that you were once my patients. Any conversation about the lifestyle I'd rather have with him in person... You and Greg really like him that much, huh?"

Abby nodded. "We do. I might be a little weirded out by the lack of available information on him, but based on everything we know, yeah, we both like him. Which reminds me, last night at Mickey's? That wasn't just the most fun I've seen *you* have in a long time, that was also the most fun I've ever seen Victor have. I mean it, you two were totally different people. It was kinda nice to see."

I was a bit shocked. I knew what she was trying to say about me. Even by my own admission I'd been a stick in the mud for the last year. But Victor?

"How was *he* different?"

Abby shrugged. "Victor's usually far more reserved. Stoic even. I've never really seen him speak unless spoken to and even then, he doesn't speak much. I mean, he's not anti-social, he's just—"

"—not that social?"

"Exactly. And it looked like you brought out the best in one another is all I'm saying."

I felt myself blush. "Thanks."

"You're welcome. Now, if you could just get him to reveal the entrance to his bat cave..."

Hmmmm. "That might be easier done than said," I said before meeting Abby's eye. "Victor offered to show me around when he returns."

"Did he now?" Abby feigned impression. "And what all, pray tell, did the good doctor do to secure such an invitation?"

Arching my eyebrow, I reached past my laptop to pull the vase of flowers forward for Abby to see. Then I smiled as her jaw dropped.

"I don't know," I preened. "But I must have done it right."

Beginning my descent into Kansas City, I turned off my phone and tried to refocus my mind before running through my checklist.

If there was one thing listening to Bella's podcast for the last hour and a half had taught me it was that there was always something to laugh at in between learning something new pertaining to sex. Given my time constraints, I figured it would be best to skip forward and sample random snippets as often as I could over the next two months. While Bella didn't seem to talk about herself all that much, I hoped to get lucky every now and again, gleaning whatever insight she inadvertently made available.

Considering the degree to which I knew she would fail if and when she ultimately tried to research me, I resolved to atone for the discrepancy as much as possible the next time we met.

I only hoped the irises were a good start for now.

Turning off my laptop two hours later, I couldn't help but exhale my disappointment. Abby had been right. Despite running multiple searches, there was very little information anywhere on the internet concerning one Victor René Maxwell. True, his poker stats and by extension the cities to which he had traveled to play in tournaments were public record. But by 2011 it was as if he had dropped off the map. Even after resurfacing two years later as founder and executive director of the To Fish Foundation, there was virtually nothing out there on him.

And even less about his employers.

Due to its private non-profit status, it came as no surprise that reporting requirements for the To Fish Foundation were far less stringent than for those that accepted public donations. But trying to run down who actually funded the charity was a series of false starts leading to dead ends, all of which was extremely frustrating because based on how the foundation was organized at least certain parts of their financials should have been publicly available. Yet none were. In fact, the best source I could find was the foundation's own website which was about as bare bones as they came.

Established by Victor in 2013 under the To Fish umbrella, the Charlotte office still served as the main headquarters. But the following year a sister branch, the Two Fish Foundation, was set up in Wilmington, Delaware by someone named Joey Dahl. Then in 2015 a third office, the Too Fish Foundation, based out of Henderson, Nevada was created by a Joseph Beveaux.

Incredibly though, there was even less personal information on the net concerning either man than there was for Victor. No social media posts, no public mentions in any local news articles, not even a listing in the online white pages. The two were even more of a ghost than Victor.

Even more perplexing, I found it odd that Joey and Joseph were listed as the only members of the To Fish Foundation's board of directors while Victor had apparently been demoted to serve as executive director of the organization he created. Of course, I knew money talked. So it stood to reason if Joey and Joseph were the foundation's primary benefactors—even if they joined later—for them to be listed first made sense. What didn't was who they were and after two hours of searching with so little to show for it, I was beyond frustrated with trying to find out.

So... *That's enough for tonight.*

Resigning myself to the unknown for the moment, I took one last look at Victor's irises before heading to bed. I considered taking the vase with me so the flowers would be the first thing I saw when I woke. But I knew I had a stop to make first.

Pausing outside my spare bedroom door, I briefly questioned whether I should before turning the knob and flipping on the light... revealing the most eclectic room in my home. While the standard queen bed, nightstands and desk were the only things taking up floor space, the walls were almost completely covered by my favorite puzzles.

Framed jigsaws I had completed over the years of the *Mona Lisa,* the Virgin River Narrows, Dali's *Persistence of Memory,* Venezuela's Angel Falls, the Taj Mahal and about a dozen others served as the only decor. My parents slept here whenever they visited and strange though it may have appeared to anyone else, I knew my puzzles made them nostalgic. Of course, the family portrait of the three of us they had made for me to assemble when I was seven was their favorite.

But the tablet propped on its stand on the desk was mine.

Pulling out the desk chair I plopped down, fired up the iPad Pro, opened my jigsaw app and did my best to ignore the obvious... that putting puzzles together was the closest thing to an addiction I had ever experienced. Both crutch and solace, puzzles were the safe place I had run to whenever another child was mean to me, usually because I had such a difficult time relating to anyone.

My early childhood visual acumen, such as it was, had been explained to me in numerous ways over the years. None stuck more so than being told I had eyes like an eagle. And while I was old enough to understand that being bird-brained was a pejorative, I was assured in my case it was a compliment. Just not by any of my peers.

Back then puzzles offered me an escape from all of my youthful problems, a way to disassociate, calm and rebalance my emotions by restoring a natural order to an artificially created disorder. Only now, organizing random pieces on a screen provided me the parallel avenue I needed to properly arrange my thought process.

Using a tablet was far more efficient and less cluttered than working on an actual puzzle and in mere seconds I was in an all-too-familiar zone. Piling the pieces by color while separating those for the frame, my thoughts began to drift, swimming in a sea of questions while my fingers mindlessly swiped left and right as I began to do what I sometimes did best, overthink things.

Because Victor hadn't immediately said yes, I had to wonder did he really not want what I was offering him? Or did he just not want it from me? Was there a specific incident in his past that left him so internally scarred it manifested as an unhealthy self-restraint of his own desires and actions? Or was his adherence to some overly restrictive moral code he seemed to possess simply such a successful coping mechanism that it was his default setting?

Whatever the answers, the behavioral psychologist in me knew I shouldn't be surprised. There was a range and a limit to what was normal even when it came to something as diverse as sex. Among humans, no common behavior deviated more widely and despite how different Victor was, I knew we all had our limits.

But I also knew that in both an overall as well as a specific sense, I was offering Victor what many men wanted: unlimited, on-demand sex. I'd never say no to virtually anything and he knew it. So what more could he want? *What does a man like Victor— There are no men like Victor. We're all— Answers. He wants answers. The same as I do.*

Rolling my eyes, I took a deep breath. I was overcomplicating simple things for no good reason. More worrisome, in the back of my mind I also wondered what a man who apparently cherished his privacy might think of a woman who had spent so many years voluntarily giving up her own. Granted, like most psychologists I was notoriously stingy when it came to revealing too much about myself. But unlike most, I had gone far more public in putting myself out there. Although I no longer was, I wasn't sure how Victor would feel when he realized the degree to which I had.

Tossing my head back, I cracked my neck. I had every piece to the puzzle's frame separated so only about three minutes left before I was done for the night. As my fingers continued to fly, I felt the rush begin. Even with just the frame, there came a moment when all the pieces and separate sections I'd been working on suddenly started coming together, faster and faster, like an approaching orgasm. The kind of moment that gave me mixed feelings when, lost among the fever and excitement, a subtle melancholy began to creep in as I became aware the end of the puzzle was near. And while all I wanted to do was go back to the beginning, the best I could do was philosophize about it.

Starting with the acknowledgement that it was not my fault.

Because I was born with off-the-chart visual acuity, I literally could not help being detail-oriented. If there was the slightest discrepancy in pigment, texture, pattern, shade, anything, I spotted it. Not only did nothing escape my notice, nothing compared to the thousand little *Aha! Gotcha!* moments of both pairing and making the perfect match when putting together a puzzle. It wasn't a thrill just to find the right piece but also to finally put it in its place, with the uniquely progressive highs always propelling me to search for the next piece and the next and the...

I could stop myself, of course. I wasn't addicted to that degree. But it never took long before I didn't want to and the minutes became hours. In fact, I shuddered to think of how many days, perhaps even entire *weeks* of my life I had wasted putting puzzles together. Of course, even when I did it was of little consolation to acknowledge that I had actually achieved my goal of obtaining a firsthand understanding of addiction.

It had allowed me to know what it felt like to feel helpless. Hopeless. Lost.

Embarrassed.

It had allowed me to know what it felt like to have a one-track mind and experience a complete loss of willpower as I found or made whatever excuse necessary to continue feeding for as long as possible the very addiction I had purposefully created. To try and convince myself *Just one more piece* or *Just one more section... and then I'll stop.*

Worse still, despite the different focus of our obsessions, I felt my ability to honestly empathize with my patients contributed immensely to my professional success. The notion that former addicts made for better therapists, at least to me did *seem* to literally be true. Unfortunately, believing the intentional destruction of my favorite form of escapism was for the greater good only made my sacrifice moderately easier to bear.

Thankfully though, my addiction never included the compulsion to start which made my particular situation more akin to being a lifelong alcoholic despite decades of successful sobriety. While I retained complete control over whether I sat down to begin solving a puzzle or not, once I started one my willpower to stop was lost. Eventually though, much like an alcoholic succumbing to a blackout, I would lay my tablet down as soon as I had become sufficiently disgusted with myself for failing once again to overcome my weakness.

True, I had quit cold turkey more times than I could count. But since the subject of my addiction was so unlike any other, I couldn't bring myself to consider cold turkey a barometer of success. In my mind, I wouldn't be completely cured until I could once again solve a puzzle while simultaneously maintaining control, retaining the ability to quit at any given moment.

Only I didn't have that yet and hadn't for a very long time.

With the frame done I shut down my tablet and headed for my bedroom as the same old dated images began playing back in my head. Intentionally grabbing my tablet and starting a new puzzle every time I felt the least bit anxious. Segregating the pieces to the frame until I had sifted through every single one of the thousand and twenty-four.

Then separating the four sides. Building each. Putting them together. Checking to see if I had beat my best time in the jigsaw app's counter. Then and only then would I stop.

And just like that, another twenty minutes of my life wasted. Another twenty spent without a lick of control. And the only problem? It still worked. I could actually feel my blood pressure lower each time as I zoned out the way avid readers do when lost in a good book. My anxiety would disappear while my focus, clarity of thought and determination returned as my mind finally became ordered enough again to think properly in the process.

Brushing my teeth, I pondered my dilemma for the umpteenth time as I avoided looking at myself in the mirror. In all honesty, I knew I needed to seek help. But from whom? Despite being trained not to judge, my colleagues were every bit as human as I was. Professionally they might be able to help but privately they would definitely have a laugh. Not that I would blame them. After all, what kind of person develops an uncontrollable urge to put together jigsaw puzzles?

Of course, I could always lie, say I had developed my addiction accidentally. But I knew my patients were shortchanging themselves by not being completely honest with me and I had no desire to do the same... *No.* That wasn't it.

I was too ashamed to do so.

I stood my toothbrush up along the back of the counter in the same position I left it... much like myself. Still addicted. Still lacking the willpower to begin to overcome my problem. Still too proud to do anything about it. Not that it mattered. No one and nothing was being hurt but my inner pride.

Determined as always to address the issue sometime in the future, I pushed the thought from my mind as I crawled into bed happy that at least for tonight my excuse for delay had an addendum. And his name was Victor Maxwell.

Snuggling my heating blanket tighter around my body and feet as images of Victor and I having sex replayed in my head, somehow I still had enough wherewithal to allow myself to dream.

Hmmmmmm. Dr. Bella Maxwell...

II

Sex *n* **1 :** *either of two divisions into which organisms are grouped according to their reproductive roles or the qualities which differentiate them* **2 :** *copulation.*

Friday
February 7, 2020
6:55pm, 27° & cloudy

Sitting at the restaurant's dining table alone, I waited for my waiter to walk away before releasing a huge sigh of relief I didn't realize I had been holding back. With a full two-thirds of my identities and their tax implications now completely reconciled with the IRS I had to admit… I was actually making out okay.

Victor Maxwell's had taken the longest, of course, but since it was the one I had used the most that only made sense. Thankfully, my lawyers and I were done with that third well before I left Charlotte. If my rectification of Joseph Beveaux's tax records went as well starting next week in Vegas as Joey Dahl's had gone here in Kansas City, I'd be home free four weeks from today.

And better yet, I'd be back with Bella.

With time to kill waiting for my medium-well ribeye to arrive, I pulled some paperwork from my briefcase to recheck some numbers before Monday rolled around then plugged in my AirPods to listen to another podcast. No matter how many I had heard so far, I couldn't get enough.

Every time I tuned in, before I had the opportunity to digest Bella's words the sound of her voice reminded me yet again of how undeniably special the woman truly was. Knowing that her recordings were up to four years old made me realize that Bella had long been the type of person possessed by that certain je ne sais quoi which other people gravitated toward. Each and every broadcast, she just seemed to ooze that rare but natural *it* factor so few human beings had. The kind so easy to detect yet difficult to define.

Whether it was calmly knowing just how and when to have her guests laughing at all the right moments or empathizing with her callers as she spun their negatives into positives, Bella always found a way to connect with people no matter their station or problem in life. And I had to admit, though I was a bit jealous, her camaraderie with Andy was extraordinarily good.

Through almost a month of listening—during which I covered the first season and a half of her podcasts—it was clear not only had the two been friends before the show started, but that their relationship had grown even closer along the way. And their time on the show seemed to play a big part in that.

Their deliveries and responses to one another became so instantaneous it often felt like listening to someone talk back and forth with their self. And while that also allowed them to cover a lot of ground in a short amount of time, their best comedic moments were those most unscripted.

Returning from their affiliate-sponsored breaks, every so often the two had a habit of going on-air a little earlier than expected, as if they had mistimed the delay of the live podcast. While some listeners were suspicious simply because Andy's filter was still engaged, I wasn't so sure. From what I could tell, they genuinely seemed to be caught off-guard. Regardless, to hear pieces of their private, unfiltered conversations were at times hilariously revealing.

Much like the one I picked up on as I waited for my meal.

"Look," Andy's voice boomed after the commercial, "I'm just not into ropes, okay? I'm just weird like that."

"Hey, I'm not judging," Bella replied. "And trust me, if there's one thing my line of work has taught me, it's that everyone is weird in one way or another."

"Right?" Andy agreed before pausing. "Of course, I will admit the whisk sounds like fun."

"I don't know. Maybe with the right ma—"

"—Aaaaand we're back," Andy announced.

"Oh… Welcome back everyone," Bella said, recovering smoothly and continuing as if nothing had happened. "Thank you for sticking with us—"

"—And speaking of sticky—"

"—That's right, because as I said before the break, our next segment is all about... the cumshot. What's it made of and how to do something about it. So let's start with the basics. By now I'm sure you all have heard the snickering about sperm being a good source of protein... But have you ever really asked yourself just how much?"

"I know I haven't."

"Would you believe an average of fifteen grams per serving? That's about two and half times the amount in a large raw egg."

"Yeah, but I'll bet one's always going to taste a lot worse than the other, huh?"

"That's right, Andy. And while there's not much anyone can do about the taste of a raw chicken egg, there's plenty you guys can do about the taste of your huevos rancheros."

Andy chuckled. "Yeah, I can't begin to tell you the number of times a woman has told me the chocolate coating makes it go down easier."

"Yes, well, not everyone prefers vanilla latte creamer in their light roast coffee like I do."

"French?"

"Madagascar."

"Why can't I ever remember that?"

"It's okay, the important thing is you try. And for all my listeners out there, if you'd like to try, too, here's what you can do to put a little fizz in your jizz. First off, know that—and this part should *come* as no surprise—"

"—Nice one—"

"—Thank you. I felt it apropos—the majority of cum's terrible taste is due to the presence of toxins. The good news is these can be eliminated simply by refraining from things like cigarettes and alcohol. But if you want to completely flush them from your system, exercising regularly can also help clear your body of most of those residual contaminants.

"Then, once you've gotten rid of the bad, you can start to toss in some good. Cinnamon, lemon, parsley, peppermint and wheatgrass are all great sweeteners, but if you really want to kick it up a notch, incorporate some naturally sugary fruits into your diet. Pineapple, blueberries, plums and kiwis are known to work best. If you don't believe me, just ask anybody who's been with a Hawaiian man."

"Is that why Don Ho was so popular?" Andy asked.

"Don who?"

"Oh, my God, just forget I said anything."

"Ohhhh-kaaaaay... Where was I—Oh, that's right. Cranberries and other foods which aid in balancing pH levels also improve semen. As does drinking more water and alkalizing your body."

"What about celery?" Andy asked. "I've read some pornstars swear by it. Is that why?"

"Actually, celery is most likely eaten to increase the *volume* of their loads. And considering it's more or less just thick water, that makes sense. But celery is also loaded with vitamin C which is good for ridding the body and semen of salt. Not to mention, while we're at it, cutting out red meat can rid a man of his salty taste, too.

"As for other bad foods to avoid, anything high in sulfur like broccoli, cabbage and cauliflower, while yes healthy for you, *won't* help your flavor. So it's probably best to enjoy those in moderation. The same goes for caffeine, processed foods, onions, garlic and asparagus, which can all lead to a bitter taste. In fact, if it's bad for your breath, it's bad for your partner's as well. If you know what I mean."

"No gargling with garlic goo. Got it."

Bella sighed. "Andy, what would I do without you?"

"Awwww. You flatter me, Doc—"

"—That's not what I mea—"

"—But I know my place. Around here you're the star and I'm just a glorified sex trophy."

"Sex trophy?" Bella sounded confused. "Is that like the trophy wife of someone's sex life?"

"Not exactly. But even if it was why can't it mean the trophy *husband* of your sex life? Why do women get to be the only people regarded as a trophy in a relationship?"

"Probably because there are so few men out there worthy of being called a trophy in the first place?" Bella retorted.

Andy fell quiet for a respectful second. "I take it your blind date didn't go so well last night?"

Though half engrossed in a slew of five and sometimes six figure number crunching, I was suddenly all ears. Roughly seventy-five podcasts in, Bella's personal life had been discussed so rarely that the barest mention was all it took to grab my full attention. But I refused to get my hopes up. I'd been let down too many times already.

"Do you know how some guys can't keep their hands to themselves?" she asked. "This one couldn't do that with his feet."

Andy was shocked. "What?! On the first date? That's not right. Everybody knows there's a mandatory three date minimum for some foot play."

"Yes, well, I guess some guys are just premature," Bella said sarcastically before her tone turned sweet. "Which leads us to our first return caller of the evening. Hello, Doug and welcome back."

The podcast's phone line clicked live followed by an enthusiastic male voice.

"Hi, Doc! Thanks for taking my call again!"

I chuckled. Doug sounded young and immature. And definitely a bit too happy for a phone-in.

"Well, thank you for calling back. Now, for those of you not tuned in last week, Doug called to discuss a problem he has suffered from all his life—premature ejaculation—which, according to estimates, one in four men experience at least once during some point in their lives. Those who live with the condition can understandably feel a great deal of anxiety and stress, even embarrassment. And as you might imagine, this kind of emotional turmoil can manifest itself throughout other areas of their lives leading to feelings of complete helplessness and a total lack of control—"

"—Not that they had any in the first—"

"—Annnnndy—"

"—My bad, Doc."

Bella exhaled her tolerance in a sigh. "It's okay. But even better, it's okay for Doug and others like him because as I said last week, today there are many, extremely effective, all-natural products on the market that truly can and do help with this particular ailment. In fact, I told Doug about one last week—royal honey jelly—and I'm hoping, Doug, you're calling back in with a progress report?"

"Oh no, Doc, the other night my girlfriend and I bypassed 'progress' at the thirty second mark. I'm calling you with a hundred percent, mission accomplished report!"

"That's great, Doug."

"Yeah, it is! I mean the first time we had sex I lasted a full five minutes!"

"Get 'em, tiger," Andy chuckled.

"Hell, yeah!" Doug continued, undeterred. "Shoot, the second time I almost made it twice that. My girl didn't know what hit her, but it was me! Well, me and that royal honey jelly, anyway."

Crowd noise cued up by Andy suddenly cheered Doug's accomplishment before fading out.

"Doug," Bella asked, "did you start with the ten-gram packets like I suggested?"

"Yup, I did exactly like you said."

"Well, if you didn't suffer any allergic reactions *and* you think you could handle it, I think you can safely consider stepping up to the twenty-gram dosage should you decide to order more."

"Oh, I don't know, Doc. I might be able to handle it, but I'm not sure about my girlfriend. It's like I said last week, you have no idea how bad my premature ejaculation has always been. I mean the first time a girl put her hand down my pants my spooge was already turning cold by the time she actually touched my dick."

Silence filled the air as Bella was obviously at a loss for words.

"So you were as fast as they come is what you're saying," Andy offered.

"Andy," Bella warned. "Be nice."

"That is nice. If I was being mean I'd have said Doug was once a no pump chump."

"Harsh... but fair," Doug agreed.

"See, Doc? Real recognize real, don't it, Dougie?"

"Yeah, boyeeeeeee!"

I shook my head. Some days I just wanted to weep for our species. *If only it was worth—*

"Okay, so who had the rib-eye?"

Startled, I looked over my shoulder to find an attractive female server smiling at me as she held a tray with my meal. I noticed her passing my table and smiling a few times over the last quarter hour. I'd smiled politely back but did my best to ignore her just as I had during the other three visits I'd made over the last month. But since I was the only one at the table all I could do now was smile again at her obvious joke.

"That would be mine," I said as I did my best to appear unaware of her flirt. "Thank you."

Keeping our small talk to a professional minimum I was glad when she went away. I wasn't in the market, but I was in the mood. I hadn't busted a nut in a month and my condition was starting to get to me. But as long as a wet dream didn't claim it first, I was saving myself until I got home for Bella.

Grabbing my knife and fork I started working out my frustration on my steak. I rarely ate red meat but there was no way I could pass up a few rib-eyes while in Kansas City. And with everyone in such an overly friendly mood because of their football team's winning streak—especially given their last game—I was really going to miss the place.

But when my server walked by and smiled again for no reason, I started chewing a little faster.

Yeah, I gotta get outta here, I thought as I turned the rest of them back toward Bella. *Just one more month... one more...*

I couldn't wait any longer. And lucky for me, not only was I already naked, it was close enough to my usual bedtime.

Turning my heating blanket on, I pulled back the comforter and climbed into bed beneath both. With my head and back propped by pillows, I closed my eyes then slowly began touching myself, my heart racing slightly ahead of my hands as they reached for my breasts.

Small, almost imperceptible tingles began to build within me, spreading out as they simultaneously cascaded down my arms to my fingertips, through my legs to my toes and across my stomach to my groin. Altogether the effects made me flush, causing all of my finest hairs to stiffen, each of which further forced me to become hyper aware of my body whether I wanted to or not.

But oh, how I wanted to.

Pressing my palms up and over the undersides of my breasts, I continued their journey until my nipples were directly beneath their centers. Gathering my fingers inward, I narrowed them together so my thumb and index could give each nub a brief, teasing tug. Loving how I could always count on their manipulation to quickly turn me on, I continued to massage myself all over for several seconds, allowing firm rubs to taper off into light caresses before ramping up the intensity again, over and over, a little higher and stronger each time.

Exploring my body, my hands slowly took on a life of their own as they tried to keep up with the growing needs of my various parts. Screaming for attention and desperate to be touched, their anticipation and subsequent relief, no matter how temporary, quickly began to spiral into an overload of stimulation. Struggling to maintain a steady pace yet no longer able to ignore my pussy's aching demand for attention, my right hand finally had to head south.

The first touch of my clitoris sent a small shockwave of euphoria through me which triggered my first internal clench, a flexing just inside my walls. Pausing for a second to enjoy the sensation, I began to rub myself more vigorously as my entire body reacted. Ultra-sensitive to the pace, my left hand steadied against the mattress as my right quickened my four fingertip circular motion atop my pelvis, just above my clit, increasing the tingling sensations that continued to travel up inside me.

Worked up to my highest degree of horniness thus far, when my calves started to reflex a few seconds later, I couldn't help but lean into myself. Needing something, anything, I reached out, my left hand grabbing onto whatever was available. A pillow. The comforter and heating blanket. Even my own flesh.

As my pace continued to quicken, I tried to relax into the sensation so that it could take over... but I couldn't. Instead, I had to fight my own urges, the clenching and holding both in and outside my body. Switching to use the press of my middle finger only, I concentrated the energy directed at my clit until the tingling moved even deeper within. Of course, using just one finger allowed me to feel my wetness far more easily. And my wetness now reminded me of only one thing.

Which was when my fantasizing started to assume control.

Allowing the black canvas of my mind to fill itself with images of Victor's hands came so easily. Their overall shape. The different lengths of his nice, self-manicured fingers. The smooth texture of his skin. His fine blonde hairs that were virtually unnoticeable... and the healthy, meandering bulge of his veins that definitely weren't.

While the memory failed to compare to the reality, slowing down and caressing myself helped and gave me enough time to conjure several moments when Victor had leisurely run his hands across my body in between our acts of actually having sex. Then, as now, he had put me into a state of simultaneously relaxed yet excited ecstasy to the point where I couldn't tell if he was responding to my body's wants... or creating them just to give himself the chance to fulfill them.

Either way, my mind continued to drift.

Murmuring to myself, I knew I had never had someone get to know me so well, so fast. Never had a man purposefully listen to my body while also being naturally attuned to it the way Victor had been. It had taken me twenty-nine years to meet a man like him. Would I one day meet another? Perhaps. I was still young enough. And if my patients had taught me anything it was that it was never too late in life for almost anything.

But at the moment I didn't want to ever experience the need to try and find another.

I just wanted Victor... just as much... as I wanted him... to want...

Meeeeee...

The wave of ecstasy took me by surprise as my body regained control over my mind. I had sensed the buildup in my background. I was still in a state of pre-orgasmic bliss but suddenly in even more need of relief. Alternating back and forth between the indirect pressure of all four fingertips and the direct contact of just one, I felt both my wetness and warmth increase.

Rubbing myself incrementally faster, I would get so close to coming, couldn't, then had to relax in an attempt to refocus. Then the ever wider circles I made began to be interrupted by further loss of control as my hand became erratic. Intermingled with my usual motion, I turned some of my massages downward, running completely over my clit before pulling back up. Out of sync, it still felt good yet when I couldn't handle the buildup but also couldn't come, I found myself switching to using just one finger sliding slowly through my slit followed by several circular motions using all four fingers, winding tighter and tighter with both techniques centered solely on my swelling button. Again and again I did this with the duration between each shorter each time as I pressed harder and harder until finally I was there.

That final moment just before orgasm when the level of wetness and heat right behind my clit suddenly reached their highest levels allowing me to come.

Like a huge wave crashing against my shore and washing higher through me, every last vestige of tension that had built within me was suddenly released.

All the pin pricks in my fingers, legs and body, even my calves, everywhere that had been tight from clenching became relaxed as the wave subsided before rushing back out to sea.

Drained of energy, I felt momentarily sleepy, a sensation interrupted only by anything touching me which caused a short, gentle burst of renewed tension that quickly released again, pairing itself with a light twitch... until they, too, were gone.

Relaxing for several seconds, I finally pulled the comforter around me, turned over onto my side, bunched my pillow... beneath my head... and then... so... was... I.

Monday
February 10, 2020
6:17pm, 59° & partly cloudy

I set my glass of Johnny Walker Blue Label on the nightstand before plopping down on the D Suite's king-size bed. Tucking an extra pillow behind my head I tried to relax and decompress. Despite flying into Atlantic Aviation's Las Vegas FBO early last night I was still more than a little jetlagged. Sleepy like it was past my bedtime already, my body felt every minute of the gain in an hour I had forced upon it. Given my desire for more time in this world, the irony felt facetiously poetic.

Of course, my lack of familiarity with the hotel didn't help much either. Normally I stayed on the Strip whenever I visited Vegas but since this trip was strictly business and the D Hotel was within walking distance of the office building I'd be visiting for the next four weeks, the choice was a no-brainer. Plus, I always seemed to run lucky whenever I played poker back in the day at Fitzgerald's, the D's predecessor. But no matter how good I was currently running, going up against the IRS I'd still take all I could get.

Massaging my temples to the contrary, I was actually pretty pleased. My first day here dealing with Joseph Beveaux's tax issues had gone better than expected, much the same as had my entire month in Kansas City taking care of Joey Dahl's. Of course, a lot of that wasn't just because I had done very little wrong. In fact, when all was said and done there was an overall possibility the IRS would owe me a refund. *Would* if not for whatever fine they were ultimately going to levy against me.

But I'd take it because as expensive as it was probably going to be, one way or another I always knew this day would come. No, money wasn't the issue. I was more than prepared to pay the piper. I just wasn't sure going public would be worth it. Only time would tell. And with Bella in the mix—

Despite my trepidation, the sudden thought of her in my life at this juncture made me smile.

Not once in the last month had she inquired where I was or what I was doing. Not that it would have mattered. I could have lied about what I had going on just as she could about whatever she had back in Charlotte. Instead, we both just seemed to implicitly trust one another.

Even so, I made sure we stayed in frequent contact with a short text or call first thing in the morning and last at night along with a random couple throughout the day whenever the mood hit me. And thankfully enough, Bella always seemed to enjoy returning the favor.

Missing her, I pulled my phone out and resumed her podcast from where I last left off.

"So, before we begin wrapping up our show," Bella cooed apologetically, "it's time to take a question or two from our chatroom. I'd like to thank those of you who submitted your queries for tonight's Q&A. This segment is one of our more popular and without you it just wouldn't be the same... So, Andy. How many listeners asked a question this evening?"

"A hundred fifty-seven," Andy boomed.

"Wow! One hundred and fifty-seven. It seems just yesterday we were lucky to get seven."

"Speaking of getting lucky, last night—"

"—Noooobody wants to hear about another random airhead you were able to con into going back to your apartment. This is a Q&A not a T&A segment."

"Yeah, but it's a Q&A that's all about T&—"

"—Just the same. Now give me question number... forty-two."

Andy sighed before deadpanning. "Douglas Adams' fans rejoice... Question number forty-two comes from loser—"

"—What did I tell you about denigrating our—"

"—Sorry, sorry *user*name... Jillian Mehoff."

Bella remained silent for a second. "Wow, what a classy twist on a trashy classic. Which reminds me, it's been a while since we've heard from any of our Hughs."

"I believe the proper pronunciation now is 'Yuuuuuge.'"

"Never. And just for those few listeners who might not know, jilling is to ladies what jacking is to lads... although I'm sure most of you are smart enough to have figured that out."

"I'm a little ashamed to admit that I've never heard the expression," Andy chimed back in. "But I'm not ashamed to say I *like* it."

"Which I'll bet doesn't *come* as a surprise to anyone."

"You did that on purpose."

"Yes, I did. So, what's Jillian's question?"

Andy cleared his throat. "Jillian writes 'Dear Doc. You obviously possess enough intelligence to write a book about sex and sex addiction. Why did you choose to create a podcast instead?"

"First of all, thank you for the compliment, Jillian. And I hope you will be just as interested in buying a copy of my book after I someday write one because I do plan on it. Eventually."

"Spoken like a true writer," Andy quipped.

"But to be perfectly honest, at the moment I don't feel I have enough material experience—be it personal or professional—to comfortably write anything definitive about either subject that hasn't already been written. A podcast, on the other hand, is both different and easier. This format not only gives people an opportunity to share their experiences, we all get to have a little fun along the way. Speaking of which, who's game for a little experiment, a magic trick if you will?"

"Ooh-ooh-ooh! Me! Me! Me!" Andy broke in, shouting like an excited kid. "But not with the violet wand. You turned it up too high last time."

"Hmph. Don't you wish," Bella chuckled. "But don't worry, the only electricity involved this time will be everyone's shock at my awe as I show you a way to understand how *your* opposite sex thinks. Ready?"

"Go."

"Okay everyone, take a few seconds and figure out how many people you have slept with."

"A few seconds? Damn, Doc. How fast do you think some of us can count?"

"Do your best, Andy. And everyone else, do your best, too." Several seconds of dead air followed. "Okay," Bella continued. "Does everybody have a number in their head? Are you ready?"

"Ready or not! Here I—"

"—Annnnndy—"

"—Sorry, Doc. Yeah, I'm ready."

"Okay. Abracadabra. If you are a male your number ends in either a five or a zero. If you are a female, your number does not."

Silence again filled the air until—

"Damn, woman! What kind of sorcery is this?"

"Relax," Bella said calmly. "Breathe in, breathe out. It's not sorcery."

Andy paused. "Then... how did you know? I sure never told you—"

"—I simply played the odds. You see studies have shown when this question is posed to both men and women, 80% of males *estimate* their number of conquests, rounding to the nearest 5%. This is as opposed to the 80% of females who actually *count* each of their individual lovers. And since 80% of numbers do not end in either a five or a zero, there you go. But the numbers aren't the point.

"The point is, in a roundabout, *Men Are from Mars, Women Are from Venus* kind of way, *how* each gender answers that particular question is how the *opposite* gender typically thinks. It's how we solve problems. So, if you ask a guy how to get from one city to another, he'll usually tell you something like 'Go east on road A, then north on interstate B until you go...' You get the picture. He'll break the directions down road by road. But ask a female the same question and she'll more than likely say something like 'It's over that way, toward the beach.' Both answers are correct but as human beings we strive to be more accurate about the things that matter more to us.

"And *that's* the telling part. You see, women tend to take sex deeper to heart. We associate and conflate sex more with our feelings compared to men and in turn we are more selective about our partners because sex *matters* more to us. This is why we are willing to devote the time and energy to actually count our lovers. We want to be exact because it matters to us.

"Of course, if you pay any attention to global advertising, that might sound strange because even though the saying goes 'Sex sells,' let's be honest. It should say 'Sex sells *to men'* which gives the impression sex matters more to men. Which is true, but only superficially, which is what advertising is all about tapping in to—"

"—I know what I'd like to ta—"

"—See what I mean?"

"No. What?... Ohhhhh. Sorry, Doc."

"It's okay, Andy," Bella chuckled. "And that's because men like yourself, if you'll pardon me for stereotyping for a second, you by and large tend to take the Babe Ruth approach when it comes to women. The glory of having your name at the top of the charts is worth the ignominy of it also being at the bottom."

"Hold up, you lost me."

"In addition to being the home run king, Babe Ruth was also the strike out king. But no one talks about that."

Andy paused. "Huh. You think I'd know that."

"That's okay, too. But, speaking of things you'd think you'd know but probably don't, join us next week when we travel to beautiful—"

"—Brazil?!"

"Ohhhh. Wrong on both hemispheres. But that's what you get for not taking that right turn in Albuquerque. No, Southeast Asia. More specifically, Vietnam, where we're going to explore the joys of ear-picking."

"Ewwwww. I thought this was a podcast about sex."

"It is. So it just might interest you to know that there is actually a G-spot in our ears when, touched just right... Well, it's a G-spot. What do you think happens," Bella giggled.

"Hold up, hold up, hold up," Andy protested. "I mean I'll cop to feeling a really nice tickle from a Q-tip a time or two, but it's nothing like hitting the G-spot—"

"—Had your's hit a time or two now, have you?" Bella teased.

Andy paused. "No, but I've definitely hit that shit enough times to know... Hey, wait. You're right. Now that I think about it, I've been with a couple of freaks who damn near got off on that."

"Ughhhhhh," Bella moaned. "People are not freaks just because— you know what? Never mind."

Chuckling to myself I turned off the podcast. One month in and I'd learned no matter how much I thought I knew about sex, there was plenty I'd never heard nor dreamed of. I'd also gotten used to how by the end of the podcast,

Bella was typically at her wit's end with Andy.

And after a month of digging, so was I.

Although Andy Chastain was Facebook Friends with Greg and Abby, online he had no connection to Bella. The silhouetted picture of Andy du Payne I had first seen was also the only one that had ever seemingly been taken. And oddly enough, it was from Bella's final podcast.

While maintaining a chronological listening order I'd nevertheless allowed curiosity to get the better of me. Every so often I found myself investigating Andy Chastain a bit longer than I was proud to admit. Whether from unconscious jealousy or because he was simply the most likely candidate to be Andy du Payne, I couldn't shake wanting to learn as much about the guy as possible.

And I had to at least partially give him his due.

Chastain was more a commercial-gym lizard than your stereotypical meathead-and-potatoes-bro-gym bro. The pretty boy type who was all about looking good and posing even better. Which of course didn't make him a bad person. But it also didn't make him the type who seemed capable of coming across even momentarily the way Andy du Payne often did because at the risk of judging a book by its cover... Chastain just didn't appear to be that sharp.

Even more confusing, I couldn't reconcile his need for a second job. The only explanation I could come up with for his working a nine-to-five in addition to being co-owner of a small chain of exclusive fitness clubs... was that he didn't co-own all that much.

Massaging my temples until I regained enough energy I sat up and against my better judgment downed the remainder of my whisky. The semi-blasphemous guilt I felt for not taking the time to savor the taste was a small price to pay for helping to momentarily forget all about the two Andys as I turned to thoughts about what to do for dinner.

Going out held no appeal. While I typically had no problem with people staring at me because of my height, the thought of strolling down Fremont Street and getting gawked at by all the looky-loo tour-asses not to mention the character acts themselves was enough to give me a headache. And running down to one of the hotel's many restaurants meant risking another run-in with the casino's host who had cornered me upon arrival yesterday. Unfortunately for her I was no more in the mood for gambling now as I was then. Not that I could blame her for trying.

With professional football done for the year, the media's focus had turned to debating either the potential threat of the Wuhan virus or the political correctness of its label and seemingly not much else. Talk of quarantining patients inevitably led to speculation by the news network's talking heads that mass gatherings should be cancelled in order to effectively combat the spread or "flatten the curve" as they began to lockstep call it. And of course, with an increasingly obvious national shortage of N95 masks and terms like "pandemic" and "remote learning" working their way into the everyday vernacular, it was no surprise businesses within the entertainment and gambling industries were starting to get nervous. Lifeblood of Vegas or not, if America didn't get a handle on the virus casino shutdowns were imminent.

Deciding on the easiest way out, I dialed up and ordered room service then gave in to my paranoia and promptly washed my hands just in case. From what I had seen The D's cleaning staff had done an excellent job so far, going above and beyond to make sure my room's common surfaces were thoroughly disinfected. But with my date with Bella less than a month away, I didn't feel like taking any chances.

Stretching back out on the hotel bed while waiting for my food to arrive, I couldn't help but wonder what she was getting into tonight until I glanced at the clock.

Hmph. Probably bed.

Getting ready to turn in for the evening I found myself gazing into the bathroom mirror as I mindlessly brushed my hair out. I'd been daydreaming again and was surprised to suddenly see me coming back from a thousand-yard stare so long I easily saw past myself. With my makeup already off and my teeth cleaned, I shook my head to snap out of it, put the brush down and headed to bed.

My daydream had started like most had over the last month. Envisioning my first time back with Victor. Where and how it might go. Who would speak first.

What each of us might say. The possibilities at this point were endless... or so it seemed in my head.

I couldn't wait to touch Victor again. To feel his touch in return. To discover if his kiss still had the same passion for me or did it just stem from the one in his pants. Because although once upon a time that might not have mattered... now it did.

Whichever answer Victor ended up giving me about becoming my Master, the mere thought suddenly had my juices flowing and I needed a distraction in order to stop. I was still sore from having masturbated three times already using a new, wider vibrator I had ordered three weeks ago which had finally arrived in the day's mail. Shipping companies had so quickly begun prioritizing supplies for first responders to the coronavirus that all non-essentials had been pushed to the back of the line in order to make room.

Though how a vibrating dildo could ever be deemed non-essential...

I rolled my eyes before I began to seriously contemplate a fourth go-round, choosing instead to climb into bed and fire up my laptop as a diversion.

I'd actually spent a fair amount of time over the last month researching cryptocurrencies. From their history and various purposes to the current state of the market and future projections, I figured it might behoove me to get a better handle on something Victor not only seemed so interested in but also felt was so important.

Though personally, I was fascinated more by some of the crazier stories associated with the vast amount of wealth involved with many of the coins.

I couldn't get over the true story of the first transaction using bitcoin to pay for two large pizzas in May of 2010. At the time each coin was worth about $0.003, so with the pizzas costing $30 total, 10,000 were needed to pay for them. Of course, no pizza parlors were accepting bitcoin as payment so, after agreeing online, one guy offered to use his own cash to pay for the pizzas then personally deliver them to the buyer who happened to live in the same city. They then exchanged 10,000 bitcoin online from one crypto wallet to the other making it the first legitimate cryptocurrency purchase in history.

The thing was up until that moment bitcoins had no real usage for anything else, so no one had any idea if they were worth holding on to. But eventually they were.

In December of 2017, the price of one bitcoin reached its all-time high just shy of $20,000. Had the guy held on to his $30 worth of bitcoin for just seven and a half years, his holdings would have been worth almost $200 million. Meaning he had paid the equivalent of $100 million... per pizza!

Finally realizing just how much money could be made in cryptocurrency, I thought back to what Victor had said about buying his first bitcoins after poker's Black Friday. Not that I knew how much he initially purchased, but I began to wonder what the price of one was right around that time. I'd only held off investigating further because something about knowing the answer felt as if I might be violating his privacy.

But, with the overwhelming desire to get my mind off the even bigger one between my legs, I gave in and began to run the appropriate searches. While I couldn't find an exact breakdown of daily prices dating back that far, I did locate a monthly price chart for bitcoin for 2011... which made my jaw drop.

Victor had purchased his first crypto somewhere in the neighborhood of $0.75 each.

Struggling to do the math, I quickly calculated that every $20 of bitcoin he might have purchased would have netted him an easy $500,000 provided he had been able to hold on and not sell for about nine and a half years. *I guess you could say that's when I started to dabble,* I recalled him saying as my mind continued to blow.

Wondering what Victor might have been in the market to afford in 2011, I suddenly remembered what Abby said about him earning an easy six figures playing poker back then. The question was *how* much money would a guy pulling down *that* much money per year... consider to be dabbling? And more specifically, a guy like Victor?

With very little to go on, the memory of Victor paying for my drinks at Mickey's popped into my head. The nonchalant way he had passed enough cash to the bartender to cover my tab without really bothering to count it. Granted, it was only one example. But...

Damn. How much is Victor really worth?

Hearing myself think, I put my head in my hand before trying to bury it a bit further in my shame.

Priceless... that's how much.

Turning my laptop off, I suddenly felt the urge to do anything whatsoever to ignore my private embarrassment. Thankfully, I had just the thing.

Sunday
February 16, 2020
11:59 pm, 43° & cloudy

I couldn't sleep.

With society's increasing angst concerning the spread of Covid-19—as the news had begun calling it all week after taking their lead from the World Health Organization—not to mention my building excitement to see Bella again in less than three weeks, I figured trouble sleeping was to be expected. I just wasn't used to it.

Grabbing my phone off the nightstand, I briefly considered queueing up one of my favorite new segments of Bella's YouTube channel, "The Balls Of Ballin' Ballers." A bit ahead of my listening schedule because of all the delays and adjustments made necessary by the coronavirus, I'd watched parts of about a dozen or so episodes in the last few days and each one was a little more outrageous than the last.

The original installment had started accidentally enough with the podcast's first guest appearance. A starting point guard I had never heard of for a professional basketball team had joined Bella via video chat for a half hour discussion of what life was like on the road with groupies in every city at his beck and call. After regaling her audience with some truly bawdy stories, Andy—who'd been uncharacteristically quiet for almost the entire segment—decided to finally chime in.

Saying he wanted to talk about the pink elephant in the room, he asked if the reports were true. I had no idea what he was referring to but after a little digging later I discovered Bella's guest, while a senior standout in college, had to sit out his team's conference championship game. While the official reason given was a hamstring injury, rumors ran rampant at the time that he was suffering from the onset of elephantitis of the nuts. A rumor which the young man had always denied.

"But were you?" Andy had asked.

Shocked not just because she hadn't heard the story but because Andy had the audacity to ask, Bella apologized profusely and assured her guest he didn't have to answer. But as much of an asshole as Andy came across in that moment, he had also figured correctly. Enough years had passed. The point guard was older, more mature and had obviously reached that age when people truly cared less of what others thought about them. Plus, he was in the perfect setting. So, he finally admitted the truth. Yes, the towel in his lap as he rode the bench the whole game was really covering up the fact he had testicles the size of baseballs.

With very little fanfare that probably would have been the end of his and the podcast's story if not for the next night when he scored a career high triple-double during the last game of the season allowing his team to squeak into the playoffs for the first time in a decade. Interviewed court side afterward about what possessed him to play such lights out basketball, the point guard had a good laugh then gave thanks and an emphatic shoutout to Bella's podcast for helping relieve such a heavy weight off his shoulders that he had been tired of carrying around for far too long.

Not only did his nationally televised praise in front of a primetime audience help increase the size of Bella's listenership, it also prompted several other athletes to tune in, some of whom asked to be her guest because they wanted to one-up some of the point guard's craziest sex stories. Then too the timing worked out well as promotions for Bella's third season were already running, touting the upcoming launch of her new YouTube channel.

Of course, with the exception of the series finale which I had yet to watch, I was disappointed to learn that Andy stayed not just off-camera but also entirely off-set, choosing instead to remain a disembodied voice by dialing into the YouTube show each night. The same couldn't be said for Bella's guests because if there was one thing celebrity athletes loved more than being heard it was being seen.

But then a funny thing happened.

Shortly after each new interview, Bella's guests would inexplicably play one of the best games of their life, sometimes posting the kind of stats that broke team records. It didn't always happen on their first game following their appearance, but it did soon enough after for the pattern to be undeniable. And that's when other athletes—being an overly superstitious bunch—began to jump on Bella's bandwagon in droves.

Across all major sports, the celebrity status of Bella's special guest stars continued to rise higher, week after week. It didn't matter that few if any had an embarrassing admission of their own they wanted to reveal. Simply appearing via video chat on her show to tell some of the most unbelievable sex stories was enough to do the trick.

And thus "The Balls Of Ballin' Ballers" was born.

Of course, I did have one small problem with the segment. Before long some of the athlete's stories began to seem a little too contrived. Embellishing was one thing, but outright concocting was another. Making matters worse, my bullshit detector for them seemed to go off simultaneously with Andy's which made for an uneasy kinship I could live without.

Mentally restless yet a bit too tired for tall tales or awkward affinities, I opted instead to restart the last show right where I had left off.

Bella looked great as always, poised behind her desk with her hair up. Looking down at the monitor in front of her every so often instead of into the camera beyond it gave the impression she could actually see Andy even though her audience could not because of the way the screen was facing. It made for an interesting visual for a show that was based mostly on talk. A beautiful woman switching back and forth between talking to a bodiless computer and her invisible audience.

"But that's just me," I caught Andy's booming voice saying just after hitting play. "What about you, Doc? What turns you on?"

Immediately my ears perked up even though I knew better than to let my hope follow.

"Come now, Andy, you of all people should know a lady never tells."

"Well, do you at least like the taste?"

Bella paused for what sounded like an eternity. "I would not know."

"Don't you mean 'I do not know?'"

"Maybe," Bella smiled coyly. "Or maybe I just really like the word 'would.'

Which reminds me our next segment is about morning wood. So—seeing how you are the resident cock jock around here, Andy—why don't you start us off by telling us a little something about your morning wood."

"First, there's nothing little about it."

Bella huffed her doubt. "You're trying to say papí's packing, is he?"

"And second," Andy continued, uncharacteristically ignoring her for once, "even a little can be enough *if* you know how to use it right."

"It sounds like someone's compensating..." Bella sung slowly.

"It sounds like someone needs a little morning wood..." Andy sung back.

"Hey! Who's the shrink here?"

"The one who needs a little morning wood?"

Bella rolled her eyes. "You're not right."

"You're right," Andy agreed a little too amicably. "Maybe it's the one who needs *more* than a little morning wood?"

"Hey! I might be a lot of things, but I'm no size queen."

"What do you want to bet that nightstand drawer of yours begs to differ?"

Bella peered down indignantly into her screen. "What are you trying to say?"

"I'm saying when scrolling through vibrating dildos on Amazon you've never once thought to yourself, 'Oooooooh, now there's a nice looking four-incher.' That's what."

Bella looked mildly shocked. "Do they even make those?"

"How the hell would I know?"

"Oh, that's right. Hey, did you know vibrators are still illegal in Mississippi and Alabama?"

"No... but that would explain a lot."

"Andy, you need to stop insulting certain segments of our audience," Bella said to her computer before turning to address the main camera. "Folks, I apologize. And... I'd like to make it up to you with a joke. It's about this patient I once had, a guy who knew next to nothing about the male anatomy. In fact, it took me forever to explain to him that there was a vas deferens between his testicles and his penis..."

"Psychiatry jokes. Yeaaaaaaaaay..." Andy's voice trailed off like someone falling from a cliff.

"Oh, come on," Bella protested. "That was funny."

"Doc, any joke that makes you think that much isn't funny. You're smart enough to know that."

"Fine, then how about why are blondes always pissed when they get their driver's licenses?"

"Doc, I don't care if you are a blonde, this is how hate crimes star—"

"—Because they always get an 'F' in Sex."

Andy paused for a few seconds. "You know, it's ironic. When this show first started, I actually worried you might end up being ashamed to be associated with me."

"Why is that—Ohhhhh. You're trying to say my jokes are that bad, huh? Okay, how about this one? Do you know why it's okay to be addicted to the hokey pokey? Because eventually you just turn yourself around."

As quick as he could, Andy cued the drums and cymbal. *Buh, dum, dum, tinggggg!*

"You're no fun," Bella rolled her eyes.

"N—"

"—Not that it matters," Bella cut her cohost off, "because as I just remembered, according to our latest follower count, people think *we* make a great team."

"Is that so?"

"It is. In fact, during the week—between last Thursday's episode and tonight—we surpassed our first half a million followers on Twitter and I, for one, am honored. So, thank you, everyone. I promise to continue to do my best and be worthy of your time.

"Of course, I did not achieve this milestone alone. My name might be on the title, but I think everyone knows this is just as much Andy's show as it is mine. So—despite his stick-in-the-mud attitude tonight—I'd like to say a special thanks to you, Andy du Payne. Would you like to say anything?"

"What can I say?" the deity boomed with disinterest. "People are obviously big fans of inappropriate public discussions. I'm glad to play my part."

"You're actually proud of that role, are you?"

"Well, it's not my favorite but it's a close second."

"Oh, yeah? So what's your first?"

Andy paused just long enough to think about it. "Probably whenever I role play with my flavor of the week. I make sure I'm Burger King and they're McDonalds."

Bella was quiet for a second. "I'm afraid to as—"

"—I get it my way and they *love* it!"

Bella's second pause was longer. "You really need to stop stealing things off the internet."

"Please," Andy whined. "That joke's been around so long it's more like recycling than stealing. Besides, thaaaaat's what I'm here for, Doc. *You* provide the sexual relief while *I* give good comic. After all, every Laurel needs his hard-on."

"Who?"

"Really? I go full DP, smashing two in one and you don't even— *Ugh!* I swear, sometimes I think you kids these days are more deprived than you are depraved."

"Some of us are only depraved because we're deprived," Bella retorted flippantly.

"And who's fault is—"

"—Don't give me that," Bella cut him off before pushing a button on her computer's keyboard. "Next caller, you're in with Quinn. How can I help you?"

As Bella seamlessly switched back into her Doc-mode, I slowly began to lose interest in the remainder of the episode. I was curious but I also knew it was pointless to continue listening just to determine whether she was actually as frustrated with Andy as she sounded. Far too often they bickered like sister and brother who, just as often, seemed to have completely forgotten all about their fight by their next interaction.

But what did interest me was the repetition of Andy's implication. It wasn't the first time he had alluded to Bella being intentionally celibate. Though that was assuming that was the truth.

Despite how close they sounded, Andy seemed to have no clue about Bella's life as a Sex Slave, which on its surface wasn't all that far-fetched. Even though Bella had allowed me to know about her on our first night together, I had to imagine the lifestyle wasn't something people in the BDSM world were prone to advertise. And even if Bella wasn't outright lying, it was possible Andy was just missing the obvious.

Thinking back to my last few years in foster care, I recalled how some of the older kids on the verge of aging out of the system began dealing drugs. With their current support system scheduled to be cut off like a delinquent utility bill and most not looking at much of a future, for many the choice had been an easy one. Not wishing to go that route myself, I remembered it had also slowly dawned on me how the subculture had actually always existed around me. I had just been too naïve to see it.

So what was I missing here?

One thing that time also taught me was the level of truth to the saying about birds of a feather. Back then once I knew who was dealing drugs it wasn't too hard to figure out who they were dealing to. Likewise, someone had to have first introduced Bella to BDSM. I figured her job alone probably brought her into contact with an untold number of people capable of initiating her into that world.

Of course, it didn't take much to realize the formerly sex-addicted Costellos were prime candidates.

The more I thought about it, Abby fit the bill of what I expected from a Sex Slave. Quiet as the meekest mouse, I had rarely seen her more than a few feet away from Greg's side. But what didn't jibe was *he* seemed to be there to serve *her,* not her for him. Not that that proved anything, of course. Just because he might have been her Master didn't mean he had to be a domineering asshole about it. Then again just because I had my suspicions didn't mean they were remotely probable.

My problem was I only knew for sure of three people Bella truly knew, one of whom was still a faceless voice and none of it enough to go on. And pondering further was only going to give me a headache.

Still not tired enough to go to sleep, I opened up my email to mindlessly review a set of tax documents my lawyers and I would be submitting the next morning to the IRS. With only a few weeks to go before returning to Charlotte, I took solace in the fact that it wouldn't be much longer before I reached the final episode on Bella's YouTube channel when I'd get my first and only full look at Andy.

No. Not Andy... *Andy du Payne.*

Shuddering at the notion that he could have ever been Bella's Master with a name like that...

Damnit.

Was that why Bella wasn't into pain? Because Andy du *Payne* was? Had there been something between them at some point? Something more personal? And if so, had he done something to hurt her? Or was I just jumping to conclusions? Imagining things that weren't really there just because I was tired and not thinking straight?

Real or not, I shook my head, glad I honestly couldn't see the two of them together… yet slightly worried it might be because a large part of me really didn't want to.

Monday
February 17, 2020
11:02 am, 49° & mostly cloudy

Fidgeting back and forth between my phone and second cup of coffee, I alternated between glancing at the flowers on my dining room table and the test results on my laptop I had just received.

And I wondered exactly how I should tell Victor about them.

The last thing I wanted to do was screw things up. It sounded like everything was going well for him in Vegas with the IRS. He'd never been very forthcoming with any particulars about why exactly he needed to deal with their offices in two different cities and I hadn't wanted to pry. For the moment, I also didn't want to be responsible for upsetting him with a suggestion he might be opposed to, but I knew the longer I waited the more difficult it might make it for him in the end.

Deciding to preface my text with a simple request to talk later by phone whenever he got a break, I still wasn't sure how best to explain myself. Of course at the same time I knew if I just went with it, I'd think of something. I always did.

I only hoped Victor would be understanding regardless of the choice he eventually made.

Setting my cup down, I grabbed my phone and opened the Lock Screen… just as his text came through.

Doing my best to be understanding, I excused myself from the phalanx of lawyers and made my way to the nearest break room which thankfully was empty. The downtime was unexpected, but I could still make use of it.

After taking a seat I slipped my AirPods in and on a whim decided to randomly fire up one of Bella's earlier podcasts instead of continuing forward with her YouTube episodes. Sliding the cursor to somewhere in the middle, I let go.

"Okay, so here's what you might call a 'psychological hack,'" I caught Bella saying. "But before I explain, I want you to think about first blowing up an inner tube pool float... then later deflating it. Which was easier? Inflating it? Or letting all the air out? The latter, right? So, with that in mind, here's the tip: If you find yourself having to give someone both good and bad news of fairly equal value, you should always give them the *good* news first.

"The reason for this is elevating someone's mood only to deflate it back down will tend to leave them feeling better *overall* than if you were to do the opposite, deflating them with the bad news first before trying to build them back up with the good. That's because negative news affects us to a greater degree than positive news does.

"Think of it this way. We say, 'depression can set in' but have you ever heard anyone say 'happiness can set in?' No, because happiness doesn't grab and maintain a hold on us the way depression can. And that's because our brains are built for one thing, survival. This is why bad and sad things not only tend to teach us more than good or happy things do, they also leave deeper marks by etching themselves into our earliest memories..."

Smiling to myself, I wished Bella could see me. As had happened so often already, I loved running across moments that reminded me of our time together. And not just the sex. Increasingly, it was our conversations I was reminded of most.

Suddenly remembering there was no time like the present, I snapped a quick selfie of my smile and texted it to Bella with the message *Just because.* Surprisingly, the bubbles of her reply popped up less than two seconds later. First to come through was a single blushing emoji. Followed a few seconds later by her message.

Your timing is impeccable. You must have felt me thinking about you. I literally just opened my phone to text you when your photo came through. Do you have a second to talk?

I punched buttons as fast as I could to reply.

"I guess you do," Bella answered along with the laugh I missed. "Although I figured you would be in one of your meetings by now."

Her comment caught me by surprise. Though I had been in Las Vegas for a full week I still had to actively think about how that now put Bella two hours ahead of me.

"We're getting a late start. We're about an hour behind already," I informed her while doing my best not to sound too gruff. While being late was one of my personal pet peeves, these days certain circumstances were understandable. "One of the head IRS lawyers overseeing my case had to fly home to Seattle last night because of Covid."

"Oh, God, I hope everyone there is okay."

"We're all fine. His wife's a doctor who came in contact with a patient over the weekend. She's having to quarantine so he needs to be there for his kids until her test results come back. Although apparently, he's still going to participate. At the moment we're all on break while he tries to figure out his Zoom."

"Oh. Well, I'm glad you're safe and hopefully his wife is as well."

"Thanks. I just hope the test is accurate. I'm sure everyone is trying their best but this thing is still so new it sounds like they're all just winging it until they can get a better handle on it."

"I hope they do, too," Bella said softly. "They just closed public schools here in Charlotte for the next two weeks and when I spoke to Abby and Greg last night, they said they're expecting to be forced into closing down their gyms sometime in the next week or so."

"Damn, I'm sorry to hear that."

"Me, too, but I'm sure they'll be okay. Luckily most of their clients eventually sign up with a personal trainer from a network they've built before transitioning to working out with them from home, one-on-one. That's where their real bread and butter is."

I was surprised. Not only had Bella and I not discussed Abby or Greg much in the last month, I was unaware of this secondary aspect to their business. "So their gyms are just gateways to their main business which is concierge fitness trainers who work for them like private contractors?"

"More or less. That's why each location is fairly small and exclusive."

"Sounds like a lot of work but also a smart business plan."

"Actually, considering their target customers, the smartest thing they did was bring in someone to serve as the public face of the company." Bella let out a small snort. "Though in my opinion the guy's an absolute douche."

Oh, sh— I suddenly realized Bella was talking about Andy Chastain. She just had to be. *I mean, who el—* "So I take it you've met him?" I asked, trying my best to chuckle naturally.

"You could say that. I wish *I couldn't,* but unfortunately I can't."

This time my chuckle came easy. "That bad, was it?"

"Let's just say I'd forget the entire experience if I could."

Oh, so that *bad.* "Okay." Sensing the slight rise in Bella's tone and getting nowhere anyway, I decided to change subjects. "So, what were you going to text me about?"

"Ha..." Bella half-huffed, her laugh trailing off a bit nervously as she obviously remembered what she had forgot. "Ummm... Ironically enough, I was just about to text and ask you to call me later. I wanted to tell you about a test I went for last week..."

Uh...

I don't know what came over me first, the drop of my stomach or the cold sweat everywhere else. In retrospect, if Bella had said the same words to me a few weeks earlier my first thought might have been she was about to tell me she was positive for an STD. But for some reason, the way things stood now, my first thought was she was about to tell me she was pregnant. With our child. Because one of our condoms must have failed.

And I wasn't sure what I thought about that.

Dual emotions clashed within me, competing against one another as if my soul was some kind of trophy. On Team Positive, elation jumped to the fore by instantly acknowledging that out of all the women with whom I had ever been involved, Bella was the only one with which I could possibly bring myself to entertain the idea of creating a child. Backing that recognition up was a little voice in the back of my head screaming at the top of its lungs, confidently cheerleading its support and assurance that we'd make great parents.

Unfortunately, Team Negative countered by sucker punching me with a fistful of brutal honesty to the face. *What makes you think you know her?!* it screamed before cackling as I went down. *You just met!*

"You don't say," my suddenly parched throat rasped as I struggled to get back to my corner.

Looking around to get my bearings I noticed a clock on a wall indicating the time was just after nine in the morning. Meaning... *It's seven, no... eleven in the morning there...* The math felt complicated, like I needed a stiff drink to dull the sudden onset of throb in my temples. Like I couldn't think clearly. Then again who could with all that ringin—

"Relax," Bella cooed. "It was just my annual check-up which included screens for gonorrhea, the clap, HIV, et cetera. I just got my results. I'm clean, of course, but I was thinking... if you are, too... then *maybe* we could skip using condoms next time?"

I wasn't sure what the idea did more, throw me or thrill me. "Um..."

"I'll text you my results," Bella added quickly, "and you can do the same once you get yours."

"Okay. Sure. It sounds like a great idea actually." *But—* "But, uh, what about birth control?"

"I've got it covered. I had my OB-GYN put in a new IUD while I was there."

"Okay, then," my slightly anxious side heard me cave to my brave. "I'll see if I can find a clinic on my lunch break later today. I'll... text you the results as soon as I get them."

To the subtle sounds of Bella possibly doing the same, I breathed easier. Despite every cell in my brain wondering if I was making the right choice, every bone in my body was more than excited at the prospect of bareback sex with her. One in particular which suddenly had me smiling.

"Good," Bella said. "So... what's the smile for?"

I blinked. How could she possibly kn— "Oh. You mean, the picture I just texted you. Um, well, I was listening to one of your podcasts—"

"—You *were?"* Bella squealed. She sounded as genuinely surprised as honored. "Which one?"

"One from a little over midway through your second season. You explained how it's best to give good news before bad. It reminded me of our conversation during our ride back to Charlotte."

"How I knew your earliest memories were more than likely negative ones?"

"Exactly."

"Mmmmm," Bella purred. "I do miss getting to talk to you for long stretches of time like that."

"So do I," I admitted. "But the good news is our wait is almost over."

"It is... but of course we already know that... Wait. This isn't a precursor to your way of breaking bad news to me, is it?"

It wasn't, but at that moment, I suddenly remembered there was—

"Actually, there is something I've been meaning to tell you. I know I promised you an entire weekend dedicated to staying in bed when I get back—"

"—Please don't tell me you're canceling," Bella cut me off.

"Ummm..."

I tried not to laugh. The unfamiliar consternation in Bella's voice was almost as perceptible as the change in her diction. It amused me how she lapsed into using contractions much more liberally whenever she got the least bit riled. Lucky for her—

"No. Actually I wanted to invite you to join me for something. I forgot I have a prior commitment that Saturday out at the Whitewater Center. It shouldn't take more than a few hours... And I'd love it if you'd go with me. What do you say?"

Putting my cup of coffee down, I couldn't believe Victor would ask me something like that.

"Do you know what I am looking at right now?" I asked in reply, knowing that he didn't.

"Ummmmm... no. Not really."

"The dozen purple roses you got me for Valentine's Day. They're sitting on my dining room table and along with the irises are some of the most beautiful flowers I've ever received."

I could hear Victor smile. "You have a funny way of saying 'Yes.' But I like it."

"Mmmmmmm, I'm glad you do."

A sudden commotion in the background brought on a small growl from

Victor.

"I'm sorry to have to cut this short but it looks like they're calling everyone back to the conference room. You have a wonderful day, okay?"

Awww— "Thank you. You do as well."

Disconnecting our call left me feeling anything but. Though disappointed we couldn't talk longer, I was amazed at how much deeper my relationship with Victor had become in such a short amount of time. The thought of where it might go when he returned in three weeks sent a sudden surge of wetness to pool between my legs.

Fighting the horniness because my second teletherapy appointment of the day was due to call in about fifteen minutes, I made a mental note to research the Whitewater Center when I found the time. Trying to compose myself, I suddenly remembered Victor had agreed to sex without a condom. The second surge made me glance at my bedroom door.

Screw it. Fifteen minutes was more than enough.

Tuesday
February 25, 2020
3:30pm, 63° & cloudy

Disconnecting from my last teletherapy appointment of the day, I contemplated going outside to take advantage of the day's above average temperature. Most days I would have gone for a quick stroll to a large park just one block away, over on Main Street, where kids and their families always seemed to be playing. But since my laptop was already open and with cloud cover so thick there was no sunshine to enjoy, I opted instead to open a new tab in my browser and run a search for future applications of cryptocurrencies.

While neither history nor finance had ever been of particular interest to me, the more I had researched both bit- and altcoins the last couple of weeks the more fascinated I had become by the world they were poised to build.

I'd heard my father remark more than once over the last few years how surprised he was not just to have lived long enough to see the technology of the *Dick Tracy* cartoons become a reality, but that it had arrived much sooner than he ever dreamed it could. It was his delight that made me curious. What would I live to see transform in my lifetime which might awe me to the same degree?

I'd already lived to see entire industries that existed prior to the internet—communication, entertainment, gaming, information, media and transportation—become transformed by the creation of the World Wide Web. I'd seen email give way to text messaging and VHS lose to DVD before being supplanted by streaming. I'd watched search engines come and go while companies like Uber and Lyft drove taxi companies away, seemingly forever.

But none of that compared to what I discovered digital and cryptocurrencies were about to do.

If the projections I read were correct, we were only a few years away from clocking in on a job to trigger our pay to stream directly into our bank accounts on a minute-by-minute basis. Not only was waiting for a week from Friday to get paid for the previous two weeks worth of work about to become a thing of the past, taxes could be imposed in real-time as well. Gone were soon to be the days of providing governments the interest free loans of refunds or being charged for them via yearly assessments.

And while many of the ways we currently did things were going to change whether we liked it or not, cryptocurrencies had the everyday potential to be just as optionally pervasive as well.

By the time self-driving cars were predicted to be the norm, so would preprogramming them to communicate and negotiate with one another. Want the slow guy in front of you to get over so you can go somewhere faster? Who needs toll roads when you and anyone else can offer him a nickel to move aside at his car's earliest opportunity?

The possibilities for the potential of cryptocurrencies were as staggering as they seemed endless. The only problem was cryptocurrency's true usefulness had yet to transpire. Not that it was crypto's fault.

During one of my first forays into the subject, I ran across an analogy that described digital assets' current dilemma brilliantly when the author of the article pointed out that cars were built long before roads were ready for them. That back then, trails for horseback riding between towns or worse, ruts for wagons, were the norm. While the cars worked well enough, their intended paths had to first be smoothed out for better usage.

Likewise, today's payment rails were too slow and costly. It took time and money to move *actual* money from point A to Z. And while cryptos were designed to quickly and cheaply bypass every point between B and Y, the moves from A to B and Y to Z known as "the last mile" just weren't ready.

But that was just where things currently stood. I wanted to know where they were going.

Checking to see what my browser had to say, it didn't surprise me to read a suggestion that cryptocurrencies would render both paper money and billing obsolete in the not too distant future. Yet the timing of the mention was a little troubling. While certain the two weren't related, I had heard that several area businesses had been reporting coin change shortages. With people spending less because of Covid-19, the situation was understandable. But regardless of the reason, the coincidence made me wonder just how distant a cashless society might be.

And what that might mean for banks...

Segueing off the thought, I recalled Victor mentioning certain digital assets had been developed specifically for banks to use. Running a quick search, I found only a couple. And though greatly outnumbered by the vast amount of coins in the cryptosphere, they were noticeably among the biggest.

One in particular.

Referred to again and again as The Coin That Shall Not Be Named, it was difficult to ignore. With a market cap worth several billion dollars when its price was multiplied by its circulating supply, the coin was designed to move like an email. Like small packets of information zipping across the internet, each transaction could move across the world in about 3 seconds costing less than a thousandth of a penny. The thing was virtually free.

And yet no one wanted to talk about it.

High level executives from many of the world's largest and most influential financial institutions studiously avoided saying its name, declining to go down any road during a discussion in which it might be brought up. And those who did often became visibly uncomfortable.

I watched several YouTube videos where time after time major CEOs, presidents of central banks around the world and directors of the US Federal Reserve all seemed to wither under the spotlight and become very uncomfortable whenever the coin was mentioned. It was as if no one wanted to be responsible for letting the cat out of the bag first. When it came to the coin they all seemed to have inside knowledge that none of them wanted to share. And for good reason.

The price of the coin was still unbelievably low.

Damn...

Stretched out on the hotel's bed after a late dinner, I cued up one of Bella's

YouTube shows. The episode didn't have a Ballers' segment, but I wasn't in the mood for one as the last few days I'd really enjoyed listening to her call-in segments. Not all her of her callers were like Doug. Most were actually quite normal. Though the last one I had been listening to was a bit of an outlier.

Picking up where I left off, Bella had just finished learning that forty-two year old Carol from Iowa, while not a virgin, nevertheless believed herself to be asexual because the sights of sex made her squeamish. As a result, she had very little sexual experience but was curious if Bella could still help her. There was a man she was interested in and should things ever progress that far, she wanted to be ready.

"So, just to be sure I am hearing you correctly, you are actually interested in having sex with this man, possibly at some point in the future. Is that what you're saying, Carol?"

"Well... yeah," Carol said. "That's exactly what I'm saying."

"Okay, good. Then the first thing I want you to do is to stop thinking of yourself as asexual, okay? Despite what many people might think, being asexual doesn't mean someone has little to no sex nor does it even refer to someone who doesn't enjoy sex. It has nothing to do with activity level or enjoyment. Being 'asexual' means someone doesn't experience sexual attraction. You do, therefore you are not asexual. Do you understand that?"

"When you explain it that way, sure."

"Good," Bella continued, "because I could hear in the way you used that word to describe yourself that you felt it had negative connotations and I don't want you thinking of yourself negatively. Okay?"

"Okay."

"Good. Now, with regard to your next issue, have you considered using a blindfold?"

"I have..."

"But?"

"But that's way too kinky for me. Plus, if I'm being honest, I've had so few sexual experiences I'm not really sure what I'm doing. And if I couldn't see, I think that would make it even worse."

"I see... Tell me something, Carol. Thinking about everything except for what you witnessed during them, did you enjoy the sexual encounters you've had so far?"

"I did."

"Good, then I think I can help. Tell me, are you're up to the challenge of a quick experiment?"

"If you think it will help."

"Great! So, the first thing I need for you to do is tell me what are three of your favorite fruits?"

"Ummmm, apples. Bananas... and strawberries."

"Good. Now next I need for you to close your eyes."

"Okay... they're closed."

"Good. Now imagine an apple in your hands. Roll it around. Feel it. Touch it. Notice the shape and texture."

"Okay."

"Now do the same thing to the banana... Then the strawberry... Now imagine the apple and strawberry cut in two and the banana peeled. Smell each of them... Then taste them, one by one.

"Now, with your eyes still closed, I want you to think about the best sexual encounter you've ever had, the best out of all of them even though you've only had a few. But I want you to reimagine doing it again only with your eyes closed. Imagine feeling your lover's body, but not seeing it... Imagine smelling their skin, without seeing any. Imagine tasting their skin, their lips as you kissed them, but with your eyes closed. Block out the part you don't need to re-experience the wonders you have felt already. Allow yourself to feel, listen, touch, smell and taste... but don't open your eyes to see. If the sights of sex diminish your enjoyment, eliminate them. Don't let it ruin the parts you do like.

"The next time you have sex, if you can arrange it, have it in a place that is as dark as possible. Close your eyes as often as you need to... and then lose yourself in all the other sensations that you enjoy so much. Do you think you can do that?"

"Maybe. But don't you think he might find that weird?"

Bella smiled as she bowed her head just a bit. "Let me tell you something about myself that's a little different from other people. When it comes to food, I'm all about the texture. It doesn't matter if I think something *tastes* delicious. If it *feels* wrong in my mouth, I won't like it no matter how delicious I think it tastes. And I *really* don't like foods that contrast with themselves. Take tomatoes, for example. I hate them raw because they are both firm as well as juicy. But purée them into ketchup or spaghetti sauce, even salsa, and I love them.

"What I'm trying to say is it's perfectly okay to be particular about something. If the sights that go along with sex turn you off, then I say turn *them* off. There's still plenty of ways you can enjoy sex without experiencing any aspect of it that you don't."

"Wow. You know, I've never actually thought of it that way. Thanks, Doc."

"That's what I'm here for, Carol. And you're welcome. Now you go and try to come well."

Disconnecting the call, Andy also played a sound resembling a game show contestant making a bad decision. After squabbling for a bit over the timing of Bella's joke and Andy's effect, Bella started to put an end to the segment by looking back into the main camera.

"Hold up, Doc," Andy protested. "I don't think we should take a break after a lame, snoozer of a call not to mention how you ended it."

"There was nothing wro—"

"—*And* since you already brought up ketchup and next week's show is all about fellat—"

"—Oh, no! That's not happening!"

"But it's the perfect story and an even better teaser."

"Yes, but you forget, *my parents* listen to this podcast."

"Mister and Misses Quinn? Do you mind turning off the podcast for about ten minutes? Thank you... There? See how easy that was?"

"You aren't right."

"And *you* aren't the type of person to leave her audience hanging. Now are you?"

Bella growled. "Mom. Dad. Turn it off. Seriously."

As she paused a few more seconds, I made sure my volume was turned completely up. I couldn't believe after all this time I was about to hear something so personal. Especially if it was ab—

"When I was a child," Bella began, "I... didn't get invited to parties very much. So once, when I was, I got really excited about it. It was a birthday party for a classmate, held during the summer at a neighborhood park. Nothing out of the ordinary. Play, eat lunch, have cake, open presents. The usual.

"But what really excited me was learning that for lunch, they weren't just going to serve my favorite, hot dogs, they had one I'd never seen or heard of before... A foot long."

"Awwww, yeah," Andy interjected.

"Shut up... So, I'm standing in line, ready to get mine only there's this idiot adult preparing what each kid wants. I want to make it myself, but I don't want to be rude. So, I say, 'ketchup only, please.' And what does the adult do? She puts the ketchup in the *bottom* of the bun and then the hot dog on *top* of that.

"I'm—well, it doesn't matter what age I was, I was too young to call her out for her stupidity. So I took my hot dog, said thank you and walked away toward where I was going to sit at the picnic table. Only I don't want to wait. I want to know if there's anything better about a foot long compared to a regular hot—"

"—Oh, there is, trust m—"

"—Shut up!" Bella groaned as she tried to calm down. "So, as I'm walking to my seat, I start to take my first bite... when I trip on a tree root. I stumble, but catch myself. I don't fall... but suddenly I'm standing there with the tail end of the foot long hanging out of my mouth which I've caught with my teeth.

"Kids are laughing, parents look horrified and I'm thinking what the heck is the big deal? So, I pull the hot dog from my mouth. Which some of the kids thought was cool. And, well, let's just say I'd never known what that felt like. So, I put it back in and then... you get the picture... So, let this be a lesson, everyone. Condiments go *on top* of the hot dog. Putting them underneath makes it easier for it to slide out of the bun which is why only idiots eat them that way... There? Are you happy now?"

"Honestly," Andy said, "I thought you might just point out that one out of every three people lack a gag reflex. I figured it would be a great way to end the show to get everyone excited for next week. But if you want to use the opportunity to brag about your deep-throating skills, hey, it's your show."

I could actually hear Bella shake her head. "Serves me right... Okay, when we get back, understanding the importance of consent. Or what every straight man understands after accidentally stepping inside a gay bar. And for all my littles out there, don't you worry. I have not forgot about you. I know you're listening and I have something extra special coming up, just for you when we return. So, stay tuned. Andy and I will be back to play in two plus two."

As outro music faded to commercial break, I decided to do the same and prepare for bed. Though not right away.

Closing out the podcast, I tapped a few buttons to go on Safari. As exhausted as I was from another long day of haggling with so many lawyers and accountants—as we all did our best to cope with the mounting pressures and repercussions from Covid-19's continued spread—there was no way I was going to fall asleep without satisfying the most important question suddenly burning in my mind.

What the hell *is a little?*

My eyes kept losing focus as I drifted in and out of the throes of the most intense carnal pleasure I had ever known.

Riding the waves within me, my entire being floated up and down, sinking deeper into ecstasy before lifting back even higher in euphoria. Again and again and again the swells ebbed only to return, carrying me ever closer to my own personal waterfall.

Helpless to stanch the flow, my body flooded uncontrollably, the moisture and wetness gushing in a heated rush, adding to the ocean of liquidity surrounding us. Despite how full Victor filled me, when I exploded the pressure behind my juices was strong enough such that much of it escaped around the sides of his thickness. Within seconds the wet, distinctive sucking and splashing sound emanating from between my legs was enough to put Victor over the edge. As we came together, I suddenly felt his cum add to mine.

Pump after pump after pump, Victor filled me as he continued to pound me between my legs. I loved how his orgasm only made him fuck me faster and harder... but this time he didn't slow, didn't stop.

Lacing his fingers over the top of my head, Victor pushed my entire body toward the foot of the bed, sliding me effortlessly across the silk sheets only to force me back with the thrust of his hips. Again and again and again he used the near frictionless sheen to rock our bodies together before ricocheting apart. Yet not only was his dick not getting softer, I could swear I felt him grow harder.

Opening my eyes, I found him looking at me with so many untold emotions in his cerulean pools, all yearning to be expressed.

Love. Lust. Need. Want. Desire. Heat...

In desperation he covered my mouth with his own, kissing me as best the remainder of his passion would allow.

Wrapping my arms and legs around him, my hands grasped his back and my ankles crossed behind his knees, I lifted myself up as I locked him down. Making him mine.

It was strange. I don't know when the hotel came in to change our sheets to silk. And I guess our condom must have broken. But that didn't make sense, either...

I opened my eyes. I was excited but exhausted. But not enough to stop me from noticing I was in my own bedroom. *But why...* Oh. It was only a dream.

Damn.

Friday
February 28, 2020
6:14pm, 66° & mostly cloudy

Just as I was opening the door to my hotel room, my cellphone rang. Since I wasn't expecting a call but did expect Bella to be in bed already, I started not to bother digging it out of my pocket. Between real estate agents trying to buy my house and politicians trying to buy my vote, I was sick of damn robocalls.

With the Super Tuesday primaries just four days away, the number of daily calls from the candidate's campaigns that I was receiving bordered on harassment. Making it worse, their spiels were pointless. My absentee ballot had already been cast. And although it was a vote against the other candidate instead of one for my own, regardless of the eventual winner, all I really wanted was to be left alone.

Suddenly realizing that was no longer the same case it used to be, I pulled the phone from my pocket just in case. And was glad I did.

"Hey," I answered, putting the phone on speaker. "I thought you'd be in bed by now."

"Oh, I'm in bed," Bella teased, making me chuckle.

"You know what I mean."

"I do," she said. "But I couldn't fall asleep without asking you something. Two somethings, actually."

"And what's that?" I asked as I hung my coat in the closet.

"Well, before I forget *again,* let me start with the personal question I forgot to ask you about the last two times we've talked and then I'll get to the one that's kept me up."

"Okay. Shoot."

"I was wondering what sparked your interest in etymologies?"

As I sat on the edge of the bed and began taking off my shoes and socks, I laughed at the memory. "It wasn't a what, it was a who, my ninth-grade English teacher. It was the only subject I wasn't doing well in because to me it was the most boring. My teacher thought it was strange because he knew just how much I loved to read. So, after holding me over after class one day he explained there were stories behind each and every word that existed called etymologies. Well, I'd never heard the word before so, being a bit of a smartass at the time, I said, 'Well, if that's true, then what's the etymology of the word etymology?'"

"No, you didn't."

"Oh, yes, I did. I remember thinking at the time that I was being chicken-or-the-egg-clever, but then my teacher simply smiled at me and said, 'It's Greek.' Now, that might not have mattered to a lot of kids, but only a few days before this he caught me with a copy of *The Iliad* and *The Odyssey* in my lap instead of paying attention in class."

"Ahhhh. Big fan of Greek mythology, were you?"

"Huge. And from that day forward, one of etymologies as well."

"Hmph. That's pretty interesting."

"As interesting as the second thing? Whatever it is that's kept you up past your bedtime?"

"Well," Bella said, "you tell me."

"I was looking into what you said about cryptocurrencies being able to do away with a need for banks. Is that because of CBDCs?"

I heard Victor chuckle. "That's part of it. Once the US develops a central bank digital currency, there won't be a reason for retail and commercial banks to hold our money on deposit anymore. The central banks, our Federal Reserve, will do that for us."

"You mean the *government* will hold our money?"

"No, remember the Federal Reserve isn't part of the government."

"Okay, but what you're still saying is that everyone in America will eventually use them. So we'll all have the same bank?"

"Exactly. They will hold the money that we use to buy things with from stores that bank with them, too. In all honesty, it'll be a far more efficient and cheaper system than we have now."

"But then what happens to retail and commercial banks?"

"Theoretically, they'd survive primarily as lending institutions."

"Theoretically?"

"Well, if defi doesn't do them in first."

"Defi? I've seen that term a couple of times, but I didn't research it. What is it exactly?"

"It's short for decentralized finance. Long story short anyone can go online and apply for a loan which will be funded by anyone who deems you qualified and agrees to your terms. It basically means anyone can act as a bank and lend money."

"You're kidding. How would that work?"

"Well, let's say you need $100,000. You might find one person to loan you all of it or 50,000 people each of whom would be willing to lend you $2 worth of various cryptos each. Kind of like a gofundme only with payback terms."

Wow. The implications seemed as obvious as they were preposterous. "But if you're right and CBDCs and defi are coming, then retail and commercial banks..." I couldn't finish. But Victor could.

"Will be going the way of the dodo."

Damn. When Victor told me the first time, I believed him even though I didn't quite understand how it could be possible. But now that I did... I didn't want to believe him.

"If that happens, it could devastate a city like Charlotte."

"Trust me, I know," Victor lamented, his voice as soft as it was serious. "I've given it a lot of thought. Charlotte could be less than ten years away from becoming the next Detroit."

I hated to think of it, but Victor was right. The banking industry was as important to Charlotte as the oil industry was to Houston.

"And if it does? What then?"

"I don't know," Victor admitted. "But as with everything in life, it's always best to be prepared."

Wednesday
March 4, 2020
7:57pm, 65° & clear

After setting my empty dinner tray in the hallway outside my door, I brushed my teeth then got ready for bed.

Making sure that both the clock on the nightstand and my phone's alarms were set for 4:00 so I could hit The D's gym before heading to the IRS as I'd done each morning since arriving, I shook my head in gratitude. Though it was in all likelihood somewhere in the state already, Nevada had yet to register a positive case of Covid-19. For the moment, amenities like the gym were still unrestricted and I needed all the distraction I could get.

Between my hotel room, the D's gym and the IRS office, I'd neither went anywhere nor did anything else for almost a solid month. Which was why—with only two days to go before I returned to Charlotte—I was well ahead of the schedule I had set for listening to and viewing Bella's podcasts. Determined to save her final episode for tomorrow night I decided to use the SKIP button to sample snippets from the bonus compilation chapter, *The Very Best of Andy du Payne.*

Given the effect the coronavirus was starting to have on the little bit of society I was forced to interact with, I could use a laugh or two.

Propping a couple extra pillows behind my head, I grabbed my phone from the nightstand then pulled up the segment. After tapping PLAY I held my finger above the SKIP button then closed my eyes. I wasn't all that tired, but I figured I'd hold out listening to Bella, Andy and their guests as long as I could until I fell asleep.

"I swear," I heard Bella say first, "I don't know how you drink coffee out of a mug that big."

"What can I say?" Andy said. "I. Like. Big. Cups and I cannot lie..."

Silence. Then... "That sounds familiar. Is it from a song or something?"

"Wow! Are you really that—"

"—Ha! Got you!"

Andy's sigh filled the air. "Serves me right. Never trust a big butt and a smile."

"Nice one—"

"—Aaaaand we're back." SKIP.

"A true hallmark of the narrow-minded is how adamant they can be about their beliefs."

"My, my, my. I'm impressed by how reasonable you managed to make yourself sound while stating that, Andy."

"Yeah, well, nobody likes a hypocrite." SKIP.

"Hi, Doc. This is Paul from Pomona. First time caller, long time 'Dict and I've—"

You've gotta be kidding me. Really? SKIP.

"Don't forget, boys and girls," Andy's digitized voice warned, "May is the official Masturbation Month. So do your part and lend a hand, okay?"

"Or two if you're lucky enough for that to be a requirement," Bella cooed.

"But you said size didn't matter."

"We all have to say that. It's in the girl code."

"Ouch." SKIP.

Despite the synthesized bass electronica, Andy's voice seemed softer as it filled the air.

"How will you know when your man loves you? You'll know when he makes a mix tape of songs he thinks you'd like. You'll know he loves you even more when those songs are ones you've shared together at some point... But you'll know he can't possibly love you any more when he tells you your voice is the most beautiful song he's ever heard."

"Awwwwww, Andy, you big softy. I think I might cry."

"Yeah, well, you're a chick, so..."

"Aaaaaaaand he's back, ladies and gentlemen." SKIP.

"And now a PSA from the one and only Andy du Payne."

"Okay, everyone. It's October so in honor of breast cancer awareness there will be no more sucking on titties for the rest of the month. Instead, you are only allowed to suck on... wait for it... BOObies!!" Andy followed his joke with a long, maniacal laugh that suddenly came to a dead stop. "Seriously, go get 'em checked, ladies. It could save your life." SKIP.

"Hey, you never know," Andy said. "Some people these days meet online playing some random game like Ruzzle then end up living happily ever after. Who's to say it can't happen?"

"Probably a bit more likely with Words With Friends, but I get your point." SKIP.

"Today's episode is going to be dicklicious!!!" Andy bellowed emphatically. "We've got DLT going all up and *down* on the menu. That's a Dick Lettuce and Tomato sandwich for all you new-*cummers* by the way, where the dick is nice and mean—"

"—nice and mean. Good thing there's nothing confusing about—"

"—and the lettuce and tomato, well what's a sandwich without all the appropriate accoutrements, amirite?"

"Why do I get the feeling you never go light on the mayo?"

"Oh, nooooooo. You know Papi likes to spread it on *nice and thick.*"

"You are not right in the head."

"Hey, just because my normal isn't your normal doesn't make me *ab*normal... and vice to the versa, capisce?"

Finally realizing what Bella had been referring to on our drive back to Charlotte when I brought up distributed ledger technology, I shook my head and smiled. SKIP.

"I made a list. Are you ready? And just so I don't offend anyone by implying who should be listed last, it's in alphabetical order: Alternaqueers, art fags, bears, bottoms, catchers, circuit boys, club kids, cubs, drag queens, gay listers, gaysians, gypsters, gorillas, jocks, muscle Marys, otters, pitchers, power gays, queens, show queens, tops, trannies, tweeters, twinks and twunks—"

"—Oh, my—" Bella chimed in.

"—velvet mafia, versatiles and wolves. So, did I leave anybody out?"

A male caller huffed petulantly into his end of the phone. "Not that I can think of."

"You know," Andy said, "for people who eschew labels you people sure do seem fond of them."

"Excuse me? *You* people?'"

"Yes, you people, Sebastian. You've been calling in here for two years, loud and proud. What? Are you not gay now? Yes, you are and I'm here to tell you I don't mind if you're loud. I don't mind if you're proud. But putting those two together every single freaking time you open your mouth—well, maybe not *every* time—I'm sorry but that shit gets on everybody's nerves."

"So much for don't ask, don't tell," the caller replied indignantly.

"That's because twenty years later it's become a much more highly evolved policy called don't know, don't freakin' care. Listen, it's simple. No one cares if you're homosexual. No one cares if you're heterosexual. All most people care about is you express your sexuality—*any* sexuality—in private."

"It's not like we're hurting anyone."

"Neither is anyone masturbating in their car with their tongue hanging out of their mouth, but you don't think that shit's appropriate, now do you?"

"No, but—"

"—No-no-no! I can't believe I'm saying this but no buts! The answer is no! If making other people feel uncomfortable is wrong, then public displays of *any* overt sexuality is wrong. I know there's a lot of people that don't like me specifically for how I speak, but if it's wrong for me to offend people with my words why isn't it also wrong for people to offend me with their actions? That's because it is! It's wrong. So keep that shit in your pants until you're somewhere it's appropriate to remove them, ok? Loving affection is fine, lewd groping is not."

"Yes, but where do *you* draw the line and why do *you* get to draw it?"

"I don't. The majority of people do. But you don't hear the majority of people in this world complaining about PDAs as long as they don't cross the line between affection and sexuality."

"Maybe you don't because you're straight, but it's a different story if you're homosexual."

"You are absolutely right. I will give you that. I agree, homosexuals are still far more likely to be shamed for PDAs than heterosexuals which is entirely wrong. But do you not agree with me that times are a changing and that people and their opinions are changing, too?" SKIP.

"So, what's the strangest relationship you have ever had, Andy?"

"I was once involved with this woman. Chick was certifiably psycho—"

"—Annndy—"

"—Sorry. She had OCD. You know the kind of person that rubs everyone the wrong way, but God forbid you touch *them?* Anyway, she needed everything arranged just so in order to function. Everything had to be on a schedule and on a list. Including, you guessed it, sex."

"That doesn't sound like fun."

"Depends on your definition. For the four weeks I tolerated her, we had Missionary Mondays, Taboo Tuesdays, Wet Dream Wednesdays, Thin Lizzy Thursdays—the two-finger type, not the band or anti-depressants—Freaky Fridays—not to be confused with Taboo Tuesdays or the movie—Satisfaction Saturdays and last but not least my personal favorite Give It A Rest Already Sundays."

"Well... at least it sounds like she tried."

Andy suddenly sounded contrite. "I gotta give the crazy bitch that. She really did." SKIP.

"I'd like to propose my own new term," Bella announced. "The End Send. The text or email you use to break off a relationship."

"Email? Jeez Louise, Grandma, how old are you?"

"I have an old soul. Why do you keep taking the fun out of things? What is with you today?... When is the last time you got laid?"

"This morning, thank you very much."

"That bad, was it?"

"Bitch—"

"—Asshole."

"Love you—"

"—Mean it. Ok, moving right along. POs. I know some of you guys love them, but can they be better? We'll explore that probe-ability right after these messages from a couple of our sponsors. So, don't go away and we'll be back right up your backside before you know it." SKIP SKIP SKIP.

"Look," Andy sighed in exasperation, "all I'm saying is why waste time developing my own personality when anyone can stream one for free off the internet these days?"

"So form over substance is what you're advocating?"

"Don't be ridiculous. Pornos have no substance. That's part of their beauty."

"Did you just—"

"—Aaaand we're back."

"You did that on purpose."

"Yeah, but we're still back, so get your ass to work." SKIP.

"What's your favorite place to be with your significant other, Andy?"

"Together."

"Awwww, you big softie."

"Not according to Dave in the chat, I'm not."

"Really? And what does Dave have to say?"

"He says on a daily basis I tend to 'vacillate between being a tool and a fool.'"

"'Vacillate?' Really?"

"Yeah. I think he's trying to impress you."

"Well, that's sweet. It's also a good opportunity for me to remind everyone that unlike the first few months, I no longer read our chat during the actual podcast. I do, however, read it in its entirety after the show, so please, just like your orgasms, keep your comments coming. However, as I'm sure those of you who have been with us from the start realize, our chat room has grown rather large. Therefore, from this point forward, Andy won't just moderate. He and he alone will get to pick and choose what gets through to me and on air. So be nice.

"And speaking of being nice, I'd like to make an announcement. It's been brought to my attention that in a few cities some of you have formed small meet-up chapters ostensibly to come together—"

"—Was that pun intended?"

"Yes—in order to benefit certain local charities in each of your areas. I'm also aware that there's been a lot of talk in the chat that I might try to legally stop you from affiliating your activities with my podcast. Which is why I am announcing that I will *not.* As long as your get-togethers are truly for charity, you will always have my blessing. This world will never have enough people trying to do some good and I for one won't stand in your way. And, on an even lighter note, I also want to say I consider it an honor you have decided to call yourselves 'Doc's'Dicts.'" SKIP.

"Trust me," Andy said, "the only good thing about getting older is more and more of the opposite sex starts looking attractive."

"Are you talking about The Villages again?"

"No, but hey! Shoutout to the STD capital of America! Way to go, boomers."

"Annnnndy—"

"—What? They're a bunch of geriatric heathens who think protection is no longer necessary. I mean I guess when you're that close to knocking on death's door you might as well go out knocking them boots bareback style. Tell me I'm wrong."

"You aren't right in the head that's for damn sure." SKIP.

"I'm bi-sexual but I prefer gay porn," Andy joked as he often did during his Diddle Riddles, "a fact about me most who know find confusing. So diddle riddle me this: Which confuses you most? To be straight yet prefer gay porn? To be gay yet prefer straight porn? To be asexual yet love all porn? Or to be bi-sexual yet hate all porn?"

What the he— I was too tired to think that much. SKIP.

"Look," Andy said. "I can sum up everything you need to know about pussy in two sentences. Pussy is not a charity. One way or another, you're gonna pay for it."

"My, my, my, Andy, how unbelievably misogynistic of you."

"If it wasn't such a public service announcement, you might think so, huh?"

"Where do you come up with this s— You know what? Never mind. Next caller." SKIP.

"Ok," Andy said, "it's pretty obvious I don't have the Doc's brains, so when it comes to her Word of The Day, I'm not even going to try to compete. Instead, I'm going to bring this segment down to my level for a few. But don't worry, what I lack in quality I make sure to make up for in quantity. So, words that mean the same thing as penis. Here's what I know. Feel free to compare but not ashamed if you don't measure up. After all, we can't all be from Jamaica. Ready?

"Dick, cock, schlong, dong, peter, johnson—no, not Peter Johnson—rod, bone, woody, stiffy, phallus and tallywacker. Now let's do the ladies because let's face it, the ladies looooove when we do them. And what do we do? Their vagina, pussy, twat—no true lady's favorites cunt or snatch—box, hole, quim, gash, slit, slot, muff, trim and coochie. Yes, I know I'm showing my age. No, I don't care. Hell, kids these days can't even develop their own fashion sense, always hitting up the retread recycle bin. Why is everybody afraid to try something different? The last decade with any originality was the 80s and no, you genetic X abnormalities, 90s grunge *doesn't* count. There's nothing edgy about emulating a homeless lumberjack then trying to slap a 'fashion' label on it after someone even lazier than you decided to copy you... Wait a minute, where was I?"

"Coochie," Bella deadpan reminded everyone.

"That's right! And what do we get when we put the two together? Sperm, ejaculate, cum, wad, load, seed, spunk and goo—where do you think spooge comes from?—and as always the ever classy nut sauce. So, now that everyone is properly desensitized to the fact that all of these are just words..."

Oh my God. SKIP.

"Remember guys," Andy boomed, "swiping right doesn't give you any right whatsoever."

"So, wait a minute. It's swipe right for yes and hot or left for no and not?"

"You really don't know that?"

"I hear enough about them from my patients but personally no, I've never used any of those swipable apps."

"'Swipable?' Is that even a word?"

"I don't know. You'll have to ask auto-correct, but you'll have to do it later because it's time to take a break. However, when we return it's time for some pet play."

"Hey, hey, hey! Get back in your cage, PETA. It's not what you think." SKIP.

"Hey," Andy said, his voice smoother than usual, "if you need a vaginatarian, *I'm* your man."

Bella sighed. "That is just wrong on so many levels." SKIP.

"Listen," Bella said, her voice more compassionate than normal, "I am not saying it is wrong to love someone more than yourself. Parents, just to use an example, do it all the time and no one in their right mind would argue that is unhealthy. But by the same token, it is also okay to reach a point in a relationship where you love someone more than you do yourself. To give your time and your life not just *to* that person but also *for* that person.

"But the *sequence* to doing so is the most important component to the likely success of such a relationship. Before you should try to find or even hope to run into such a worthy individual, you *need to love yourself first.* You need to feel the vast majority of your very own work-in-progress that is you... is nearly complete. *You* need to be in a place where *you* feel the need to only add a few finishing touches to yourself on occasion with 'on occasion' being the operative phrase.

"Then and only then, if you still want to have a successful relationship, should you begin to open yourself to finding a partner. Think about it. Unless you are someone with a heart of gold and the patience of Job, how long are *you* willing to wait for someone to get themselves together? Probably not long, not long enough for a relationship to be successful, anyway. And if *you* are not willing to wait that long, what makes you think anyone else will or even should put forth the necessary effort for you?"

"Wow," Andy deadpanned. "What a long-winded way to say, 'Get your shit together.' No wonder our podcasts run so long." SKIP.

"Look," Bella admitted, "I know I'm going off topic for a second here, but I honestly don't have a problem with a certain level of gold digging. Why? You know who invented gold digging? Men. Know why? To attract women who wanted gold to make jewelry which would make them more attractive to, you guessed it, men."

"Humans are nothing if not a vicious cycle," Andy opined.

"All I'm saying is there is nothing wrong with a woman finding a man's wealth as attractive as his health. Women and men find one another attractive for a variety of reasons but only a few of those overlap. True, only the shallowest people concentrate on just one aspect. And just so we're clear, it's the *singularity* of their focus that makes them shallow, not the object of it. But those women who also take a man's wealth into consideration alongside so many other factors shouldn't be tainted by association to gold-diggers any more than any self-respecting woman who is overly libidinous should be linked with those who aren't self-respecting."

"Hey. Hoes gonna hoe, you know?" SKIP.

"Today I decided I want to do something new. Andy, I would appreciate it if *you* would choose today's Word of The Day for us to discu—"

"—Fecalphiliac."

Bella's long, drawn out pause of silence preceded her sigh.

"And so, sadly, today marks the *last* day I will ever ask Andy..."

"But you aaaasked."

Another pause. "Did you just say, 'you asked' or 'you ass?'"

Andy chuckled. "Don't you just love ambiguity?" SKIP.

"You know what?" Bella asked. "I have to be honest. When working with some of my patients, I've never liked the designation 'Sex Slave' that some of them have used. It makes me uncomfortable. The label carries too many negative connotations. While I will admit that it is the most accurate denotation there is, the term means so many different things to different people. Most people, of course, understand it to refer to a person who is used for the sexual gratification of another. Setting aside any discussion about their willingness for another time... have you ever stopped and considered the description can actually be self-reflective? That is the person who *is* a Sex Slave is a slave to their *own* desire for sex? A slave to their overall id, if you will."

"Hey Doc," Andy said, "I'm sorry to interrupt, but I've always wondered something. Is id short for libido?"

"No. Actually, as weird as this might sound, if anything libido is a shortened form of id."

"Huh?"

Despite how tired I had grown, I still chuckled. As confident as Andy often seemed, whenever the deity sounded confused it struck me as funny.

"Libido refers specifically to one's *sexual* desire," Bella explained. "It's a very narrow definition focused solely on sex. A person's id, on the other hand, is the unconscious source of our demands for immediate satisfaction of *any* of our primitive needs. It's responsible for that instinctive impulse we feel whenever we crave instant gratification."

"Sounds pretty sexual, if you ask me."

"Which is why most people erroneously interchange the two words, I know. However, it's the id that compels us to choose fight or flight. It's also the overriding force which overcomes all of our commonsense resistance to buying anything in the checkout aisle. But it's our libido that has us masturbating the first chance we get no matter how inappropriate the locale. Or, I don't know, maybe going home with just anyone after two when the lights go on in the club."

"Spoken like a woman with more than a few regrets."

"Hey! I went to college, but I never stayed out that late... not often anyway...

maybe once or twice."

"Methinks the lady—"

"—I wasn't talking about myself," Bella clapped back. "Next caller."

Shaking my head as I turned my phone off for the night, I realized Bella wasn't the only one who'd had enough. I needed some sleep.

Thursday
March 5, 2020
9:01pm, 49° & cloudy

I was too excited to sleep.

Tomorrow was the day.

Our day.

I couldn't believe it was almost here. And part of me wanted so badly to flash forward.

I expected this time tomorrow night, Victor and I would be laying somewhere, a tangled heap of limbs. Naked. Spent and exhausted. Aching, much as I did now, for even more.

Yet there was another part of me that I had to admit was afraid.

Tomorrow I would find out exactly what I had gotten myself into. If I could explain myself well enough. If Victor could be as understanding as he seemed. If he could forgive me.

Once again, I ran my explanation through my heart. But they were still just words.

I only hoped when the opportunity finally arrived tomorrow evening, I could maintain my composure enough to accurately filter them through my brain before processing them with my mouth.

I hoped Victor would have the ability to feel my intentions... provided he could see past my inactions.

I took a deep breath, hoping it might help.

A deception by omission. It seemed so insignificant at the time. *Compared to now, anyway.*

And yet now was almost upon me.

Provided I could ever fall asleep.

Tossing my comforter aside, I got up and headed for my kitchen. The half glass of Cab might not have worked but it was still early enough to make it a whole.

I couldn't believe it was finally here.

My last night to watch Bella's YouTube channel.

And first night to get my first real look at Andy du Payne.

I could always view more later, of course. Due to my time constraints for the last two months, there were still complete episodes and several hours worth of material I had yet to check out. And while I could watch more during my flight home tomorrow, the expected tail winds projected to push me east were going to be stronger than any I had flown in thus far. I doubted my return trip would be able to afford any distractions.

At the moment, however, a distraction was what I needed most.

My lawyers, accountants and I had wrapped the day on a high note. As expected, the IRS owed me a bit of a refund for overpaying my taxes under all three of my names. While it wasn't enough to cover the amount I was advised to expect from the fine they were set to impose tomorrow morning before I departed for Charlotte, there were worse things in life. I'd live. *Hopefully.*

I shook my head to break up the negativity. Trying not to think about the new problems I could have on my plate going forward, I fired up Bella's podcast/YouTube finale and hit PLAY.

And right away could tell something was different.

Much like every episode, Bella opened by radiating her beautiful smile into the camera. She was even seated behind a desk with her microphone in front of her, the same as before. But gone were the computer monitor she used to address Andy along with the framed Taj Mahal and *Mona Lisa* pictures that were always hung behind her. In fact, she was in a different room altogether.

Backdropped by a shelf full of books, Bella appeared to be in a professional office of some sort. More than likely hers, I could see from one wall to another given how wide the camera's angle was set unlike how narrowly focused it had always been.

Yet even more shocking than the two new settings were the two figures flanking her.

On Bella's left sat Shawn Royale who I vaguely recalled had been a fairly flamboyant, all-pro wide receiver for some professional football team out west. While I wouldn't have recognized him if not for his picture in the episode's thumbnail, I wouldn't have even known who he was if not for a helmet-to-helmet tackle he took on field during a game years ago.

If memory served me correctly not only did it happen near the time of Bella's show, the hit to his head was so vicious it left him permanently paralyzed from the neck down. Only now, stretched out on a beautifully upholstered chaise lounge chair obviously intended for Bella's patients, Shawn Royale appeared anything but either.

Relaxing comfortably with both hands behind his head like he owned the place, his appearance was special in that he was the first live, in-studio guest Bella had ever hosted. And while that fact had been widely advertised for the week leading up to the show, it was her second guest the majority of her regular audience had tuned in to see.

Because on Bella's right was The Invisible Andy.

His anonymity protected behind the same heavily frosted panel of glass in the only picture I had ever been able to find, I was once again bothered by the lack of doubt in my mind that I was looking at Greg Costello. Despite being restricted by its size, even the way the backlit figure moved about the small, custom built enclosure to shield his identity reminded me of the man.

Dumbfounded that I could be so wrong, that Greg had been Andy all along, I stared in shock as Bella commenced with the show. Thanking her audience for joining her in her new location. Announcing then welcoming her first, live guest complete with canned applause. And last but certainly not least, introducing the man everyone had been waiting to see, Mr. Andy du Payne.

Amazingly though, for the next two hours Bella's final show carried on like most of her others. The only two real differences were that her other guests had not only broadcast from their own homes, but each had only joined the podcast for The Balls Of Ballin' Ballers segment. Shawn wasn't only present for the entire show, he participated throughout.

Well, those two differences and Andy's odd presence behind the glass, anyway.

His attendance explained as a trial run that he might or might not resume the following season, Andy didn't say nearly as much as he typically did. And he moved around behind the glass even less than that. While I assumed he couldn't see out any better than the camera could see in, that only made his statuesque posture seem even more bizarre.

Although many in the chat that night were vocally disappointed in his subdued demeanor, Andy and Shawn did get into it a few times. While I wasn't all that familiar with professional football—no matter how many times in my life I had been mistaken for a player—I did know that successful wide receivers like Shawn tended to be cocky divas who didn't appreciate sharing the spotlight. Chalking up their minor jaw-jacking moments to just that, I didn't make much more of it.

When suddenly the podcast was over.

Bella thanked Shawn and Andy and bid her fans farewell after encouraging them to return for her fourth season following a two-week Christmas break. She gave no indication the show would be her last, not even a hint of the possibility. Which told me what I expected all along.

Something must have happened.

Scanning over the thank-you messages from her most active, long-time listeners I read through a few of the more speculative posts about what might have transpired. It was easy to dismiss Bella deciding they couldn't work together any longer because she was mad at Andy for being more combative with Shawn than any other guest. Even if that were true, I knew she would have explained it as such and not left her fans, especially her beloved 'Dicts, hanging.

Likewise, it was easy to reject the probability that Bella was somehow so despondent over Shawn's injury—which according to the post occurred just two days after the interview, breaking the lucky streak associated with an appearance—that she decided to hang up her microphone. And while Shawn inferred a few times that the streak was a partial motivation for him to be her guest, I had a hard time believing it was enough to make Bella feel any level of responsibility for what happened to him. Especially one deep enough to ditch her show altogether.

No, there had to be something else. Something everyone had missed.

Backing out of her farewell messages page, I rechecked her website to look for any kind of clue. And then I found it.

I remembered the first time I saw it I had assumed it was simply a message board for Bella's fans to converse outside of her shows. Instead, the tab 'Dear 'Dicts' opened a message to her fans.

Dear 'Dicts,

It's not you, it's me. Cliché, I know, but true nonetheless. And while most breakups occur because people simply grow apart, that's not the case with us. If anything, I feel closer to you than ever and I can only hope you feel the same.

Yes, I still love you and I always will. You have validated the purpose of my life and given it immense meaning and I will forever be thankful for the role each of you have played. While it may have been you who sought my assistance, it was you who helped me more than you will ever know.

And flawed though we both might be, neither of us did anything wrong.

Sometimes things happen in life. Circumstances we can't predict can lead to occurrences we can't control... often because we failed to predict them. But when those circumstances remain out of our control, sometimes it is necessary to take a step back, perhaps even to reduce those elements in our lives we do have control over in order to concentrate on the ones we do not.

So it's time for me to practice what I've tried to preach. To focus on myself and my well-being. To take care of me... so that one day I might again help take care of you.

Until that time...

Thank you for the memories,

Doc

And just like that, Bella's podcasts and YouTube channel were done. She never produced another episode much less a statement of further clarification about why she shut her show down. Though her website remained active for her 'Dicts to continue interacting, the page had quickly turned into nothing more than an abandoned shrine of farewell wishes and thanks from her most ardent supporters as everyone went their separate ways.

III

Love *n* **1 :** *strong affection* **2 :** *warm attachment* **3 :** *beloved person*

Friday
March 6, 2020
5:11pm, 54° & windy

I glanced at the photo slotted between the top corner of my bedroom's full-length mirror and its frame. A pre-girls-night-out with Abby selfie from two years and forty-five pounds ago, my hair and makeup looked almost perfect. Complementing my smile, my favorite little black dress had revealed just the right amount of cleavage, all of which had battled the bronze glow of my skin for attention.

And now here I was, two years later, standing in front of the same mirror. With the exception of the dress, I looked *exactly* the same.

Two-a-day workouts, every day for the past eight weeks had been rough at first. The pounds I had shed just prior to meeting Victor had been the easiest as they were just water weight. While I had done it a few times even before that, putting in so much effort with very little to show for it had, in the beginning, been disheartening. But I understood how the human body worked so I simply kept at it.

Twenty minutes of morning yoga gave way to forty of strength and weight training followed by a rigorous half hour of cardio. Reversing the process in the evening followed by an epsom salt bath not only made for a great night's sleep, it helped double my results. But still, I knew I was lucky.

My one saving grace in becoming overweight was that I had gained it uniformly. Even at my heaviest, I didn't have any specific problem areas. I had simply more than less ballooned all over. But those days were behind me now as I was resolved to never again use food as a means of comfort.

Studying my reflection, I allowed myself one last moment of smug satisfaction. In the last two months I had not only lost thirty pounds, I had also gained a few muscles. My body wasn't just slim and trim, it was toned and honed.

While I had to cut my sunbathing trip to Saint Marteen short to beat the anticipated travel ban due to the spread of the Covid-19 virus, the full week's worth of natural tanning I managed to squeeze in was more than enough. And the dark bronze of my skin looked even better paired with the golden sun drench in my hair. I looked and felt healthier than I had in a long time. Not only did I find myself wondering what Victor would think about the new me, the truth was, I wondered myself.

Did I do it for him? Or did I do it for me?

I had already been on the path toward better health prior to our night together, so I knew Victor wasn't the impetus for the changes I had made. But ever since then, getting back in shape solely for this weekend had become my mini obsession. I knew a good man when I saw one and if Victor was still anything like he was... he was going to be mine. The type of man most women would consider an absolute heartbreaker, in the last two months Victor had continued to set the bar of what I was looking for higher than I had ever dared dream.

And he did it right when I wasn't looking...

Looking back, the idea was hard to contemplate. All I had wanted to do that night was get myself laid. A simple wham, bam, thank you, Dan. That had been my plan and if I had just stuck to it... *Ohhhhh!* I shook my head, berating myself again for what I swore once more would be the last time as my mind turned to the far more pressing matter before me.

What if he doesn't want me like I want him?

The thought had been nagging me for weeks. Had allowing Victor to role play as my Master gone too far? The sex had been the best I'd ever had and I was pretty sure it was right up there for him, too.

But what if that's all he wants now? What if that's the only reason he still wants to see me?

I had no problem with Victor using me to fulfill his own desires. He had taken me to a place sexually where I felt no guilt or shame. A place that was purely and unapologetically hedonistic. And in return, I wanted him to feel exactly the same.

Recalling one of her therapy sessions from back in the day, Abby had been right about the freedom that comes with allowing oneself to be used as a Sex Slave. Every time I found myself fantasizing over the memory, I was quickly reminded that our entire night together had been a total, liberating rush. Images of Victor standing over me, fucking my mouth in a way no man ever had then later riding him to the best orgasm of my life. The surprising amount of wetness he generated between my legs and the way the sound spurred him to pound down on top of me even harder. I even remembered the Williamsburg blue, opaque glaze of his eyes, that steely look of unadulterated lust that came over him as he gripped my ass even tighter while fucking me from behind...

The memories still gave me goosebumps.

Allowing Victor to use me solely for his pleasure, to gladly let him take me in any and every way he wanted had created something between us I never knew could exist. In those moments I felt what he felt as I know he did I. Our bodies and minds had been so in sync each of us seemed able to anticipate when and how the other would moan... because it wasn't just the sex that was incredible.

It was the connection.

The level of our inner connectedness had been as high as the moment immediately preceding my orgasm. But it had lasted so much longer. *Oh, so much long—*

Realizing I was starting to make myself wet from thinking about it, I shook my head. I had to stop. We were meeting in less than an hour at SoCo Bar in The Westin Charlotte for what I hoped would be an entire weekend of more mind-blowing sex and I needed to get my game face on. I hadn't shown Victor one shred of self-doubt our first night together and I wasn't going to this weekend either.

Not that I honestly felt I had to worry about it.

Every single day of the last sixty, Victor had made sure a message beginning with the words "Ciao, Bella" was waiting for me when I woke up. Most often his missives came in the form of a simple text or a longer email. Sometimes sexual sometimes not, each message was brimmed by a silver lining of optimism to say the least.

Then, almost as if just to mix things up, every so often I would receive something more poignant. A scenic picture, inspirational quote, link to a song or a meaningful word from the online *Dictionary of Obscure Sorrows.* Sweet nothings that had quickly become far sweeter everythings to me. I never knew what would be waiting for me or what to expect each morning when I grabbed my phone until all of a sudden I ironically found myself full of expectations.

And that's when it hit me.

I realized I had forgotten what it felt like, to wake each day excited to find out not just what Victor had in store for me... but what life did. Excited again to figure out the best way I could help my patients. Excited about eating better, working out as hard as I could and getting the results I wanted. I was even excited by how good growing healthier made me feel each day translated into how peacefully I slept each night.

I finally knew what the saying "Everything felt new again" meant because I was living inside their quotation marks. I felt reborn, like my life was starting over only this time I had a head start. I was older and wiser yet still had plenty of my youth left. Plenty of living left to do.

And to feel that way again... gave me hope. Possibly more than I had ever had before.

And even better, I was fairly certain Victor felt the same.

Occasionally reading or hearing his opinions on our only night together I realized I had given him something he didn't just want, it was something he dreamt about having again and again. For him it wasn't just about having his way with me... it was about having his way *with* me. Both of us simultaneously in the moment together. Our energy shared, flowing back and forth. Sexual. Sensual. Adoring. Uplifting. Caring... Teetering on the precipice of loving.

And I was the first woman he had ever been with like that. The first woman he had ever truly *had* like that. I could see it, tell it, sense it. I knew it without having to ask him...

Because I felt the same.

That was why for most of the last two months I had agonized over the second first impression I wanted to make. Casual-and-carefree me? Bold-and-sexy me? Or I-want-to-be-your-Sex Slave-for-life-but-can't-explain-why-for-the-life-of-me me? Refusing to settle, I ultimately decided to just be myself and go with a casual and carefree attitude to show him my boldest and sexiest best as I tried to make him want me as his Sex Slave for life.

Aware you only get a second chance once, I figured I might as well give it everything I had.

And looking at my figure in the mirror, I truly felt I was about to.

Knowing full well that a person's eyes are often first and foremost drawn toward another's most prominent features, I had found the perfect dress to take full advantage of my derrière.

Wandering just a few days ago through one of the many exclusive boutiques in the historic district of Dilworth just south of uptown Charlotte, I remembered being filled with a wonderful though unfamiliar feeling. It had been odd to realize that never once in my life had I worn anything in an attempt to accentuate my backside. Not that I was ashamed of it. I just naturally had more junk in my trunk for a woman my size.

No, it was the way other people, both men and women, often seemed to treat me a bit differently because of it. Whether it was a quick glance or an outright stare, when I felt people take notice of me strictly because of my ass, I couldn't help but to begin prejudging those who did as somehow shallow. Fighting my own hypocrisy for doing so and not wishing to feel that way about anyone, I often chose my clothes to mute the obvious, downplaying myself in the process which, as a psychologist, I knew was unhealthy.

But searching for just the right dress in which to meet Victor again, I had reveled in the fact that I had never felt strongly enough about a man to purposefully flaunt my ass as an asset. So when I spotted the purple gown hidden behind a larger dress on the rack, my pulse started to race with a strange, never-felt-before sense of hope as my hands separated the two for a better look.

I could tell immediately that the color was exactly what I wanted. But as I pushed its hanger back, my heart flew over the moon. It was all I could do not to squeal in delight.

Perfect!

Topping each sleeveless shoulder, an overlying, sheer purple piece of silver embroidered fabric stretched down to the mid abdominal area. The dress tastefully hung beneath it, covering what would have otherwise been exposed cleavage as the top parted perfectly in a V between the breasts. Draped just below the see-through neckline, gently layered waves of ruche satin fabric clung to the body-hugging spandex. The tighter horizontal ruffles across the waist progressively loosened as they dipped lower, ending just below the hips where the remainder of the material flowed to the floor, smooth in the front and widely pleated in the back. The full-length maxi party dress even had a zippered, thigh high slit along the frontside of the left leg, providing for a sexy or modest option.

Not that I felt like there was any real choice between the two.

Without a doubt, the gown was everything I had been looking for and more. Fit for a red carpet affair, it exuded both class and sex appeal, revealing just enough while leaving the rest to imagination. And though I already owned a matching pair of heels and earrings, I used the opportunity as an excuse to shop for something new... just because it felt so wonderful to feel girly again.

Looking at my image in the mirror, I turned to the side to check out my butt once more and smiled. While no panty line was visible, I knew that was to be expected. No woman in her right mind would have worn anything larger than a G-string in this gown.

Not that signs of my underwear's absence were what I was admiring anyway.

Perfectly bubbled, two straight months of squat exercises had definitely paid off, not just in the lift of my cheeks but also in the firmness of my thighs. My only complaint, if I could call it that, was the body-hugging dress stretched so well it made my rear appear even more pronounced. I didn't think Victor would mind but I didn't want it distracting too much from my hair which I had spent an hour and a half curling until I achieved the exact look I had envisioned for our first evening back together.

Satisfied overall, I smoothed out my dress along my hips one last time before grabbing my clutch and weekend bag, then locking the door behind me.

While on more than one occasion Victor had floated the idea of my joining him at his place for a full, two-week self-quarantine when he returned, each time I found a way to graciously decline. Given the other families that lived on the foundation's grounds, I knew Victor was going to take the precaution with or without me before being around them again. I just thought it best not to let him plan anything too far ahead when it came to me.

Especially since I still had so much left to reveal to him.

I only hoped he took it the right way.

Twenty-five minutes later, after handing my car keys to the underground parking garage valet and ignoring his gawk, I suddenly developed a small case of the butterflies. For two solid months I had done nothing but think about this night until finally it was here. Would it go as I hoped? Would Victor take me as I was? But more importantly...

Will he want to keep me the way I am?

Savoring my last sip of Johnny Walker before swallowing, I tried to relax. As my watch counted down each passing minute, I ironically found myself getting further and further wound up. Which made no sense. Despite the fact I hadn't laid eyes on Bella for almost two solid months, it wasn't as if I didn't know what to expect. We had communicated in one form or another every single day since I'd left Charlotte.

Whether by phone, text, email or an occasional note attached to a bouquet of flowers, I'd done my best to vary my messages so as to prevent any kind of routine pattern from developing. And although I was no fan of Bella's rule forbidding any video chats, in this moment I was definitely reaping at least one reward for our perseverance.

I absolutely could not wait to lay my eyes on the woman again.

Of course, there were other things I was excited about as well.

I thought back to a month ago when Bella suggested we each take an STD test then swap results so that we could forgo using a condom. Discussing it further later she admitted to feeling comfortable enough to trust me to stay celibate between the time of my test and our meeting. I had agreed to the same but refrained from telling her I almost felt comfortable enough for us to skip the test altogether.

Now—thankful for our mutually clean bills of health—I was grateful she seemed as devoted to giving our relationship a real chance as I was.

That was why—oddly enough after spending so much of my free time over the last two months thinking about her as I prepared for this weekend— it really shouldn't have surprised me just how much of our one night together that I remembered.

Yet it did.

Though barely a full day's worth, my memories of Bella were incredibly powerful. Far more so than of any other woman I had ever known.

I could still vividly recall just how fine Bella's hairs felt as my fingers laced through them. How smooth her skin was to the touch. How her mouth and tongue tasted, her breath so personally particular and inviting. *Just like her pussy. Mmmmmm...* As the memory of that perfect sensation began to tingle my tongue—making my mouth water even more than it already was—I recalled exactly how Bella smelled, causing me to inhale and close my eyes.

Holding my breath, not wanting to release any part of her, it dawned on me how reversed my mental process was. And perhaps how damaged my brain might still be some fifteen years after my accident. After all, smells usually evoked memories, not the other way around.

Opening my eyes to exhale, I stared off into space. Oblivious to those around me, I fingered the rim of my empty tumbler, still bothered by how something else didn't make sense. Thinking back on our night together in Jacksonville, I remembered how looking at Bella had produced such an odd juxtaposition of entangled thoughts, each a paradox of the last.

The woman had been so self-confident that her self-confidence seemed almost an afterthought. I remembered how from her choice in Cabernet Sauvignon to the minimalism of her accessories, she had exuded nothing but class. So she clearly took a certain amount of pride in her looks. Yet her being a bit overweight belied some factor that I couldn't quite put my finger on. It certainly wasn't a delayed hereditary trait. She wasn't big boned. The sheer slenderness of her wrists and ankles had shown me that much.

So why had a woman—who clearly still cared about her fashion appearance—ceased caring to the same degree about her physical one? What happened to her in the year between the time she signed off on her podcast and when we met?

As surface level and shallow as my curiosity and concern might have seemed, even to me, I knew changes in one's physical appearance were often manifestations of deeper issues or unforeseen developments. While the only coinciding event I knew of was Bella's abrupt cancellation of her podcast, even I had to admit the two still might not have been related.

Worse still, I knew the biggest inconsistency I saw in her was something born of my own prejudice. Not that I had ever given the idea much thought, but I still couldn't get it out of my head that Bella was simply not the type of person that immediately sprung to my mind upon hearing the term Sex Slave.

Oh, it had been there inside her. The look in her eyes, her complete abandonment to feverishly satisfy my every desire with more lust than I had ever experienced had definitely been there. But how did a woman with so much class, so much inner peace, calm and contentment also possess some internal switch that allowed her to perform as well as *become* a complete one-eighty of her outer self in the sack?

I wasn't knocking it, of course. I had never been more turned on by a woman in my entire life than I had been with Bella. The controlled animal she had unleashed in herself had freed the barely controllable one in me. But my problem with learning to control my animalistic nature aside, what bothered me the most was that I failed to understand Bella's desire to go to such an extreme.

I had to keep reminding myself that she *wanted* to be a Sex Slave. Undeniably, that was her unequivocal choice. She had found what had made her happy and I had no intention of trying to change that by quelling her desires. But until I understood why she had them... I couldn't be happy about them with her.

And that, I knew, was my problem.

Even though we hadn't been together, hadn't so much as laid eyes on one another for the last two months, I still wasn't sharing in that part of her happiness. I had no doubt I possessed the ability to give her what made her happy—as she so obviously did for me—but until I felt I understood her motivation, until we could share in one another's complete happiness, I couldn't see a future together. And at this point I had to admit... I wanted to. I really, really wanted to.

Of course, the ironic thing was... I had my own sharing I needed to be able to do, too.

But will Bella be able to handle it?

If only briefly, I knew I was going to be a spectacle. That much I was prepared to handle.

While I knew our plan was to rendezvous at the bar, what I didn't know was exactly what we were going to do after we met. For the weekend, Victor had given me enough of an itinerary of our plans for me to pack accordingly. But for tonight, I had far less of an idea of what he had in mind. Though he tried to convince me not to worry about it, until a few weeks ago he still hadn't told me how I needed to dress.

And then he did.

"Imagine we are going to a cocktail party for the biggest charity event put on by the world's wealthiest people," Victor had requested. "Immediately after which we're going to gamble in the high roller room of the world's most expensive casino. Dress prepared for something like that."

So I had.

Had I been ten years younger, people probably would have assumed I was going to prom. But as I was neither, the relatively few guests I encountered in The Westin lobby after exiting the elevator looked at me as if I were a lost chanteuse, searching for a piano to lay across and a microphone to suck on. Or perhaps it was just my imagination. Because that's how it felt.

Either way, there was no going back now. The bar was just around the next corner. A few more steps and I would be there.

But will he?

I could tell she was coming before I saw her.

Offset the rear corner of the ground floor lobby where I sat, The Westin Charlotte's SoCo bar was sporadically crowded on three of its four sides. Businessmen and women filled the stools and couches as others mingled. A few appeared to be networking after a conference while others were obviously winding down their work week with a few drinks. While the backdrop in the center of the bar along with several hanging partitions shielded the rest of the reception area from view, further to the side where I sat waiting the surrounding partitions blocked it almost entirely.

Not that it mattered.

Even if I hadn't heard the approaching click of her heels on the marble floor, when two guys simultaneously whipsawed their heads to get a better view, triggering a couple more to do the same, I knew it had to be Bella.

But not even their popping eyes prepared me for just how bella she truly was.

Two steps into the Soco Bar's main entrance area I turned to find Victor sitting in the corner, not only waiting for me, but obviously expecting me. Shivering just once, small thrills began to race up my spine like a cacophony of voices, all shouting simultaneously and repeatedly to be heard above the rest.

He's here!

He's looking for me!

He's even hotter than before! How is that possible?

Oh, my God, that smile! It's for me?!

Wow! His suit! That has to be custom-tail—

My thoughts were interrupted by my own ecstatic shock as I realized not only had I froze in place upon seeing Victor, but because within seconds he stood to his full height. Heading straight for me, I was surprised I had forgotten just how tall the man was.

Of course, some of that definitely had to do with his suit.

Dark and double breasted with a faint checkered pattern, the cut was definitely English. High up under his pits and crotch, Victor's arms and legs looked thinner thus longer. Paired with a crisp white shirt and diagonally striped grey and black, Windsor knotted tie, I couldn't tell whether he had come from adjourning a boardroom or toasting a groom just moments ago. All I knew was that without a doubt he was even more devastatingly handsome than the first time we met.

And the look in his eyes as they stayed glued to mine...

Awe. Appreciation. Hunger. Desire. Want. Need. Lust.

I'd never had a man engage me in such mutual apodyopsis before in my entire life. It wasn't possible because I had never before felt the same for anyone. That he appeared as momentarily lost in its throes as I was...

I didn't have time to enjoy the feeling further as Victor's long legs closed the final gap between us. Reaching down, he took my face in his hands and kissed me as if we were the only two people in the entire place.

And for several seconds, he had me feeling like we were.

Gone was the din of the crowd. Gone was anyone staring at my ass or how I was dressed. Gone was everyone but Victor and myself as everything faded into the background of our kiss. And as his lips devoured mine, I was shocked to feel all the same emotions so obviously going through him.

Joy. Relief. Passion.

He's missed me! Oh my God, this is really happening! Oh my God, his lips! How I've missed his lips...

Rejoicing in the feel of his hands, reveling in the touch of his mouth, I lost myself in the moment as I fed both Victor's hunger and my own. Lips, tongues, hands... time. After time, after time.

Until slowly we stopped and opened our eyes. All four of them smiling before we both did as well.

Taking a small step back, Victor took my hand and raised it to his lips for a kiss. Completely oblivious to our scene, his confidence along with the degree to which he was so thoroughly present in the moment was every bit as intoxicating as his cologne. As was the personal taste of his breath, the unique flavor of which I could still detect even through the whisky he had obviously just been drinking.

Oh, how I missed—

"Ciao, Bella," Victor said softly.

His voice. His. In person. Not through the phone—

"Hi," was the only word my mouth could muster.

His eyes on mine, Victor nodded his understanding.

"Come with me."

Not a request, just a polite, simple command.

Keeping my hand in his, he began to lead the way back toward the elevators. Following as quickly as I could, only then did I become aware of several people turning their heads, quickly looking away as if they had not been watching us the entire time.

As if, I smiled to myself.

"Come with me."

I could hear my heart pulsing so loudly in my ears I couldn't help but wonder if Bella felt it in my hand. As if that weren't bad enough, I had to force myself to pace my stride on the way to the elevators. It had been far too long since I had last walked hand in hand with a woman.

I struggled to remember the last time. Was it when Bella and I were together in Jacksonville? Had I held her hand as we made our way from her car to my hotel room then? I couldn't remember. Didn't know. Couldn't think properly.

All I knew as a I pressed the Up button was that I wanted to be alone with her. Wanted nothing but some privacy. Any privacy.

Yet as we stood there waiting for the elevator together alone, I realized just how torn I was.

Keeping my hands off of her was going to be difficult. Mindful of her admonition against public humiliation, even though it appeared we were going to be alone for the ride up, I knew a hotel as posh as The Westin would definitely have at least one security camera in the elevator. Bella would know that, too, but dear God was it going to be hard to keep my hands to myself.

Luckily, just before our elevator dinged I realized my resolve wouldn't be put to the test as a woman stepped forward to ride with us. After holding the door for the two of them, I ducked my head, stepped inside and pressed the button for the penthouse on the 25th floor, noticing that the woman had already selected the 21st floor.

Four floors alone. I can handle that.

Slipping my hand over Bella's, I gave her one last look and a smile. But as I assumed the bored elevator passenger position, I began to wonder what was going to happen once the other woman got off on her floor. Would Bella be bold enough to make a move on me right then and there? Or would she do as I was doing, quietly harnessing the obvious sexual tension of the moment for what was undoubtedly going to be a delayed yet explosive release?

As the woman exited on twenty-one, I squeezed Bella's hand a little tighter but stayed stock still. Sensing only the smallest amount of disappointment in her posture, she nevertheless followed my lead and remained motionless.

Twenty seconds later, I opened the door to our room... which was just how I left it.

No sooner had the door shut than Victor grabbed me from behind and spun me around. With his mouth on mine our hands became a frenzied mess as we tangled with one another. As fast as I could, I had his coat unbuttoned and was just beginning to slide it back and off his broad shoulders when Victor suddenly lifted me bodily in his arms.

Despite how my heels had given the position of our kiss in the lobby such a new, exciting feel, allowing me to feel both taller and more confident, being swept up by Victor reminded me of just how strong he was. Three strides were all he took to place me standing before him in front of the room's credenza. In our frenzy, I hardly noticed that the leather executive chair was already conveniently pushed to the side, out of our way.

Beyond the wall of windows on our left, a sudden flash of lightning illuminated the suite. As the thunder rolled several seconds behind, Victor's right hand slipped between my legs.

Running his fingers up my right thigh, I watched his face for the moment.

Expecting to find Bella's panties sopping wet, I was surprised when my fingertips brushed against the bare softness of her folds. So surprised, I pulled back despite myself.

"You're not wearing any..." I said, unable to continue as I realized she had been naked under her cocktail dress all along.

Obviously enjoying her little moment, Bella practically cooed.

"Considering how well our first time went, I wanted to pick up right where we left off."

Giving Bella a second to revel triumphantly in her tease, I lifted both her skirt and her without warning up onto the desk, sitting her on her ass and spreading her legs with my body as I got down on my knees, lowering my face directly to her crotch.

My God, her smell...

Clamping my mouth on her clit, I wasted no time plunging my tongue inside her, eliciting the most beautiful high-pitched moan I had ever heard a woman make. Lapping from her like a dog in heat, my nose barely registered the tickle from the soft wisps of her small strip of pubic hair.

Reaching behind me blindly, my hand found then deftly rolled the chair to the desk beneath me, allowing me to sit. As I made myself comfortable, Bella did the same, leaning back to support herself with her left hand as her right pulled my head closer against her while those gorgeous high heels of hers came to rest atop the chair on either side of my head.

Again and again I licked her. Tasted her. Tongued her as deeply as I possibly could while both my hands moved behind and underneath her ass cheeks. Marveling at how firm each now was while fitting just as perfectly in my hands as they had before, I pulled her tighter against my mouth, allowing her to lean back and spread her legs even further for me.

As Bella's moans turned to wails, her wetness increased to the point I knew she was ready. Sliding my right hand forward, I inserted two fingers inside her as my mouth engulfed her clitoris. With my middle finger applying pressure against one side of her G-spot, my index finger stroked the other side in a steady, come-hither motion. Coupling the manual stimulation to the pace of my tongue swirling around her clit caused Bella to buck uncontrollably against my mouth until she finally came.

Again and again I made her jerk, allowing her only a split second of relaxation before I triggered yet another spasm until I knew she couldn't take it anymore. Her pussy still raw and her body shaking in ever smaller quivers, I looked up to watch as she opened her eyes, her heat still evident in them.

It was all the look I needed.

Relinquishing his oral grip on my sex, Victor stood and gathered me up, lifting and carrying me easily in his powerful arms over to the window. As I wrapped my legs around his torso for balance, I suddenly realized just how much I ached to have him inside me. So when his hands dropped their support from under my butt allowing my body to drag down, I couldn't help myself as I spread my legs to all but dry hump the bulge in his pants.

"Mmmmmm," he hummed. "I guess I'm not the only one ready for more."

Deftly running his left hand up my back and into my hair momentarily distracted me from the feel of his right hand as it slid quickly around and under my butt cheek. Equally playful as he was rough, Victor gripped a handful of my hair while slipping two fingers inside my wetness again.

"Are you Bella? Are you ready for more?"

"Yes, please," I begged.

"Please, what?" he retorted.

Not just his tone but his words shocked me. Two solid months of communication and not once had Victor undutifully broached the topic per my request. Still...

How could I forg—

"Yes, please, Master."

Victor grinned but said nothing as he used both of his grips on my body to spin me around to face the glass. Guiding my head slowly forward as he bent me over, I instinctively reached out to brace myself against the window while arching my back and ass in the process. Adjusting my position with a simple sidestep, I spread my legs a bit further as both his fingers and several emotions started to well within me.

Gazing down on the cityscape below, I suddenly realized I had never been so high up in a building in my life. I was equally awestruck by the countless pinpoints of light as I was the first thunderstorm still slowly approaching from the west. There was something about towering over the former while being on par with the latter that infused me with a feeling of empowerment over the world. But at the same time, the backdrop of the dimly lit room as well as the flashes of cloud-to-cloud and cloud-to-ground lightning each made me feel fully exposed for all the world to see. I knew we were on the 25th floor, but I couldn't help to feel as if I were a public spectacle.

As if that wasn't bad enough, the overly analytical slice of my brain that wouldn't turn off was vaguely aware the next storm was probably somewhere over my house. Seeming to sense my thoughts and feelings, Victor withdrew his fingers then leaned forward to my ear as I heard him unzip his pants behind me.

"I know you said no public humiliation, Bella. But do you trust me?"

"Yes," I said, the word flowing with emotion as I was quickly growing incapable of thought. Because while I might not have understood his question, I did know my answer. "Yes, I trust you."

"Good."

And with that Victor slid my dress up over my hips until it bunched along my waist.

Pressed against the glass, naked from the waist down for all the world to see, my psyche and soul exploded. I had been undeniably specific, no public humiliation. True, twenty-five floors high, no one below would be able to discern what we were doing. Even our location on the southern edge of the inner city guaranteed that there were only a few high-rises near enough from which anyone could possibly see—

—Oh my God...

If I was going to last sixty seconds, it was going to take every ounce of willpower I had to hold off for fifty. Two solids months without sex and I was all but beside myself. And while jelqing had all the hallmarks of masturbation, it had had none of the payoffs. Add to it the sight of Bella's bare, perfectly curved ass propped by her high heels eagerly awaiting my next move and I suddenly couldn't take it anymore.

With a single, swift swipe, I wet the head of my cock between the folds of her lips then thrust forward, slamming into Bella so hard and fast our bodies sounded every bit as loud as the last clap of thunder. Burying myself as deeply into her as she would have me, I grabbed her by the waist to hold us both still.

For two months I had been imagining what this moment would feel like. To be inside Bella again, to feel her wrapped around my cock. Closing my eyes as they rolled back into my head, I paused us both to savor the sensation.

One second.

Two.

Three.

And then little by little, I began to withdraw from her. Emptying her hole as I emptied her whole before finally pushing myself back inside where it felt I belonged.

As one thrust became two and two became four, I consciously began to tamp down against the orgasm already rising within me. Physically clenching my PC muscle along with my teeth, I attempted to concentrate on two things: the firm grip I had on Bella's cheeks and the relentless pounding I was putting on her pussy. With each thrust my mind grew more and more dim until I ceased to exist in any part of my body but my cock.

As each inch slipped furiously in and out of her walls, I suddenly could no longer feel her ass in my hands, see her hair shaking atop her head or hear her squeals of rising delight. Fucking her harder and harder, nothing existed except the few square inches where our bodies repeatedly separated before fusing back together. Lost in the sensation, my burgeoning orgasm suddenly went parabolic, leaving me no choice but to completely withdraw from Bella in order to stop it.

"No no no no no no no—"

Bella's plaintive whine crashed through my senses, startling me.

"No, what?" I gritted through my teeth as I desperately pinched down on my impending orgasm. I wasn't done. It was too soo—

"I need your dick..."

What?—Oh, God. I had been so focused on my orgasm, I failed to realize Bella was so close to hers.

"I need your dick. In me. Please," she whispered. "Please put your dick back in me... *Please!"*

I had never heard a woman so desperate for my cock. Had never taken a woman to the knee-quivering state Bella was now in. Had never—

Fuck it!

With no need to aim, I slammed mercilessly back into Bella, causing her to cry out. Quickly reaching forward, I grabbed both her hands from the window and spread them backward. Pulling her away just enough to prevent her head from hitting the glass, I used her arms like reins as I proceeded to pummel her for all we were worth.

Neither of us lasted and damn if I cared.

As sheets of rain backlit by lightning lashed the windows mere inches in front of my face, I came. Hard. Again and again. Multiple orgasms rocked my core, each spreading out in waves that sapped my strength as they carried my willpower with them. As the shake of my knees, clench of my abdominal muscles, aching hardness of my nipples and countless other sensations continued to heighten, each began to compete with my diminishing ability to simply stay upright as I drenched Victor with my juices.

And then it was his turn.

On a downstroke, I felt the first spurt from his dick flood the gap between us, filling me with the heat of his cum. Letting out a cry but not letting up, each of his next two ejaculations occurred at the top of his thrusts. Piercing me like hot needles, both splashes shot even deeper inside me, triggering waves to ripple through me.

Hearing me cry as my legs began to buckle, Victor released my hands so that his were free to scoop me up behind my knees. Lifting my feet several inches off the floor, I felt myself impaled, suspended by his hands every bit as much as I was by his dick. The unfamiliar sensation produced yet another orgasm so strong that the muscles lining my vagina momentarily seized in the middle of a contraction and refused to give in to the tremors that so desperately tried to escape my confines.

Riding the wave of ecstasy, I arched my head to my left and reached back over my shoulder, my right hand encircling Victor's neck in an effort both to hang on as well as balance my weight in his arms. Rocking me up and down on the slipperiness of his dick, he slowly decreased our tempo and allowed me to regather my strength. Sliding fully inside me one last time, he gently relaxed his support under my knees, giving me time to regain my footing. Standing before the window again, my legs spread as before, his lips on my ear surprised me.

"Bella," he whispered simply but in such a way I couldn't discern whether he was saying my name... or describing our experience.

As I took a deep breath and reveled in the rarity of my confusion, Victor slid himself from within me. The ache of his sudden absence was mitigated by the tantalizing shock at the sheer volume of hot cum that began to run down my legs. As two streams of his semen oozed down my inner thighs, Victor wrapped his arms around my shoulders and torso, embracing me in a cocoon that felt wonderfully protective.

"My Bella," he whispered.

Glancing back at me over her shoulder, Bella slowly swiveled to face me. Amazed yet grateful she managed to keep her high heels on, I loved how her height brought us closer together. Leaning her ample chest forward, she swayed her back until I knew her bare flesh had to be pressed against the glass.

"My Master," she replied with only a mild hint of obedience.

"Hmmmmm. I almost forgot that part."

"You'll get used to it... if you want."

Oh, I most definitely want, I thought before pulling her to me to kiss her, passionately at first, but more gently as time passed. Releasing one another's lips, we did nothing but gaze into the other's eyes for several seconds, the kind that seemed to go on and on and...

"So... what now?" she finally asked.

Detecting a bit of trepidation in her voice because my nonverbal answer was obviously less than she was hoping for, I smiled and reached up to stroke the side of her cheek before brushing a curl behind her ear. "I'm glad you asked."

Running my hands slowly down across her covered breasts until they reached her waist, I stretched Bella's dress back down along her sides, pulling it snug at the bottom. Finished, I began to reach for my cock when I noticed how perfectly still she was holding, just watching me. The look in her eyes made me smile.

"Would you like to put my cock away?"

"No," she said without any hesitation, causing me to damn near crack up in laughter as I suddenly recalled how quick witted her responses could be.

"Yeah," I finally admitted as she chuckled with me. "I don't want to put it away either... So, you do it for me."

Without saying a word, Bella gently took me in her hand, guided and pushed me back into my pants, then dutifully and carefully zipped me up.

"I hope this doesn't mean we're done already," she pouted playfully.

"We're not," I said. "But we're done here. We're leaving."

Bella's shock was immediate. "Wait, what?"

"'Wait, what?'" I teasingly mimicked her in return. "Is that any way to talk to your Master?"

Bella's confusion stunted her response. "No... I mean, no, but... but you haven't exactly *agreed* to be my Master yet."

"No," I said. "Not yet... So let's go somewhere where we can talk about it."

Without waiting for a reply, I took her by the hand and began to lead us toward the door when I suddenly remembered something.

As Victor began to lead me by the hand, a thousand questions erupted in my head.

Why are we leaving? I thought this weekend was only supposed to be about sex? Has he decided he wants to be my Master? I thought he was only going to give me an answer after... Where are we going? Oh God, I didn't get to show—

When Victor suddenly stopped, my confusion only got worse.

"Ooops, I almost forgot," he said before releasing my hand and walking back over to the window. Looking up into the top right corner, he reached out and scratched something with his finger. On his third try, his nail caught and a thin sheet of plastic film began peeling off the glass. See-through from our side, the opposite that had been facing the exterior was both dark and completely reflective. Pulling down and to the right until it was fully detached, Victor balled the one-way cellophane mirror into a large, crinkled wad before tossing it into the wastebasket by the credenza.

I couldn't keep my jaw from dropping.

"No public humiliation, you said... And I told you you could trust me," he said with a wink.

As Victor grabbed my hand again and began to lead us toward the door, I stood on the tiptoes of my heels and pulled him down to me, smothering him with my best thank-you kiss. At that point, I no longer cared where we were going.

I would follow the man anywhere.

After retrieving Bella's suitcase from the trunk of her car, we tossed it in mine then headed north out of uptown on the Brookshire Freeway.

With the next wave of the approaching storm still a bit off to our west, we spent most of the twenty-five minute car ride holding hands. But after informing Bella we were going to my house, we also spent most of it in silence. Which was fine. We'd spent so much of the last two months communicating in different ways that now all we really seemed to want to do was just touch and be in one another's presence. At least it felt that way to me as our fingers stroked the other's hand.

Turning right onto my road, I felt my heart quicken just a bit in anticipation because I'd also spent all of the last two months imagining how Bella's first visit to my house might go... and how there were a few things I still hadn't told her.

"Ummm," I started, "this might sound a little weird, but before we get to my place, I need to make a quick stop."

Bella, already looking at me, simply smiled and nodded her okay. Caressing the back of her hand in response, I reveled in the trust she was placing in me. I only hoped it would continue.

After the third house on the left, I turned down the side driveway of the fourth. By the time we passed the right rear of the house, Rick was standing there waiting. In his black and yellow Caterpillar ball cap, white tee shirt, denim bib overalls and steel-toed work boots, he looked just like I left him.

Twenty-eight and just as short and scruffy as ever, Richard Crockett had been a recon ranger for the US Army until he lost most of his left leg to an infection he incurred while traipsing through the jungles of Guatemala. I'd met him several years ago at the VA hospital where he was being outfitted for a prosthetic. After a pleasant conversation and a few background checks, I had the To Fish Foundation hire him for the job he had now.

Pulling to a stop alongside, I rolled down my window.

"Welcome back..." Rick started to say before realizing I wasn't alone. The surprise in his eyes that I had someone, hell *any*one, with me could not have been more unmistakable. Not to mention I was holding her hand. "Boss," he finished before recovering nicely. Despite his poker face, it was clear that he recognized Bella from my request two months ago. I'd only asked for her address, but I knew he'd probably dig a little further. "Ma'am," he nodded and drawled politely, laying both on a little thick.

I rolled my eyes. "What did I... never mind. Rick Crockett, I'd like you to meet Dr. Bella Quinn."

Rick nodded again but this time with a smile. "It's a pleasure to meet you, Dr. Quinn."

Yep, he remembers, I grimaced with the straightest face I could, thankful Bella didn't seem to notice either.

"It's nice to meet you, Rick. But please, call me Bella."

Rick bowed his head just a bit. "As you wish."

I rolled my eyes again. "So, is everyone ready?"

"As we'll ever be," Rick reported. "I think the kids are a lil' disappointed you can't play with 'em for another coupla weeks but other than that, everybody's in good spirits."

"Good," I said. "And my packages?"

"In the back a the Raptor, just like ya asked."

"Thanks."

"Don't mention it... We're still on for tomorrow mornin' at the Whitewater Center, right?"

"If you don't mind."

"Are you kiddin'? It'd be my pleasure. Plus, it'll be an even trade. You're still coverin' for me after, right?"

"With Nixie? I told you I would."

"Just makin' sure. I mean, I can always leave her here. I just figured it'd be a good opportunity to let her socialize. And I'd really like to get a couple courses in before they shut the place down."

I couldn't blame the man. Not only was the US National Whitewater Center one of my favorite places in all of Charlotte, opening weekend was one of its best. With so many people happy to get back to outdoor activities after staying inside much of the winter, the first day alone was enough to do wonders for the soul. And while Covid-19 had begun closing certain indoor businesses like gyms and restaurants where people couldn't avoid close proximity, large outdoor venues like the Whitewater Center weren't being affected.

Yet.

However, seeing Rick take a quick glance at Bella, it took me a second to realize he thought my plans might have changed because of her. Granted, she was the first woman anyone I currently knew had ever seen me with... but I didn't think that was enough for him to doubt I'd go back on my word. So I shot him a look.

"No worries. It's all good."

Rick glanced down a second time to where Victor's hand was joined with mine before looking back up at Victor with the smallest yet most obvious shit-eating grin I'd ever seen.

"I bet it is," he deadpanned.

Victor fought his chuckle briefly before giving up. "Dick," he mumbled below his breath.

"Boss," Rick shot back.

Remaining quiet, part of me relished their good-natured banter. Something about seeing Victor in a new light, his natural interaction with someone I didn't know, brought my butterflies back.

Victor shook his head while chuckling. "So, what time would you like to meet in the morning?"

Taking a quick glance again at our hands, Rick gave a little lip shrug. "Water release isn't until 11:30. So how about 10:30? Top of the steps by the spire?"

"That'll work," Victor said just as a bit of a strong gust of wind whipped the air. "You'd better get inside before the next storm gets here."

"Why? Titanium's not electrically conductive... is it?"

"I don't know. But do you really want to stand here and find out the hard way?"

"Ummm. No, not really... It's good to have you back, Boss," Rick said graciously then smiled warmly before tipping his head toward me. "And it was good to meet you, Bella."

I smiled and nodded back. "Likewise, Rick."

Victor rolled his eyes one last time. "I'll see you tomorrow."

Bowing in exaggeration, Rick nodded. "I'm at your service."

Shaking his head, Victor smiled in that way of his I couldn't quite put my finger on as he started to chuckle again... a little longer than normal, I thought.

I drove away as my window rolled up.

Pulling under the trees behind Rick's house, I turned right onto the fairly well concealed cobblestoned driveway. Motion sensing pathway lights began illuminating ahead of us, leading our way through the woods toward the gate. Bella seemed captivated by the sight. Given how pitch black everything else around us was, I couldn't blame her.

"Rick really seems to like you," she mused without looking at me.

I gave a small smile but said nothing. My hiring Rick had saved him from spending the rest of his life lost somewhere in a civil service job which he had been resigned to entering when we met. The man was grateful above all else.

"And you like him, too," she continued after cutting her eyes in my direction for a second.

Yeah, well. "I pay him more than I ask of him to do and in return he does more than I ask of him. It works out for the both of us."

"And what exactly does he do for you?"

"Pretty much anything I ask. For the most part, he's my private groundskeeper, but because you have to pass through here to get there, you could say he's also the foundation's security guard."

Turning left, I stopped just before a break in the wall of bamboo that had begun paralleling our drive. Automatically the two halves of the overly ornate, black wrought iron gate in front of us began to separate, each sliding and retracting into a slit within the bamboo wall. Pulling just a few feet past the entrance I paused and waited for the gates to close before driving on.

"Well, that was interesting," Bella offered before falling silent again.

"The bamboo stretches around the entire property," I explained.

Bella nodded curtly but still said nothing. I began to ask her if she was going to ask me why... when suddenly it dawned on me why she wasn't. It made sense.

"I understand you probably found out a few things about me over the last two months... Things I haven't told you yet myself."

On the outside, I tried to appear calm, cool and collected. On the in, I was anything but.

Much like our only night together, there was plenty Victor and I had left unspoken over the last two months. I knew that once he returned to Charlotte we'd eventually address some of those issues. I just never envisioned any of those conversations taking place in a car.

But if that was how he wanted to roll with it...

"True," I said, "but that only makes us even." Victor nodded once in concession before I countered, "Although to be fair, 'a few' is an overstatement."

Victor chuckled, smiling as he did so in a way that set me instantly at ease.

"About five years ago," he said, "I started hiring anti-SEO companies to suppress anything about me on the internet."

Hmmmmm, I thought while saying nothing.

"Aren't you going to ask me why?""

I gently shook my head. "No. I am sure you have your reasons. *Why* you might or might not want to share them is the real question."

Victor blinked. "Well, if that's not a nice little twist on Reverse Psychology 101, I don't know what is."

Yes, but... Refusing to give in, I cocked my head. "That still doesn't mean it's not true."

Tipping his head down, Victor's smile turned a bit wry. "I could say the same thing about your desire to be a Sex Slave."

My heart fluttered. He was right, of course, but I was surprised nonetheless. With the exception of our moment in The Westin hotel room, he had honored my wish perfectly for the last two months by never once broaching the subject. I knew one of us would eventually. But to do so now, in the car, wasn't how I had envisioned it. And still didn't.

"You could. But why don't we save that conversation for somewhere a little more— Look out!"

Victor slammed on the brakes, bringing the car to a halt well enough to miss hitting the large white-tailed deer passing in front of us. Watching until it disappeared into the surrounding woods, I noticed oddly that it did so rather slowly.

"It didn't seem scared."

"She has no reason to be," Victor said as we continued forward. "There are no predators here. The bamboo that surrounds this place keeps the coyotes out. Nor can they get through the gate."

Hmmm. "Even so, she was still moving pretty slow."

Victor smiled at me. "That's because she's pretty pregnant."

"Awwwwww."

I didn't have the heart to explain to Bella that I safeguarded the deer population on my property for the possibility that I might have to one day eat Bambi. Hopefully that day would never come but until it did there really was no point in elaborating.

Driving on, a break in the woods and clouds allowed the nearly full moon to showcase the horse fields and stables off to our right. I could tell by the unsurprised way she looked at them that Bella somehow knew about them, too. Which was fine.

I'd given plenty of thought to just how much of my life's secrets I was prepared to divulge to her this weekend. Part of me felt a bit guilty about being able to explore the online treasure trove of information about her past. Her podcasts and videos often invoked the same feeling I imagined people got from seeing another person's childhood photos. Which sadly, as a former ward of the state, was something I'd never be able to offer Bella.

Sharing more about my present self felt the best way to right the scales between us. Smiling to myself I realized just how happy I was that didn't have to wait any longer.

Soon...

Half a minute later, I turned right onto the first driveway exiting the woods. The one that led to the back of my house.

As beautiful as I found the front, I figured Bella would get a bigger kick out of the rear.

"You've got a ten-car garage?" I asked in awe. Though I already suspected as much, to see it in person was something else. Not that the size and design of the house weren't impressive enough.

The grand French countryside-inspired mansion was far more massive from the ground than it appeared from above in the satellite image. I estimated each side of the decagonally arranged chateau was about seventy feet wide. Steep pitched slate roofing towered above beautifully designed stone sides, each of which was lit perfectly by hidden landscape lighting. And though the estate appeared to be mostly two-story, in the subterranean courtyard where we were sitting it looked more like three.

With four bays in front of us and three to either side, Victor had parked us face-forward in between them on the center of the driveway's in-ground automobile turntable. A simple push of a button on his keychain had started the process of fully rotating the Mercedes and us into position.

With just a tinge of embarrassment, Victor smiled. "Not exactly."

I watched as he reached up and pushed a button on the overhead console to what I assumed would be one of the garage doors. Instead, all ten began to lift in unison. Simultaneously, the interior lights flickered to life revealing each bay was not one but two vehicles deep.

Spaciously designed, better equipped and more immaculate than any luxury dealership I had ever seen, Victor's high-tech shop was every grease monkey's wet dream. I was in awe well before taking stock of the full collection.

Staring in disbelief at the array, I counted from left to right a '65 ½ Mustang Fastback, a '68 Camaro SS with an RS package, a '78 Jeep CJ7 and a Plymouth Prowler next to an empty spot into which Victor began backing the AMG. A fairly new F-150 Raptor was lined up next with its bed full of boxes, just as Rick promised. And just beyond the pickup truck, a new Acura NSX, Mustang Shelby GT500, a '74 Coupe DeVille and a '63 Corvette, which I recalled was his father's favorite, rounded out the display.

Not bothering to wait for Victor to come around and open my door, I exited and stepped deeper inside for a better look. As beautiful as the front row was the back was far more impressive.

Elevated on commercial-grade lifts and wrapped in inflated, plastic bubbles to protect them from the humidity I spotted a Rolls-Royce Dawn Black Badge, Bugatti Chiron, Koenigsegg Agera, McLaren P1, Pagani Huayra, Lamborghini Aventador, Ferrari SF90 Stradale, Aston Martin DBS Superleggera and a Bentley Mulsanne. The last car, a Mercedes-Benz McLaren in the far corner, would have grabbed my attention more than anything else if not for the one oddity in the whole fleet.

Popping the AMG's trunk, Victor smiled, watching as I rescanned the garage just to be sure. I couldn't believe I had forgotten all about it. But there it was, plain as it had been that first day.

"Why is your Jeep the only one in here with a custom paint job?" I asked.

Victor looked around as he grabbed both my bag and a box from the AMG's rear. Placing both under his left arm, he shrugged.

"Probably because it's the first vehicle I ever owned and the only one I restored myself. Years ago, when it came time to choose the paint, I really liked what Plymouth had created for the Prowler, so I went with it." A funny look came over Victor's face. "Just out of curiosity, why do you ask?"

Unprepared for the moment, I went with the simplest explanation that came to mind. "Every once in a while, I see a person's aura. The first time I saw you at Mickey's... I saw yours."

Surprisingly, Victor was only mildly shocked. "And you're saying it was dark purple? Like the one on my Jeep?" I nodded as Victor's expression softened. "Hmph. I guess that explains why I've always been drawn to it. It's always been my favorite color."

"You don't think it's weird that I can see auras?"

"No. I'm not sure it can be explained either, but that doesn't make it weird."

Grateful for Victor's understanding, I smiled to which he smiled back.

"Now come on, it's time you saw the rest of the house," he said before taking a step into my personal space. "Unless, of course, you want to stay here looking at the foundation's cars all night."

I didn't. But... "These aren't yours?"

"Yes and no. They're mine, but the ones in plastic I bought for future auctions to benefit the foundation."

Wow. The cars on the back row had to be worth several million dollars. Not that it mattered. "You can't drive most of them, anyway, can you?" I asked softly.

Victor appeared touched that I recognized his dilemma.

"Oh, I can drive them, just—"

"—not comfortably," we said together before laughing.

Taking a glance at the McLaren in the corner, I wondered, "Which is your favorite in here?"

Slowly narrowing his eyes until they smoldered, Victor dropped his voice to match.

"The one with the exceptional rear suspension."

I felt my eyes widen and nostrils flare before I could catch myself. *Oh, yeah?* Not to be outdone, I slowly shifted my weight by taking a small step, thrusting my hip out just a touch in the process as my bare left leg parted the slit in my dress.

"Well, you know, they do say some... ch*ass*is... tend to stick out... a little more than others."

Victor tilted his head to the side as his eyes tracked my curves. "Yes, some most definitely do."

Suddenly aware of the number of car hoods around us, I started to panic a bit. As much as I enjoyed our audible foreplay, before we had sex again there was something I needed Victor to know. And now was neither the time nor place.

Taking his free right hand in my left, I said, "Come on. Show me your house."

Shaking his head just once, Victor began leading the way to the center of the back wall. What appeared to be two windowed doors like those leading into a restaurant's kitchen turned out to be the entrance to an elevator. But more interesting than that was the beautiful, gold gilded plaque above it.

As Victor pressed the elevator's button, immediately opening the doors, I held back just long enough to read the white chalk on slate black board. Like Victor's tattoo, the Latin was written in calligraphy.

For a man's house is his castle and each man's home is his safest refuge. — Sir Edward Coke, I translated silently.

Interesting.

Alone in the elevator, I atoned for The Westin by kissing Bella as passionately as I could... could for a guy with a suitcase and a box under one arm anyway. Stepping onto the main floor and triggering several lights to turn on, I hoped our kiss would be enough to hold her for a few.

"I'd give you the grand tour," I apologized, "but I need to take care of something first. It'll probably take me about ten, fifteen minutes tops. In the meantime, feel free to look around and make yourself at home."

"Victor, I... I wouldn't feel ri—"

"—It's okay," I assured her. "All lighting in the house is motion sensor activated so don't worry about turning anything on or off. I'll come find you once I'm done. Okay?"

"But—"

"—Bella, listen, if we're going to try and make this work, the sooner you're comfortable here, the easier it'll be for both of us. While you're here, my house is your house. Do you understand me?"

When Bella started to protest again, I put up my hand.

"Don't worry. You can't invade my privacy. If you see a drawer or cabinet you're curious about, open it. I won't mind. I have nothing to hide from you," I said then chuckled before I could catch myself. "And full confidence not even you are likely to find those things I have hidden."

Bella blinked, slightly taken aback.

"But who knows. Maybe we'll both be surprised."

Victor pulled me close, cupped my face in his hand then leaned down to kiss me. Half expecting something more perfunctory, I was surprised to feel his passion followed by the subtle, lingering melancholy preceding a reluctant goodbye. Raising my left hand with his right to his lips, the next words through them were less surprising.

"Ciao, Bella," he said with a smile before turning and walking away.

I watched until Victor rounded the first corner then listened as the clicking sound of his footsteps echoed down the designer hardwood floor, receding until they disappeared. Then I looked around.

My God, this is a big house.

Slightly intimidated, I looked down the hall in the opposite direction. To my left and directly opposite the elevator was a shorter hallway leading to solid glass doors, the other side of which I could see the pool area all lit up.

The favorite part of his house, Victor had made more than a few mentions of it over the last two months. So much so, I had really been looking forward to seeing it with him. Figuring I might learn more from the inside instead of the out and resigned to wait, I decided to save the pool for last. Slightly disappointed, I glanced up in exasperation long enough to notice a second plaque hanging above the elevator doors. Identical to the first, the only difference was the Latin inscription.

'The world is a book and those who do not travel read only a page. —Saint Augustine of Hippo.' How beautiful, I thought before realizing how fitting the quote was for an exit to the garage.

Feeling more relaxed, I took a second to enjoy the sensation. Victor definitely had a way of taking me out of my comfort zone while simultaneously making me feel secure that was unlike anything I had ever experienced. Unfortunately, starting with my very first glance around, I couldn't help my wandering eye as it went on the lookout for anything with a woman's touch still attached.

But from the lamps on the tables lining the halls to the artwork adorning the walls, everything about Victor's place seemed to err on the side of masculine... much as the furnishing's subtle yet matching gold accents, like those on the plaques, also placed everything firmly on the side of the rich.

It was interesting to note, however, that there seemed to be little to no truly personal ornaments anywhere. No souvenir photos from vacations or trinkets from a road trip. Nothing exclusive enough to pertain only to Victor. Of course...

There must be something somewhere.

Suddenly giddy at the prospect of snooping with permission, I spun and headed down the hall.

True to Victor's word, recessed lights in the ceiling and along the bottom edge of the walls began to flicker ahead of me, illuminating my path through the semi-darkness. A good twenty yards from the elevator, I reached the first opening where, strangely enough, the short hall to my right had an incredibly low hung ceiling. Knowing that Victor was six-eight, I guessed the height to be around seven foot. But even more interesting than that was what was above it.

Just as with the elevator, another gilded plaque hung over the entryway, only this one framed a Latin quote from Lucius Annaeus Seneca. "A gem cannot be polished without friction, nor a man perfected without trials." Intrigued as to what room the quote hinted, I stepped down the hall and opened the door.

Bright fluorescent lights switched on automatically revealing an enormous personal gym. Every piece of professional grade exercise equipment imaginable filled the room which appeared even larger due to all the mirrors along the walls. And at about fifteen feet high the ceilings made me realize Victor's house might not have a second story to it at all.

Despite the gym's pristine cleanliness, when my nose caught a faint whiff of Victor's sweat, the pheromones automatically triggered my instinct to inhale. *Mmmmmmm.* And the thought of him working his muscles in here...

Turning around before I got too worked up, I found above the exit the same plaque with a quote by Marcus Tullius Cicero. "It is exercise alone that supports the spirits and keeps the mind in vigor."

Closing the door behind me, I found it interesting that Victor had chosen two Romans to quote for his weight room. Curious as to what might be next, I quickened my pace.

Waiting for me above the next low-slung entrance was a line I recognized from *The Art of War.* "Victorious warriors win first and then go to war, while defeated warriors go to war first and then seek to win." As I thought about the possible significance of Sun Tzu's quote beginning with Victor's name, I opened the door at the end of the hall. A large, high ceiling dojo with multi-discipline sparring stations took up each of the room's four corners with plenty of floor space in between.

Turning to leave I glanced above the door to quickly translate a quote by Alexander the Great. "I am not afraid of an army of lions led by a sheep; I am afraid of an army of sheep led by a lion."

Two rooms and four quotes deep, as luxurious of a house as Victor's was turning out to be, I suddenly found myself more excited by the unique glimpse into the man each of the quotes he had selected were providing me.

Pausing at the next entrance in delight I read, "A reader lives a thousand lives before he dies... The man who never reads lives only one." *George R. R. Martin,* I smiled. *One of the masters himself.*

Fully expecting to open the door at the end of the short hall and discover a library, I was pleasantly surprised to find one of the most comfortable reading nooks I had ever seen. While the wall of floor-to-ceiling windows at the end of the room looked out over the garden, the rest of the room was filled by every sitting apparatus imaginable. From recliner to loveseat, couch to chaise and hammock to papasan, Victor had outfitted the room with at least one comfortable reading position to fit every mood. Even the lighting for each was perfectly arranged.

Gazing above the door I found a quote by a man I didn't recognize, Jim Rohn. "Reading is essential for those who seek to rise above the ordinary." Making a mental note to research the author, I started to make my way back down the hall.

Turning right, I began to wonder what was taking Victor so long. As much as I enjoyed seeing his place on my own, I found myself wishing he were by my side... and not just so I could ask him questions about each room and the quotes above them.

Pausing at the next entrance, a quote from Mark Twain greeted me. "Truth is stranger than fiction, but it is because Fiction is obliged to stick to possibilities; Truth isn't." Eyes wide, I stepped toward the end of the hall, curious as to what type of room such a quote could portend.

The first thing I noticed was just how large the space was. A dark, rich, multi-tray wooden ceiling towered two stories overhead, supported by floor-to-ceiling bookshelves along the nearest three walls. Several large, windowed French doors at the far end led out to a balcony overlooking the garden below, the perfect backdrop for the small writer's desk centered just before it.

But as beautiful as the library was, nothing captivated me the way its book collection did.

With sliding ladders along the walls, each and every shelf was almost filled to capacity. While a few were decorated with small statues or ornate vases, nearly every single one was lined by nothing but books. Running my fingers along the spines as I strolled slowly past, I found sections for fiction and non-fiction, do-it-yourself and operating manuals, poetry and playwrights, histories and biographies. Swiveling my head, taking it all in and finding myself astounded by the sheer volume of literature before me, I suddenly noticed one shelf at the bottom of one of the corners that appeared different than the rest. Something about it seemed just as out of place as... Victor's Jeep.

Walking over for a better look, I realized the shelf contained more than a dozen notebook binders. Handwritten labels slipped into the holders along each spine indicated Screen and Teleplays, Novels, Poems, Concert Tickets, Movie Tickets, Certificates and Awards. There was even one marked Personal Journal. Scanning each title, I started to reach for one.

"Why am I not surprised," Victor asked, startling me from behind enough to jerk back my hand, "to find you looking at that shelf out of all those in this room?"

Turning to plead my case, I realized he appeared far more casual. Although he was still wearing his jacket, his tie was missing with his shirt unbuttoned far enough for me to catch a glimpse of his tattoo.

Trying to still my rapidly beating heart for more than one reason, I started to apologize. "I didn't mean to pry—"

"—Don't," Victor shook his head as he walked toward me. "You weren't prying. I told you, mi casa su casa. Remember? I have nothing to hide."

Stepping into my personal space, Victor bent down to kiss me, setting me instantly at ease.

"Thank you," I said.

"De nada."

I smiled. It felt so good to feel his arms around me again. And for him to brush my hair away from my face. *God, how I missed—*

"So, what were you about to read," Victor asked as he slowly released me from his embrace, "before I so rudely interrupted?"

"Actually, I was about to check out your certificates, if that's okay?"

Victor nodded with only the slightest hint of reluctance. "Be my guest."

Studying him for a second longer, I pulled the binder out and flipped it open to reveal several sheets of protective plastic covers. According to the handwritten cover sheet, the certificates Victor had earned over the years were compiled in chronological order. Skimming through the list I saw he held licenses in various states for bartender, masseuse, personal trainer, exercise physiologist and nutritionist, first aid, lifeguard and scuba along with a culinary arts degree. Unexpectedly I saw that he was also an actuary, a CPA, a notary and a hang gliding instructor. But none of those caught my attention more than his last certification.

"You have a pilot's license?"

"I do," I blinked.

I heard the concern in Bella's voice but didn't want to guess as to what she was thinking as she looked up at me.

"If you tell me you know how to fly or, God forbid, *own* a damn helicopt—"

"—No, no, no," I laughed. "Nothing that dangerous."

Searching my face, Bella waited a few beats before answering. "Good."

Nodding, I said nothing further and watched as she thankfully let the subject go. The truth was ever since our night at Mickey's I'd been dreading this eventual conversation. Bella's fear of both heights and flying admission had been brief but—as it was in direct opposition to my joy—it had also been more than enough to catch my attention.

More importantly, of course, I knew nothing escaped hers.

But given the worsening spread of Covid-19 and my impending, self-imposed quarantine, the point was moot for the moment. Despite how much of the last two months I had allowed myself to fantasize about joining the one-through-seven-mile-high clubs with Bella, I saw no need to begin trying to encourage her to conquer her fear. There would be plenty of time for that later provided she still wanted to be with me.

Besides, I still had a little more work to do regarding her other one.

"So, these other ones," I said, pointing back at the binders. "Are they a collection of your favorites or something?"

"No, those are things I've written," Victor shrugged. "But they're more like a lifetime's accumulation of unfinished works-in-progress with no deadline."

"Wow. I had no idea you were so prolific. You never mentioned having an interest in writing."

"That's because I'd make a horrible writer. Like I said, those are mostly incomplete."

The thought made me laugh. "You know, I've actually counseled more than a few authors over the years. The vast majority of the things they've written stay perpetually unfinished... Which, now that I think about it, is partly why some of them sought my help."

Victor smirked. "Yeah, I know that feeling."

I glanced at his binders again. "Are you sure you don't mind?"

"Help yourself."

Eyeballing his Personal Journal, something made me opt for his Poems instead. I opened the cover to find another handwritten, chronological list of... some interesting titles. Scanning quickly, I finally turned to *Ah, The Allure And Alleviation Of Allegorical Alliteration* to find... a blank page.

"I was going to write a twenty-five line poem," Victor explained before I could ask, "using each letter of the alphabet alliteratively. I got as far as the title."

"Well, at least it was a good one," I laughed as Victor smiled.

"Thanks. I like to think I'm capable of putting a little thought into one."

I nodded in agreement as a sudden recollection of our conversation at Mickey's about our favorite authors made me wonder. "Who's your favorite poet, by the way?"

Victor started to say something before catching himself. Whatever it was made him laugh.

"Oh, God, I'll tell you but if you think I'm being facetious I won't blame you."

"Who?"

Victor did his best to look me straight. "E.E. Cummings."

It took me a second. "Are you for real?"

"Remind me to read you 'she Being Brand/ -New' one day and you'll know I am."

Making a mental note to do just that, I shook my head as I turned back to the notebook. Finally deciding to check out his earliest works, I flipped to the first page causing Victor to clear his throat.

"Before you read that one," he said, "I should probably explain something."

"Okay."

"It's about the place from which it was written. I think the context is important."

I nodded softly. "When it comes to poetry, it almost always is."

"That first one... When I was maybe eleven or twelve years old, I went through my first true growth spurt. I grew over eight inches in about two months."

"Eight in two months?" As a doctor, I knew the rate of a typical growth spurt. Victor's had been on the extreme high end. "My God... That must have been excruciating."

"It was." Victor pursed his lips as he relived the memory. "Every night I bolted out of a dead sleep and tried to jump up on whichever leg was cramping. Of course, I was too young to understand what was happening, so it wasn't long before I actually feared falling asleep. And even though my growing pains eventually subsided, my fear never did... to the point where I developed chronic insomnia." Victor shook his head. "Anyway, a few years before I won emancipation, I was depressed enough to write my first poem for an English assignment."

Looking down, I began to read.

"The Nocturnal Panic Attack of the Chronic Insomniac"

Like a throbbing contusion
The confusion of illusion
Is a pain in the brain
Enough to drive one insane
But since the unexamined life
Is one lived in vain
I toss in my bed
With thoughts in my head
So complex and deep
I'm denied true sleep

Until finally I cry
And admit with a sigh
My only wish is to die
Just so I can stop asking myself...
Why, God, why?

Wow...

I looked up at Victor. "How old were you when you wrote this?"

"Fourteen. Maybe fifteen."

"Victor, that's incredible. It's beautiful in a kind of haunting way, but it really is incredible."

Victor shrugged. "Words of a tortured youth. What are you going to do, you know?"

"I'm just glad you survived. Foster care, insomnia, depression, not to—"

Victor waved a hand, politely but dismissively cutting me short. "Childhood. We all had one."

"Yes, but..." My words trailed off as I let go of the thought. While a child psychologist like myself could have a field day with a poem like his, Victor was right. He was no longer that kid and his writing nothing more than a moment in time. I handed him the binder which he took back wistfully.

"You know, now that I think about it," Victor mused, "that poem was the initial reason I became motivated to seek my emancipation."

"How so?"

"My teacher referred me to the school's guidance counselor because of it."

In my attempt not to laugh, I let out a snort. Which made me laugh. During which I snorted. And then I just lost it.

"Oh God, I'm so sorry!" Unable to contain myself, my laughter grew. I felt horrible because I knew was laughing at my own snorts, not at what Victor had said. Thankfully, he seemed to understand as he began to laugh wholeheartedly with me until we both finally regained control. I had to take a deep breath before letting it out. "I'm so sorry. I really am."

"It's ok," Victor chuckled. "As a psychologist, I'd have to imagine a poem like that would be cause for concern."

"It would. Couple a couple years of insomnia with typical teenage depression with growing up in foster care and a poem like that... Honestly, you're lucky your teacher didn't try to have you temporarily committed."

Victor shook his head but smiled. "No, he didn't go that far. But his inability to read it with the same foresight you just did irked the hell out of me. It made me realize one of the things I was most tired of was having adults exercise such a large control over my life when most cared so little for me in the first place. So, when I was forced to change schools about a month later, the first thing I did was ask my new counselor to explain everything I needed to do to achieve emancipation. Lucky for me, he was also the ROTC program commander. He's the one who pointed me in the direction of the Marine Corps."

Looking around at the library's opulence, I couldn't help but smile.

"Well, as bad as all that sounds, with the exception of your training injury it appears your life has pretty much been roses ever since."

Victor smiled. "More or less."

"Less?" I waved at the room. "You've built all this. You do what you want for a living, not what you have to. And to top it all off, you're as hot as you are handsome. Am I missing something?"

"No... but I am."

"What?"

Victor smiled sweetly but said nothing.

The right woman with which to share it.

Of course, as prepared as I liked to be, I wasn't prepared to say that yet. After all, while I hoped Bella's tour of my house and life were helping to answer any questions she might have about me, I still had some of my own. But time and place meant they could wait for the moment.

"Come on," I said, nodding toward the door, "I'll show you the rest of the house."

Taking Bella by the hand we were in the hallway before she said anything.

"By the way, why are the ceilings in these hallways so low—"

My heart leapt into my throat, nearly choking me. *How the hell does she know—*

"—Wait! I forgot to read the plaque."

Releasing my hand, I watched Bella re-enter the library before turning to look up as I tried to calm back down. The unexpected hit of adrenaline sent my heart beating like a jackhammer.

"'I never let my schooling interfere with my education,'" she translated. "A second from Mark Twain. Nice."

"Enjoying my quotes, are you?" I asked, trying not to appear as if I was recovering from anything as Bella retook my hand.

As quickly as possible, I turned and began leading us toward the next roo—*No, not that one yet. Damnit.* I wasn't thinking straight. Maybe Bella wouldn't notice skipping it if I just kept our conversation going while walking past. After all, she was following my lead. *So lead.*

"... really have been," I heard her say. "They blend nicely with your décor. But it's kind of a shame they're written in Latin so fewer people can read them. I assume you had them custom made?"

Breathing easier, I chuckled at the memory. At least it was something to talk about.

"I did. I thought about ordering them with different jokes or corny clichés, but I was afraid someday someone other than myself might actually be able to translate them." I shrugged. "Then they, not to mention I, would have looked foolish." I just needed a few more steps.

"Well then, I guess it's a good thing you appreciate quotes more than clichés."

I agreed. But I had to say something. Any second Bella was going to look up at the next quote.

"Why? What's wrong with clichés?" I asked as I kept on stepping.

"Really?" Bella asked a bit incredulously.

No, not— "Yes, really," I said. We were past the entrance, heading to the next one. But if I didn't keep talking, I feared Bella might notice. "People only dismiss clichés because everyone repeats them a little too often, but that's a shame. I think people fail to respect clichés for standing the test of time. I mean just because they're second tier to quotes such that no one bothers to remember the first person to have spoken or written about them doesn't make them any less worthy."

Bella shot me a look.

"Okay, maybe a little less worthy."

She grinned, unknowingly setting me instantly at ease. "You're so easy."

"And you love it," I winked.

I rolled my eyes. I did, but...

"All I'm saying, Mr. Maxwell, is that while I wouldn't put anything past you, if above your bedroom door is some Disney quote about that being where the magic happens, I might need to amend my definition of a dealbreaker."

Victor smirked in that secretive way of his.

"In that case, I think you're in for a surprise."

Taking in his words for a second, I jumped in front and boldly reached out to palm his crotch as I looked him in the eye.

"There's only one prize I'm interested in."

Not to be outdone I stepped forward, invading Bella's personal space in return before I paused, grew serious then said, "Hasn't anyone ever told you to never end your sentences with a preposition?"

Bella gave me a look of mock shock. "Why, no, I've never had anyone tell me that... before."

Managing to hold our expressions for two seconds, we simultaneously busted out laughing.

"I swear," I said once I could, "I don't think I've ever had so much fun getting out-cheesed before."

"Mmmmmmm, me either," Bella said before giving my cock a quick squeeze. Finally moving her hand away, I took it and put it back.

"No one said you had to stop."

The look in Bella's eyes coupled with the reflexive bite on her lower lip said it all. In the span of a heartbeat the woman's motor was up and running so fast I was reminded that it probably never stopped.

Half of me wanted to stop. Just not the half touching Victor's growing bulge.

Summoning every ounce of strength I had, I pulled away a second time. Before we had sex again, I had to let Victor know. Softening my expression on purpose, I asked, "Do you mind showing me your pool first?"

My question caught him as off guard as I knew it would.

"Um... Sure."

Leading the way to open one of the exterior French doors, Victor allowed me to exit first before taking my hand and directing us around the nearby waterfall and grotto. Walking around the pool's edge, we continued toward the small beach on the other side, the sound of small waves lapping over the sand soothing us as we went.

"So, this is your happy place," I mused.

"During the summer," Victor admitted.

I noticed his tone sounded a bit reluctant as he invited me to sit with him in one of the hammocks strung between two palm trees. As he removed his shoes and socks, I kicked off my heels then squeezed in beside him. The sand between my toes felt like heaven. As did his hand retaking mine.

"As you might have noticed, my house wraps entirely around the pool area."

"I have," I said. "It's different, but I like how it gives you complete privacy."

Victor nodded. "I designed it that way. I'm... a bit of a nudist when it comes to laying out." He paused for a second. "Think you could handle that? Spending all day in the sun, naked out here with me?"

I inhaled sharply. The idea of Victor strolling around here all summer long, completely naked... and a hypothetical invitation to do so with him. I had to take my shot. It was time.

Pushing myself up out of the hammock I took a few steps forward before turning around.

"I don't know. Do you think you could?"

For two months I had anguished over how I was going to play this moment, how it might go down. Would I come clean and confess at the Soco Bar before things went any further? Wait for the privacy of our hotel room to prevent my big reveal from causing a public scene? Or just try to forget all about it and go with the flow? Trust I'd think of something the way I always did?

Only nothing I had envisioned came to pass. Instead, Victor's mere presence once again captivated me such that I had completely forgotten about my tattoo. Now, suddenly, here that moment was, presenting itself to me in a singularly perfect way in an unbelievably beautiful setting that I never thought possible.

"Are you sure you're ready for this?" I asked softly with a cryptic smile of my own. After all, two could play—

"—As ready as I'll ever be."

The excitement in Victor's grin made me feel a little sorry for how oblivious he might one day feel whenever he thought back to tonight.

"Do you like this dress?"

Victor's smile turned to bewilderment. "What?"

"I said—"

"—I heard you... Um, no, actually. I don't *like* your dress. I *love* your dress."

Mmmmmm. "Good answer. Me, too."

Turning my back, I swept my hair gently over my shoulder and out of the way. Without a word, Victor took my cue and rose from the hammock.

Butterflies hardened my nipples as soon as I felt his fingertips brush the nape of my neck, just before they tugged, steady and slow down my back. Amplified somehow above the flow of the grotto's waterfall, the distinct sound of my zipper coming undone filled the air. And while I couldn't see his expression behind me, I got the impression Victor was savoring the moment every bit as much as I was.

The kind of moment that felt like a dream within a dream...

When his fingers finally reached my lower back, I crossed my arms over my breasts and slowly turned around. Meeting Victor's eye, I stepped back to give him a better look before pulling my dress forward and down. Extracting my hands through the sleeves, I simultaneously shimmied the opening in the back past my rear. Then, as seductively as possible, I lowered the top of the front with my hands... tracking Victor's eyes as they went from my own to my neck... down my bare chest... as I watched for my moment.

"Think you could handle that? Spending all day in the sun, naked out here with me?"

Her reaction was greater than I had hoped for, her excitement obvious and even better than that. I couldn't get enough of just how quickly Bella's sexual drive was ready and raring to go. And part of me had to admit I enjoyed using my knowledge of it to tease her.

Turning her head in a slow burn, Bella fixed me with a smile before pushing herself up out of the hammock. I loved that whatever she had allowed me to goad her into, I was about to deserve. Whatever or whoever was about to come, I had definitely asked for it.

Turning around to face me from about six feet away, Bella smiled. "I don't know. Do you think you could?"

I smiled but said nothing.

"Are you sure you're ready for this?" Bella smiled back.

God, yes. "As ready as I'll ever be," I grinned.

"Do you like this dress?"

Um. "What?"

"I said—"

"—I heard you... Um, no, actually. I don't *like* your dress. I *love* your dress."

Bella's smile was delicious. "Good answer. Me, too."

Turning her back to me, she swept her hair aside, exposing the rear of her dress. Her intention was clear. My duty even more so.

One step and I was on her, towering behind her. With my hands steady on the outside and on the verge of shaking on the in, I took a second to brush my fingertips along the soft, fine hairs at the base of her long, beautiful neck. But then I could wait no more.

After turning and taking a half step back, Bella allowed the front of her dress to spill forward just enough. Then she slipped each arm from its sleeve before beginning to slide her entire dress past her hips and over her ass.

I was able to maintain eye contact until her breasts spilled free.

I wanted her to stop right there, for the top of her dress to keep covering her stomach, to not ruin what my eyes were seeing with what they were about to... when her dress suddenly slid entirely off.

Revealing that her tattoo was gone.

I shook my eyes and stared. It hadn't been removed. Not by laser. There was no scarring. It was as if it had faded completely away only to leave behind one of the tightest stomachs I had ever seen on a woman.

In fact, now that she was completely naked, I could truly see just how great a shape Bella was in. From her legs and arms, stomach and thighs, everything about the woman—physically, at least—appeared to be in tip-top condition. Yet in that moment, I realized just how much it didn't matter. I wasn't any more or less attracted to her than I had been two minutes or two months ago. But no matter how smoking hot she now looked. I just couldn't get over the unexpected absence of her tattoo.

"Wha—"

"—I never lied to you," she said, her eyes imploring mine. "But… I've never been a Sex Slave… Nor have I ever had a Master."

Not knowing what to say, I waited for Bella to continue. The look on her face told me she was far from done.

"For a long time, I wondered… fantasized, actually, about what it would be like to be a Sex Slave. But I could never work up the nerve to explore the possibility."

As Bella took a deep breath, I rose and took off my jacket. It wasn't that cold and the threat of any storm seemed to have passed, but there was no way I could continue listening with her standing there, completely naked. I wanted nothing more than to get my hands and mouth all over her, but she obviously had so much more to say. Sex could wait.

Covering her shoulders with my coat, I gathered Bella in my arms as she looked up at me.

"About a year ago I… went through something. The *what's* not as important as *how* I failed to handle it. I lost confidence in myself, stopped trusting my own judgment. Not the type of things conducive to life as a therapist."

"Was that when you ended your podcast so abruptly?" I asked as gently as I could.

Bella nodded. "A few days prior, I tried outlining the fourth season's opener. My show was never scripted but the format was always pre-planned. But every time I thought about how I was going to discuss a segment, it felt like putting on a charade." Exhaling a deep breath, Bella bowed her head. "I lost so much belief in myself I just decided it was better to end the show altogether."

Giving her a second, I finally raised her chin with my hand.

"That was a pretty significant life change for a what that's not important enough to explain."

Victor was right. However, I wasn't sure I could explain well enough the type of situation one had to be there to understand. Of course, there was only one way to find out.

"As I'm sure you saw on my podcasts, I've known more than a few professional athletes. Most were simply teammates of some of my patients looking for a little media exposure. But a couple of them actually became my patients."

I continued to explain how even though the athletes were my patients for various reasons including but not limited to sex addiction, the sports team each played for were my actual clients as they footed the bill.

"Only some of these guys were smart enough to leverage their position. They'd only agree to counseling if they could appear as my guest first. And, on a case-by-case basis, for the most part I didn't have a problem with that. The upside to my podcast aside, my interviews generally allowed me to establish a good rapport with them before delving into our counseling and therapy sessions."

I took a deep breath.

"So one day, at the request of a client, I agreed to take on a patient with a similar demand. Only this time I was privately warned by several people that it was a bad idea. That despite their image, this particular athlete had a reputation of being a sexual predator. But after doing my due diligence, I failed to find any evidence to support their opinions. Which I have to admit intrigued me."

Sensing how much more I had to say, Victor turned and led us back over to sit on the hammock. Not only was I grateful for his patience and understanding, I suddenly felt more relaxed. Being naked yet covered in the comfort of his jacket felt rather nice, too. As did his hand on mine.

"I realized," I continued, "if those who knew him were right, then this person was a true sociopath. But because I didn't know that for sure, I agreed to take him on."

Half impressed, half concerned, Victor cocked his head.

"The interview actually went really well... So well, in fact, that when he returned half an hour later claiming to have lost his phone, I allowed him into my office to look for it despite being alone at that point."

Victor's eyes suddenly turned serious as I noticed his breathing slowed.

"You're talking about Shawn Royale."

I nodded. It didn't surprise me that Victor had listened to enough of my podcasts over the last two months to put the timeline together. And from a doctor/patient privilege perspective, it also didn't matter that he knew who I was talking about as Shawn had never officially become my patient.

But more important than either...

"He never touched me," I assured Victor.

"But he tried."

His voice was tight. Monotone yet filled with the type of emotion that both warmed yet made my blood run cold, there was almost no doubt in my mind Victor would damn near kill the guy if he could get his hands on him. Thankfully, there was no longer a reason.

"Only for a second," I explained, trying not to relive the memory any more than I had to. Failing miserably, I took a deep breath. "It was like someone flipped a switch. A minute or so after I shut the door, out of the blue he started unbuttoning his shirt. Asked me if I was ready for him. Said he knew I wanted him, that he could tell by the way I had acted during the podcast. And if you could have heard the way he was talking..."

I shook off a shiver before allowing it to take hold.

"Once I realized my denials were pointless and he intended to rape me, I managed to keep my desk between us. We circled it a time or two before I managed to think of a way out."

"What'd you do?" Victor asked.

With his voice a bit softer than before, the sound of his compassion set me a bit more at ease.

"I stopped as if I had suddenly remembered something then asked him if he really planned to rape me on camera. For a split second, he thought I was talking about my podcast camera. But when he realized it was turned off I told him no, that I had hidden cameras for my other patients so that I could replay their sessions whenever I might need to. I didn't, though he didn't know that... But thank God, I was convincing enough that he believed me and left."

"You bluffed your way out of a possible rape?" Victor asked. The touch of admiration in his voice was hard to miss.

I gave a small nod. "Of course, after he left was when I fell apart." Surprised, Victor stayed silent and waited for me to continue. "I wanted to call the police, but I knew, because he never laid a finger on me, that no crime had been committed. I knew legally I didn't have a leg to stand on."

Tears welled in the corner of my eyes which I quickly blinked my way through.

"My podcasts were live on Thursday nights. Between then and Sunday, I agonized over what to do. I worried he was out there hurting someone else. I felt powerless to stop it but responsible at the same time for doing nothing at all."

"And then karma got to him," Victor said.

I nodded, happy that he knew about Shawn's injury and that I didn't need to explain further. Not about that, anyway.

"Of course, it felt like karma got to me, too."

Before Victor could ask, I continued to explain how, beyond beating myself up for doing nothing for those two intervening days, I began to doubt myself. My decisions and opinions. My advice for others and personal goals for myself. Everything, really.

"Which eventually led to depression and feeling like no one could possibly understand what I was going through. So I tried to fill those voids by comforting myself with food. And when that didn't work, I decided to get a head start on my midlife crisis by buying my dream car twenty years too early. Only that didn't work either."

Victor relinquished my hand in order to put his arm around me. Drawing me close, he looked down as I looked up.

"But by the time we met," he said gently, "something obviously had. You certainly didn't seem to be suffering from depression our first night together in Jacksonville."

I half smiled, pleased that Victor had noticed.

"Back in November, I took Abby up on her invitation to play poker with her and Greg. But by then I was a good forty pounds heavier than the last time I had done anything remotely social... And then no one offered to buy me a drink." I tried not to sound as shallow or petulant as I felt. But... "It was a blow to my ego. I mean, I was at a bar with a bunch of single guys and not one..." I rolled my eyes. "Fortunately, not only did it serve me right, later I learned Greg had explicitly warned every guy in the place that I was off limits."

Victor's eyes popped for a second as he started to say something but then wisely thought better of it.

I shook my head. "It doesn't matter. It was enough to convince me to start regaining control of my life starting with my health. By the time we met, I was in a far better place."

As Victor gazed at me for a few seconds, I could see the agreement in his eyes. But when they slowly dropped to my stomach—

—*Oh!* How was it I kept forgetting...

I nodded. "So good, in fact, that yes, I decided to take a shot at fulfilling my ultimate sexual fantasy."

I did my best not to sound as incredulous as I felt.

"Are you telling me you got a temporary tattoo solely for the purpose of a one-night stand? Just so you could experiment, maybe give your fantasy a trial run?"

Bella nodded softly. "As crazy as it sounds... yes."

But— "Weren't you at all worried..."

"No. Trust me, I wasn't going home with anyone I didn't trust enough in the first place. And I always knew the degree to which I explained my tattoo was going to depend on who he was and had shown himself to be... If I chose wrong, I could always just say that it was a temporary mistake."

"But... why?"

Bella looked confused. "I just—"

"—No, I mean why, what... motivates you to feel that way?"

"You mean a desire to be used for someone else's personal, sexual gratification?"

"Well... yeah."

Bella chuckled. "I don't."

"But you said—"

"—What I mean is that's not how *I* see it. Yes, in bed I'm willing to completely surrender myself to another. But for me, what I get in return is far more important."

"And what's that?"

Bella smiled softly. Taking my free hand in hers, she intertwined our fingers, lacing them together in their own, unique embrace. I loved how small hers were yet how perfectly they fit in mine.

I took Victor's hand to give me a second to think. No matter how often I had thought about why I wanted to be a Sex Slave, I'd never vocalized my rationale. Not even to myself.

Because my answer was an intangible feeling, a desire so uniquely personal that there was only one in all of existence, I knew no one but myself could ever adequately describe it. And although I never had and still wasn't sure I could, here, in Victor's presence... it felt like now or never.

"You have to understand, before I met you it was all just theoretical to me. What I wanted, what I thought it might be like, what I expected it to be like and what I hoped for... were all slightly different things. But then came our night together. And now I know the truth of it."

"And what's that?" Victor asked softly.

"It's a little hard to describe," I started honestly, "probably because the answer is two-fold. Both journey and destination... During the act, the journey, I can feel myself slipping away but moving in the direction of finding myself. By temporarily suspending my own wants and desires, I fill them with yours. Only mine never truly go away. I'm still me. I still possess them. But without having to carry their weight, I can accept so much more. And in so doing, have more than I had.

"Along the way I shed my thoughts and feelings, both good and bad, to the point where it feels like I've started anew. I rid myself of ego and fear. Of certainty and doubt. Joy and pain. I empty myself until I have only one thing left. Lust. Lust which burns through me like fuel until it, too, is gone.

"And when it is, I've arrived at my destination. That thin line that separates thoughts from feelings while being void of either yet entirely surrounded and defined by both. That hollow in the center of nothing which is still substantive enough to be considered something.

"It's a state of being and nothing else. And its duration, no matter how fleeting, no matter how short a time I can grab hold of it before my fingers slip through it because it was never anything physical to begin with... is worth it to me."

Feeling unbearably light, like a weight had somehow just been removed from my soul, I exhaled as Victor smiled into my eyes for several seconds before finally speaking.

"It sounds to me like you described it just fine."

"Yes, well you seem to have that effect on me," I preened.

"So the feeling's mutual? Good."

Something in the sexiness of Victor's subsequent wink emboldened me. *Good, indeed.*

"So, what's next?" I asked suggestively.

"Hmmmmmm..." he hummed before his eyes suddenly grew playfully wide. "I know. How'd you like to *come* with me?"

"Mmmmmmm. I thought you'd never ask."

Victor stood and spun, keeping our hands joined. "Ladies first," he said as he helped me stand.

After grabbing my dress and our shoes, Victor led us back toward the grotto at the other end of the pool as my excitement began to grow. I couldn't wait, not only to see his bedroom and read the plaques above his door, but to—

With my hand in his, Victor suddenly swerved us from our path to duck behind the grotto's waterfall. Though possible to swim back here, our paved walkway ended along the smooth rock wall in the alcove. Or so I thought.

Pushing with his hand against the last part of the wall, Victor revealed the last few feet to actually be a door which opened into... a massage room.

Recalling that Victor had once been a licensed masseuse, I felt my nipples stiffen as the dim lighting that flickered on revealed a wide, cream colored table. Centered in the middle of the spacious cave within a cave, the plush foam and leather table was surrounded by every accessory associated with a full-fledged professional massage parlor. Scented candles and aromatherapy sticks, oil warmers and fresh linens. There was even a sink along its soundproof textured, tranquil art decorated walls. The room had it all including a Japanese shoji screen standing in the corner to discretely change one's clothes.

But— "I thought," I started but couldn't finish just as Victor did, lighting some of the candles.

"You thought what?" he asked slyly as he paired his phone to a speaker in one of the corners.

When the smooth sound of the calmest, most ethereal jazz I'd ever heard began filling the air, all I could do was shake my head slightly and say, "Nothing."

I smiled. Part of me felt like I knew what Bella was thinking. That we were finally headed to my bedroom. And ultimately, we were.

But— "I thought," I said as I took a step into her personal space, "seeing how you were already naked, you might enjoy a full body massage. Tell me. Have you ever had one?"

Standing before me and looking up, Bella had no problem meeting my eye. And then some.

"No, I can't say as I ever have... Then again, I'm also not really 'already naked' either."

Her tone was as sultry and sassy as her attitude and I loved it. *Hmmmm.*

Using my right index, I slipped my fingertip under the lapel of my jacket, ran it down slowly until it brushed against Bella's right nipple, eliciting a small gasp for breath... And then I pulled it away. Forward... and to her side... then off her shoulder, exposing the right half of her naked body. And then I did her left.

"So, what's your excuse now?" I asked once my jacket was crumpled around her feet.

Bella cocked her eye. "I never said I had one."

To which I cocked mine.

"Master," she breathed in quick reply as her pupils dilated.

I smiled. Wry and knowing. "Lay on the table for me. Face down."

Pausing just long enough to in and exhale, Bella turned and did as I said, her obedience only slightly less immediate as it was delicious to see. Watching the beauty of her naked body climb up on the table, it took every ounce of restraint I had not to reach out and touch her bare skin somewhere. But as her face pushed down into the cradle and her arms settled into the hanging rest, I knew I wouldn't have to contain myself much longer.

After turning on one of the electric bottle warmers, I splashed several drops of grapefruit extract onto a container of solid coconut oil. Working the clean, lightly scented mixture in, I made sure my hands were nice and warm before applying both to Bella's bare back. It had been a long time since I had given a woman a massage and even longer since I had given one meaningful enough for me to remember.

Ignoring my training at first, I did my best to listen to Bella's body, her subtle reactions to my variances in pressure, placement and pace as over and over I worked more oil across her skin, reveling in my ability to touch her any and everywhere we both desired. Her arms and shoulders, legs and calves, back and neck. I even made sure to rub out a small knot just below her left shoulder blade that was so tight I could actually hear it pop as it rolled beneath my thumbs. And with nowhere off-limits, I did my best to cover her all over in oil as much as possible before massaging any one location in too sexual a manner, especially her magnificently shaped buttocks.

But eventually Bella turned to such complete putty in my hands I was left with only two directions in which to go. A further all-over massage which was only going to lull her, drooling toward a deeper sleep... or one targeting her erogenous zones, stimulating her back toward wakefulness.

Bending down until my mouth was just inches from her ear, I whispered, "I'll be right back."

With barely enough energy left to respond, Bella murmured her acknowledgment as I walked over to grab the metal bottle in the warmer. Holding it with a washcloth so as not to scald my hand, I pumped several squirts directly onto the heels of her feet. With a large, rising inhale and subsequent exhale of her shoulders as she sighed, Bella's toes curled even as her arches flexed.

Quickly working the water-based lube around the tops of her feet and between her toes, I smiled as I watched her try not to squirm.

I went from being slightly embarrassed yet grateful Victor couldn't tell I was drooling to being on the verge of orgasm in about two seconds flat.

Of course, as relaxed as I was, I was already about ninety percent of the way there.

Victor's hands felt like ten magic wands wrapped in the warmest, roughest silk imaginable. Pushing, rubbing, gliding, caressing, smoothing, pressing, gripping... over and over again. Whether the man was kneading my flesh or concentrating on working the tension out of my muscles, everywhere he touched me turned more liquid than I already was.

Despite having very little fat left, I could feel my flesh flowing forward of his splayed fingers, four individual rivulets slowly gathered together to form one solid wave. Back and forth, up and down my body his hands and my gratification traveled as I increasingly went out of my mind in the best of ways.

I was so comfortable, so relaxed in Victor's presence that it barely dawned on me that I was completely naked. Barely registered that the man had unfettered access to my body, especially given all he seemed to want and do was slide me deeper and deeper into my own personal pleasure coma.

True, I got ahead of myself, getting excited when he began massaging my ass. Spreading my cheeks. Pulling them up and sideways, down and in before rolling back out. But he never went further, never touched me anywhere more intimate than on my inner thighs. And even more surprising was how suddenly thankful I felt. Thankful that he was treating those areas exactly as he had all my other muscle groups, as places to be relieved of tension. Because it felt indescribably wonderful...

But when the hot oil hit the bottom of my feet the rush of liquid pleasure coursing through my body traveled up my legs and tried to empty itself between them.

Clenching my pussy as I tried to block my deluge, it was all I could do not to writhe in ecstasy as I silently praised Victor for being so intuitive. As he began spreading the oil all over my feet, feeding both the warmth and rush of my blood, I remembered one of our nightly discussions from just a few weeks prior.

Little by little he had done an amazing job of slowly feeling me out over the last two months whenever the topic of our conversation turned sexual. Asking all the right questions in all the right ways. Listening to my responses and correctly extrapolating them with others... Getting me to reveal erogenous zones he hadn't had enough time to detect on our first night together.

I thought I had done a pretty good job of denying any interest in my feet. And the honest truth was I really didn't even enjoy the thought of anyone but myself touching them. Yet at the same time Victor had coerced me into admitting how sensitive they were. Easily tickled. Easily sore from spending too much time in heels.

So as the sting of the hot oil dispersed, spreading into a flood of radiating heat, something in me just went with it.

Suddenly my sensitivity transformed from apprehension to anticipation, revulsion to desire. Everywhere Victor touched me made me want even more from his hands and fingers even though I didn't want them to go. Everywhere he touched me I wanted to say *There, right there...* But no sooner had he hit just the right spot then he found another... and another...

I had no idea my feet could hold so much tension until I felt its release. No idea a part of my body that typically felt anything other than bad could actually feel so good. No idea that a part I didn't like to think about could be all that I could.

Although I lost track of time, I estimated Victor spent at least five minutes on each foot, probably more given his responsiveness to the moans and groans I failed to stifle. So, when it became abundantly clear he was done with my second foot, I didn't know whether to cry or cry out...

Until he spoke.

"I'm going to wash my hands," I whispered into Bella's ear. "I want you to relax until you find the strength to turn over. There is no rush. We have all night."

Hearing and watching Bella sink deeper into the massage table as she exhaled made me smile. Given the untold years since I had last given a woman a massage, I was more than pleased to realize I still had the touch. But more specifically I was even happier I had it for Bella.

As I washed my hands under the incredibly hot, soapy water, I found myself grateful we were so well matched when it came to massage. I had enough experience to know no matter how well things went in the bedroom between two people, a massage could be a different story. Thankfully, Bella had been so vocally and visually responsive to my touch that she had actually made the first half of our session a pleasurable experience for me as well.

Drying off my hands I turned to find her still face down. Stepping over to the side of the table as quietly as possible, I stood there just looking at her. Admiring her new shape. Appreciating the work, time and dedication she must have devoted in the last two months to achieve it. Feeling honored to realize at least on some level she probably did so for me.

Recalling her requirement against any form of video chatting, I couldn't help but wonder if it was because she hadn't wanted me to see her progress. That she had wanted to surprise me. Knowing it was possible, when the shame for my own narcissism began to rear its ugly head, I felt relieved when Bella suddenly stirred alive.

Slipping her arms out of the rest she pushed herself up slowly from the table, paused to gather her strength... then began to roll over. She seemed only mildly surprised to find me standing there.

"Mmmmmmm, how long was I out?"

"I don't know," I said. "Were you?"

Bella smiled lazily up at me through her nearly closed eyes. "Felt like it."

Laying supine before me with the back of her head nestled neatly into the cradle, her eyes rolled to join it before shutting entirely again along with a depleted exhale.

I couldn't wait to touch her, slather the rest of her with the invigoratingly scented oil and get back to running my hands all over her. Instead, of course, I just stood there, savoring the moment. Reveling in my first good look at Bella's naked front. Her perfect nipples and breasts. Her taut, unblemished stomach. Her landing strip alighting atop her clit.

Compared to the rising level of my lust, my fascination and thankfulness for the absence of her tattoo were almost nonexistent.

"What are you waiting for?" Bella asked.

Startled, I looked over to find her eyes were still closed.

"Nothing," I replied.

Grabbing the container of coconut oil, I added a few more drops of the extract before using the heat of my hand to melt and stir the mixture together. *Hmmmmm. Where to put the first— I know.*

Considering how I ended at one end, I moved around to stand above Bella's head then smoothed the first palmful of oil along both sides of her elongated neck. Massaging gently, I worked my way down across her shoulders and arms, applying a liberal amount of oil as often as needed.

Doing my best to make the topside of Bella's massage as non-sexual as the back, I worked quickly down her chest and stomach, hips and legs. I concentrated solely on oiling her up until I reached her ankles where I reversed my direction and intent.

Molding her calves two-handed, one at a time for quite a while finally gave way to my using a deep tissue massage technique on her quadriceps. Applying sustained pressure to slow, deep strokes, I did my best to target Bella's connective tissues and the inner layers of her muscles. But as I broke up what little remaining tension I found, I discovered my own beginning to build.

As my hands moved ever closer northward, I began to doubt I could resist touching her sexually for much longer. Not with what appeared to be wetness between her legs. Not with my hands and fingers so close. And definitely not with her pelvis undulating ever so slightly the closer I came...

I couldn't take it anymore.

Leveraging the length of my arms, I kept my hands on Bella's legs as I moved the rest of me back to her head before bending down to her ear.

"Would you like to finish this in my bedroom?"

Bella's eyes flew open. Wide and surprised, all she could do was nod as I moved to her side to help her off the table. Giving her time to find her legs I took mine to walk around the room and blow out the candles. I went slow, trying to give myself time to cool off.

But when the last wick was out and I turned to find Bella looking at me with that undeniable look in her eye... well, there was only one thing to do.

My legs felt like jelly, especially at my ankles, knees and hips. Though the rest of me felt just fine, by the time Victor finished blowing out the candles, one part in particular was feeling far better than most.

Turning around to find me staring at him, Victor cracked me one of his all-knowing smiles that I found sexier every time he did. Only this one was a little different.

With his eyes never leaving mine, he paused for only a beat or two then made a point to slowly unbutton his sleeveless vest before slipping it off. When he continued with his shirt, I could actually feel my eyes fail to contain my excitement.

Taking in his torso, chest, arms and his entire tattoo, I couldn't believe this moment was the most I had seen Victor naked so far tonight. I had envisioned making love completely naked in bed in a room at The Westin so often over the last two months that when it didn't happen, I had thrown all my other expectations and plans out the window with it.

So, when Victor's hands dropped to his pants, my eyes went with them.

The pop of the button. The pull of his zipper. The push of his waistband down off his hips.

The first thing my eyes took in was the dark navy blue of the loose fitting silk boxers he was wearing... the satin shimmer caused by the bulge swinging beneath—

—Is that his...

My body realized the head of Victor's penis was hanging out, just below the cut of his underwear, before my brain did. Despite the rush of heat hitting my pelvis, I had a hard time believing what I was seeing. But glancing up to find Victor looking at me with a borderline smirk on his face... told me I should. Though for the life of me I couldn't remember him being that lo—

With his thumbs at his sides, Victor peeled off his boxers. And he was.

Oh, my, was he.

Two months. Every day. Two hundred reps.

That's what Bella's jelqing instructions recommended so that's what I did. But that wasn't the hard part. Nor was finding the better part of half an hour to do it.

No, holding back from becoming erect, stanching the flow of fantasies swirling through my brain and doing everything in my power not to visualize Bella naked as I semi-jerked off each day was.

But, true to her word and following her directions to the letter, my efforts had paid off. Not that I'd taken the time to find a ruler but knowing myself better than anyone else, my cock was definitely longer and even a bit thicker than it used to be.

The look in Bella's eyes assured me of that.

Looking back up at Victor I found his smirk had grown... too.

Even more though, I loved how perfectly our eyes communicated without saying a word.

"You didn't need to do that," I assured him.

"Need? No," Victor said before stepping back into my personal space. "Want?... Yes."

Exhaling my acquiescence to his desire, I reached out to begin getting him as excited as I felt. So it was a surprise when Victor took my hand.

"Let's take this to my bedroom," he said before leaning down to whisper. "I *need* to make love to you."

Nodding gently, I allowed Victor to lead me by the hand. Completely naked, neither of us spoke a word as we exited his massage room hideaway, slipped out from under the grotto's waterfall, walked past his pool and back through a set of French doors we had yet to use at the other end.

Ever the gentleman, Victor slowed to give me enough time to read the quote above the hallway to what I presumed was his bedroom. While the entrance was twice as wide as the others, an identical plaque, though wider as well, hung just as the others did.

Only this one contained no quote.

"Tomorrow. Sunday at the latest," Victor broke our silence when we paused a few steps further, just outside his closed bedroom doors, "I'll explain certain things about myself and my life... that I hope will make sense. Just as you did about your tattoo."

I nodded my understanding but felt a bit of anxiety as Victor reached out for one of the doorknobs. Thankfully, he didn't open it right away.

"For the moment, just know this," he continued. "The quotes you've been reading were designed for three things. Entering, they give you something to think about. Exiting, something to remember... My bedroom has neither because..."

I was surprised when Victor paused, slightly embarrassed.

"Well, I guess you could say I just don't think the words have been written yet."

And with that Victor reached down and opened both doors simultaneously to reveal one of the largest and most opulent bedrooms I'd ever seen.

From the light yet regal blue color of his walls to the four poster bed at the far end that was so large it had to be custom made, everything in the room was fit for a king. The rich, dark wood flooring even complimented the matching designer rugs and tapestries so well that for a brief moment or two I was worried I'd found the first feminine influence in the whole house. Setting that fear aside for the time being, a second popped in my head as Victor began leading me over to the bed.

Noticing my overnight bag in one of the room's corners just before we stopped at the foot, I couldn't help but to give Victor's hand a small squeeze as I got my first good look at just how luxurious his bedding ensemble was. All of the decorative pillows as well as the plush microfiber suede comforter with silk embroidery looked incredibly... stainable.

"Ummm..." I hesitated just enough to get Victor's attention. "I'd..." *Oh, God. How do I say this?* "... hate to ruin your mattress like the one we did in Jacksonville."

A reassuring smile quickly spread across Victor's face. "Remember the box in the back of my trunk?" I nodded. "Waterproof mattress protector." My eyes went wide as Victor nodded toward the bed. "It's already on. That's what I was doing while you were taking your tour."

Looking from Victor to the bed then back again, I pinched my bottom lip with my teeth.

"Let's see if it works."

It worked. And then some.

Of course, among the enduring mysteries that defined each individual woman, it was also one of the easiest to solve.

It was simple, really. Most men needed excitement and the proper amount of friction to achieve orgasm and not much else. Women required it, too, of course. But many also needed to preface their excitement with relaxation.

Whether it be a clean or simply uncluttered home, the dishes put away, the laundry done or maybe just the monthly bills paid, taking care of the needs of a woman's mind first often went a long way toward taking care of her body's second.

Which was why, knowing full well she couldn't destroy my mattress, Bella thankfully felt free enough to try and destroy me instead.

The two of us spent hours making love, having sex and flat out fucking. One minute treating one another's body as if each was a playground. The next a buffet. Only the park never closed and the smorgasbord, much like Bella and I, kept on coming.

I'd never known a woman could be so pliable in my hands. Whether with regard to the number of sexual positions we found ourselves rotating through without even thinking about it or the ever-increasing intensity of our passion for one another, not even our first time together in Jacksonville could compare.

Thinking back to that night, I recalled a few, brief feelings of competitiveness. Momentary desires to try and outdo whatever Bella had already done with her former Masters. Taking her to then trying to push her a little beyond the physical limits of the roughest sex she still retained the ability to enjoy. To use her as thoroughly as possible without crossing any threshold leading toward abuse.

Not only had she allowed me then, it was as if she was encouraging me even more so now.

Perhaps it was the inevitable consequence of our two month buildup. Or the surprise erasure of Bella's tattoo along with the knowledge that I was the first to both know and have the honor to treat her as she truly desired. Or maybe it was because a part of her finally felt free. All I knew was the sex between us over the last couple of hours had been more animalistic than anything I had ever known.

And never more so than when Bella's floodgates opened.

I always noticed it in her face and eyes first. A surprised look of disbelief that it could even happen again, often especially so soon after the last. Then came the shock of acknowledgment that *Oh, yes, it was...* followed by a collage of facial expressions like no other.

A crushing escalation of pressure.

An overwhelming sense of anticipation.

The contorted ache for release.

All ending in an explosion of emotions that exited Bella's body in a feral catharsis of muscle-tensing, hand-clenching, finger-gripping, body-heated wetness.

Splashing us as we slapped against one another, regardless if she was on top or I behind.

Drenching me whenever she sat fully, her juice so abundant it drained down both sides of my legs as well as between them.

But she wasn't squirting. Those faces and the gushing that followed were somewhat different as I'd discovered by manually manipulating her once using my hand and fingers.

No, Bella's surplus of liquid pleasure came straight from her overload of excitement.

And she, as well as it... were all mine.

With Victor on his back, I slid into the crook of his arm as I draped the left side of my body across his top. Laying my head over his pectoral muscle, it wasn't long before the steady drumbeat of his heart put me in a trance. Hypnotized by the beautiful sounds of his personal metronome, I found myself reminiscing for some reason about my job.

Having grown up feeling like somewhat of an outcast, I remembered being pleasantly surprised to discover during my therapy sessions with my female patients that I had more in common with other women than I ever suspected. Even the types with whom I would never have imagined myself identifying.

Like most of them, I yearned for a partner in life who was multifaceted, capable and kind. A man who was true to his word but understanding when I changed my mind. One with just enough overconfidence for me to tap into whenever I needed to borrow a little extra. The type of man who kept up his appearance without being motivated by vanity. Someone empathic enough to simply listen without judgment, treating others as he wanted to be treated. Who didn't always try to help fix my problems but instead supported me as I solved them on my own. Someone who made me laugh, both on purpose and on rarer occasions, spontaneously not-by-design.

But perhaps most of all, someone who deemed me worthy of their time as I did them.

After Victor rolled onto his side facing me and the pattern to his breathing transitioned to autonomous, I turned onto my side, slowly so as not to wake him. When my back finally pressed against his side, I curled his arm over my shoulder, wrapping it between my arms and breasts.

Gazing at the contours of his muscles and tattoo as I fell asleep to the sounds of his gentle snore, my mind drifted back to the day I got inked.

Unlike my tat, the memory was still fresh. After all, it was only about three months old...

... "Oooh, I like this one."

I pointed on the page at a kanji that caught my eye. Most of the Japanese characters I had seen so far had an English interpretation underneath, but not this one.

Abby glanced over at the symbol and immediately snickered. "You dirty little slut."

"Whaaaat?" I complained again. After her third time making the same exact comment, whether pulling my leg or not, she was starting to take the fun out of my search.

For the last fifteen minutes, we'd been relaxing on an overly comfy, velour covered couch, flipping through several large binders of Sex Slave tattoos scattered across the coffee table in front of us. Each album was filled with so many different types of drawings and photos of actual tattoos that the variety alone was a bit overwhelming. But because it was midday on a Monday we had the entire place to ourselves and the personal privacy in such a public setting felt oddly relaxing.

Its gothic and damask décor to the contrary, Masterpeace Tattoos on Central Avenue had turned out to be much cleaner—almost to the point of being clinical—than I had expected. That alone had already eased my anxiety tremendously.

It also helped that the owner, Delilah, was a close, personal friend of Abby's. Because she was the only artist Abby had ever used, there was a singular, underlying style to all of Abby's tats that I felt matched the beauty of her soul. Though to be completely honest, the work of a few dozen artists would have been a better match for Abby's semi-schizophrenic changes in personality.

"Only you'd pick a tattoo that says that," she continued to tease.

"What?! I have no idea what it even means."

"Even better. You should get it. Carpe yourself some diem, damn it!"

I rolled my eyes. "You're no help."

"What does it matter?" Abby shrugged. "You're getting it in *temp ink* for God's sake. It'll be gone in a month or so. Besides, how likely are you to meet a guy who's gonna be able to interpret whatever you choose?"

"You've got a point," I hated to admit.

"I know I do. So don't worry about it, okay? Like I said, it's not about the tattoo. It's about the story you want the tattoo to tell, the fantasy you want it to create."

All I could do was shake my head. Despite once being *her* sex therapist, Abby usually gave me great advice when it came to sex. Even in our therapy sessions, she had always been the crazy-cool mom/big sister/best friend/mentor I'd never had. So when I told her my plan to let my freak flag fly again in Jacksonville, she was quick to suggest I get either a henna or temporary ink tattoo and concoct a story around it. I thought she was crazy at first, but after awhile her idea kind of grew on me.

"I mean why not? Hell, if men can settle for any port in a storm, we ought to be able to grab any lighthouse on the shore. Besides, if you're gonna get a little, you might as well live a little, girl," had been Abby's advice at the time.

Of course, her hair had been a shockingly respectable nutmeg brown that week. Today it was road hazard neon orange. All of which was jelled rock hard and twisted straight up. It was harder to take the same advice from someone who looked like a lit matchstick.

"What if I don't know the story I want to tell?" I asked as I turned my page in exasperation.

"Ha! Who's in denial now, Doctor?... Hey, have you ever realized just how much Doc-tor sounds like Dick-her?" Abby suddenly began cocking her head from side to side like a deranged metronome. "Doctor Dick Her. Dick her, doctor. Doctor Dick Her. Dick her, doctor."

Despite myself, I howled in laughter. On Abby's on days, the woman was a riot-a-minute and just one of the many reasons I loved her. "Girl, you ain't right."

"Never was, never will be but thank you for trying... Ooooh, what about this one?"

Abby pointed to an actual photograph in her book. In it, a female had swept her hair off the back of her neck to reveal a very plain, standard looking UPC barcode hidden discreetly beneath. Dot matrix font numbers printed below the vertical black lines made the image all the more stark.

A former patient had once mentioned this particular tattoo during their therapy sessions, but I had never actually seen one. Supposedly there was a website where people could voluntarily become a certifiably registered Sex Slave, complete with their own unique barcode and corresponding number.

"Just think of the shit you could make up about this," she said.

The thought made me wrinkle my nose. "Not my cup of tea."

"Didn't you stop drinking tea?"

I nodded. For the last week, although I had yet to alter my eating habits, I'd had nothing to drink except for water and orange juice. Gone were my daily sodas and sweet tea along with six pounds I never intended to see again. I was proud of myself, even if it was all water weight thus far. *A girl has to start somewhere,* I thought as I tried to ignore the fact on I was on my fourth start.

Grimacing, I flipped the page.

What— "—the hell is this?"

"What the hell is what?"

I leaned my book over for Abby to see. While the left page had yet another colorful purple heart with a key hole cutout, the right page contained a large drawing of three small, pale blue orbs arranged in a triangular pattern. Connected by a series of perfectly straight lines, one leg used one while the other two used two. With the balls melting and the lines dripping with radioactive blood, it looked like something a psychotic chemist might draw and nothing like I had seen so far. Even Abby appeared stumped.

"I have no idea," she shrugged. "Might mean something to the artist. Might not. So for you it can mean whatever you want."

Whatever I want.

The words gonged in my head like church bells because whatever I wanted was exactly what I was looking for in a tattoo. My problem with all the others I had seen so far were that they came with pre-attached meanings. This one didn't. It was a blank slate that could truly mean whatever I wanted it to mean. And what I truly wanted mine to mean was private, my desire so secret, I hadn't even shared it completely with Abby. But on the off chance I found the right man to share it with, I needed the type of tattoo that would be a definite conversation starter.

"This is the one," I declared.

Abby tried to suppress her surprise. "Interesting. Not exactly what I would have pegged you for regardless of any hidden meaning... Ok, I'll let Delilah know you're ready," she said as she got up and headed back behind a set of heavy curtains to one of the parlor's rooms, leaving me to study my soon-to-be first, albeit temporary, tattoo alone.

Tracing along the strange lines with my finger, I knew there was the possibility that just a few weeks from now some guy I had never met and probably never see again would be the only person to ever see this on my body.

I wondered if I'd find one worthy of giving my full explanation. And if so, might I be brave enough to explain it... And if I did, might he be brave enough to handle it?

… Tucking Victor's hand in beneath my chin just before falling asleep, I smiled, grateful to hold two of the three answers I had hoped to find.

Saturday
March 7, 2020
7:57am, 50° & partly cloudy

Morning horniness, at least for me, was always unique.

As my mind and body struggled to rouse from their combined slumber, each began to discover that certain areas had already jumped the gun and grabbed an early lead. Shocked by their head start, I faced my first choice of the day. Either catch up or give up.

And personally, I felt sleep was overrated.

Waking to the feel of skin on skin, Bella's naked arm draped across my chest, her feet curled around mine, absorbing their warmth... the unbelievably intense ache of my cock should have come as no surprise, yet it was. Without needing to touch myself I knew was as hard as I could get. I could feel the skin along my penis stretched as tight as it would go as the heat of my blood flowed, racing throughout my largest appendage in the vainest of efforts to cool itself off.

I wanted to fuck.

I wanted to rage.

I wanted to create then destroy Bella's wetness for all I was worth. I wanted to use a fistful of her flesh in each of my hands, reining her in to properly mount her only to slap her backside with my open palm whenever she bucked too hard or not enough. I wanted to hear the sounds her mouth and body made as they responded to my directions, feel the tactile sensation wherever we both touched.

Instead, I laid there.

Listening to the rhythmic sounds of her breathing. Watching the steady rise and deep fall of her shoulder correspond to the lift and press of her chest against part of my own. Inhaling the musk still infusing the bed from our last round of sex just before we fell asleep late last night.

Wondering how I was going to tell her I would be her Master if she still wanted to have me.

My intention was to tell her either later tonight or some time tomorrow. I didn't need more time than that because a part of me knew my decision had long been made. I wanted Bella and it was time she knew just how much.

Reaching across with my free hand, I brushed her hair back, uncovering her face... and causing just enough of a stir for her to open her eyes.

Waking beside a man for only the second time in my life felt almost as much of a dream as did the first. But while number one lit my body afire, number two melted my heart, puddling me all over. Finding Victor's baby blues gazing down, his smile in them the first thing I got to see was... indescribable.

"Good morning," he murmured, his morning voice a tad bit huskier than his normal.

"Mmmmmm," I smiled. "Good morning."

"How did you sleep?"

"Well. How about you?"

"Hmmm," he purred, his smile growing in tandem. "I haven't slept that good in two months."

I chuckled, agreeing with his compliment.

"I could get used to this," I said truthfully yet hopeful I wasn't overstepping a bound.

"So could I," Victor concurred far too quickly to be a platitude.

Excited by his inference, I stretched my arms and legs, extending my body fully until everything ended with a yawn. Suddenly depleted of strength, I allowed myself to fully relax... which thankfully Victor took as an invitation to begin touching me.

Running his fingertips along the naked skin of my bare arm, I could tell by the control he exerted over his leisurely pace that he was horny. *Good.*

Watching how where his eyes began to roam didn't always track with where he was pleasuring my body induced the most incredible sensations. Tactile in one spot, palpable in the other, it wasn't long before I felt alive all over.

Which made it a shame when he spoke.

"Do me a favor and close your eyes."

I tried not to show my disappointment. "But I just opened them." Reaching out, I ran one of my fingers across his chest. "And I like what they see."

Tearing his eyes away from my body to direct his gaze back to mine, my groin flushed from his look of assurance.

"Trust me. I'll make it worth it."

My breath caught, leaving me with just enough for, "Oho-kay."

Bewildered about what could be coming next but trusting him completely, I shut my eyes.

"Thank you," he intoned.

With last night's massage still fresh in my memory and the heightened sensation of his hands soothing their way around my body taking command of so much of my attention, I almost failed to notice that Victor's voice sounded deeper.

Almost.

"Now," he said slowly, his voice calm, gentle yet somehow still authoritative, "I want you to think about a morning in your past when you were awakened a little too early by a sound. A time when you woke, nestled under your covers, face down, hugging your pillow. But the noise didn't go away. So, you reached for another pillow... and put it loosely over your head to drown out the sound. Have you ever done that?"

"Sure," I crooned. I wasn't sure where Victor was going, but I liked the memory.

"Do you remember what it felt like to lay there, to drift back off to sleep?"

"Mmmmmm. I do."

"What did it feel like? Tell me."

With my eyes closed, it wasn't hard to remember. "It felt warm. Safe... Like I didn't have a care in the world."

"Good," Victor said, his voice still warm and inviting. "Now open your eyes."

Bella did as I asked, opening her eyes with a smile that was more dreamy than quizzical.

"Would you mind assuming that position for me? Face down in a pillow. With another over your head?"

Only the faintest of beats passed before she agreed. "No, not at all."

"Not at all, what?"

Bella's eyes widened as she inhaled.

"Not at all, Master."

Looking directly into her eyes until she realized I had nothing left to say, Bella turned over, burrowed under the comforter and buried her face into a pillow before pulling a second atop her head.

Damn.

It was almost a shame she was incapable of seeing how much her acquiescence made me smile.

Sinking face first into the luxuriously soft, king size pillow while pulling a second over my head, I basked in the pleasure of being simultaneously relaxed yet turned on. Nursing the throes of my mini massage coma, the stroke of Victor's hands as they had caressed my body still had me floating on cloud nine, caring neither for past nor future, my sole concentration focused on the presence and path of his fingertips.

For what seemed an eternity, I stayed locked into the absolute *now* of each and every moment.

But with the sudden realization that Victor clearly wanted to use me, to possibly fulfill what felt like the beginning of a fantasy, all I could think about was what was coming next? What was he about to have me do? Or do to me?

"Now, I want you to again imagine that you've just been awakened by a noise," Victor crooned. Even through the pillow, I could tell his speech was slightly slower and deeper, almost hypnotic. "It's early," he continued. "Too early to wake. So, you've covered your ears and you're going back to sleep," he said as his voice grew softer and more measured. "You're going back to sleep," he said as I felt him leave the bed, "and only your Master's touch has the power to awaken you."

As I relaxed and snuggled deeper into the comfort of my cocoon, I sensed Victor move to the foot of the bed. For the first ten seconds of silence, my level of self-awareness rose until I suddenly exhaled, releasing myself from my own captivity. A few seconds later, I felt the comforter around my feet begin to lift. Slowly at first, pausing to reveal my feet, then further and further, inch by inch he uncovered me. Teasing me by making sure the highest edge of my nakedness kept contact with the comforter, my butterflies began to flutter ever so slightly just before my ass was laid completely bare.

"Mmmmmmm," he moaned as he joined me in my renewed anticipation. Climbing onto the bed, I felt his knees on either side of my legs before he continued to unwrap me.

Pausing just under my cheeks, his pace slowed even further as I felt his hands press against the outside of my legs. Lifting the cloth and kneading me simultaneously, he continued north, his gasp almost inaudible as my entire lower half was finally unveiled.

"Would you look at that?" I heard Victor murmur to himself.

With the bottom edge of the comforter straddling my upper hips, I felt like I was in two worlds at once. Cooler, naked, exposed and vulnerable from my waist down, I was warm, covered, isolated yet safe from my waist up. The dichotomy somehow encouraged all my concentration, all my focus to my nether region, to where all my feelings were rushing, carrying my blood and consciousness with them.

How Victor slid his hand under my pelvis without my feeling it I'd never know. Yet suddenly he was lifting me, there, with his hand. With my head still in the pillows, my hips rose ever higher until my lower back and ass were arched fully in the air. Their weight became solely supported by my knees when they locked just before Victor removed his hand entirely from beneath me.

"Perfect," I heard him say.

And then nothing.

Several still seconds of silence passed as my upper body grew warmer while my lower cooled. The temperature difference and the anticipation heightened my senses to such a degree that I practically bucked when Victor's warm fingers first touched my clit. Pressing his thumb firmly against my ass, his tips and palm began rubbing me ever so gently in the same slow, circular motion I used on myself. Round and round he went, taking his time, never increasing his speed, going slow, just the way I liked.

Despite the cushion covering my ears, I could clearly hear the wet sounds Victor so intentionally caused my body to make. Losing myself in the sensations, I closed my mouth, gathering it around a piece of the pillow beneath me. Stifling my whimpers became more difficult as I felt Victor reposition himself behind me, directly between the spread of my calves. But when, without a word he withdrew his hand and pressed his dick into me, not even the density of the goose down could muzzle my moan.

"Ohhhhhh, God," Bella cried into and underneath her pillows, echoing my thought exactly.

Smoothing my hands across the backside of her flesh, I kneaded each of her ass cheeks until they were molded firmly inside my grip. Relishing the control, I closed my eyes, joining her in the absence of visual stimulation and began to withdraw and thrust as slowly as I could. In and out, in and out I went, over and over, holding to the slowest rhythm I could maintain without driving myself mad in the process.

But after several minutes, when Bella finally tried to move in an effort to quicken our pace, I stilled and opened my eyes then quickly gave her right buttock a good slap. Just enough to sting, not enough to hurt, yet more than enough to do the trick. Instantly, she froze.

"Don't move," I commanded before slowly resuming my pace.

"Ooookay?"

"Okay, what?"

"Ooookay, Maaaster..."

Hearing not just hesitancy but also a slight tinge of confusion in Bella's voice reminded me that this, too, was new to her. But what she said she wanted was to be used for my pleasure. And to me that meant I was going to have to teach her not to interfere.

Gripping her ass a bit harder, I slowed my pace to both compensate and get her attention.

"Listen to me, Bella. The only thing I want to do right now is fuck your sweet, tight little pussy. So you can go back to sleep or feel free to cum all you want. I don't care. But you are to remain perfectly still until I say otherwise, do you understand?"

"Yes, Master," she whined.

"What was that? I didn't hear you."

"Yes, Master," she whined louder.

"Good girl."

Releasing my hold on Bella's ass, I closed my eyes and folded my fingers behind my head.

Truth be told, I wasn't all that comfortable with what I had just done. After spending so long working her up, I knew denying Bella what she wanted was wrong. But what she said she wanted also included being used solely for my pleasure. My only problem was I hadn't really treated any woman that way before in my life.

But the only way I figured I could get through this was like this. With Bella's head buried in the pillows, me not looking at what I was doing. Which was hard to do when what I was doing felt so fucking fantastic. Yet it had to be this way. Bella was right. If I was going to ultimately cherish her to the degree she wanted to be cherished, I had to be able to use her the way I was most afraid. And to do so, I had to make this as impersonal as possible.

Of course, I also understood the mechanics of the female orgasm. I knew exactly what I was doing by keeping my pace so perfectly constant. Rocking back and forth, I did everything I could to never vary my strokes. Like most men, I could go slow like this all night. And a large part of me wanted to. I loved nothing more than fucking. Loved it so much I never wanted it to end. I actually preferred not to cum. Most of the time I just wanted to fuck and fuck and fuck...

But most women could only take so much for so long and I certainly couldn't blame them. We were all beholden to our bodies, after all. Especially when it came to certain parts.

I knew well that a woman's vaginal walls won't begin to contract and expand uncontrollably until her internal muscles fail to keep up. When the pace of involuntary contraction from intrusion is eclipsed by the involuntary relaxation from withdrawal.

I knew not before the amount of pleasure from the relief of Bella's pain was greater than the pain at the beginning of her pleasure would her vaginal muscles begin to spasm in tandem, both from her anticipation as well as her desire for prolongation. And I knew overlapping faster and faster, leaving less and less time between them, her spasms would eventually unite, becoming one in climax.

But by steadying the frequency of my thrusts and withdrawals, I knew I was modulating Bella's spasms. Controlling her body's response with my own. Denying her release as I forced her to accept the repetitious way I stoked her desire.

I knew it was only temporary. But I could not tell if that made it better.

Several minutes into Victor taking me from behind, my mind was numb, reduced like a sauce left simmering too long on a stove. Fragments of disjointed thoughts struggled to bubble free, popping at the surface in between bouts of the most singularly focused moments of sheer physical ecstasy I had ever experienced.

In and out Victor infringed upon before rescinding against me, the rawest parts of our flesh pulling along one another as we slid to and fro. Unable to discern whether the pleasure of his advances or aches from his withdrawals teased me more, my mind flowed back and forth with both... tethered to my body... enjoying the tug-of-war... deliriously trapped in their middle.

Gone was my awareness of the disparity in temperature. Absent was my disregard for any deeper meaning to or future repercussions from allowing myself to be so impersonally used.

Yet fully present in the moment like the gift it was... was I.

I wasn't sure when I released Bella's ass from my grip.

So lost in the sensations of being inside her, I temporarily lost track of the rest of my surroundings until I realized the top of each of Bella's feet were cupped in each of my hands. Angled like an upside down stirrup, I raised her ankles higher and pushed as deeply into her as I could go without pressing up against her backside. Lowering her calves just a bit allowed her to move forward and away from me, in the perfect position for my next thrust.

Back and forth we went, rocking together wheelbarrow style. Her wailing. My grunting. Over and over and over again.

Until I looked down.

Down to see the place where we were joined. Down to see where all the wet noise of excitement was coming from. Down to one of the most beautiful sights in all the fucking world.

My...

Grabbing Bella by the outside of her hips I rammed into her hard enough to elicit a small yelp. Throttling my strength just a touch, my next thrust was better prepared for and received than the first. Sensing Bella brace herself as she wiggled her ass a bit higher to accommodate my intensity only added to my increasing excitement as I continued to be mesmerized by the sight of my cock slipping in and out of her pussy.

Holding her tight for dear life, I slammed into her as hard as I felt her body could handle it. Over and over and over again, fucking her so hard I felt like *I* had to hold on, feeling the energy, the power, the emotion building between our bodies. It took every ounce of my control not to let go.

Only to realize I couldn't.

I couldn't cum. I knew it. I felt it. My ability to achieve orgasm wasn't accruing. No matter how hard I fucked, no matter how hard I gave it to her, the buildup, *that* buildup, wasn't happening. It wasn't there.

But just as quickly I realized where it was.

Taking my hands off Bella's hips and slowing just long enough, I whipped the comforter away, completely exposing the rest of her body. Sensing her shock in how still she became, I grabbed the pillow off the top of her head and flung it aside, too.

I had never been fucked so hard in my life. Including every time by Victor.

Laying there so comfortably on my knees in the most submissive position I'd ever experienced, the pillow and comforter sensory deprivation were anything but. In fact, they were magnifiers.

Every time Victor crashed into me, I heard our collision, *felt* my juices splash my back and buttocks. The occasional hint of Victor's woodsy cologne embedded in the pillow beneath me smelled like a dash of seasoning sprinkled over the aromatic essence of his natural body I tasted in the bedsheet balled in my mouth.

But nowhere were my senses more overloaded than in my brain.

With the pleasure between my legs intense enough to repeatedly force my eyes to the back of my head, my mind tormented me by filling in the blanks. Somehow I could *see* the angle of Victor's hands as they gripped my flesh. His veins elevated on their tops, crossing his wrists, spreading along his forearms, up his biceps, the balls of his shoulders until...

The look on his face as he looked down at me splayed before him was almost indescribable. Determination. Hunger. Want. Desperation. Lust.

Need.

Every minuscule change in pressure of Victor's grip, I *saw* his expression change in my head. Understood their foreshadowing effects on his pace. His rhythm. His pleas—

The comforter came off with barely a warning. The sudden loss of body heat that came with it was less shocking than Victor's action itself. Stunned, I had no idea what he wanted me to do so I did nothing. But by the time he took the pillow off and tossed it aside there was only one thing I wanted.

"Don't stop," I pleaded. "Oh God, please don't stop."

Raising up on my hands and twisting my head back over my shoulder, I couldn't believe the look of absolute lust ingrained upon Victor's face. His eyes, usually so brilliant and blue, were like steel coated in ice, their resolve so severe it sent a rush of blood fleeing to his groin that was so hot I could feel it inside me.

My body didn't have time for a buildup. But between the unexpected expression in Victor's eyes and surge of heat searing my pussy, it exploded anyway. But not like I ever had.

My orgasm was a total release of wetness, a gushing not from one place as I usually felt, but from all over, everywhere inside me. Nor was I wracked by shudders and contractions the way I normally came. Instead I collapsed, my head hitting the pillow, my strength gone, my weight above my knees giving way as my hips fell lower, increasing the pressure of Victor's body inside mine.

Thankfully, the change in our angle of contact along with the incredibly loud splashing sounds emanating between us spurred Victor's excitement to a whole new level.

Selfishly riding wave after internal wave of my own orgasm, I was grateful to hear him grunt and groan, his grip and thrusts quickly increasing beyond what I could handle. Perfectly willing yet completely incapable of doing anything else, I surrendered my body to Victor, crawled inside my mind and just let him have it.

She was done with me but not I with her.

Had I kept Bella under the pillow and comforter, I had no doubt I could have fucked her all damn day. And one day in the future I just might. But as we had places to go and people to see, I needed to see her for myself.

All of her.

The differing ways Bella took me on, taking me in, always amenable and pliable to any angle or pace I desired, ready to match or exceed any rhythm, even the astonished look in her eyes that always preceded her orgasms just before they overwhelmed her, all of it pushed me toward my edge.

But only she had the power to shove me over.

Now, naked and exposed, half supine yet completely spent before me, her hips suddenly angled differently where we were fastened, the pressure in my balls began to boil over.

Emptying myself inside her, my juice mixed with hers as I struggled to hold on to her hips for dear life. With each successive spurt pumping a little less than the last, I slowly relaxed my grips on her ass until my orgasm was done.

Drained both physically and mentally, my emotions took over as I found myself desiring to be even further connected to her. Pressing my weight gently forward, I forced Bella flat as I took care to lay as lightly above her as I could. With me still fully inside, she lifted up just enough to maximize the contact of our skin, murmuring and sighing as she did so.

With my chin above her head, I used my right hand to sweep her hair from between us so we could touch one another even more.

We laid like that for quite a while.

So long in fact, I remembered our breathing was in sync just before I dozed off. But at some point we must have shifted because when I woke a few minutes later, Victor was slightly behind my side on my left. Finding his right arm wrapped around me, his hand curled around mine was almost as wonderful as realizing he was still inside me even though he was now soft.

Nuzzling the top of my head in the crook of Victor's neck, under his chin, I reveled in the moment. The last time I had felt so cherished and protected I was a young girl. But never in my life had I known the sensation simultaneously combined with feeling so sated and desired.

And the sentiment behind it was one I never wanted to end.

Feeling Victor stir behind me, I took a deep breath as he tilted his head to kiss the top of my mine.

"Are you ready to start our day together?"

"Yes," I exhaled with a smile. *Yes, I am.*

As we sat still in traffic, Bella glanced around at all the activity along the sides of the road.

Mountain bikers zipped around the long-distance runners wherever their paths crossed along the single track and all-weather trails as each tried to steer clear of the wayward day hikers using both. At the same time, I was doing my best to avoid the line of families too impatient to wait yet not too lazy to tote their blankets and chairs in by foot.

Luckily, the end of the line of vehicles waiting to pay to park stopped deeper inside the US National Whitewater Center's entrance than it typically did around this time on opening day. Not by much but more than enough for a frequent visitor like myself to notice. Of course, with Covid-19 so heavily in the news, a slightly lower turnout than expected made sense.

From our vantage point in my Raptor, high above most of the vehicles ahead of us, I could see the line was moving decently fast. I estimated we'd be parked and inside within the next ten minutes which was plenty of time.

Because although I had already explained to Bella all about my promise to watch Nixie, what I hadn't finished yet was warning her all about Rick.

"All I'm saying," I repeated as I glanced at her sideways while slowly inching the 4x4 forward, "is when it comes to Rick it'd be wise to steer clear of any topic that comes anywhere close to being a conspiracy theory. Trust me. He's been known to get carried away."

"Why?" Bella asked before suddenly making a face. "Does he *really* have a titanium plate in his head?"

It took me a second to realize what— "Oh, you mean last night? When he asked me if titanium was conductive. You thought he— No. Rick has a titanium prosthetic for one of his legs."

"Oh."

"Though your idea makes more sense," I laughed before cutting my eyes at her one last time. "Seriously, though. You've been warned."

Acknowledging me with a half nod, half shrug, Bella went back to people watching.

Not long after I accepted Victor's invite to The US National Whitewater Center, I went online to learn more about it. Though I knew it was a bit of a Mecca for those dedicated to an active lifestyle, I had never driven anywhere near the place despite living only fifteen minutes away.

Thankfully, three minutes on the website told me pretty much everything I needed to know.

Spread across thirteen hundred acres, the facility's main draw was the world's largest, man-made recirculating whitewater course. Nearly three-quarters of a mile long, the river was divided into two channels, each with differing levels of difficulty. While rafters and kayakers traveled from around the region to repeatedly tackle the artificially created class II-IV rapids, with over two dozen additional recreational activities to choose from there was more than just a little something for everyone.

Calmer ponds were available for the less adventurous to try stand-up paddle boarding, flatwater kayaking or canoeing while for those seeking solace from the crowds, fifty miles of mountain biking, hiking, jogging and walking trails wound through the surrounding forest. Yet, no matter what anyone came to do, frequent festivals and a live music pavilion along with plenty of craft beers on tap gave visitors more than enough reasons to stick around afterwards and socialize.

Marketing hype aside, the place really did sound like an outdoor enthusiast's idea of paradise.

Unfortunately, as I continued scrolling I also discovered a couple of activities that worried me. According to the pictures and descriptions, several courses of rope bridges courses stretched high up from one suspended platform to another, occasionally criss-crossing above the rafters' heads before disappearing into the woods. As if those weren't terrifying enough, a four-story tower erected on the ground's highest elevation served as the drop-off point for a thousand-foot zip line.

Yet as I stood holding hands with Victor at the top of the concrete steps overlooking one of the Whitewater Center's two main entrances, whatever fear I felt quickly faded as I became awestruck by my first real look at it all.

With the entrance situated on a ridge and higher than everything else around, I could see almost the entire facility spread out below. And with the sun still low in the sky behind us, the waterways, rock walls, zip lines and walking trails were all lit by an almost preternatural serenity undisturbed even by the several hundred people milling about, most of whom were excitedly preparing for one activity or another.

All of whom seemed to be in a really good mood.

As older kids and their parents scaled different paths up the forty-foot high rock climbing walls to which they were harnessed, a little further down several younger children scrambled across small boulders built especially for them. While many of the visitors were still signing waiver forms or paying for their activity passes, others already had their own blankets and lawn chairs set up for the day on the grassy areas between the wide concrete walking paths. Surprisingly, a few had even strung up their own hammocks where they found spots. The large number of people walking around with a dog on a leash was something else I didn't expect to see.

Noticing how the waterways in the background were mostly dry, I recalled that Rick had said the water release was at 11:30, a little less than an hour from now. Which made me wonder—

"There they are," Victor said as he pointed toward the bottom of the steps below us.

Looking much different than he did last night, it took me a few seconds to spot Rick in the crowd coming toward us. Sporting a wick dry athletic shirt over loose basketball shorts and a small backpack hanging off one shoulder, I was almost as surprised to see his lower left leg was equipped with a black, blade-style prosthesis as were the back two on the leashed dog with him.

"Stay there a sec," Rick called up to us. "Nixie could use the practice."

Leading the way, the Belgian Malinois trotting behind Rick did its best not to hold them up. In fact, it was pretty heartwarming to see a couple of children acknowledge and encourage the animal's efforts and success with small cheers when they reached the top.

"Good girl," Rick said as he gave the dog a few rubs under her neck before turning to me. "Dr. Bella Quinn, I'd like you to meet Ms. Nixie Fairchild."

Tickled by her name, I bent over just a bit. "Hello, Nixie," I said, prompting the dog to look at Rick who then nodded. Almost dutifully, Nixie offered me her front left paw which I took and shook. "Well, aren't you sweet!"

"How long have you been here?" Victor asked.

"Oh, just long enough to say hi to a few regulars," Rick said before turning to me. "So, are ya ready for the grand tour?"

Blinking my surprise, Rick looked up at Victor. "You didn't tell her?"

"Oh, I warned her about you plenty," Victor half smirked. "But about the tour, no." Turning to me, he continued, "I have something I need to attend to for about an hour so I've asked Rick if he would be so kind as to show you around. Do you mind?"

Under any other circumstance, I would have. And that was despite the part of me that was actually relieved.

While Victor had assured me we were only going to watch Nixie and be spectators during our visit, I was secretly worried he might try to encourage me to give one of the zip lines a try. Though well aware of my fear of heights, he also seemed to have a knack for pushing me just enough out of my comfort zone for it to still be tolerable. I just really didn't want one of his favorite spots in all of Charlotte to be somewhere we both failed.

Of course truth be told, I was more disappointed than anything else. Ever since researching the Whitewater Center I had often imagined happily strolling around the place simply holding hands with Victor. And while there would still be plenty of time for that later, I also knew I could trust him. Not only wasn't he handing me off to just anyone, I was sure he had a good enough reason for it as well.

"Not at all," I said before pulling Victor down for a quick kiss.

"Thanks," he said before turning to Rick. "I'll meet you on the Biergarten bridge in time for water release." Victor leaned down to scratch Nixie's head. "If you beat me there, save me a spot, okay?" Nixie replied by wagging her tail as Victor turned back to me, taking my hand. "And I'll see *you* in an hour... Ciao, Bella," he said before kissing me again.

As he turned and walked back toward where we had parked the Raptor just minutes ago, I couldn't help to wonder where Victor was going. But as my new chaperone swept his arm out toward the rest of Whitewater Center, I decided not to dwell on it.

"Shall we?" Rick asked.

The day, and especially the place, were just too beautiful.

I hated leaving Bella's side, but there simply was no other way. Not that I was worried.

I'd texted Rick strict instructions earlier in the morning. Go grab a couple bottles of water. Walk around the right side of the park first. Take time sightseeing.

Given the distance between where I had parked and what I had to do, I'd be done in under an hour. And though the facility could be easily circumnavigated in about half that time, stopping to check out everything there was to do would take a good deal more.

I only needed enough.

After explaining how bringing in outside food or beverages were just about the Whitewater Center's only restrictions, Rick picked up three bottles of water at a concession stand, handed me one then began to lead us around. Heading toward a covered, open air stage, he explained that the river channel on our right was for the most challenging rapids. Rodeo rafting, he called it.

"But don't worry. People rarely fall in. And even when they do, the water's only waist deep."

While I appreciated Rick's attempt to pacify my look of concern, I had also seen the website photos of how turbulent the water could be.

If you say so...

It took some time before we crossed the next bridge to head counterclockwise around the Center. As they passed by, so many kids kneeled down to pet and love on Nixie I sensed even she grew tired of all the stopping and starting the attention caused. But once we were on the outer perimeter with a wider berth, the pedestrian crowd thinned out, allowing us a far more leisurely stroll.

True to Victor's word, Rick kept me entertained. As he filled me in on all the incomplete screenplays, novels and short stories he had been writing over the years and how he and Victor had first bonded over a discussion of one, I couldn't help but gaze around. In a place as big as the Whitewater Center... there was just so much to see... In fact...

"Is that a tent?" I interrupted.

"Probably," Rick replied before peering off into the woods where I was pointing. "Yeah, it is. Camping overnight isn't allowed but plenty of people spend the whole day here. Pitching a tent gives them somewhere to get out of the sun and relax."

Wow. I'd never heard of a recreational facility to allow such a thing. Then again, I'd never been to one like the Whitewater Center either.

Strolling a bit further, we paused and stepped to the water's edge where a gentle stream flowing down the river ahead of us emptied into the lower pond. Directly across the water on the man-made island, five rock climbing walls stretched toward the sky. Starting at the edge of an elongated, brilliant blue swimming pool, the walls towered upward as they arched increasingly out over the water. Fittingly, taken altogether the curves resembled the whitewater of cresting waves.

"Do you know how high those walls are?" I asked.

"The smallest is twenty feet, the tallest forty-five." Rick caught my look. "The pool is about twenty feet deep on the shallow end which is more than enough for a fall from the top."

Unlike the rock walls and spire at the main entrance, I noticed this particular attraction was closed. Realizing that was probably because the swimming pool was still too cold to use, I also noticed another difference. There were no climbing contraptions at the top.

"And you don't use a harness or ropes? There's nothing to stop a fall but the water?"

I was looking at it but I still had a hard time believing it. *Why would anyone in their right—*

"—That's what Deep Water Solo Climbing is all about… I take it you're not a fan."

"If it has anything to do with heights or flights or anything else you can fall from, no I am not." I looked at the top. "Do you and Victor really climb those things until you fall off? On purpose?"

Rick nodded. "We usually race one another to see who can make it to the top first. But 'cause a Covid, I don't think we'll get to do that again any time soon."

Shaking our heads for entirely different reasons, we started back on the path with Nixie leading the way. Walking past an obstacle course leading into the woods on our right, I noticed several parents monitoring their children as the kids attempted to walk along a wall of rope netting without allowing their feet to touch the ground. Which reminded me…

"Victor mentioned all the families living at the foundation have already self-quarantined for two weeks. How's that going?"

Rick shrugged as we continued around the bend. "About as well as can be expected, I suppose. People are anxious, you know, fear of the unknown and all that. But everyone there's prepared to ride it out for a while if they have to. What about you?"

"Me?" The question caught me by surprise. I wasn't sure if I was being asked *how* I was or *what* I planned on doing, but the former sounded easier to answer. "Oh, you know... so far, so good."

Rick grimaced in mock exasperation. "That's 2020 for ya. At this rate it won't be long before 'So far, so good' is the new 'Awesome!'"

I nodded. Just two and a half months old, it had definitely been a strange year. Part of me was already starting to dread whatever April might bring. Trying not to think about it, I watched Rick take a long, wistful look around, his gaze sweeping over a large portion of the Whitewater Center's crowd.

"You know," he continued, "I don't know what's going to happen next, but history hasn't been too kind to people who're kept cooped up for too long. Humans just ain't built for it."

"No, we are not," I agreed.

"I heard someone the other day talk about how we need to start 'social distancin'" which, while I understand, still doesn't sound like a great idea." Rick turned to look me in the eye. "People need people, ya know?"

I nodded at the subtle implication, then smiled with a deeper appreciation of why Victor seemed to like Rick so much. And I had to admit, I did, too. Despite the slow, down home, Southern drawl he occasionally lapsed into, he was obviously quite intelligent. "Some of us more than others," I assured him before reaching down to tousle Nixie's ears.

Continuing to walk around the far back side of the Whitewater Center, I did my best to ignore the sounds of guests screaming as they stepped off the controlled fall side of the Zip line tower in the woods. Harnessed in or not, I remembered reading on the website that the platform was a hundred feet high.

No, thanks, I thought as Rick bent down to pour Nixie some water into a small bowl he pulled from his bag. Recalling that the Catawba River was just off to our right, hidden behind the woods, I tried to spot it through the foliage. Anything to forget the falling bodies just yards away.

"So," Rick asked, "did the Boss get a chance to give you a tour of To Fish this morning before y'all got out here?"

Welcoming the distraction even if the question did come out of the blue, I shook my head.

"But I think he's planning to later today or perhaps tomorrow. Why?"

Rick smiled. "Just a word to the wise. If he suggests playing a game in the clubhouse, decline."

Um... "What game?"

"All of 'em."

"No, I mean what kind of a game?"

"Oh, we've got all kinds in there. Pool, darts, foosball, air hockey."

You've gotta be— "The foundation's clubhouse has all those games?"

Rick nodded. "And more. And the Boss beats everyone at 'em. He plays so often no one can touch him. And he takes it easy on nobody and I mean no body."

Hmmmm... "What about shuffleboard?"

Rick rolled his eyes and nodded. "That's actually his best game."

That— Rolling my eyes in commiseration, I wondered. "If he's that good, why do you think he plays so often? Surely not to get better or for the thrill of beating anyone."

"Oh, no. In fact, the Boss doesn't gloat at all. That's just not his style."

"So why then?"

Rick pursed his lips for a split second before relaxing. Recognizing the clear signs of reluctance, I started to let him off the hook. But he had known Victor far longer than I had. Not only was his opinion valuable, I was sure he'd stay quiet if he felt it necessary.

"How much has the Boss told you about his childhood?" he finally asked.

"You mean about being raised in foster care?"

Rick chuckled. "He mighta grown up in it, but I'm pretty sure the Boss raised hisself."

I nodded my agreement. "So what about it?"

"Boss once told me when he was a kid, he made a promise to himself. That when he grew up, he'd play all the games he could that he never had the money for... or adults who loved him to play with."

Wow. "He said that?"

Rick nodded. "I know he's just the foundation's Executive Director. But he didn't provide to have that clubhouse built for himself. He had it built for the kids that live there."

"So they wouldn't have to grow up without... the way he did," I concluded.

Rick nodded respectfully.

Damn.

Standing above the soon-to-be rapids on the bridge leading to the Pump House Biergarten, I heard them approach before I saw them. Well, I heard Rick, anyway.

"You tell me," he semi-demanded of Bella as she walked Nixie up the steps my way. "What *good* reason does the *President* have for giving the press *the slip* for *half an hour* when he's in a *thousand room* hotel with *plenty* of privacy, sending his *motorcade* as a decoy, disrupting five o'clock traffic on a *Friday* in a heavily congested, metropolitan area, inconveniencing *everyone,* only to use Marine One *anyway* in order to fly from the hotel's *rooftop* to his next fundraiser *thrown for the flimsiest of reasons,* might I remind you, by the *sleaziest music producer this country has ever known?"*

Incapable of saying anything despite her mouth being wide open, Bella looked at me for help.

"You poked the bear anyway, didn't you?"

Looking from me to Rick, both Rick and Bella turned back toward me in unison with the same look on their face.

"Nooope!" they practically shouted together before high-fiving one another and laughing hard. Rick in particular.

"Oh, my God! Did you see the look on the Boss' face?" he asked, doubling over.

I just looked down at the man. "Oh, you're going to pay for that one."

Rick put his hands up. "Hey, now," he laughed. "That wasn't *my* idea."

Leaning up to give me a laughing kiss, Bella apologized. "I'm sorry. I couldn't resist."

Narrowing my expression, I gave Bella a stare. "Oh. Even better."

As Bella's eyes grew wide with wonder as to what I meant, people all around us—on the bridge and on both sides of the waterway beneath us—began to chant, softly at first but growing louder each second.

"Ten... nine... eight... seven... six... *five... four... three... two... One!"*

Cheers and laughter competed with a great deal of clapping as water began flowing down the channel below us, steadily at first but then picking up the pace as the upper pond began to swell with the overflow running our way. Nodding as she turned her head around to take it all in, I was glad to see Bella smile just as big, if not bigger than, those celebrating.

Grinning a melancholy bit to ourselves, Rick and I had attended enough opening day water release moments to know this one, though a little less crowded, was a little more special. We both knew, outdoors or not, given the way things were progressing, it wouldn't be long before Covid-19 shut the Whitewater Center down, too. However, at least for the moment, it was clear the coronavirus had been relegated to the back of everyone's minds instead of the fore.

Strolling around for an hour and a half with Nixie on her leash in one hand and Victor in my other, part of me felt like I was living in a domesticated fairy tale. Whether we were or not, I could tell from the look in other people's eyes that they thought Victor and I were just a couple walking their dog much like many of the others we came across. When quite a few paused to chat with us, I was once again reminded why I loved living in the South. Everywhere you went, the people were just so friendly.

Simple though it may have seemed—and eager to get back to more horizontal activities—I was nonetheless a little sad to meet back up with Rick on the Biergarten bridge when he was done navigating a couple of the Whitewater Center's more advanced rope courses. While I was sure he didn't want to take up any more of Victor's time, he assured us he also had a personal reason.

"Not only does it look like we might get a little rain, I want to get back to working on my screenplay. I came up with this great idea for a scene last night and I can't wait to—"

"—Hold up," Victor said. "Screenplay? What happened to the novel you were writing?"

"Novels take forever to finish," Rick said with a wave of his hand. "Plus, there's no money in it. But the movie I'm writing now? *Guaranteed* blockbuster."

"Let me guess," Victor groaned with a smile. "It's about a conspiracy theory that—"

"—Nope!" Rick cut him off. "It's about a reality TV show... that *investigates* conspiracy theories."

"Tell me you're kidding."

"What? Are you kidding? *Think* about how big my target market will be! People who watch reality shows *and* those who are into conspiracy theories!"

Victor shook his head. "Well, at least 'the person who writes for fools is always sure of a large audience.'"

Rick cocked his head and thought for a second. "Twain?"

"Schopenhauer."

"Damn. Wasn't even close. My second guess woulda been Hemingway."

"Regardless of who said it," I chimed in, "don't you listen to him, Rick. I think your movie idea sounds like a great one."

"Thank you," Rick said as Victor hit me with a slow burn... which Rick caught. "And on that note," he joked before extending his hand. "Bella, it's been a pleasure. I hope to see you again sometime soon."

"Likewise," I said, shaking his hand. "And thank *you* for showing me around." As Victor and Rick said goodbye, I bent over and gave the shepherd's head a quick ruffle. "And thank *you* for being such a good guard dog today, Nixie."

Leading her gently with the leash, I watched as Rick and Nixie made their way down off the Biergarten bridge then head toward the parking area.

Nonchalantly sidling closer on my left side, Victor's voice dropped low enough so only I could hear him over the sloshing whitewater churning beneath us.

"You know, you're a little pushy for a wannabe Sex Slave."

Goosebumps ran instantly down my arms and across the back of my neck. The slight tingling sensation even extended all the way to my nipples as I turned to find Victor leaning down against the bridge's rail, his face inches from my own. Determined not to cede him the upper hand, my eyebrow arched to my defense.

"I notice you say that with a smile," I challenged him.

"Well, I didn't say I didn't like it."

"So then... you're saying it's something you want..."

Victor allowed my words to linger as he tried to determine whether I was stating or asking. Finally smirking, I thought he was throwing in the towel until he spoke.

"Keep it up," he cautioned, "and I'm going to punctuate the backside of your narrative with my exclamation point a whole lot sooner than you're probably anticipating I will."

Struggling to hold my composure in the face of his abrupt, creative boldness, I murmured for a second or two, drawing out the moment until my thoughts recovered. Given the setting, it was easy for me to hush my voice as well. "Mmmmmm, such... big words. Think you can back them up?"

"Are you challenging me?"

"Perhaps."

Victor grinned as he fixed me with his eyes. "Think you'll get away with it? Here?"

"Absolutely," I retorted in defiance before realizing I hadn't really thought things through. "I mean... this... is a public place. And you know my rule about public humiliation." *Nice save.*

Victor's eyes swept the crowd around us, taking it in in one long panorama. Then, after a brief pause, he shrugged, seemingly in defeat.

"Oh, well. No real privacy here. I guess you'll have to wait after all."

Emboldened by my sudden upper hand, I made a face. "Giving up so easy? Tsk tsk. What's a man's words worth these days? Oh well. Promises, promises..."

Suddenly Victor's smile slowly began to spread into that special grin of his. *Uh-oh.*

"My dear, Bella," he said, his eyes lit even brighter, "have you learned nothing about me yet? *Challenge* accepted."

Slipping his right hand into my left, Victor spun and began to lead us down off the bridge. Trailing in his wake as he positioned himself in front of me, my mind started to race, wondering where we were going. Not that it looked all that threatening, but with the darkest cloud in the sky starting to drift over us, most patrons were beginning to seek shelter under the nearest gazebos and patios as well as the Biergarten.

Weaving our way through the crowd, I was struck by how incredibly self-aware Victor was of his own size. Whenever he purposely claimed the right of way, people moved out of ours. Yet wherever he saw an opening, he accommodated others by politely threading us around them. I could not remember the last time I felt so safe within such a large crowd. And though I wasn't yet prepared to believe Victor was mine, at that moment I was completely his.

Reveling in the company of my masculine complement, I was also grateful to be so securely tethered to the strength of Victor's hand as he guided us toward the Whitewater Center's exit on the far left... where I vaguely recalled a path coming down from the parking lot on the ridge above was located.

Is that where he's taking us?

Were we going to have sex in his truck? Because even with tinted windows and overcast skies, the idea didn't thrill me. While the Whitewater Center was geared toward those with a physically active lifestyle, it was obviously also a very family-oriented place. Doing it in the pouring rain where no one would be paying attention, I *might* be able to handle. But the clouds above us weren't all that omin—

Wait a minute.

Instead of taking the last path up the hill on our left, Victor led us straight ahead. Stepping through a clearing in the trees, I felt the faintest of raindrops begin to fall. Turning to grin back at me with that know-it-all look of his, I realized Victor probably knew what I had been thinking, thus expecting. Tamping down my sigh of relief yet still unaware of where we were going, I was grateful this edge of the property was far less populated.

After turning right on yet another cleared path behind the trees, Victor led us left onto a small trail leading into the woods.

As my eyes slowly adjusted to the sudden absence of sunlight, I realized that very few of the fifty-foot tall pine trees back here had any branches below ten feet high. This made it easier to see about half a dozen or so tents scattered both left and right, none closer than ten yards from another. A sign marked *Hot Yoga* on one of the trees stood in front of an empty clearing on the forest floor. But a good fifty yards beyond that clearing was what really caught my eye.

Set well apart from everything else and darkened by the shade of the canopy was a large, verdant-camouflage printed tent.

So that was what was in the back of the truck.

Twisting to look back at me with that wicked little grin of his, Victor said nothing as he led us toward his makeshift getaway. Smiling in silence, I let the smell of live pine, dead wood and nutrient rich earth fill my nostrils as the sound of drizzle began to intensify into a light rain. Barely registering a few drops under so much foliage, the white noise quickly became almost hypnotic, relaxing me as I breathed in deeply. The moment felt both magical and surreal as I found myself thinking back to the first night Victor and I had met and how he had known what the word petrichor meant.

Reaching the front of the tent while still holding my hand, he used his free one to push open the partition's flap.

Ever the gentleman...

I stepped aside to let Bella enter first. Wide enough to sleep eight, I had arranged an elevated, queen sized air mattress covered in silk sheets and pillows in the center. With little room left to move, Bella quickly laid down on the bed as I ducked inside and zipped the door closed behind us. Although the tent was high enough for average sized individuals to stand upright, I had to stay stooped.

Trying to avoid the sight of what sounded like her beginning to roll around like a cat in heat, I focused on the four corners of the tent where I began turning on each of the small, portable dehumidifiers I had stationed. While it might not have been all that warm outside, that didn't mean it wasn't about to get hot in here.

With the final A/C activated, I turned to find Bella on her back, propped up by her elbows, just staring at me lovingly.

"It must have taken you several trips to bring all this down here."

I wrinkled my nose. "Nothing I couldn't handle."

"Thank you."

"You're welcome. Besides, like I told you, I like to be prepared."

Bella's eyes smiled as she shook her head. "Well, you have certainly done a fine job of that... Thank you."

"Again, you're well... cum," I said slowly, driving home the point that the tent wasn't meant for camping or relaxing. It was erected for sex. And as I watched the heat build in Bella's eyes, I started to become as well.

Kneeling down to remove her socks and shoes, a small look of concern crossed her face.

"I'm not sure how quiet I'm going to be able to be," she said as she watched me.

"That'll be part of the fun. Being made to feel things that make you want to cry out," I said as I reached up to slide her shorts and panties off together. I couldn't resist gazing upon her lips as they came into view. *Da—*

"—Fighting your natural urge," I said quickly, surrendering to my own for a moment as I placed my face between her legs close enough to inhale the faintness of her scent. Realizing she wasn't ready yet, I climbed further atop the bed and her body, lifting her shirt over her breasts and head as she leaned forward for me.

"Leaving it nowhere to go," I said, laying her shirt gently aside before helping to remove her sports bra and spilling the magnificence of her breasts free. "Keeping it bottled up so it intensifies everything else you're feeling..."

I paused for several seconds allowing my eyes to feast on Bella's entire nakedness before rejoining her eyes. I could tell she wanted me to touch her so badly, I almost felt guilty for taking my time. "Remember earlier when I had you put the pillow over your head, denying you sight? Now, I want you to deny yourself from making a sound. I want you to hold it in until you can't handle it anymore and you explode."

"Is that all?" Bella whined through her bated breath.

"If I do it right, that'll be enough. But if anyone hears you, that's on you and your inability to contain your inner self... or it's on me and my ability to unleash it."

Bella's eyes flared with a sudden burst of excitement. "Are you challenging me?"

"No," I said then smirked before I backed off to stand at the foot of the bed, fixing her with my eyes. "Now I'm challenging you."

Reaching down with both my hands I plucked the bottom of my fitted tee shirt. Drawing it up as slowly as I could over my head, I flexed my abdominal muscles for all they were worth.

I had always done my best not to pride myself too much on my body. Having never known my biological father, I figured I just lucked out in nature over nurture. But if there was one area of my physique to which I had dedicated myself more than any other, it was my core.

Twisting to the side ever so slightly, I watched as Bella's gaze made its way from my stomach over to my obliques. The little extra light that seemed to brighten her eyes made me smile as I kicked off my shoes using only my feet. Enjoying my audience as she enjoyed her show, I reached for the front of my swim trunks and slowly untied the bow. Standing as tall as the tent allowed, I slid them over my erection then down and off, relishing the subconscious way Bella bit her lower lip when my cock sprang into view. Watching her still, I slowly kicked back and raised one foot to remove first one sock followed by the other.

By then Bella was practically beside herself in heat.

And ready to do anything I say.

The knowledge—nay, the power—was heady. To know without a shadow of a doubt she would do virtually anything I asked was such a turn on I couldn't help but begin to stroke my cock, teasing her even more.

"I'm going to throw you a bone," I said with just a touch of wry. "I want you to ride me. I want you to control everything. But I don't want you to worry about pleasuring me. Focus only on yourself. Yet remain completely quiet. Can you do that for me?"

"Yes," Bella breathed.

"Yes, what?"

Her eyes went wild. "Yes, Master."

Giving her one last pointed look, she moved to the side as I laid down in the center of the mattress, allowing her to climb atop me. True to my word, I made no attempt to touch or help her.

Whether Victor knew it or not, my pussy was beyond ready for him. Just shy of squirting, I don't think I had ever been so wet before being touched.

In one fell swoop, my hand guided his massive dick, slipping it inside me before my right knee even touched the bed. As I lowered myself, straddling and spreading for him as wide as I could, Victor groaned and bucked. With his hands clasped behind his head, my vagina flooded, tensed and relaxed as I relished his reaction, his surprise that I had taken him so quickly.

"My God, woman..."

The look in Victor's eyes turned wild as he fought to control the squirm of his hips.

Not going to help me, huh?

Squeezing my inner walls, I bounced up, sliding along the length of his shaft and torquing him with a slight, spiraling twist.

"Aaaaaaghhhh," he moaned as quietly as he could while slamming his hands to his sides. Gripping the silk in his fists and giving up so as not to be overcome by the pleasure, I watched as his eyes rolled to the back of his head as they closed. The clench of his jaw spurred me to retake him, riding and grinding him again and again.

Over and over, I fucked Victor for all I was worth. Exclusively using my upper leg muscles so with nowhere to put my hands, I lost track of them until I felt one running through my own hair as the other kneaded my breast, tugging and pinching my nipple. Struggling to remain quiet as my body's ache began to give way to ecstasy in waves that seemed to build one atop the other, I jolted upright when I felt Victor's hand cover my mouth as his other pressed against the back of my head.

Lost, unaware my eyes had even closed, I opened them to see the wild-eyed passion in his own. With my head clamped firmly between his grip, Victor bucked, hard, his dick driving deeper in me than it had ever been. The piercing stab of pain subsided immediately into opposing pleasure only to be replaced by the anguish of momentarily feeling him begin to exit my body. The sensations were simultaneously too much yet not enough.

Again and again, harder and deeper he bucked back into me, the sound of our midsections clapping ever louder as the pressure welled within me. Finally reaching my breaking point, I felt my flood release, my juices crashing down onto Victor as he splashed through them. Five, six, seven more thrusts he pounded up into me, triggering a tremor every time, each only slightly weaker than the one before it.

Drained of all self-control I sank, my entire body collapsing onto Victor with the exception of my hips. The strength of his thrusts continued to bounce my ass into the air only for it to fall and bounce back higher against the next one.

Thankfully, I sensed his orgasm approach as his speed increased even more. And even more thankfully I knew the man well enough to know by now he was not going to hold this one back.

The first shot of his cum filled me with a polarizing sensation. With his hand still firmly covering my mouth, I wanted to cry out. But seeing the look on Victor's face, realizing he was the one swallowing his own noise, his own desire to call out...

Oh my God...

The mixture of feelings, the sensations, our wetness joining between us, the pungent smell of pine, earth, our sex and the sporadic sound of raindrops tapping all over our tent I now had enough wherewithal to detect... My body shattered again into little pieces, not as severely as my first time, but more out of its desire to share in Victor's experience simultaneously.

Crumbling together in a post-coitus heap of arms and legs, I felt his hands begin to gently rub my back. The sensation along with the hypnotically soothing sound of the rain were the only two things I was aware of for quite some time as my mind began to float.

How does he keep doing this to me?

How was it every time we were together, I ended up in a state where all I wanted to do was stay that way, for nothing to change? To lay there just like this forever with him? He was all the nourishment my mind, body and soul needed and given the number of times he took my breath away I wasn't quite so sure I still needed oxygen anymore in order to survive.

Not if I could stay... just like this...

Stirring with a murmur to stop myself from falling asleep, I raised up just enough to look down into Victor's eyes. Nodding and smiling, neither of us spoke in unspoken agreement as we were now wont to do.

Yeah...

With his right hand, Victor reached up to the side of my face and brushed back a lock of my hair, curling it up, over and behind my ear, causing my cheeks to flush.

"Why do you always do that?"

"Because I love looking into your eyes," I said quietly but without hesitation. "Being able to see as much of your face as possible. Your expressions and the feelings I see you going through behind them... Like the ones you're having right now."

I didn't mean to make Bella blush further—actually didn't think it was possible—but she did.

Laying her head back down upon my chest, I felt her settle in and close her eyes. Doing the same, I listened as the rain began to taper off as my eyes grew heavy. I had no doubt we were about to fall asleep together. Which was fine. We had no itinerary.

Drifting off I realized that, even though I couldn't see them at the moment, every time I looked into Bella's eyes, they seemed to go a little deeper than the last. Like we were carving out... our own personal niche... into one... another's... souls...

How... beautiful...

"I don't know about that. And I'm still not entirely convinced your Eruditious win was legitimate, by the way."

"Still sore I slipped one by you before I slipped one in you?" Victor chuckled as his face quickly contorted into a *Surprise!-Gotcha!* expression, earning him a playful slap on his chest. Giving me a quick kiss and hug as a consolation, his movements produced a pleasant sway to the hammock... much gentler than the ones we'd made earlier.

After waking from our nap, packing up the tent and leaving the Whitewater Center to retrieve my car from The Westin, we'd made our way as fast as possible back to Victor's house where, being unable to contain ourselves any longer, we stripped one another naked poolside before Victor bypassed any semblance of foreplay and promptly bent me over his hammock. Giving it to me for quite a while from behind, I was more than delighted when he repositioned me face up on the swing's edge and used it like a basket, hoisting me in the air while he stood and rocked into me over and over again, fucking me against the taut, bouncing nylon wall.

Regaining my wits several minutes after we were done, I honestly wondered if we'd jarred the roots of either palm tree a little loose in the process. Mine certainly felt like it.

Only now, utilizing the entire hammock as we laid together, limbs sprawled across one another while we relaxed, Victor sighed.

"You've got to admit, the words he's created have a beautiful ring to them."

I couldn't help but nod in agreement as I thought back to our game that first night...

... "Apodyopsis..."

It took me a second to remember the word's meaning, a delay I chalked up to my surprise at Victor's deliberate brazenness. Despite being surrounded by the disinterested buzz of Mickey's patrons, up until that moment all of our sexual innuendos had been far more subtle. Victor was obviously trying to ratchet up a notch.

Not to be outdone, I paused long enough to give him a once over, much as he had just done me, before lowering my voice as well.

"The act of mentally undressing a person with one's eyes," I answered.

The complete lack of surprise on Victor's face was enough to make my ego swell from his tacit praise. Whether he meant it as a challenge or a compliment, apodyopsis was no softball.

"Hmph. Seems like we've finally found a game in which we are evenly matched," he conceded.

Wry fought smug for my smile, yet somehow my tone managed to temper both.

"So far."

Victor acknowledged my point with a simple shake of his head. "Two-to-two," he said before pausing to look down to his left.

I tried not to smile as I realized Victor was in effect talking to himself. A sure giveaway among normally wired, right-handed people, his movement was also indicative of someone about to speak truly meaning whatever word he had selected was real.

Smiling, he raised his head and fixed me with the powder blue softness of his eyes. Saying nothing, each passing second seemed to slow so that by the time ten had passed, so had an eternity. And although I tried my best to hide it, his patience had me on pins and needles by the time he finally spoke.

"Rubatosis."

Ruba-what?

"Rubatosis," he said again after I said nothing. "R-U—"

"—I can deduce the spelling," I interjected. "But just because it sounds like a real word—"

"—I assure you, it is."

Victor's voice was as calm as it was confident. Although I had never heard of rubatosis, I had no doubt he knew what it meant, especially given his actions before speaking. And while he could be bluffing...

"I believe you," I admitted, "but I can't define it. I've never heard of the word."

Victor bowed his head slightly. "Rubatosis is the unsettling awareness of your own heartbeat."

Despite my years of medical training, especially with regard to self-awareness, I was still stumped.

"I tell you what," I started. "I'll cede you the point *if...* you can tell me what dictionary contains the word rubatosis."

Victor's grin grew so big he was practically beside himself. "You're going to love this. It's called *The Dictionary of Obscure Sorrows."*

Obscure Sorrows? What the— "I've never heard of it."

"'Just because you've never heard of something doesn't mean it fails to exist....'"

My jaw dropped at Victor's twist on my father's gentle jab, but stopped when his voice trailed off as he made a face.

"Although you know on second thought," he continued, "maybe it doesn't."

"Excuse me?"

"Exist," Victor said before gritting his teeth and explaining. "Technically *The Dictionary of Obscure Sorrows* is both a website and YouTube channel. It's a dictionary, just not in typical book form yet. The guy that's creating it is still in the process of compiling everything together. It's taken him years because he researches the etymologies including the suffixes and prefixes that are at the root of the emotion each word is meant to describe."

Hmmmm. "So, it's a work-in-progress dictionary... but one entirely... about emotions?"

"Exactly. Only unlike a standard dictionary, all the words in *The Dictionary of Obscure Sorrows* are neologisms created specifically to define emotions which don't already have a one-word, descriptive term."

"Like rubatosis?"

Victor nodded as I thought about it for a second. God only knew I had experienced the unsettled awareness of my own heartbeat more than a few times and I was sure most everyone else had, too. In fact, the more I thought about it, I was surprised that there wasn't already a word for a feeling so universal.

"It sounds interesting," I said. "So, how many more words from this obscure dictionary do you know?"

As Victor bowed his head slightly again, his smile took on the most beautifully wicked gleam.

"More than enough to spank you with..."

... True to his word, Victor ended up beating me, eighteen to two.

My final word—zeugma—had been just enough to stump him. But with the exception of apodyopsis, I had no idea what occhiolism, énouement, chrysalism, sonder, monachopsis, nodus tollens, exulansis or ellipsism meant. Nor, at the time, rubatosis.

Part of me didn't know what was more infuriating, that Victor had beaten me at my own game or that he had actually made it easier for me by only selecting all real words just as I had for him and yet I still hadn't stood a chance. Of course, since then I had perused the online version of *The Dictionary of Obscure Sorrows* more than once. Although it was one of the plainest of some of the most beautifully spelled words I had ever read, I really loved the definition of sonder.

"You're right," I mused. "They really do have a beautiful ring to them. I just can't believe I hadn't heard of it sooner. If I had, trust me, you wouldn't have beaten me."

Victor grinned. "I have zero doubt," he said graciously.

"Mmmmmmmmmm," Bella purred before extending one of her legs over the side. Kicking back and forth a few times, our hammock started to sway in rhythm. "So... what do you want to do for the rest of the evening?"

"You."

Lacing the fingers from one of her hands in mine, she chuckled. "You... got it. What else?"

Shifting my body, and thus Bella's, to the side just a bit, I turned us to better capture the last few minutes of the day's sun. While the afternoon clouds had broken up nicely before clearing out, my hammocks weren't optimally positioned for this early in the year. Soon we'd be in the shadow of my roof.

Gazing down at Bella's stomach, I began to fantasize about what it would be like to have her naked and poolside with me all this coming summer. To have the ability to just take her any time I wanted her... which, the more I thought about it, I wasn't even sure I could handle. I mean how much was going to be enough?

Reaching out, I started to trail one of my fingertips lightly along the lines of Bella's body. Using little more than a feather's touch, I drew my own pattern on her, directed solely by her reactions.

Shoulder to shoulder produced an inhale. Down her arm let it out. Over to a nipple where she tried to hold her next breath. Down her stomach where she quivered it out. Then shifted her pelvis.

And I met her eyes.

"Just you."

Making good on his promise, Victor made me breakfast in bed... for dinner.

Delicious plant-based, protein pancakes with lite syrup. Turkey sausage. Egg white omelets with spinach and feta. Whole grain toast with strawberry preserves. And a banana.

We worked up such an appetite, each of us had two helpings. And while I had water, Victor teasingly opted for pineapple juice.

Barely clearing our room service dinner trays or giving our food time to settle, it wasn't long before we were absolutely spent from sex again. Then, changing the bedsheets one last time, we crawled together back beneath the covers, silently yet mutually acknowledging we were finally done for the night. Doing so, coupled with Victor's smile as I caught him glancing at my stomach one last time before turning out the lights, was all I needed to remember...

"... I'm not gonna sugarcoat it for you, girl," Abby said above the electric noise of the tattoo gun as it stabbed my stomach, "this is messed up right here. I mean it and no, I'm not just talking about that gnarly-ass tat you picked out. Seriously. You need to find yourself some friends that don't need a therapist before you end up needing to see one yourself. This is bad."

"I don't need new friends. Besides, aren't you the one who told me good things come in small, *crazy* packages?"

"No. I said good things cum and cum and cum. Not that your way doesn't sound right, too."

I rolled my eyes. I'd already grown bored by the actual tattooing process which I had expected to be far more painful but wasn't. As usual, my mind had worried needlessly. The needle was much more an annoyance than a source of pain and Abby's blatant honesty was a welcome distraction from the monotony. As for her other comment...

"Yes, well you know my feelings about therapy."

"Yeah yeah yeah, everybody could use a therapist because in the grand, Sylvia-Plath-scheme-of-things we're all dying and need all the help we can get before we do, yada yada yada."

Abby turned her head to the side then stuck a finger down her throat before loudly gagging. While most of her antics were over the top, mock regurgitation was one of the few repetitive mannerisms she ever exhibited. Recognizing that they were also a prototypical reaction to stress, a part of me couldn't help but slip into Doc mode.

"What is wrong with you today? Why are you getting so worked up? You knew I was going to do this. Hell, it was practically your idea, remember?"

"I know, I know," she groaned.

"So what is your major malfunction then?... Do you and Greg need some couples counseling or something?"

I was joking, of course, but the only time Abby became this exasperated anymore was when something was wrong with her relationship with Greg. Only I had just had dinner with them the previous evening and had noticed nothing amiss. I got the feeling something specific was eating at her.

In fact, I almost knew Abby too well sometimes. While her mood could always turn on a dime, I usually saw it coming. At the moment, not so much. Something was up but judging by her Debbie Downer expression, it was something deeper than I realized. Even her exhale said as much.

"I'm dry."

Oh. "Oh..." *Ohhhhh*— "Abby, I am so—"

"—Save it. Last night was the first and God willing *only* time it's happened. I'm fine. It is what it is."

I nodded softly but I could tell by the tone of her voice neither she nor it wasn't. Based on her non-reaction reaction, I could tell Delilah sensed it, too, though to her professional credit, she managed to continue as if we weren't even there. On the other hand, as Abby's albeit former therapist, I felt obligated to say something.

"Then why—"

"—It's Greg."

Whatever I was expecting Abby to say next, it wasn't that. "Oh," was all I could offer again.

"No, 'oh.' You don't understand."

No. "You're right, I don't. Greg isn't the type of man to get upset by something that's not—"

"—He's *not.* That's just *it. He's* more okay with and far more accepting of it than *I* am. Ridiculously so, I might add."

I couldn't help but make a face. If anyone could be ridiculous...

"And you're upset about that?" I asked, trying to take the Doc out of my voice as I kept the friend in.

"Yes— No... I don't know. Yes. I want Greg to care as much as I do..."

"But?"

"But we've never had to use lube for sex before last night, not once. *Ever.* And I'm just not ready to ride off into my KY sunset yet and I sure as fuck don't want him saddling up either."

Now I got it. From day one of our sessions, Abby had made no apologies for her desire to find a monogamously sex-centered relationship. She was an independent woman proud to be so self-sufficient that she had worked herself into having only one dependency left in her life. That singular uniqueness actually made sex even more special to her and she wasn't prepared to have anything about it change. Still...

"Abby, all women eventu—"

"*—Girl,* do I look like *'all women'* to you?"

Before I could stop myself, my eyes flew to the bonfire blazing above Abby's head. Even Delilah couldn't contain her hiccup of a laugh before biting her tongue with me.

"See there? Case closed." Abby rolled her eyes then exhaled. "I know I shouldn't complain. You're right, Greg's great. I'm the one who's a basket case and I'm sure I'll get over it... eventually." She sighed. "I'm sorry. I didn't mean to give you two such a depressing preview of your future."

Delilah snorted. "Please. In my own way I've been a woman before my time for the last few years already."

I was a little taken aback. Delilah was closer to my age, maybe a year or two older at most. For her to be going through vaginal atrophy meant she was premature by a couple of decades, not a few years. She seemed to register my shock.

"I can't remember the last time I was with someone who took enough time to get me there first," she explained.

Ah. That made more sense. "At least you've *had* a last time," I offered in sisterly commiseration. "Of course, if I can ever lose some of this weight, maybe one day I'll have one, too."

"You need to get rid of that Hot-n-Now app first," Abby said. "That's what you need to lose."

"Hey! You leave Krispy Kreme alone."

"You first."

After rolling my eyes, I looked at Delilah. "A word of advice. Never become friends with a woman who actually *owns* a gym."

Abby rolled her head once before hitting me with her deadpan eyes. "Try being one with a *psycho* therapist some time."

I started to retort... but then realized she got me.

Damn...

... Curling my feet around Victor's as I tucked his hand between my breasts, I breathed in the smell of the fresh sheets.

While I had nothing against the scent of clean, part of me missed the smell of Victor's pheromones infusing the linens along with all the wetness he'd induced from my body.

Content until morning when I'd get to wake and experience both again, I smiled as I thought about how thoughtful he had been to actually purchase a mattress protector.

Drifting off, I wondered if he intended to need it for longer than just this weekend...

I knew he still had... something important to tell me... I just hoped... his answer... was... yes...

Sunday
March 8, 2020
8:57 am, 57° & mostly sunny

After good morning sex and breakfast in bed, I took Bella for a drive around my property, pointing out various buildings and locations as we went.

We stopped by the stables and grabbed some apples to feed a few of the horses out in the field. Skipped a few rocks across the pond as I filled her in on all the varieties of fish with which I had it stocked. Said a few socially distant hellos, introducing Bella to a couple of the families who lived there and were outside enjoying the warm, bright morning sunshine, too.

And all the while, I held her hand.

Giving her a quick tour of the animal rescue/veterinary clinic, I wasn't surprised when Bella noticed then commented on how well-equipped it was that the mini hospital could have doubled for a triage center. Nor did I find it remarkable when she calculated that the adjacent greenhouse and the fruits and vegetables growing in it were capable of feeding almost two dozen people per year... roughly the same number that lived here.

But it did surprise me when she elected to stay mum as I showed her around the foundation's warehouse. While I didn't expect the small improvement store worth of tools and building supplies to pique her curiosity, I figured she'd at least inquire about all the solar panels. After all, there were more than enough to completely cover the roofs of not just every house on the property, but mine, too.

Of course, when I finally suggested we head back to my place to get naked and enjoy my pool for the day, *that's* when Bella decided to surprise me.

"What about the clubhouse?"

I shook my head. *Rick.* There was no telling what he had told her. Though I could guess.

"First off," I replied, "if you want another piece of me, I'd prefer to give it to you somewhere I can guarantee our privacy because second," I said as Bella's eyes bulged just a bit, "there's probably a few kids playing games in there by now."

"In that case," Bella demurred as she hugged me around my waist, "I'd love to go get naked poolside with you."

Pulling her in tight, I looked down and gave her the eye. "You say it like you have the option."

Pushing back a bit, Bella cocked her head. "That's because until you've made a formal decision... I do."

Her spunk made me smile. I had no doubt Bella knew what my answer was going to be. But she was right. I had yet to vocalize it. But that was only because—

"It's time I told you something... But I need to show you something first."

In less than ten minutes, Victor had us standing a few feet back from a hallway entrance to one of the rooms in his house somewhere near where we must have stopped on Friday night. I definitely didn't remember reading the plaque.

"'An investment in knowledge pays the best interest.' Benjamin Franklin," I read. "Nice."

Smiling just a bit too wryly, Victor stepped forward and reached up. Giving the plaque's bottom right corner a small push, I was shocked when the bottom edge sprung outward. Powered by a small gas cylinder on each side and hinged at the top, the plaque appeared to be nothing but an ingenious way to conceal the cache of weaponry in the cutout behind it. Handguns, automatic rifles, knives. All hidden by the custom artwork. Looking from it to Victor, I was speechless.

"Yes, all of them are like this," he said before pulling the plaque back down and into place.

"But... why?"

Victor inhaled. "It's... complicated."

Not based on what I had seen. In fact, some of it made sense. "Are you... the foundation... Are you people preppers?"

Victor laughed though he tried not to. "Not exactly... We're... fully prepped."

Okay, I thought even though part of me didn't get it. I mean Rick, not to mention the two families I had met earlier this morning, they all seemed—

"Do you remember when I told you after my parents died," Victor continued, "I was allowed to take one toy with me? And I took the model of the '63 Corvette?"

A bit confused, I could only nod.

"While I was at their funeral, someone stole it. One of the other foster kids in the home took it and I never saw it again. I was heartbroken at first, but it turned out to be a valuable lesson. It taught me the importance of hiding the few things I had. At least until I got smart enough to realize that better than hiding something... was never allowing anyone to know I had something at all."

Following Victor by the hand, I was dying with anticipation by the time he opened the door at the end of the hallway where he stepped aside, ushering me to enter first.

Unlike every other in the house, the room was much smaller and windowless. That no lights flickered on automatically was just as surprising as the amount of illumination from the bank of computer monitors at the far end. Seven screens—stacked three over four—curved around a glass workstation with the oscillating light from their savers bouncing off the polished black tiled floors.

As we walked toward the back, I noticed how the remainder of the room was completely bare, almost as if to be purposefully void of any distractions.

"Shield your eyes for a second," Victor said once we reached the desk. Nudging the mouse next to the keyboard, he brought the displays to life.

Despite holding my hand in front of my face, the sudden blaze was still so glaring it took my eyes a few seconds to adjust. But when they did, I could see that most of the screens were filled with...

"Are those..."

"Cryptocurrency exchange trading apps? The bottom four, yes. The top three are just market-state visualizations."

Dismissing the scrolling numbers and candled graphs along the bottom, I took a quick glance at the flanking, static monitors on top. On one, several red and green rectangles of various sizes appeared to show the market dominance and 24-hr price change of hundreds of cryptocurrencies. On the other, a chart of the Coin That Shall Not Be Named displayed the current trade volume among all the exchanges where it could be bought and sold.

But it was the third monitor that really grabbed my attention.

Over a solid black background, an electric blue outline of the upper six continents laid flat like a map. The flags of several countries along with their corresponding 3-letter monetary designation were arrayed at the bottom of the graphic. But what looked really cool were all the different sized blue balls with a white X in their center streaming out of certain flags at various speeds. Like tracer fire from a cannon, each shot was aimed at then faded out upon reaching its target country. While most flowed from the American flag labeled usd, decent strands shot out of the mxn, krw and jpy flags as well.

The geek in me was stoked.

"What is this?"

"Fiat leak," Victor said with a smile. "One of the best visual representations of just how much money is flowing into each cryptocurrency in real-time. Pretty cool, huh?"

Mesmerized, I could only nod.

Turning to one of the computers, Victor pulled a thumb drive attached to a cord from his pocket and plugged it into one of the USB ports. Using an app on one of the bottom monitors, he began switching back and forth between working with it and fidgeting with the device as he talked.

"One of the reasons I didn't want you getting into any conspiracy theories with Rick yesterday... well, I'm sure you've probably read or heard a few about Covid."

"Hard not to," I nodded. "I think the biggest one I've read is that China created then released it to kill our economy in order to hurt the President's chance at reelection." Victor made a face. "What do you think?"

"I think anything is possible," he shrugged. "But regardless of the past, I'm more concerned with what is likely to happen in the future. I think Covid-19 has the potential to cause more global disruption than anything since 9/11. And anything with the potential to create that much chaos is going to give way—

eventually—to the need for rebalancing."

"Kind of like a market correction?"

I could see the pride in Victor's eyes. "Exactly... And once that time comes, the moves necessary to shift the market back in the direction of global equilibrium are going to create enormous financial opportunities... for those people smart enough to recognize them first."

I knew Bella had investigated cryptocurrencies on occasion over the last couple of months. But I wasn't sure how much she knew.

"Every country in the world is currently in a race to transition their monetary system from fiat to digital," I explained. "To try and do away with cash and all its inefficiencies as much as possible. In all likelihood China's CBDC will go fully live, some time within the next year which will give them a first mover advantage while a US CBDC is still years away from becoming a reality. The US is actually so far behind in the race that we've painted ourselves into a corner. The way I see it, our only way out is for the government to turn to the private sector. Which it will, eventually. Though not that it really matters as far as I'm concerned."

"Why not?"

"Because CBDCs are designed only to transact business inside each country's borders."

"So? Surely China will need some of our CBDCs to do business here as we will there."

"Yes. But there will always be an imbalance to that equation as one country will need more than the other, so then what?" Seeing Bella's confusion, I decided on another tack. "During Napolean's time it was said that when Paris sneezed all of Europe caught a cold. Today people say when the US sneezes the *entire world* catches a cold. The reason for that is simple.

"The American greenback is the largest monetary system on the planet. Our dollars are accepted as payment in more places than anywhere else on earth. When India buys oil from Saudi Arabia, they pay for it in US dollars. After all there's only so many rupees Saudi Arabians actually need and vice versa for that matter between any two countries.

"This makes our money, in effect, the most sought after bridge currency in the world. It's the most liquid, with almost every country using it to do business with one another. But in order for India and other countries to buy those dollars, the US has to print more than we need here at home. This inflates our currency, devaluing our dollar's buying power which is our sneeze. Then, when our government enacts policies to restrengthen the dollar's value, it makes it more expensive for other countries to buy which in turn hurts them. And they catch a cold."

"Okay, that makes sense. But what are you saying? That the solution is cryptocurrency?"

Victor nodded. "It's going to be. We'll still have our dollars to use here even though they'll become a CBDC. But the rest of the world will stop using our money—which they can't control—for cross-border payments to another country. And they'll do it by switching to a cryptocurrency which *no one* can control."

"What do you mean 'no one?'"

"Many cryptos, by design, have a limited supply. Not only can no more be created, most are deflationary because they actually destroy a small piece every time they get used in a transaction."

"Okay, but what about whales?"

Victor looked as shocked as he did pleased. "Wow, you really did do your research. But what exactly did you learn a whale is, in terms of investing?"

"An investor with a ton of money."

Victor nodded. "So named because when a whale moves in the ocean everything around it does, too. Especially smaller fish that get too close. In financial markets, whales often own such a large percentage of the market that whenever they buy or sell, the rest of the market moves in reaction.

"A whales' influence, however, depends on the percentage of space he or she takes up. A whale in the Pacific Ocean with a large volume of water, not really a big deal to a fish in the Indian Ocean. But put a whale in a lagoon or a pond and all of a sudden water starts washing up onto the shore. But what's really interesting are the three ways to *become* a whale.

"The first is for a person or an entity like a hedge fund to already have so much influence in other markets that their entry into a new one, no matter how little they buy, causes the market to move just because everyone gets so excited by their new involvement.

"The second way is for an existing player in the market to step up and invest such a large amount of money they end up owning a chunk big enough to make them a major player. But, if you don't have a large amount of money to begin with, anyone can still become a whale the third way—"

"—By being early. Buying a huge percentage when the price is still low."

Victor beamed at me and I could see it in his eyes. He wasn't just proud I knew the answer.

He was pleased I knew his secret.

Bella's smile widened then grew even bigger after turning to look at my fiatleak monitor. The confirmation in her eyes that she knew exactly what I was talking about before I even said it was a beautiful thing to see.

"You're going to buy The Coin That Shall Not Be Named."

Mmmmm. I liked how Bella made a statement instead of asked a question. But she was still partially wrong.

"No. I'm going to buy *more* of it." I detached the Nano X from my computer before looking into Bella's eyes. "Even though I already have more than enough now."

Taking Bella's hand, I gently twisted her wrist to place the device into her open palm.

"Do you know what this is?"

It looked like a thumb drive. A little longer, heavier and a bit fancier than most, but a thumb drive nonetheless. Flipping it over for a closer look, light from one of the monitors caught it at just the right angle for me to read the laser-etched inscription on one side of the metallic casing. It was written in Latin.

Of course.

"Vires in numeris," I said.

"Strength in numbers," we said together.

"That," Victor nodded toward my hand, "is a hardware wallet."

I remembered reading about them. "The type that holds cryptocurrencies?"

Victor cocked his head. "Yes. And no. Technically, cryptocurrencies never leave their ledgers. Hardware wallets hold private keys used to gain access to cryptocurrencies." He nodded at the device in my hand. "Open it up and push both buttons at the same time."

Sliding the drive out from under its cover I realized the swiveled hinge was actually a button. At the other end of the drive another of the same size was the only feature visible until I pressed both, lighting up the small digital display between them. The word *Ledger* was quickly followed by a prompt to enter a PIN code. I'm not sure what I was expecting but I must have looked confused.

"Think of it like this," Victor said. "While you can hold cash in your purse, how do you usually access and spend the money in your bank account?"

Ummm. "Using my debit card."

"Right. Which is uniquely numbered just for you. But your money isn't kept *in* your actual card any more than cryptocurrency coins are kept *in* a hardware wallet. Both are just devices used to access the money you own."

"I see."

Victor glanced down at the flash drive still in my palm before looking again at me.

"Tell me. If someone you knew and loved were being held for ransom and the kidnappers contacted you for money they knew you had in the bank—let's say $100,000—how would you get it?"

To say Victor's question threw me was an understatement.

"Ummmm... I guess I'd go to my bank... and see how fast I could withdraw my money."

"Right. Except many banks don't keep $100,000 cash on hand at their branches. And even if they did anything over $10,000 triggers delays for questions, possibly by law enforcement. The kind of things that prevent most kidnappings from being lucrative enough to attempt for so much risk."

I nodded even though I wasn't exactly sure where Victor was going with this.

"What's the largest amount of cash you've ever carried in your purse?"

Remembering the time my father guided me through an auction back when I was in college, I started to understand the connection.

"Forty-five hundred dollars," I said. "When I bought my first car."

"Did it make you nervous? Carrying that much cash?"

"Yes and no. My dad was with me, but yeah. I was still a little worried about being robbed."

Victor looked down pointedly at the flash drive in my hand. His meaning was crystal clear.

"How much is in this wallet?" I asked as I felt my nerves wake.

Victor shrugged. "I haven't checked the market today, but since I haven't received any alerts on my phone, either... I'd say between all the various coins on there..." Victor paused then slowly smiled. "You're currently holding a hundred million dollars."

My eyes went wide, first at Victor then at the flash drive in my hand which within seconds I felt start to sweat. Or maybe it was my imagination. Not that it mattered.

One hundred mill—

I wasn't sure which was worse. How Bella suddenly stood so starkly still or how she started to turn white. Either way, a part of me hoped her reaction meant she might more easily understand what I had to say next.

Taking the thumb drive from her hand, I was surprised to hear her exhale.

"Are you okay?" I asked.

"Yes. I... I just... never... Do you really have a hundred million dollars worth of cryptocurrency in that wallet?"

Bella looked up at me in awe as I nodded. It wasn't the smartest thing I'd ever done, placing so much money in a single location, but I'd wanted to make enough of an impression upon her that she would understand my position. And what would be hers—

"—So you're really a whale?" she asked before I could continue.

"Ummm..."

Well, damn. I guess I might as well explain that part now, too.

"No," I said before hesitating to take a breath of my own. "I was three."

Jaw down, eyes up and even wider than before, I listened as Victor calmly explained how he was born Joey Gunnar Dahl to a Swedish teenage runaway who placed him up for adoption just after his birth. Renamed Joseph Rene Beveaux a week later by his adoptive parents, Victor lived unaware of his original name until gathering all the necessary paperwork for his emancipation at seventeen.

"You wouldn't believe my shock the first time I saw my original birth certificate," he said. "Growing up in foster care, I never really had anything to call my own. So, when I found out not even my name was really mine... it made me want to create one that was. So I did."

It wasn't until a year after successfully petitioning the court that Victor realized someone must have failed to update his records properly after he received a reminder letter from the Selective Service addressed not to him but to Joseph Beveaux.

"I didn't think much of it at the time. After all, the government knew me. My paychecks from the Marines were made out to Victor Maxwell so I figured that was all I needed to worry about. I never even bothered to respond and correct them. I probably threw the letter in the trash."

But, Victor continued, less than a year later he found himself suffering from a traumatic brain injury, a failed porn star and doing odd jobs in LA until he was hired as a private investigator's assistant. Just a few months before his life would take a turn for the weird.

One of his last weeks on the job, he learned the Selective Service gets the names for those eligible to register from several different lists. Places like public high schools and the Departments of Education and Motor Vehicles. But they also pulled from the Social Security Administration.

"Bear in mind at that time I was still pissed off at the military—and by extension the federal government. So, in my own juvenile way, I thought it might be fun to stick it to Uncle Sam by opening up a couple of bank accounts in my former names. After all, I had the birth certificates and social security number to match."

So, he did. Unknowingly giving himself a future opportunity to set off a small chain of events which would dramatically alter his life.

"At first, I was traveling around the country on occasion to play poker. Weekend road trips to Palm Springs, Vegas and Reno turned into longer jaunts to places like Vancouver whenever the tournaments were big enough. But every time I returned home to LA, I was reminded how much I hated it. So I bought an RV large enough to live in and tow my Jeep, left to play full time on the poker circuit and never looked back."

It was a bit much to digest. Fortunately, I already knew or could figure out the rest on my own.

Later, Victor bought into bitcoin early.

Made a killing.

Spread out his newfound crypto wealth into different coins using all three of his names.

And now it was all under one. His.

Which was exactly what I wanted to be...

His.

With my life story's synopsis complete, I felt a pang of guilt for not being more appreciative of the look of love in Bella's eyes. I knew somehow I'd make up for it later. But for the moment, I was going to have to be a bit more direct.

"Do you understand why I've told you all this?" I asked her, softly but seriously. "I won't be the one assuming the greatest liability. I won't be the one in the most danger."

"What do you mean?"

"With crypto, a person can walk around with $100 million in their pocket and no one would ever know. There's no problems or safeguards from a bank to deter a kidnapper from going after someone they know has that much crypto... If I'm kidnapped, I have no doubt I'll be tortured into giving up the secret keys to my Nanos. But I've always known that's a possibility, so I've always been extremely careful in the way I've done things. That's why the vast majority of my crypto trading was done using Joey and Joseph's names and bank accounts."

"You used your old names as... drops?"

I rolled my eyes. "I know. It wasn't the smartest thing I've ever done. But I figured if anyone came looking for the owner of their accounts, at least they were one layer removed from the real me. That's what I was doing for the last two months, rectifying things with the IRS."

"They caught you avoiding taxes?"

"No. I voluntarily went to them and pointed out their error. That's why, just to be safe, I always overpaid." I chuckled. "Their lawyers wouldn't admit to it, but I think that's why the IRS never came after me. It was either an honest oversight on their part or someone who should have pursued it didn't, figuring who in their right mind *over*pays their taxes by so much?"

I tried to make light of myself, but Bella was having none of it.

"But you are in your right mind. Right?"

Her concern was so touching I hated hearing the worry in her voice.

"If you're talking about my brain injury, yes. I won't deny I still have my moments, but those are fewer and further between the more time goes by."

Bella looked at me funny. "So, what are you afraid of?"

I tried not to seem sad even though I felt it inside. Why, I had no idea. I definitely didn't have a valid reason. Trying to delay the inevitable for a few more seconds, I wheeled out my desk chair for Bella to sit on as I perched myself lightly on the workstation table's edge.

"At the end of 2017," I started, "the cryptocurrency market had its biggest bull run ever."

"When the price of bitcoin almost reached $20,000," Bella said.

I nodded. "I sold off nearly every single one I still had shortly before it reached $19,000. Not only had I never had more money in my life, neither had Joey or Joseph. Between the three of 'us' *I* nearly became a billionaire."

Bella's eyes got big but to her credit she said nothing and waited for me to continue.

"I bought back in when the market corrected, of course, just like I always have. And we've been in a bear market ever since. But the next time it turns bull..."

I shook my head then leaned forward to make sure I had Bella's attention.

"There are almost eight and a half million households in America worth a million dollars. In North Carolina there's about a quarter of a million. It's fairly easy to remain anonymous among two hundred and fifty thousand people... But do you know how many billionaires live in North Carolina?"

Bella shook her head.

"Four." I paused to allow the implication to sink in before continuing. "For the last three years—ever since the bull run—I filed as many extensions as I could with the IRS. Not just for me, but for Joey and Joseph, too. But now that that's been taken care of everything is consolidated under the name—*my* name—Victor Maxwell.

"You see, until a few months ago, no one in this world knew how much crypto I possessed. Now I have no idea how many lawyers and accountants spread across three states know everything about me... including my true net worth." I paused to flip the flash drive back open. "What's in this Nano represents the largest consolidated investment I've ever made. It's a gamble, but so is everything in life."

Bella looked at me cautiously. "You're trying to say the amount of money you have makes a relationship with you a liability."

No. "Not the amount. The type."

Bella nodded, but I could see by the look on her face that she still didn't comprehend what I was implying.

"I have almost everything I could ever need here at my foundation. I rarely need to leave so I rarely do. And when I do, I'm cautious. I know how to protect myself and most of the time I stay armed... So far easier than kidnapping me... would be kidnapping someone I'm close to." I saw the light turn on in Bella's head. "Someone I'm in love with."

And then it turned on in her eyes.

Love.

The pinnacle of all human emotion when one has it. And its abyss when lost.

I only believed in love because I was created by two people who had found it. Saw it in my best friend's relationship with her husband. And heard tales from countless strangers that swore with conviction they had experienced it. But I never had.

Not until Victor came along. *Right when I wasn't looking.* Well, not for love, anyway. Yet here both were.

Looking right back at me.

Bella was quiet a little too long. If it hadn't been for the look in her eyes her increasingly rapid breaths might have worried me.

"You're in love with me?"

I nodded, too apprehensive to say anything else until she responded. But when she didn't the compulsion overwhelmed me.

I didn't know how to reply.

Outside of my family, I'd never told anyone I loved them before. And part of me was terrified.

I loved Victor, too, but if things didn't work out between us... There was no one else in the world like him. No one more perfect for me.

And if things didn't work out between us... I knew I'd never be able to love like this again.

Unable to articulate my fear, I was grateful when Victor resumed speaking, his voice softer and even more sincere.

"You're the first person I want to talk to in the morning and the last in the evening. I love having your attention and making you smile in return... I feel happy knowing that you are..." I paused to swallow the lump in my throat. "Whenever we're together, it feels like time stands still... I don't know what love means to other people, Bella, but since that's what it means to me... then, yes.

I'm in love with you."

Truth be told, there was a small part of me that felt sick to my stomach. Not because Bella wasn't immediately or emphatically reciprocating my affection. In her eyes she was. I saw and felt it.

But I worried that professing my love now might distract her from realizing the situation she could be putting herself in. The odds might have been small, but the danger wasn't.

Was it all simply in Victor's head? Or mine for that matter?

Undoubtably, I loved Victor, too. Loved everything I knew about him, anyway. Because despite just how much we talked on a daily basis over the last two months, I had to wonder, how much did I really know? What else hadn't he revealed about himself that might give me pause?

I wasn't worried about the source of his wealth or the danger it could put me in. What worried me more was how I had counseled enough couples to know most relationships failed at their outset when one or both persons idealized something in the other that wasn't really there. Was I doing that to Victor? Or he to me? Were we in love with the idea of one another? Of what could be?

Two months was more than enough time for two people to fall in love. But three nights?

No matter how great the sex over our only three together was, was it enough to sustain us? I didn't know but I was sure any attempt to find out carried with it the possibility for the greatest heartbreak of my life. The question was, was I willing to risk it?

God, yes.

"I'm in love with you, too."

I had no idea if the smile on my face matched the one in my heart. Not that it mattered.

Neither were any longer mine.

Both belonged to Bella.

Victor leaned down to kiss me as I stood to kiss him.

Sweet. Tender. Passionate. Loving. Long... and drawn out.

And as we finished and opened our eyes together, I suddenly felt new again. Much like the morning after Jacksonville when I finally knew what great sex was like and there was no going back, now I finally knew what great love felt like.

And I'd go anywhere with him.

"Come with me," I said, causing Bella to smirk. Which then made me do the same. "That's not what I— You know what, that works, too."

Laughing together, I began to lead Bella by her hand out of the room. But not before stopping so she could read the plaque above the door.

"'Mostly it is loss which teaches us about the worth of things.' Arthur Schopenhauer," Bella said before looking up at me.

"'Mostly,'" I said into her eyes. "But the worth of some things could never be more obvious."

We didn't make it down before the first hall before we were tearing off one another's clothes. The trail of shirts, shoes, pants, socks and underwear still littered the floor all the way to Victor's gym where we took off running, completely naked until we reached his bed.

Now, half an hour later, we laid there exhausted, amazed at how quickly such a state was becoming customary for us. Having finally caught our breath, Victor rolled over and propped his head up on his hand using his elbow.

"So, I started to ask you about something Friday night, but the timing wasn't appropriate."

"And *now* is?" I asked.

"Now we're both naked. When it comes to us, it doesn't get more appropriate than this."

"Touché. So, what's your question?"

"Well, it's more a statement than a question really... I can't believe Greg was your sidekick, Andy."

I couldn't help to make a face. "Greg wasn't Andy— Oh! You think just because he was there for my show with— No. Well, yes. Greg was there that night when I filmed the show from my office because I didn't want to be alone with Shawn. But Greg wasn't Andy."

Victor looked confused. "So, Andy du Payne was Greg's partner, Andy Chastain?"

"Oh, God, no. That guy was a jerk. The one and only time I was ever alone with him he flat out just asked me if I was DTF like it was no big deal."

Victor still looked confused. "Then who was Andy?"

I smiled. "Abby."

Victor's eyes popped. "You're kidding me."

I shook my head. "Wait until you meet her. I mean the real her."

"But I've already—"

"No, you've only been around her on days when she serves as Greg's Sex Slave. Wait until you see her on a day when their roles are reversed."

Victor shook his head. "If she's anything like Andy, I don't—"

I laughed. "Trust me, Andy du Payne was just a crazy character she created for the show."

"Well... it was a pretty good one."

I nodded. "Maybe one night the four of us can do dinner via video while we're quarantining? You could pick Abby's brain, talk to her about Andy."

"I'd like that. I bet it could be fun. But speaking of quarantining, what in the world are we going to do with all our free time?"

Cocking my head, I gave Victor enough of a once over to make him smile.

"That goes without saying," he said. "But let's face it. We're going to have some down time."

Hmmmm. "Not much if I have anything to say about it. But I do still have some teletherapy patients I need to see a few days a week. Maybe while I'm working you could work on finishing some of those things you've been writing or— Ooh! I know! Maybe we could write a book together."

Victor scrunched his nose. "A book? About what?"

"Well, they say you should only write about what you know. So, I'll write about sex and you write about crypto. Surely somewhere between the two there's a story we can tell."

"Maybe. But what would be the point?"

"Who said there needs to be a point? Given all the tripe that's written these days and self-published on the internet, it's obvious most people don't care if there's a point to what they read as long as they're entertained in the process."

Victor thought about it for a second before pursing his lips. "I don't know. I mean crypto is still so unknown I can see where writing about it might make sense, but people already think they know everything they need to about sex."

"Well, then we'll write about all the odd things they probably don't know."

"Like the things in your podcasts?"

"Exactly. But with some good sex scenes thrown in to tide them over and keep them even more interested." I ran my finger around Victor's stomach in a circle. "Think of all the fun we could have developing the inspiration for those."

Victor smirked. "Like we aren't going to be doing that anyway."

"Exactly my point! *Since* we're going to anyway..."

"True. But..."

"But what?"

"You're not talking about writing some tawdry, pornographic sex novel, are you?"

I rolled my eyes. "Please. I'm sure if we put our heads together, we can come up with something a bit better than that."

Victor peered down at me a little more closely. "Why do I get the feeling you already have something in mind?"

I smiled but said nothing as I watched the idea begin to take hold in his brilliant blues.

"Yeah, that might work," he finally agreed. "Hell, it might even make for a good book."

"Trust me. If we write it together, it will make for a *great* book."

"Yeah, well," he started to scoff, "let's don't try and make it *too* great. I don't mind being an anonymous author, but bestselling author is a label I can do without, thank you very much."

I arched my brows. "Narcissistic much?"

"Not really," Victor shrugged. "I just have a really big cock. Which is bigger now thanks to you," he said before grabbing himself and waving it back and forth.

I rolled my eyes. *"Please* promise me you'll stop jelqing."

"Okaaaaaay," he said before leaning down to kiss me. "But only if you promise we publish under pseudonyms should the time ever... come."

"Nice one."

"Thanks."

Hmmmmm. His idea gave me another. "What if we did that *and* used a drop? Someone who might not mind the notoriety? Along with our pseudonyms, of course."

Victor looked confused. "What's the point in using a drop if we're going to use pseudonyms?"

"In case someone discovers who's behind our pseudonyms, instead—"

"—they're led to the drop. Clever. You think I'd have thought of that."

Realizing he had and was playfully mocking me, I gave Victor a playful slap in return. But then, still unconvinced, he shook his head slightly.

"I don't know, you know. Writing under pseudonyms while pinning it on someone else. Readers might not like to be screwed with like that."

I practically snorted. "More than likely our readers will be people with a bit more interest in sex than the norm. And if that's the case then trust me, being *screwed* with is something they most definitely will enjoy no matter *how* it's done."

Victor chuckled. "I see what you did there. But who—ohhhh," he said before nodding.

"Exactly," I said, loving that he caught my drift. "Do you think he'd be interested?"

"I don't know. I'll ask him."

"Good. You do that. In the meantime," I said as I started to get up, "I am going to run home and grab enough clothes for the next two we—"

"—You won't be needing any clothes—"

"—I still have to teleconference an hour or two with some of my patients every few da—"

"—Oh, right, sorry, I forgot."

I laughed as I got out of bed. "That's okay. I know what you were thinking and I like where your mind was. Keep it there. I'll be back to entertain it," I said, leaning down to poke Victor in his stomach, "and *you* as soon as possible."

Following my poke with a kiss goodbye, our smooch went a little longer than I expected... though I wasn't complaining. Even nicer was how, when I finally turned to go, Victor held on to my hand and smiled.

"Hold up, hold up," he said. "Just because you're coming right back doesn't mean we should start forgoing formalities."

My confusion turned to surprise as Victor raised my hand to his lips for a kiss.

"Ciao, Bella," he said. With that special gleam in his eye, his smile grew a bit wider than usual.

Charmed, I replied with a smile but was a bit too stunned to say anything until I reached the bedroom door. Turning back, I just had to know.

"Why do you always look like that whenever you say that?"

"When I say what? 'Ciao, Bella?'"

I nodded which made Victor's smile turn coy.

"I don't know. How do I look?"

"Like you know something... like you're keeping a secret."

Having spent my entire life both hating and sucking at goodbyes, when the opportunity finally presented itself for me to enjoy getting one right, I couldn't resist taking it. *Plus,* I thought with a smile...

This is the moment I've been waiting for.

With his grin giving way to yet another chuckle, Victor rolled off the bed and strolled over to where I stood. After opening the door for me, he gazed down into my eyes before slowly brushing back a lock of hair from my face.

"As I'm sure you probably know, the word 'ciao' is Italian. It actually comes from the Venetian dialect where it was once pronounced 's-ciavo.' But prior to that, it was pronounced 'sclavus,' the Latin word not only for 'slave' but for

'Slav,' allegedly because the Slavic people were so often forced into slavery.

"Of course, today 'ciao' is used as a way to say goodbye as well as hello. But that dual use practice stems from an even more ancient time when the world's wealthiest individuals were constantly on guard for their lives. Never knowing who was out to get them for their money, they often trusted no one at all. This was particularly true when it came to their servants who were required to announce both their presence as well as their departure any time they entered or exited a room. Which they did by bowing and saying, 'I am at your service.' But by using the root of the word 'ciao,' what they were literally acknowledging and simultaneously declaring was... *I* am *your* slave."

Victor stared lovingly into my eyes which I felt widen as I realized...

"So, all this time you've been telling me, 'Ciao, Bella...'"

Damn...

AFTERWORD FROM MS. O

Once Mr. N and I finished our final draft, we asked five of our closest friends to read *Ciao, Bella* before posing the one question they wanted to ask us the most. We figured five questions were enough to be representative of what most of our readers might wish to know and we thought it would be a good idea to answer them here. However, four out of five basically asked us the same question: What was our writing process like?

Our answer, like our process, is fairly simple. After agreeing on the overall story, each of us gave the other twelve hours to write a passage before passing the novel back. We quickly realized the routine rhythm of life dictated that sometimes one of us was naturally going to write more than the other. And that was fine. We felt it could and did give our story an organic feel.

Once complete, we each edited the other's passages but with the original writer retaining the final decision over which edits were best to use. This allowed us to unify the flow of the story so that each passage wasn't too disparate from the other. It also allowed us to understand one another's ways of thinking along a line we had never explored before; writing together. We had a great time with it and think it worked out well.

As for the fifth question, how much of our story is true...

Well, some things are best left to the imagination. We hope you enjoyed yours as much as we did ours. Thank you for reading.

ABOUT THE AUTHORS

Mr. N and Ms. O reside in the southeastern US. They are a blissfully happy couple who share two kids, a dog and a cat... along with a love for alliteration and all things Shakespeare. They have been living a Master/Sex Slave lifestyle for the last 11 years and while they have friends who are openly active in their local BDSM community, they themselves are not and wish to remain anonymous. They ask that you please respect their privacy as you would wish yours to be respected.

www.ingramcontent.com/pod-product-compliance
Lightning Source LLC
LaVergne TN
LVHW041100080826
845145LV00007B/1640

* 9 7 8 0 5 7 8 7 8 6 1 8 6 *